PRAISE FOR

The Wild Dark Flowers

"A charming, intriguing novel. Some scenes are reminiscent of two popular TV series, *Upstairs, Downstairs*, and *Downton Abbey*, which have similar subject matter. Her research is excellent. The various battle scenes in France are completely riveting, and her portrayal of the sinking of the *Lusitania* is heartrending. This book is a perfect summer read."
　　　　　　　　　　　　　　　　　　　　—*Historical Novel Society*

"Simply delicious . . . Like *Downton* . . . as addictive as a soap opera."
　　　　　　　　　　　　　　　　　　　　　　　—*Record-Courier*

"Elizabeth Cooke has written a noble, admirable follow-up novel to *Rutherford Park* . . . Fine, fine historical fiction!"
　　　　　　　　　　　　　　　　　　　　　　　—*The Best Reviews*

"Fans of the era will seize the opportunity to immerse themselves in Cooke's world. Unlike many historical dramas set during the Great War, the second installment in Cooke's trilogy is set on the home front and the battlefield . . . Readers see what war does on and off the front lines, yet Cooke never loses focus on her characters' emotions."
　　　　　　　　　　　　　　　　　　　　　　　—*RT Book Reviews*

continued . . .

The Gates
of Rutherford

Elizabeth
Cooke

BERKLEY BOOKS, NEW YORK

BERKLEY

An imprint of Penguin Random House LLC
375 Hudson Street, New York, New York 10014

This book is an original publication of Penguin Random House LLC.

Library of Congress Cataloging-in-Publication Data

Cooke, Elizabeth, date,
The gates of Rutherford / Elizabeth Cooke.—Berkley trade paperback edition.
p. cm.
ISBN 978-0-425-27719-5
I. Title.
PR6063.C485G38 2015
823'.914—dc23
2015014272

PUBLISHING HISTORY
Berkley trade paperback edition / September 2015

PRINTED IN THE UNITED STATES OF AMERICA

10 9 8 7 6 5 4 3 2

Cover photos: woman © Edward Steichen / Vogue / Conde Nast 1925;
castle © Gentl &Hyers / Conde Nast Traveler 2007
Cover design by Diana Kolsky.
Interior text design by Laura K. Corless.

Penguin
Random
House

Chapter 1

The rain fell softly on the day that she was to be married.

All night long Charlotte had been dreaming of her old home at Rutherford Park—she thought that the sound of the downpour outside was the water rushing through the red stones of the riverbed by the bridge. It was only when she awoke that she realized she was in London, in the Chelsea house owned by the American, John Gould.

It was half past five in the morning when Charlotte let herself out of the house and into the street. Cheyne Walk was barely stirring, and the road held only a clattering echo of her own running feet. She was at the Embankment wall in just a few moments, leaning on the edge, staring at the lively grey ribbon of the Thames. *I shall be married*, she thought, *in a few hours*. She turned her face up to the rain.

It was April 1917; she was nineteen years old. And everywhere there was change. On the fields of Flanders, history was being written in the harrowing of humanity; in the pretty eighteenth century house behind her, her own mother lived in what some called sin, but what Charlotte could see was a kind of correctness, a way of holding on to life. In Yorkshire, her once happy father habitually mourned in bitterness. The world rolled and altered.

She held on to the Embankment wall, feeling its granite strength. Someone had told her that the stones of the wall here had come from Cornwall, from Lamorna Cove. It was supposed to be wildly lovely there, but she had never seen it. She had, despite her nursing service at St. Dunstan's, never seen France. Her brother, Harry, was back there now, advising the Flying Corps. She had never seen America, as Mr. Gould had done; she had never been to Italy. She had wanted to take the Grand Tour as her male ancestors had once done. But she doubted that she would now. She was to be a married woman.

She turned away from the river, trying to hold down the nonsensical impulse to throw herself into the water. She had nothing at all to be worried about, she told herself. This was just a morbid anxiety, a last-minute rush of pre-wedding nerves. She must grow up, and stop wanting some romantic notion of independence. After all, what did she have to be worried about? Michael Preston was a wonderful man, a brave man. His blindness was no barrier; they were, as he always joked, a good team. Her parents were pleased that she was about to marry into one of Kent's oldest and most respected—not to say very wealthy—families; that she would be secure and cared for. That she would live a stone's throw from her family's London house in Grosvenor Square, in a lovely little mews cottage that Michael's parents had bestowed upon them. Her father had even hinted obliquely at the grandchildren that she and Michael would provide, and she so longed to see him happy again. She was desperate not to bring further disappointment into his life.

Yet the old sense of suffocation threatened to overwhelm her.

She looked back through the trees at the houses on Cheyne Walk. John Gould now owned one of the prettiest, his gift to her mother, Octavia. They lived like two honeymooners here, and for the last six months Charlotte had come here often, absorbing both their scandal and their happiness in equal measure. She was to be married from here, and not the Grosvenor Square house where her father was now staying in solitary and temporary splendor among the dusty relics of his marriage. Now and then, in talking to him, it had become obvious that he expected his wife to eventually return to him. People called him an old fool for it, she knew. It was her older sister, Louisa, who tended to look after Father; Charlotte was drawn to her mother. But sometimes the longing for the old untouched days at Rutherford would return in her; the innocence of it all, the feeling that England would never change. The ancient conviction that the Cavendish estate of Rutherford and that charmed and luxurious way of life was eternal.

Charlotte smiled to herself. Well, they had all had that permeability knocked out of them now.

She wondered, as she looked at Cheyne Walk, at the other dramas that had played out in this London street over the centuries. In Number 16, Dante Gabriel Rossetti had lived out his final years with Fanny Cornforth; Number 4 was George Eliot's last home. Just along the way was the Chelsea Hospital and the Physic Garden. And it had been here, last October, that Charlotte had sat with her mother and told her that Michael had proposed to her. In the seventeenth-century green oasis by the Thames, Charlotte had expected Octavia to tell her that she was far too young. In retrospect, she had hoped that this was indeed what her mother was going to say. She would have returned to Michael and told him that, without her mother's approval, she could not possibly marry him, flattered as she was to have been asked. But, to her astonishment, Octavia had not objected at all. In her own half-dazed and happy state, she had simply clasped Charlotte's hands and smiled at her, and given her blessing. But it was not her mother's blessing that Charlotte had wanted. She had wanted her mother's disapproval, and an excuse not to marry at all.

It was very strange, she considered, that in all these months, it had only been John Gould, her mother's lover, who had carefully and subtly questioned her decision. "Shall you be very happy as a little wife?" he had said to her in a joking fashion last Christmas. She had looked at him gravely, the champagne glass in her hand as the dinner guests settled around the dining table on the day before Christmas Eve. "Don't you think that I could be?" she'd replied. John, in his handsome and easy way, had considered her. "You always struck me as a wild bird waiting to fly," he had commented. "Well, one can fly when one is married," she'd told him. And then had blushed scarlet. "I mean, as a couple. We could fly anywhere, anywhere at all."

If he had noticed her embarrassment, he hadn't dwelled upon it. "Come to America when this lousy war is over," he had said. "And see the house I've built for your mother on Cape Cod. I'm sure you'll like it. America, too."

Her heart had welled up inside her. Oh, she was sure that she would love the beach, the house, the country. The very words spelled out freedom and space. And of course she could go there with Michael—of course they would love to, she told John. She had then deliberately turned away from him and his piercing appraising gaze. She had spoken gaily to the woman on the other side of her; but about what, she had no idea at all.

Since then, she seemed to have been swept forward by events. Michael's parents were charming; their grand home in its beautiful gardens outside Sevenoaks was charming; Michael himself was, of course, charming. But how "charming" grated on her to the roots of her soul! How maddening she found it. How ridiculously she had painted herself into this lover's corner. Into maturity and security and all those other things that her father so approved of. She thought she should die of it.

"Stop it," she said out loud, to no one at all but herself. "What a silly, selfish fool you are."

She walked back to the house and let herself in the gate. In six hours, at midday, her father would come here in the Rolls-Royce he had lately acquired. They would be chauffeured to the parish Church of St. Margaret's at Westminster Abbey, within sight of the abbey itself and the famous clock tower of the Palace of Westminster that was familiarly called Big Ben.

There would be crowds at the church door because society weddings were food and drink to a war-weary London, and because it was seen to be a great romance, this union of the blinded war hero and the youngest child of a loyal servant of the Crown. Police on horseback would hold back the throng; there would be cheers as she emerged from the car dressed in what she—oh so privately, oh so secretly—thought was a completely idiotic costume of a white silk dress and a vast tulle veil. Her sister, Louisa, would be there at the church door, laughing prettily and scattering rose petals. And, after the ceremony, the thunder of the *Meistersinger* march on the church organ would compete with the pealing of bells of St. Margaret's. And she and Michael would stand together at the porch, smiling, arm in arm.

And all the time, she would be wanting to run.

The door of the house opened as she approached it, and there was the housemaid, looking frightened that someone was already outside as she reached to polish the door frame and the brass handle of the bell. "Oh, miss," she said, beaming when she saw that it was Charlotte. "The happiest day of your life. We are all that excited, miss, if you'll pardon me saying."

Charlotte stepped over the threshold and shook off the coat that had become saturated with rain.

"Yes," she murmured. "You're quite right, Milly. It's the happiest day of my life."

Chapter 2

The Ritz hotel commanded one of London's greatest thoroughfares, and was within sight of Green Park and Buckingham Palace. It was the new creation of César Ritz himself, and looked much like a French chateau that had been gracefully dropped in Piccadilly, complete with its modern refinements and Louis XVI furnishings.

The arrival of the Cavendish and Preston wedding party caused as much of a stir on Piccadilly as it had at the church in Westminster. A crowd gathered to watch the bride and groom emerge from the wedding car; but they were equally interested in the great and good of the nation that followed. Politicians whom they recognized only vaguely, whose top-hatted appearance was greeted with polite applause, were followed by officers in uniform, ladies of the aristocracy, and a small scattering of artists from the Slade. Murmurs of scandal and appreciation rose and fell like waves until the last guest disappeared behind the gilt-and glass doors.

Charlotte's father, William Cavendish, the seventh Earl Rutherford, was well pleased with the overall effect of the wedding, despite the Oranges and Mauves. Privately, this was what he called the artists that his estranged wife, Octavia, seemed to so admire. Still, the gallant officers were rather more impressive, and he was glad that Charlotte, despite having inherited some of her mother's more stubborn and outrageous characteristics, now appeared to be settling into a respectable life. William liked Michael Preston, and admired him for his stoicism in the face of his terrible injuries. One would hardly credit that the man was blind; his face bore no sign other than a few discolored lines around the forehead. He carried himself with dignity, and he was intelligent and modest. Such qualities might carry him far, William thought. He had even wondered if he might introduce Michael to those whom he knew in government when the war was over.

William stood now at the entrance to the large dining room and looked about himself. He and his daughter Louisa had arranged the wedding on Charlotte's behalf. Or, rather, Louisa had done the majority of the arranging and he had done all of the paying. It showed in the room. The table displays were opulent, the flowers in full bloom despite it only being April. Each table bore its white damask cloths, its silver and glass and decorations of silk and ribbon, like stage sets. He saw that, in among the color on the high table, Charlotte looked rather lost. *Dear girl*, he thought. Something had overwhelmed her robust personality at last. She seemed to be very small there among the sea of society faces, and rather pale. He caught a waiter as the man walked past. "Take a glass of champagne to the bride," he murmured. "And make sure she is served first."

He smiled with pride. Louisa sat to Charlotte's left, looking terribly pretty. Far to the right sat Octavia, Charlotte's mother. He saw that she and Louisa briefly exchanged a glance of satisfaction, and he supposed that Louisa's immaculate organization of the day perhaps had much more to do with his wife than he had supposed. Well, what did it matter? Octavia was largely shunned by society, but she had probably found a way to help her daughter. Women were subversive creatures, he thought. One never really knew. Never really knew at all.

He walked up to the top table. It took him some time; matrons of the beau monde would tend to leap up as he passed, and press him engagingly to their breasts as if he were an abandoned child. Over the last year, he had grown used to brushing them off with politeness. He was not abandoned, in his opinion. He was merely put aside for a while. Octavia—he was determined about it, determined to the point of being almost convinced—that Octavia would return to him once the American had grown tired of her. She would leave the little house in Chelsea and return to Rutherford where she belonged. He gritted his teeth and turned his face away in the meantime. She would come home. It was surely inevitable. Men like John Gould wouldn't look after another man's wife indefinitely. As for his own heart . . . he didn't like to consider it at all. He had been brought up not to linger on the subject of feelings. He would present an equable face to the world, no matter how many nights he laid awake and wondered what the hell had happened to his marriage.

As he passed the final table before he sat down, he noticed a familiar face. It was Caitlin de Souza, his son Harry's friend. She sat unmoving, her hands clasped in her lap, dressed in a somber outfit of pale brown with a lace collar.

"Caitlin, is it?" he said, and held out his hand.

"It is, your lordship."

"On leave?" Caitlin was a nurse at the front.

"Yes, sir."

"Grim as ever, I take it."

"It is terribly grim, yes."

"Heard from Harry?"

It was typical of William to talk in such abbreviated sentences. He saw no need to pontificate. He loathed small talk. Caitlin smiled, and at once he remembered why Harry, who was presently serving with the Royal Flying Corps, was so attracted to her. "He writes very often," she murmured.

William lowered his face close to hers. "Persuade the old fellow to do the same for his parents, why don't you?" he whispered. "Take it as a personal favor."

He stood back up, squeezed her hand, and walked on. To the other side of the table, directly opposite Caitlin, he had noticed the disheveled form of Christine Nesbitt. At least, she looked disheveled to him. Why did these artists never run a comb through their damned hair, he thought. And she seemed to be dressed in something like a curtain. Good Lord, it was a wonder that the Ritz had allowed her across the threshold!

It was probably Octavia who had shepherded the woman inside. Octavia had taken a liking to the Bohemian type since she had moved to Chelsea. She had even hosted an art fair in Rutherford, to raise money for the Red Cross among the wealthy of the Yorkshire set. It had been a success, of course. Everything that Octavia turned her hand to was a success. She and Charlotte had run the whole thing last November, and made a great deal of money for the cause. Still, the presence of the artists themselves had shocked him. Peacocks and sluts, he had decided. Peacocks and sluts.

Christine Nesbitt, he could see, was smiling broadly at him now. He very pointedly ignored her.

After the speeches—thankfully brief—William took himself out into the side room that overlooked a small garden. He could see Green Park above the trees, and watched its soft horizon above the traffic while he lighted his cigar. He wished that he were back at Rutherford. My God, though, what a ripping send-off might have been arranged for Charlotte there! The great house open, the gardens sumptuous in spring. First hothouse roses, the vast lawns, the terraces all bright perfection, and room to wander after the meal. Room to breathe. London suffocated him now.

The days of his political life seemed far away since his heart attack last year. He went to the House occasionally, of course, and was received with deference. He had had dinner with Lloyd George himself last month, and was pleased to have found his own opinions listened to at some length. The Americans would soon come to the war; that was becoming ever more obvious since the Kaiser had ordered his submarines back into the Atlantic. William had heard a rumor only yesterday that their announcement might be imminent. He hoped to God that it would mean the end of the bloody carnage across the Channel. This year, or next.

At the thought of America, William frowned. He glanced back at the heavily curtained room where the guests were still milling around. One favor had been granted to him today: his wife's lover, John Gould, had been absent. He had dreaded leading Charlotte into the church and finding Gould's handsome, smiling face insulting him from a family pew. He had dreaded even more seeing Octavia hanging on the man's arm. But he had been spared it. His wife had a grain of decency left in her, it seemed.

As if summoned by his thoughts, Octavia now appeared at the dining room door. His wretched heart skipped a beat as she walked towards him, smiling. She was prettier than the bride, he thought.

His wife wore dove-grey velvet, with some sort of coat affair in the same material, and an alarming hat—very tall, rather asymmetrical—in the same color. When he remembered what she wore to their own wedding those many years ago—those yards and yards of lace, that voluminous gown—a smile came to his lips. How different she was now. No longer an obedient girl, but just as slender. More so, in fact. A bell-shaped skirt revealed her ankles; around her waist the fabric belt was silver. She carried a little ivory walking cane—for affectation only. He had never seen a woman so lively, so little in need of any walking aid; her face shone with pleasure. *Gould*, he suddenly thought to himself. *It's because of that damned bastard that I am shown my own wife's smiling face.*

Still, she overwhelmed him, despite everything. Lightly kissing his cheek, she took his arm. "Shall we walk a little way? Out to the terrace perhaps? You're feeling well enough?"

"I am feeling very well," he told her.

As they walked, he could feel the spring in her step. "Do you think Charlotte looked charming?" she asked.

"Very charming."

"She fussed so, you know," Octavia mused. "About the veil, the dress. But then, she was always quite unlike Louisa." She turned to him. "Louisa's coming-out gown, do you recall, dear? And the pink ball gown, all in silk."

"I do indeed." It had cost him an absolute fortune.

"You would think that I had been dragging Charlotte across the Styx when we went to the dressmakers," Octavia laughed. "But she will look back on it with pleasure."

He doubted that.

"You did terribly well today," she said quietly. "The new car was a delightful touch. A Silver Ghost at that! It was splendid. I recall the days when you would have thought a barouche much more the thing."

"I am trying to be modern," he replied.

"And succeeding beautifully."

God, he wished that she were not so happy. Pretty compliments flew from her. He would much rather have had her silence, even the unendurable silences they once had together at Rutherford. He would have rather had her expressionless face at dinner than to dine alone, as he often did now.

He stopped walking; she looked at him inquiringly. "Shall you come to Rutherford?" he asked.

She paused, evidently considering. "Are you going back there?"

"This week."

"Then I shall come the week after," she told him. "There is something that I want to talk to you about."

William frowned. "Not that subject."

"No, dear. Not that subject."

She had suggested a divorce last year, when Gould had suddenly reappeared at Rutherford after Mary and Nash's wedding. A matter of hours merely, and she had been packing her bags. "I thought him dead," she had said simply. "So did the world. So did you. But he survived the *Lusitania*. Don't tell me that you didn't hope he would never come back, William. But he is here, and there's an end to it." She had turned a calm, serene face to him. "You may divorce me if you wish."

He had denied her. He would not see their name dragged through the court to the accompaniment of the horrific scandal that would ensue. More importantly, he would never—never, never—let her marry Gould. Dally they might . . . play the lovebirds. Even live together in their outrageous sin. He'd thought, when Gould had left two years ago, that she'd turned her face from her lover. Ridiculous in his hopes. But he would retain the reins, however slackly, in his hand. And one day she would come back, when Gould tired of her.

He was living for that day.

Octavia reached up and drew down one of the cherry blossom bows. "Such a dreary spring we've had," she murmured. "I'm glad the sun shone a little today."

"What subject, then?" he asked. "What subject are you coming to Rutherford to discuss?" He narrowed his eyes. "Where is Gould?"

"At home," she told him. "Preparing to go to France."

"What for?" William felt furiously irritated that she referred to the little Chelsea love nest as "home."

She gave him an indulgent smile. "You know full well," she said. "America is coming to the war. He is going to Arras. The push that's going on. So that he can report back to his New York newspaper. 'In the teeth of battle, the true picture of war, how we are needed' . . . all that." Her voice had traces of sarcasm and anxiety. "He says he will try to find Harry to speak to him."

At the mention of his son's name, William searched her face. "Have you heard from him?"

"Not a word this week."

"Nor I."

"John says that pilots must be trained in the States. He wonders if Harry might be sent there. As an instructor."

"To America?"

"It would keep him out of France, at least."

"It is a possibility, I suppose. If they come in."

"John doesn't doubt it."

William was not interested in what Gould thought.

Together, he and Octavia surveyed the garden in silence, watching as more petals drifted from the trees and lay discolored on the ground.

Hundreds of miles away in France, Harry Cavendish had been thinking of Rutherford early that morning.

When he was a little boy, he had used to wander the great house at night. He doubted very much that his parents had ever known. In the dark now, staring at the sky just before dawn, he tried to remember how far he had gone along the winding stairs that led down to the kitchens, or along the gallery outside the upper bedrooms, or up the forbidden narrow steps to the roof. He must have been seven or eight when he had first discovered the way out onto the lead-covered valleys between the Tudor chimneys, and seen the rolling vastness of the Yorkshire Dales spread out, pinpricked with occasional lights, below him.

Sometimes he would wake in the morning and it would be hard to guess whether those discoveries had been real or only a dream. Even then, as a small child, he was intrigued by height, and a desire to fly. To stand at the edge of the roof and launch himself outwards and feel the air rushing underneath him.

It had been another dozen years before that fascination became a reality.

He was watching the airfield now, a beaten expanse of mud that had once been grass, just behind the town of Arras. His little sister was getting married today, he thought. Charlotte, the last person on earth whom he ever imagined to be shackled to a man and give up what poor rights she had. Still . . . if it was what she wanted, who was he to criticize her? He had met Michael only once, and although the former soldier was now permanently robbed of his sight, he seemed a determined sort of chap.

Even so. Charlotte a wife. Harry looked at the first streaks of dawn in the sky, a few short lighter glimpses among the clouds heavy with snow. Seventh of April, 1917. Just north of here was cider country, fields of apple trees. Somewhere beneath him, going east, he knew that the chalky earth was being tunneled; New Zealand and English engineers burrowing among the networks of underground quarries, the *boves* of the French. Beyond them was Vimy Ridge, where bombardment had started in the last ten days of March.

You wouldn't know it now. All was silent; whatever activity was

out there—and there was plenty—was smothered in the dark hours
and by the threatening weather.

But God, his body ached. He shifted marginally from foot to
foot, feeling the jarring in his joints. His knees grated as if bone
skated over bone. It was two years since he had been shot down,
danced along the ground in a shattering kite, rolled along the edge
of a trench, and stood up somehow, yelling at the Northumbrians
who came to carry him out.

Two years since he had met Caitlin. Two years since the series of
operations in England. And, like a sickening addict, he had only
thought of being back here and flying again. Having another chance
at the Boche, skimming his old Farman over the flattened landscape.

Harry sighed, looking backwards and forwards along the line of
silent planes—those flimsy-seeming craft. The waiting was the worst;
he felt it now in the seemingly two-dimensional shapes of the planes,
their silhouettes populated by ghosts. Harry watched the young
recruits go up—they would be out as soon as they arrived—and he
would try to ignore their youth and their enthusiasm. He trained
them as best he could. But he would give them few words, because
his words were all saved for the letters he would have to write later
in the day. Fifty percent were dead within forty-eight hours of taking their first kite to the skies.

He had spent last night trying to compose something different
to the parents of the man who had crashed behind enemy lines yesterday. *"A fine fellow of utmost bravery. . . ."* Had he said that last week
or yesterday? Or the day before? A fine fellow indeed. Whoever he
was. They all seemed the same to him . . . interchangeable characters.
All about twenty, square-shouldered, the captain of the cricket team,
the kind of good egg all-rounder beloved of his school. A school that
he had left not so long ago. The description might fit any or all of
them. Fine chaps indeed, but Harry had struggled to remember this

particular recruit exactly. Had he been the one from St. Albans or Edgeworth? Haringey or Twickenham? Carlisle or Cardiff? He hadn't been able to recall him. There were just too many molded in the same form, sprung from the same background, trudging through his mind waving their grinning and youthful good-byes.

And now would come Arras.

The word was that dominance in the air was vital for reconnaissance in this battle. More important than it had ever been, to accent the element of surprise. They simply had to get up there and go deeper than they had ever anticipated, drawing out the tumble of scribbled lines below them until it all made sense, and one could verify the lines of communication and support. They had to fly low and they had to fly slow to get as much information as they could. It was bloody dangerous, as his list of letters continually proved.

But last month something very odd had happened.

Harry was used to the Luftstreitkräfte—after all, why wouldn't he be after his weeks of flying last year, and his months of observing this year?—and he thought that he recognized them almost by instinct. Thought he could sense them in the sky, feel the malignity of all of them, German and British alike, feel their dribble of decay, of fumes, of smoke and fuel, of manic obsession, of curdling courage left in the sky like streamers. He thought he knew that even better than he knew their actual shape and size or coloring—or the black and white crosses on the bodies and the tails. But he didn't know the red plane above Arras that so many now had reported in the dogfights. Manic indeed, and deadly.

Some of the recruits called it a flying circus. The maneuvers were so deliberately scheduled, like a dance. Trained like performing animals. Jumping to the crack of a whip. Snapping their spines in unnatural arches and dives. Caged and uncaged birds. Beasts of the air. Broken birds on the ground. Wings and talons.

He laughed momentarily at himself. Was he asleep, dreaming? Such bizarre pictures he had in his mind.

He looked down at his feet to steady himself, to bring himself literally back to the ground and reality. One leg was foreshortened by his injuries. They had taken away some sort of ligament and a shattered bone—he had never asked, he hated the details. His mother had fussed over him so, and for most of his recovery he had wished Caitlin back by his side. With her nursing training she was routinely expressionless and calm, giving him her sweet smile only when it truly counted. He knew that it continued to be hell for her in the hospital trains and the first aid stations, and so he supposed his minor wounds—the breaking of both legs, the endless surgeries afterwards—did not move her so much as it moved his mother and sisters.

He missed Caitlin greatly. He had not heard from her in six weeks. Louisa had written to him that she was expected as a guest at Charlotte's wedding, and he was acutely jealous. She could go to see Charlotte and the rest of his family, but she was not allowed to come and see him. That was accepted; that was all right. But to not write to him was a mystery. She had written to accept her wedding invitation, so putting pen to paper was not beyond her.

He stopped this line of thinking, noticing the bitterness in his mind. He must not blame Caitlin. In her work, she was under tremendous stress. More so even than himself. It was very good of her to make time to attend the wedding. But God . . . how he wished that it had been *their* wedding. He would make her his own, he decided. He would stop this sense of loss and prevarication once and for all. She confused and preoccupied him so much; she kept her thoughts to herself. He did not know how to read her; he only knew how much he wanted to be with her.

He glanced at his watch; tried to make out the time in the grey dawn light. Five forty. He shivered involuntarily. One was always waiting these days. For the dawn to come, for orders. For scrambles up and setting down. For the onward-rushing flights, for the scream of the artillery. And for it all to stop. Time was full of strange beginnings and endings.

He had a strange notion suddenly then that it was, indeed, all over. That the end had finally come, and that the grass had grown again over the fields, blotting out the trenches, leaving only the merest shadowed scribble in the contours. That the troop stations were all closed, and the railway had returned to the sleepy lines in the countryside that they had once been, threading between villages, traveling slowly between the orchards and houses and chugging slowly over the bridges on the rivers. Time had pulled a merciful blanket over the misery.

And that he was standing here at the very edge of time itself, propped against the frame of a door, looking out into the murk and wondering what it was that would soon meet him. Perhaps, he thought, it was true. It would be true one day, after all. And that he stood here unknowingly, a shadow of a shadow of a shadow invisible to all but himself. He thought that he was long dead, and all the planes had gone, and nothing moved at all over the earth but the cool, dark wind.

He abruptly stood straight and shook himself free of the feeling. "Enough," he hissed to himself.

He lit a cigarette, and tried not to think at all.

At the Ritz it was the middle of the afternoon, and Charlotte was alone in an upper room, pulling off the veil, the dress, and the white satin shoes.

On the bed lay the clothes she had chosen for her going-away: a long hemp skirt that finished an inch or two above the ankles, a white blouse, and a dark blue jacket. Dressed only in her underthings, she surveyed the pile and the suitcase that lay on the floor alongside. Her mother had insisted on buying her a trousseau. "Not of the old-fashioned kind," Octavia had told her. "But just a few little delicates, darling. A nightdress, petticoats, stockings. They're lovely . . . look. Nice lawn and fine cotton. Irish linen. Don't you like them?"

She had shown them to Charlotte a month ago, and Charlotte had been painfully aware of how much Octavia had restrained a natural instinct to indulge her own fashionable impulses. If it had been completely up to her mother, the trousseau would have been an avalanche of lace and silk. "It's all very utilitarian," Octavia had said, seeing her daughter's hesitation. "Nothing outrageous. I know you shouldn't feel comfortable in anything like that."

Charlotte had relented, seeing how much Octavia wanted to please her, and she had wrapped her arms around her mother, laid her head on her shoulder, and thanked her. "It's very beautiful," she had murmured.

She looked at herself in the cheval mirror now: rather awkward, very slight. Her shingled hair stuck out at odd angles. She took up a brush from the dressing table and began brushing vigorously, the bristles prickling her scalp. Octavia had wanted to bring her own maid to attend to Charlotte, but there the line had been firmly drawn. "Mother, it is 1917," Charlotte had told her sternly. "It's nonsense to be gussied up by a maid. I don't need it. I'm certain that I can dress my own hair."

But the more she stayed alone in the room, the worse things became. She couldn't fasten the skirt properly; the blouse was too voluminous. At last, not knowing what was the matter with her, and realizing that sooner or later Octavia would indeed come up to see to her, Charlotte slumped down on the bed and wept. "Mother," she murmured, and then kicked the suitcase in frustration and fury.

There was a sudden knocking at the door.

Charlotte froze, hastily rubbing away a tear. "Who is it?"

The door opened a tiny crack, and a wide, smiling face looked in at her. "It's me, pumpkin."

"Oh, Christine! Well, you might as well come in."

"Might I? It looks a perfect cavern of destruction. What a mess you've made of a decent room." And, laughing, Christine Nesbitt came into the bedroom. She was carrying a bottle of champagne and two glasses. "What's the matter?" she asked. "You've not been weeping?" She walked over to the bed. "If you have, I shouldn't blame you," she commented blithely. "Here, have a drink. You'll feel so much better."

She poured the wine, and sat down next to Charlotte. "Bottoms up. Here's to swimmin' with bow-legged wimmin."

Charlotte stared at her, then, despite herself, burst out laughing.

"That's better," Christine said. "Here's another one. May you be in a heaven an hour before the Devil knows you're dead."

"Amen."

They drank.

Charlotte had known Christine for six months. All those weeks ago, on one of her three volunteer days at St. Dunstan's Hospital, Charlotte had spotted a slight figure—she'd really thought that it was a boy at first—perched on a bench in the park, engaged in what looked like very earnest conversation with a Navy man who had recently arrived.

Charlotte had hurried across to them that morning—out of anxiety more than anything else. She had been told to keep a close watch on Joshua Smith. He was a Lewis gunner in the Naval Air Service—or rather, he had been. But Allington had trouble believing that such a life as he had lived in the last two years was now in the past. He had been in a state of confusion for some time even after his diagnosis.

"I'll go back when I can see again," he'd told her robustly on the day that he had been admitted. "It'll come back. It's only the cold."

His pilot had ditched at sea. They had quite simply run out of fuel over the Channel, way out past Dover, towards the North Sea, on the coast of Norfolk. "We got lost," he had added, smiling to himself. "That's what I reckon, lost." No one had told him any different that first day. The difference being that his pilot was dead, and Joshua blinded, slumped unconscious, had known nothing until the water hit him.

"It's the cold, the cold," he had kept saying. She had sat with him on the first evening. He had been feverish and kept removing himself from the bed. She had caught him feeling his way down the corridor, his fingers pinching the wooden rail at waist height. He'd heard her footsteps behind him. "Where am I?" he'd asked her. "In hospital at home," she'd told him, and gently taken hold of his arm.

"Don't put me back with the blind," he'd said. "I'm not blind. It's only the cold of the sea that's done it. It's temporary." And on, and on. The cold, the cold. Eventually she had got him to sit down on a chair in the corridor. The lights were all low, the gas sputtering in the gaskets.

"We went up steeply," he murmured. "Then it stopped and started to go back. It had no speed, no power. The wind was stronger than the power it had to go forward, you see." He had paused, reliving the stalling of the engine and the aching silence that took the place of the roar of the prop and the rushing of the air as they descended. "I could see it coming towards us," he continued. He spoke slowly, dreamily. "You'll not see that often, you know? I have it here in my mind." He tapped his temple with his index finger. "I have that picture—of the waves, you know—like corrugated iron, and the very color of iron. I closed my eyes as we hit, and that's what's done it. The cold shut my eyes."

She'd stayed for a long time holding his hand, and eventually he submitted to being taken back to bed.

When she had seen him again the following week, he had asked, "Is it the lady who was here on my first night?"

"It is."

"You'll have to forgive me for my stupidity," he told her. "The doctor has spoken to me." He had shrugged and spread his hands. "It's that there's no pain to speak of," he said. "You understand, no pain, not what I would class as pain, really?"

She'd hesitated by the bed.

"I thought it must have been the shock of the seawater. But of course it can't be that." Charlotte had tried not to look into his face; rather, she occupied herself by staring at a spot on the linoleum so that she would not cry at his pathetic good humor, the embarrassment at his confusion. He had tapped his hand on the counterpane and gave a little gusting sigh. "A piece of the aircraft," he said. "Not a bullet at all, not a shell. Ridiculous. So . . . I'm not quite sure what I shall do. . . ."

"That will all be explained."

"Will it?" he'd asked. "But I'm a gunner in the Navy. I'm in the Navy, you see. . . ."

Hard to let go. To imagine any other life. "My brother is with the Flying Corps in France," she'd replied.

"Is he?" There had been a long silence.

"I must get on."

"Of course," he'd replied, with that same bewildered air. "Of course."

And it had been Allington who had been sitting on the bench with Christine the very first time that Charlotte had met her.

Charlotte was wary—so many visitors just appeared and thought they were being helpful. They wandered in out of Regent's Park despite all efforts to dissuade them. Charlotte's worst fear was that she would come across some motherly women weeping over a "poor blinded boy," as she had once found.

But she need not have worried with Christine Nesbitt.

Christine had not an ounce of pathos in her, nor was she taken to weeping. But she was an avid, intelligent listener. And as she spoke, she drew.

That morning—frost was on the ground all around them—Christine had a drawing pad balanced on her lap and was sketching as she listened to Allington. As Charlotte had drawn nearer, she had heard what Allington was saying.

"When I first got in a cockpit, I shot at the enemy with two Enfield rifles," he was telling her. "Not much use. And then we got the Lewis gun." He had begun to laugh quietly to himself. "Marvelous thing, but we had to shoot through the prop. Imagine that! Shoot through the thing that was keeping you in the air. Then they invented a synchromesh gear."

Drawing rapidly, Christine had not looked up, but she asked the question. "What was that?"

"Clever. It synchronized the firing of the gun through the propeller."

"Gosh. That *is* clever."

"Made life easier."

"Of course."

Christine had then looked up at Charlotte, realizing that they were being observed. She smiled broadly.

"It's a funny thing," Allington was saying, unaware that Charlotte was close by, standing on the grass. "Of all the things I see in my mind's eye, it's the sea and the muzzle of the Lewis aimed through the propellers. The rippling look of the sea, and the rippling of the propeller. Why do you suppose that is?"

Christine did not offer any trite opinion. She sat back and thought about what Allington had said. "The two are very similar," she observed, at last. "When you think about it. They're a pattern. Rippling lines. One horizontal. One vertical. You'll have developed observation by looking through the Lewis gun lines and the propeller, won't you? So it's stayed there."

"I see it," he said. "Just like when you shut your eyes against the sun, you see patterns of whatever was there."

"Shadows and lines."

"Yes, quite." Allington smiled. He had a pleasant face, if one did not look too closely at his scars—the fretwork of lines that radiated over his forehead and brows. Then he seemed to realize Charlotte's presence, and turned around.

"It's Nurse Cavendish." She was allowed to call herself this, halfway through her VAD training. "Shall we walk back? The doctor's rounds will be very shortly."

She had glanced at the drawing pad before she left.

Christine had not drawn Allington. She had drawn his vision of the sea.

Charlotte gazed at Christine now above the rim of her glass. "Did you draw me today?"

"I didn't bring anything. But I shall if you like. You and Michael together, a portrait?"

"I suppose that's the done thing. I'll ask Father to commission a portrait. He can afford you. I can't."

Christine laughed. She had become well known in the last few months, after she had painted Dora Carrington. "Shall I be outrageously expensive?"

"Outrageously."

"Oh good," Christine said. "It will pay my bills all winter. Will he mind?"

"Father?" Charlotte considered. "You know, he doesn't seem to mind anything much. Not at all how he used to be. It's sweet, but odd. He seems like a volcano that's gone silent. I don't know what would rouse him. I sometimes fear it."

"That he'll blow his top? Over what?"

"Who knows, if Mother's situation doesn't rouse him? He looks at her with such mystification. So very perplexed. I worry that one day his anger will come back."

"What will he do? Chase her up the Strand with a carving knife?"

Charlotte laughed, then her face fell. "Perhaps," she murmured. "Dear God, I hadn't considered that."

Christine put down her glass and came and sat beside Charlotte on the bed. "It was a joke, darling." She put her hand over Charlotte's, and Charlotte looked down at their intertwined fingers.

"Do you remember when Mother brought you to Rutherford last year?"

"How could I forget? Such a shock." Christine gazed up at the ceiling, smiling, remembering. She then closed her eyes. "An arts fair. I thought I was coming to one of those dreadful charity galas. You know . . . 'one of our remarkable lady artists.' The one I had been to before in Chelsea Town Hall had been run by a set of behatted matrons who asked if I would do little caricatures of guests for sixpence a time. They thought that's what I did . . . cartoons and sketches. It was purgatory."

Charlotte smiled, looking at the arch of Christine's neck, the sculptured bone of her clavicle, the thinness of the shoulders under the purple linen tunic. She had a momentary longing to reach out and touch Christine's skin. It was translucent, as if the young woman were not really flesh and blood.

"And so your Mother asked me to come to Yorkshire. I thought, Yorkshire! Where on earth is that?" She opened her eyes. Charlotte rapidly looked away.

"You were a sensation."

"Of course I was," Christine replied. "I *am* a sensation. Don't you know that?"

They smiled at each other.

"I do like your sister," Christine observed. "I've been chatting to her. She's such a sweetie, isn't she? She was so nice to me when I came to Rutherford." She leaned closer to Charlotte. "I caught her reading a letter just now in the ladies' cloakroom. Who is it that writes to her? Is it a beau?"

Charlotte frowned. "Not that I know of. Why do you think so?"

"She was so utterly absorbed. And, you know"—Christine wriggled the fingers of both hands in the air—"away with the fairies. Smiling. A certain *sort* of smile. As soon as she noticed me, she hid it away in her purse. Is it a secret romance, do you suppose?"

"I hope not. Not after Charles de Montfort and the elopement."

"My God, I'd forgotten. But she wouldn't do that again, surely."

"Louisa lives at Rutherford with Father. I can't think she's found anyone at all to be romantic with in Yorkshire. You haven't met our local chaps, have you? Hardly the types to steal a girl's heart."

Christine laughed. "Born with a silver spoon in the mouth, and so unable to string two words together? Yes, I know the type. There's plenty of those in London, too."

They sat in silence for a while, both staring at the discarded wedding dress. Eventually, Christine bestirred herself. "Shall you live with your Mother, you and Michael?"

"Oh no. We have our own house."

Christine gasped in surprise. "Your own? How wonderful." She pressed her hands together in something like an attitude of prayer. "And do you have . . . space? Of your own?"

"It isn't really very big. It's a mews. A town house."

"But you have your own bedroom?"

"No." Charlotte got up and walked to the window.

"Oh, but I suppose that doesn't matter," Christine said hastily. "It's rather cozy, isn't it? Two birds in a nest."

Charlotte leaned on the windowsill, looking down on the gardens. "Yes."

Behind her, Christine was frowning. But then she got to her feet, placing her glass on the bedside cabinet. "You must come and see me when you get back," she said. "I can't think why you've never come to my rooms before, when I've been over at your mother's house so much. Lovely parties! So . . . we'll put that right. I should like us to be much better friends, wouldn't you? Where are you off on honeymoon? Did your mother say Dorset?"

Charlotte turned. "You want me to come to your studio?"

"Well, you must if I'm to paint the two of you."

"Oh, of course. Yes. We shall. We shall telephone you when we come back."

Christine laughed. "I don't have a telephone, darling. I don't have anything much at all. You'll see when you come. Bare boards and a gas ring, and a sort of couch that I sleep on. I can't cook—I never knew how. Do you?"

"No, not at all."

"Will you have a cook at your little house?"

"Yes. Michael's mother has seen to it."

Christine heard the faint tone of irritation. She gave a hearty, gusty sigh. "Well, how lucky!" she exclaimed, trying to be jolly. "I wish I did. My aunt thinks I'm turning into a gypsy. Which is quite bothering, because she gives me an annuity, bless her. I need to keep on the right side of her. But the frowns and the wiping of fingers when she visits—it's hard to bear! Do you know what she said to me the last time she came? She said, 'I sincerely hope you will grow out of this malodorous phase, Christine.'" She let out a peal of laughter. "Malodorous! I didn't realize I was quite that bad. Actually, her own place has a whiff of the sepulchre about it. Mothballs, paneling, polish. Like an undertaker's parlor!"

Charlotte did not seem to be listening. She was absentmindedly picking up clothes from the floor and was carrying them around on one arm, as if she had no idea what she should do with them.

"So," Christine labored on. "Don't disapprove of me and my hovel, will you?"

Charlotte at last looked up at her. "No," she replied, almost puzzled. "I don't think I could ever disapprove of a little studio." She smiled wistfully. "It must be heaven."

s Christine Nesbitt went down the stairs, she met Octavia Cavendish coming up.

"Have you been to see Charlotte?" Octavia asked.

"I think she needs a mother's touch," Christine told her. "She seems quite nervous. Distracted."

"Nervous?" Octavia echoed, raising an eyebrow. "I shouldn't think so. Charlotte has never been afraid of anything in her life."

You're wrong, Christine thought. *She is now.*

But she knew better than to say so.

Chapter 3

When he reached England, no one ever asked him where he came from; only his rank, his regiment, and the place of capture. And no one ever asked him why he kept his hands clasped so tightly.

When Frederick Wilhelm Reinhardt had first been a prisoner on English soil, and when they saw that he couldn't hold a cup, and that he took so long to dress himself, and that he dropped almost everything they tried to give him—they sent him to a hospital somewhere on the outskirts of an industrial town, a small place of single-story buildings.

He was with another German, and he held his arm. But he was ashamed of the other man, who shambled his way across the yard so brokenly that it seemed he was drunk. They took him to a separate room.

Frederick was very sorry to have caused trouble. The doctors had not even asked him the reason for his agonizing hands. They only tried to reason or wrestle it out of him, opening his palms and stretching the fingers and giving him a kind of exercise to do. He would obey—he always tried to obey—but often in an hour or so the clutching would come back.

The hospital, he surmised, had given up on him, after having written a great deal about him in notebooks. They sent him back to the other prisoners of war. And in time they all came here. They told him it was the north of England, and in the country. Not a city. He was glad of that.

Frederick understood in time that if he was not to attract attention, he must try not to hold his fingers together. If he had had more mastery of English, he would have tried to explain. But he had little English. Only a word or two. He was trying to learn more now that he was at a camp called Catterick.

Name and rank. Regiment. The first time that he had said his name when they arrived here, the officer writing at the table had looked up at him. "Frederick Wilhelm, eh?" he had said, and spat on the floor. "Like the Kaiser Wilhelm."

It had been dark, and raining, and everyone was deadly tired from the journey, the English guards as much as them. Frederick had felt like part of some cattle shipment, or livestock of some other kind. Now he knew what the cattle felt like on the farm at home, and he wondered if his own face showed the same expression of exhausted bewilderment that he had seen when his family had shipped cows to market. He felt like a worthless beast, pushed onto trucks, shoved into straight lines. Dark and raining: that was his first impression of the POW camp.

He wanted to say that he was sorry to have such a name as Wilhelm. He had never liked it much himself. He wanted to tell them that they could cross it out of his records if they despised it so much, if it reminded them of the Kaiser. He would have no objection. But they wrote quickly, moving on to the next man, and shouldering him aside. "I am from Holzminden," he wanted to tell them. It seemed important. To hold on to the place he was born. But of course it wasn't important to the officer writing at the table. Only name and rank. And regiment.

When he saw that there were small villages here, and farms, he felt a kind of crushing longing. He felt his own language press on his tongue, *milch, landwirt, pferd*. Was there anyone here like him, someone who had been sent back perhaps, some farmhand wounded beyond use who had returned, whose soul had gone down in the mud?

Arriving here, all the prisoners had all stood in line and wondered what it was that they were expected to do in England. Backbreaking labor. Mine work, perhaps. They had waited all night that first night, most of them not sleeping despite the weariness. Anxiety had gnawed a sore spot in his heart. All night he had heard men shuffling around him, crammed into iron-framed beds, hearing the rain drum on the corrugated iron roofs.

Could it be worse than Flanders? Could it be worse than Munster? He had been at a railway station there about a year ago, waiting for transport. And a train had come in carrying British prisoners. There had been two women waiting on the platform, and when they saw the wounded being carried out, one woman had burst into tears, and the other had spat in the face of the nearest man.

He had not the heart to blame. He wouldn't blame a British woman either for doing the same. As the night went on, he had begun to worry what would happen when the daylight came. He imagined them all swept out the next morning, unfed, bullied, and taken somewhere. Did the British shoot those who refused to work? Did they shoot those who *couldn't* work? He flexed his hands in the dark, willing them to open up. He must be able to carry something, work at something, he thought. Panic almost suffocated him there in the dark. Would he starve, here among the farms, here in a green country? Here among hills, in the kind of landscape that was so familiar to him?

But they had been marched out the next morning to a canteen, were given tea and bread and a sour kind of margarine, and marched again to the little station. Waited there, and been taken to the village, and set to work making a road. And although it had been raining in a drifting, misty fashion, it had been all right. Swamped by relief, and by memory, more than one man had stopped from time to time, both grief and relief escaping them. But they had stifled their gasps, hid their feelings even from those next to them, and had wiped their faces as if sweating and not weeping.

That day, he had learned new English words. Among them, "Waiting" and "Back up." He understood that they had put the sergeant's temper up. Or "back up," as he said. "You have put my back up, you . . ." Because he had not moved faster in the line, and because he had dropped the sledgehammer that had been thrust into his hands. And the rest of the sentence that the sergeant yelled he understood. Yes . . . "Fucking Germans" he understood already.

And he knew what "Mother" meant. He had learned that in a specific and memorable way. It wasn't so different to German, of course. "Mutter" and "Mother." They revealed the Saxon background of both countries, the bloodstock that millennia ago both armies had sprung from. Saxons and Angles and Jutes. All the same, under the skin.

And so . . . "Mother." One day in January in France in 1916 he had fallen into a task that was not his, but which his officer insisted upon by way of screams and slaps, to accompany a missionary seconded to the lines.

It had been snowing. The British had advanced the day before, and been beaten back, and there were pockets of wounded and dead all over. Their own, and the enemy. They had come upon a British boy, merely a boy. Seventeen or eighteen, he had guessed. They laid him out on a piece of trailer waiting for the horses to come to take the wounded. They chose the wood because this boy's back seemed to be broken. The missionary read from the Bible, and all the time Frederick could see the boy's eyes flitting from the Bible to the missionary's face, and back again, and then to himself. Occasionally he would let off a volley of words. The first that they heard were angry. The final few were quieter. And finally, the boy said the word that Frederick knew was "Mother."

It was not said in any kind of crying way. It was said with delight, and the boy's face had broken into a smile, a smile of astonishment as if he had seen something that they could not. Frederick thought about that often.

He dozed a little now, leaning his head surreptitiously against an iron pole that supported the station roof. Every morning they came here, a group of thirty or so of them, and were taken along the little railway line that crossed the barrack yard and out alongside the river. When they got to just outside a small village, they were off-loaded. The road that was being laid between the village and one farther along passed through a small place with a lovely church and a large wooden gate with a canopy over the top. A strange word for it, another he had learned—"lych-gate." He had asked just yesterday what it was called. "What do you want to know for, Kraut?" "I should like to know. It is good . . . nice." "Nice, is it? Got any churches where you come from?" *Gott einig* . . . is that what the man had said? Surely not. It didn't make sense anyway. "Got any . . ." Maybe that was it. But, if so, he still couldn't fathom it. The guard had laughed. "Church, don't you know church?"

He knew church. *Kinder, Kuche, Kirche.* The litany of the hausfrau, the good German woman. The good German family. He didn't speak. Didn't answer back. He smiled.

"You don't know nothing," the guard had said, in a cheerful and triumphant fashion. The English were strange. They insulted you without malice.

An hour or so later, he had tried again while they were allowed to rest. They were given water and they sat on the side of the road, on deep grass verges by the same church. He had pointed again at the gate. "Is called?"

"What—the lych-gate?"

"Yes, please. Thank you."

Lych-gate, lych-gate.

He liked being out of the camp. He supposed they were a long way from anywhere—from ports, from cities. If you ran—tried to escape—you would be walking for many miles. And over high ground. He could see hills in all directions. The houses were spread far apart, and a man on his own would be captured in no time.

He didn't want to go back, anyway. Not very much. His father had died years before, and his mother and Matthau ran the family farm. He had been his father's boy, and he felt there would be very little for him when he did eventually get back.

Perhaps he was wrong, he wondered.

Perhaps his mother cried for him . . .

At the end of the day, the train came back. It was like a kind of clockwork toy swaying along the single track. There were sixty or seventy trains a day. The open trucks were to transport the prisoners wherever they were designated to go; the closed ones often brought wounded to the camp's military hospital.

There were over seven hundred beds in that hospital—such as it was, not a brick institution, nothing fancy or large or established—but hundreds of half-brick, half-iron huts. He pitied the men inside them. The huts were cold; he knew that because he delivered coal sometimes to the big pot-bellied stoves. The staff liked to open windows to keep infection down, to circulate air, to extract the fumy dust of the fires. He had taken coal to the stores outside the hut walls, the bunkers that abutted the hut walls, and he could hear the striking clatter of iron beds on linoleum floors and the footsteps of the scurrying nurses.

He had been lucky not to be wounded. It was just his hands. . . .

Frederick Reinhardt closed his eyes, thinking, *It is April now.* April. The month of blossom. The month of green leaves.

April . . . that was the same word in English and German.

Four days after Charlotte's wedding, William and Louisa were back at Rutherford.

William had taken a motor taxi from York, as it was difficult to find a train that ran according to the timetable now. He said nothing to the cab driver; he was tired of sociability; he wanted his own bed. Louisa, too, seemed sunk deep in her own thoughts; he wondered if it were that Charlotte had been married when Louisa was the elder sister, but he did not know how to ask his daughter this. He watched her staring out of the cab window; if she caught his gaze, she smiled back at him immediately, but he could not help thinking that there was something secret in that smile, something closed to him.

Eventually, she took his hand as the cab sped out from York and into the darkening countryside. "Are you feeling well, Father?"

"Yes, perfectly."

"Looking forward to being home?"

"Yes, indeed. And what are you going to do with yourself this week?" he asked.

"I've promised Dora Henistbury-Falle that I shall help with the friendship sale that sends parcels to Yorkshire regiments. You know, chocolates and clothes and things."

"Ah, yes."

"And yourself, Father?"

"Lord Lieutenant's lunch. Seeing the land steward about the manning levels at the farms. Busy enough."

Louisa nodded once or twice, put her hand to her face. In another few minutes, she had closed her eyes. William continued to look at her in the shadows, grateful that she was with him and not with her mother. It was a remarkable change in her, this girl who had always wanted to attend a party; it was as if her abandonment by Charles de Montfort had removed part of her character entirely. But he liked the young woman who was alongside him now, and who had taken on so much of the running of the household at Rutherford. He liked her quietness, her growing sagacity. Her maturity had heightened her attractiveness, in his eyes: of course she still had the light coloring, the wide-set bright eyes, the slimness and fluidity of shape—she *looked* like Louisa, she *moved* like Louisa, but in all else she was not Louisa. Or, rather, she was a much improved version of his darling child.

She seemed content, despite their mutual isolation deep in the northern Dales. Once or twice he had asked her if she would like young people at the house; he had suggested that she arrange it. And Louisa had organized tennis teas in the summer and little dances for her friends in the winter. It had all been very jolly, very sociable. But he still couldn't help feeling that part of her—an important, personal part—was far removed from her daily life.

He had asked her, just before last Christmas, if there was anyone special that she would like to invite to luncheon. She had named a girlfriend. But not a man. He had remarked on it. "I have enough to love," she had replied. "There's Sessy . . . and you."

He had been flattered. Although love was not something mentioned very much. He did not think that the word ever needed saying, actually. That he loved his daughter, and that she loved him, was apparent. And she quite patently adored little Sessy, Harry's daughter from his brief relationship three years ago.

William did hope, nonetheless, that Louisa did not intend to become an old maid here at Rutherford. He did not want her to be alone.

He would not have wanted that, for he knew what that was like.

When the cab turned in at the huge park gates, William could feel relief coursing through him, easing away the grit and grime of the capital city that seemed to have infiltrated even his thoughts. He watched as they traveled up the drive lined with its hundred-year-old beeches, and noticed that they were just beginning to show the acid green of spring. As the drive curved round, the house came into view, and he felt, as he always felt, inordinate pride.

Rutherford was a lovely place, mellow-colored, dark terracotta now soaked with the rain, framed by the gardens. High on the roof, the medieval past was echoed in a dozen barley-twist chimneys, and to either side the rambling east and west wings spread out. Beyond the house itself, a few flickering lights betrayed the existence of the cottages belonging to the head gardener, March, and the groom and his family, the Armitages. The high walls of the kitchen garden, themselves wreathed in clematis, almost hid the lazy spirals of smoke from the cottages beyond the stables.

William took a deep, appreciative breath. All was stillness, all was calm. Every time he came home, he surprised himself by how he increasingly appreciated that security. In London, one could almost feel war lapping at the gates; sometimes one could, on a very calm day, hear the distant thunder of guns in France.

But Rutherford—at least for the time being—was safe. He glanced at the warm lights in the drawing room windows. The house, once decaying for lack of a fortune, had been saved by his marriage to Octavia. It was she—by virtue of the mills that her family owed—who had brought the wealth back to Rutherford, and turned it from a neglected place of crumbling walls and rotted windows into this place of extraordinary comfort and beauty.

The great Tudor door opened as the cab drew up in front of the steps. William saw his butler, Bradfield, marshaling the few staff that they had left to them to compose a welcome. Once, Harrison, the footman, would have been in that group—and, for a moment, William thought he glimpsed the tall and rangy figure in the shadows. But it was not so, of course. Harrison had died in the battle at La Quinque Rue in 1915; he was buried—where? In truth, William did not know where his man was buried. Perhaps that was something that one would be told when all the hell was over. It was a failing, William felt, that Harrison could not come home to rest, but what was one to do? One could not insist upon it. It was simply impractical. There were too many bodies, too many hasty burials. Two of the Rutherford gardeners had not come home at all, and were part of that "foreign field that was forever England"—or so the young poet would have it, the one who himself was buried now in Greece.

The taxicab door was opened. Louisa, immediately awake, sprang out, smiling. Mary and Jenny, the housemaids, dipped a curtsey to her. "How are we all?" he heard his daughter say.

Bradfield was paying the driver. William pulled his coat around himself, staring momentarily at the ground.

Well, England. One supposed that this was what they were all fighting for, this country of theirs. Their way of life. He had been so confident about it once, when he was the right-hand man of Grey, and honored with the Prime Minister's confidences. "The lights are going out all over Europe" Grey had murmured one night before war broke out, watching a lamplighter from the windows of his Whitehall office.

But neither of them had guessed at how many lights.

*O*nce Louisa had brushed past the welcoming staff, smiling brightly, nodding in response to questions, she ran down the whole length of the Tudor hall in the center of the house.

Her footsteps echoed as she turned to enter her father's study and library; she crossed the room quickly and opened the door to the orangerie. Just for a moment she stopped and thought of Charlotte. Darling Charlotte . . . She hoped that she would be very happy. She had sat here a hundred, perhaps a thousand times with her sister. In winter, they used to play here all the time. Harry would join in their games, playing hide-and-seek among the potted palms and the apricot trees and lemon trees until their nanny—or the fearsome housekeeper Mrs. Jocelyn—had come to herd them away from her father's sanctuary. "Your father is busy," had been the constant litany. "You must not annoy him with your noise."

And they had been so afraid of Father then—such a distant, brooding presence, like some sort of god inhabiting a book-lined Mount Olympus. He had seemed a magnificent figure to them—a glimpse at breakfast or in the half hour before dinner had been all that had been allowed. It was only since last year that Louisa had come to see her father as a real human being at all. And now, after his heart attack, and retirement from public life, he had shrunk to more approachable proportions. He still blustered, of course. Still stamped about his land ordering this and that improvement. Still took himself off to York and his clubs. Still had his guns, his shoots, his meets. But he was gentler. He was calmer. And certainly more thoughtful, although he did not confide in her.

How she and Charlotte had clung to Mother when they had been children! Octavia had been so much more a loving, tactile parent. One of Louisa's first memories was of hiding her face in her mother's long and voluminous skirts, while her mother stroked her hair. My God, how wonderful those satins and silks and crepes had smelled! Lilies of the valley, faintly. And French perfume. Always something light and fragrant, like flowers. If Louisa closed her eyes now, she could summon up Octavia's scent in a moment.

Mother visited often, but it was not the same as it had once been. Since Octavia had fled with John Gould last year, Louisa and Charlotte had been left to puzzle out the story of her mother's secret romance. The pieces had fallen into place eventually—Gould's prolonged visit while they had been in London after Louisa's presentation at Court—the preoccupied silences during the following winter. And the awkwardness between her parents. When Gould had reappeared on the scene, the scales had been wrenched from their eyes. There had been a flurry of movement when Gould reappeared at Rutherford—of overheard raised voices between her parents—of repressed scenes, of tears. And the night after her mother and Gould had left together, Louisa had found her father pacing up and down the Tudor hall in the early hours of the morning. He had looked like someone who had been assaulted or injured—his face had worn an expression of furious bewilderment. Louisa had run downstairs when she had realized that the pacing footsteps were his, and had taken his arm and guided him back to his own bedroom. He had refused to get into bed and they had sat in opposite chairs until dawn.

She took a deep breath now. Change had swept over Rutherford like a tidal wave, uprooting everything, changing everything. And in her own life, too. . . .

Suddenly galvanized again, she ran to the orangerie door, and stepped out into the garden. She ran down the herringbone path, under the pollarded lime trees, to the door in the wall that led through to the kitchen gardens.

Here she hurried down between the carefully tended rows, the forcing beds for pineapples, for melons; down past the fruit cages that would yield strawberries and raspberries in just a few weeks, inhaling the tart aroma of their leaves in the twilight. A few more steps took her to another door, leading out into the stable yard.

Here, she paused again, looking across the yard to the Armitages' cottage. She really ought not to intrude, she thought. She really ought not to be here at all.

And, as if summoned by her thoughts, the door to the cottage opened. For a moment, Josiah Armitage was framed in the light of the door. Then he closed it and progressed down the path and out into the yard. He shuffled a little as he walked. He was in his mid-seventies, and the posting of his only son, Jack, to the veterinary corps in France seemed to have broken something in him. He looked his age.

He noticed her only as he got very close to her.

"Why, Miss Louisa. Welcome 'ome." He tipped his forehead, where the peak of a cap would normally be.

"Hello, Armitage. How are you?"

"Oh, as well as can be expected."

They looked at one another in silence. Louisa felt the blood thumping in her chest. Her face was flushed, but she hoped that he would not see it.

"I wondered . . ." she began. And stopped again. She cleared her throat. "And . . . how is Mrs. Armitage?"

The old man smiled slowly. "Waiting. Like we all do." Armitage, like most Yorkshiremen of his generation, was a man of very few words.

Louisa bit her lip. She didn't know how to go on.

At last, Armitage put her out of her embarrassed misery. He fished in his pocket and brought out a very slim envelope, and held it out to her. "If you don't mind my saying," he muttered softly, "'tis a strange thing to be a messenger. I'm not right comfortable with it, miss."

She took the letter, seeing Jack's writing upon it.

"Thank you," she replied. They paused another moment. She wanted to tell Jack's father that it wasn't at all what it seemed. That there was nothing improper in the correspondence, and that her own father would not dislike letters being kept away from the house, or her scurrying through to the staff quarters to retrieve them. She wanted to say that it was all of no consequence, that it was just some kind of harmless entertainment.

But it would not be true, of course.

They both knew that.

*I*t was deathly still at Catterick.

That night there had been a thunderstorm after the warmer temperatures of the day. It was odd, because although a little more bearable, it had hardly been a summer day; the clouds had rolled in like fast grey breakers on a stormy sea, obliterating the light. It was not the kind of weather that a man would associate with thunder.

But all the same it came, and the lightning lit up the bleak barracks yards beyond the windows. Frederick did not know what went through the other men's minds but he could have guessed. The thunder was like artillery. When the storm came overhead, you could feel it reverberating in your bones just the same as when they had been at the front.

It passed within an hour. The hut was like a morgue, a hundred men stretched out and motionless and sleepless, full of memories. Ghosts walked between the beds. Ghosts they didn't want to see, or think about.

He must have fallen asleep in the early hours, and he found himself on a field at home, looking back towards the farm. He laid down in the grass and covered his face with his fingers just as he had used to do when a child, spacing his fingertips so that he saw the farm buildings in a haze of grass.

He supposed that he had been a typical child. He liked the rough and tumble of the schoolyard, and he grudged his way through lessons, not understanding much but eager to please, stumbling his way through Charlemagne and Teutonic history, and naming all the rivers of Germany, and puzzling over a little Latin. Mathematics he had liked. And botany. But botany was not a manly subject.

Nevertheless, he learned all the names of the insects on the farm, drawing them. His brother caught butterflies and pinned them, still wriggling, to a sheet, but he couldn't bring himself to do that. He liked to collect insects in matchboxes. He had a spider once with a black-and-white patterned back. He had ladybugs. He would hold them close to his face and marvel at the depth of the color on their wings; when they finally unhitched the scarlet armor plating, he was fascinated by the complicated black lace that enabled them to fly. He loved the fragile down on butterfly wings. He would lie on his back and let them walk about on his hands and arms, laboring their way along while the sun beat down on them. In his dream now, he felt a matchbox on his palm just like the ones in which he would keep his treasures. He carefully pried it open.

It was full of lice.

He felt no surprise, and no loathing. The war had taken loathing away. Lice were a fact. They came from the world into which he had been conscripted. It was not the fault of the lice that a mass of human beings had suddenly presented themselves in filthy conditions. He stared at the creatures, all no bigger than a grain of rice, inside the box—feeling once again their unbearable itch.

In all the time that he had been fighting, he had never had a bath, never had a change of clothes. The lice were constant, as continuous as the noise, the fear, the shuddering of the guns.

He looked down at his hands again, and the light went out of the dream. There was a single line across the center of his sight, and above the line was dark blue, and below the line was black. He heard a whisper, an order, that he must go up into the dark blue, and crouch down, and feel his way towards the machine gun post. It was three o'clock in the morning, and he knew that the man who was whispering to him was lost; lost in his mind, insane. But he was his officer.

He got up and slouched through the mud.

As he went he saw, bizarrely, crushed in the foul-smelling dirt, a reflection from a piece of metal. The darkness was suffocating and cold, as thick as the mud itself, a miasma, and he tried to see what the metal was—whether it was an unexploded shell, or a weapon, or shrapnel. He peered at it, astonished to see lettering on it: *Crosse & Blackwell Plum and Apple Jam*. The utterly prosaic nature of it touched him, made him want to weep.

But its presence showed that he was near the British. They threw their cans away. He'd seen them, through his periscope, throw their hard tack biscuits away, too. Biscuits so hard that no one could eat them. He doubted that the British could be as hungry as they were. He had forgotten the true taste of food, and so the sight of the tin, and the thought that discarded food might be down there among the dirt . . .

He lost concentration, and that was when it began.

The place was Pilckem Ridge.

Chapter 4

*I*t was eight o'clock in the evening, and already dark, before Charlotte and Michael arrived in Dorset. They had taken the train to Sherborne, and a taxicab to the cottage that had been loaned to them by Michael's aunt. Michael had not wanted to go to a hotel—"to be stared at" as he put it. She didn't know how he realized such things, and had once said so. He had given his little crooked smile. "The room goes very quiet," he'd told her. "One feels something like a ripple. Of interest. Of pity. That's what I can't bear."

Tonight, as the train had approached the country station, she had asked about his aunt. "We shall have to visit her, I'm afraid, despite her being as mad as a hatter," he explained. "She's not far away, in the village."

"Is the village very remote?" Charlotte had asked him last month, when they had been finalizing their arrangements. She was certainly hoping so.

"It's a nice little place, very friendly," Michael had answered.

When she had confided this to Louisa, her sister merely laughed.

"I don't see the problem," she'd exclaimed. "If you don't want visitors, bar the gate or something."

"It's not Rutherford," Charlotte had answered. "It's only a cottage. I shouldn't think anyone bars their gates. I expect people come and hang on gates instead, and expect to talk. What will I say to them? I don't want to be the subject of discussion. You know, new bride and all that. It would be so embarrassing."

"Chattering away should suit you down to the ground," Louisa had replied. "You're used to talking to all kinds of people by now, aren't you? At the hospital and so on."

Charlotte had raised an eyebrow. "It may come as a revelation to you," she said, "but I do not chatter away. Sister would shoot me for it."

"Rather defeating the object, shooting nurses?" Louisa retorted. They had been having tea at Claridge's—a rare afternoon treat on Charlotte's day off. She couldn't explain, even to Louisa, her misgivings about being permanently at Michael's side. Anyway, she had rather thought it would be tactless to say such things to Louisa, who had been so spectacularly jilted three years ago.

She had eyed Louisa secretly when her sister's head had been turned. Strange . . . Louisa didn't look at all like the spinster sister. She looked rather happy, in fact. Who would have thought it? Sociable, empty-headed Louisa, being happy to be at home in Yorkshire with Father. What changes they had all been through. It was like being on a surrealist merry-go-round.

Michael hadn't wanted to discuss the subject of their marriage at all—not in the sense of what she should be or do. He accepted that Charlotte wanted to go on working at St. Dunstan's, but had hinted that it would not be appropriate in time. She supposed that "in time" meant when she became pregnant. "You will make a topping little wife and helper," he had told her. "Everyone will love you. We shall be very happy."

Happiness. One clutched at it like air, almost as a right. But she wasn't looking for the kind of happiness that she suspected Michael was describing; the domestication, the closed-in feeling of four walls.

"We shall have adventures, shan't we?" she had asked him.

"Plenty," he had reassured her. "Although, darling, some adventures are overrated."

He had been on a so-called "adventure" in the first few weeks of the war—"over by Christmas" and all that rot—he had packed his bags with a glad heart, like so many thousands of others. He had told her as much. He had been a regular already, an officer in the Royal Field Artillery. "We all wanted to get out there in 1914," he said. "Champing at the bit. Positively fretting." He told the story with a wry smile, as he said most things. Whenever she thought of him, she thought of that twisted expression of humor. Never his blindness, never the star-shaped scar that crossed his temple and one side of his forehead in disjointed white lines.

Sitting now on the train, she leaned forward in her seat.

"What's the weather doing?" he asked.

"Trying to rain," she told him.

"We shall pass Salisbury soon."

"Yes."

"Describe it to me."

She did so—although this was only ever when he asked. She didn't want to be a running commentary on life, a human conduit. Michael had his own opinions, and firm ones at that. He could be impatient. All of this she understood.

"I remember this area so well," Michael said, when she paused in her description of countryside, the small towns and villages. "I trained here. . . ."

Salisbury Plain, with all its rolling seas of grass, its chalky uplands, was being bought up by the army. It would soon be home to military exercises rather than the larks that it was famous for until now. She pressed her face to the window glass. "Do we pass Stonehenge, do you know?"

"Not in the train."

"Amesbury?" She had read about the prehistoric monuments.

"No."

"Have you visited them?"

"Why would I?"

"I should like to see them. Might we hire a car one day?"

He laughed shortly. "Am I to trust myself to your driving?"

"I drive very well," she protested.

"If you say so."

She sat back in her seat. "Well, I shall drive alone to see Stonehenge if you think I'm so very hopeless."

"You shan't go anywhere without me," he murmured. "And that is an order."

The taxicab took them from Sherborne station through the winding lanes of North Dorset. Up a long hill at first, and then out eastwards. It was hard to see any detail, and rain spattered the windscreen. The driver was a talkative sort, rattling on about the war, telling them about his brother who was in the Middle East—"Lot of blinking fleas!" he said cheerily. "That's what's getting to him. Sitting in a hundred degrees getting bitten by fleas."

"He's seen no action?" Michael asked.

"Oh, he's seen plenty," the man replied. "You've heard of Kut, sir?"

"Mesopotamia?"

"The very same, sir." He gave a great sigh. "We never knew what country that was," he said. "Whoever heard of they places?" His Dorset accent was almost impenetrable. "Damn Ottomans trying to kill 'em. That's t'all thanks you get."

"Mesopotamia is the birthplace of civilization," Charlotte said.

"Is it?" the driver replied. "Well, you've got me there, ma'am. I always thought that was His Majesty. Good old Blighty, you'm understand? What would they Africans be without us?"

"Mesopotamia isn't Africa."

"Bain't it though?" the driver asked. "'Tis all foreign to me. What his missus wants to know is, what are we doing out there?"

The answer was on the tip of Charlotte's tongue. She had kept abreast of the war since the very first day. *We're out there because we saw a chance of extending our Empire*, she wanted to say. *Because we condemn the Kaiser for doing so, and then we do it ourselves. To save Mesopotamia from itself, to carve it up along our lines.* She had seen a picture of the new Arab league flag, and proud infantrymen holding it, and the paragraph under the photograph in the newspaper—*Our brave lads supporting the Arab uprising.*

She didn't doubt that the lads were brave. She saw evidence every day of courage and fortitude. What she doubted was that her own country was performing some sort of selfless act. She had said as much to her mother and John Gould, and Octavia had raised an eyebrow. "Don't say such things to your Father," she had commented. "He will have you down as a Bolshevik."

So Charlotte, in fact, had said nothing to anyone. Not even to Michael. And she said nothing now. Perhaps it was true that she was just a reckless little revolutionary. The idea pleased her immensely.

The taxicab dropped them at the end of a narrow track. The countryside all around them was inky black, and rain dripped from the trees overhead.

"Someone should have left us supper. There should be a light, a lamp," Michael said. "The place doesn't run to electricity. Not in this neck of the woods."

"I can see a lighted window, and a porch," Charlotte told him.

She held his arm, guiding him only slightly. After all, he was much more used to the dark than she was. As they drew closer, she could make out that the "cottage" was in fact a rather large house with a deep thatched roof. In one of the casement windows, an oil lamp had been put on the sill. From his coat pocket, Michael took out a key. "This is for the front door," he said. "It was sent with all sorts of instructions to have patience with the lock."

Eventually, they got it open. The hallway was unexpectedly cavernous, with a stair rising on the left-hand side. Taking the lamp from the porch, Charlotte walked forward. "I think the parlor is straight ahead," Michael said. "I haven't been here since I was a boy."

He was right. And on the table, a cold supper had been left for them, the sandwiches wrapped in greaseproof paper, and a plum cake resting under a large muslin dome. On the handle of the cover, someone had tied twigs of apple blossom. "Oh, how sweet," Charlotte said.

"A woman will come in every day," Michael told her. "I don't expect you to char. You do enough of that at the hospital." He was taking off his coat. "Look in the suitcase," he said. "My holdall there. There might be something to drink."

Although she was dying for hot tea rather than alcohol, Charlotte took out the bottle of champagne. "Lovely," she murmured.

"Get some glasses from the kitchen. You'll have to potter about to find it," he told her. "I have no idea where it might be."

Just for a second, she hesitated. In the hospital, she was used to being given orders. In fact, it amused her tremendously to become "Nurse" as soon as she set foot in St. Dunstan's. It was relief, somewhat, and a pleasure at times—when she was not exhausted—to be truly useful at last. But it suddenly occurred to her now that this was the very first time that a friend or a member of her family had given her an order—"Get some glasses" —in such a peremptory tone. As one would do with a servant. No smile, no kind inflection. No please or thank you. Michael's head was turned away from her; his hand beat on the arm of the chair, and his leg jittered with impatience.

"I'm just going," she said.

"I could do with a bloody drink more than anything."

Again, in the doorway, she stopped. Bloody, was it? Interesting.

The kitchen was a long, dank-smelling affair at the back of the house. She found candles and another lamp on the draining board of a little scullery beyond it. The floor was flagstone, and beyond the scullery was another tiny room, with shelves set around at waist height. Here, she saw the reason for the pervading aroma of damp. There was a stone plug in the floor, and water about six inches deep. There must be a stream underneath the house, she thought. Was there such a one in Rutherford? She didn't know. She had never inspected the kitchens at all.

"It's quite a revelation," she said to Michael when she got back with two mismatched glasses. "What is the room for with the water in it?"

"Milk churns," Michael said. "There's a farm a bit farther down. It's an overspill for them."

"Gosh," she murmured. "The things one learns."

She gave him the glasses. He had already opened the champagne in her absence and, she noticed, taken some already from the bottle. She poured, and clinked her glass with his. "What shall we drink to?" she asked.

"That's an easy one," he said. "To you."

They made their way upstairs in another half hour, leaving the remnants of their supper on the table. At the top of the stairs, there was a wide landing with doors on three sides, and a beamed ceiling. The shadows cast by the oil lamp flickered over hunting prints and a stuffed fox head—wreathed with cobwebs, Charlotte noticed.

She opened one or two doors before she found what she supposed was the main bedroom. There was a four-poster here, newly made up with fresh white sheets, but rather narrow. The posts were carved with vine leaves and fruit, and it had curtains that could be pulled all around it. "It looks to be a very old bed," she said. "Does all this belong to your aunt?"

"This was her home," Michael said. "It became too much for her, but she can't bear to part with it. She lives in a newly built villa—you know, one of those things that you see in London; bay window, little patch of garden. She's thrilled with it. She says that one of the reasons she left here was that she could hear the rats running about under the thatch."

"Oh, marvelous!"

Michael laughed. "True country life. I expect you can't rid yourselves of the blighters anywhere near a farm."

Charlotte was guiltily glad that he couldn't see the face she was pulling.

"Where are you?" he said. "Come here."

She stepped over to him. He put his arms around her and pulled her close. "You're shivering," he said.

"I'm all right."

He put his hands up to her face and manoeuvred her so that he could kiss her. When he had first done this some months ago, it had felt rather romantic; but ever since it gave her the sensation of being manipulated, as she often manipulated patients who could not do things for themselves—lifting a spoon to a mouth, a hand to a cup. He could not help it—what else was he to do? It didn't seem right to launch herself on him—it was he who needed to lead the way. She supposed they would get it right somehow. That it would become natural.

"Shall I use the bathroom first?" she asked.

"Don't expect too much," he told her. "I've no idea what Aunt Emily used for ablutions, but I suspect a tin bath and a jug of water."

It was a little better than that. In fact, it was rather pretty. There was a large Victorian bath, with claw feet and a huge showerhead contraption hanging over it. Again, the kindhearted and anonymous person had put fresh towels, in a gloriously sweet-smelling pile, on a cabinet by the door. There was a porcelain sink, and soap, and cream for the hands.

Charlotte unpacked her little case. She moved the lamp close to the sink and the mirror, and started to brush her hair.

The face that looked back at her in the reflection was very young, she thought. But not in the sense of girlish. Somehow through the past two years of nursing she had managed to keep that open, naïve-looking expression of her teenage years. "You gawk," Louisa had said to her once. "Gawk at things, like a boy. My goodness! Your mouth even hangs open!" And a peal of laughter. Louisa had always been feminine, delicate-looking. It was she, Charlotte, who stomped and stormed and ran through life. Yes indeed, she had been a gawky child. The Yorkshire word had been made for her.

Now she had lost weight, and looked—she turned now left and right, assessing herself—stringier. She was not curved or rounded at all. Sinews stood out on her shoulders as she lifted the nightdress over her head. What would Michael make of this straight, boyish body? Would he like her, the person she was beneath the layers of clothing?

No man had ever seen her naked; lately, she had barely even looked at herself. Now, in a flurry of nerves, she thought about it. Had Michael had many women? She had never asked him. She did not want to know. When he had been in France, did he use the women that the other soldiers sometimes talked about? If he had, she could not condemn him. She wondered if he had learned to be brutal in such encounters, or had some girl taught him to be kind?

She had seen so many men in the extremes of injury; tended unresponsive bodies, washed the conscious and unconscious. She had sat with them and listened to their stories sometimes for hours when she had been supposedly off duty. Although the sisters did not encourage familiarity, she nevertheless thought that she knew men pretty well. Above all, she knew their sweetness and their ability to be long-suffering. That Michael had suffered she knew, of course. And she knew how he had overcome the potential claustrophobia of the loss of his sight. He was a training officer now at St. Dunstan's; he had patience and kindness as well as that self-deprecatory, sanguine smile.

It would be all right. She gave the woman in the mirror an encouraging nod. It would be a new country, another world. It might even be pleasant.

She took a deep breath, and opened the door.

Two hundred miles away in Rutherford, Mary Richards was just going to bed.

She climbed the back stairs from the kitchen, up several flights between the narrow, whitewashed walls. The servants' quarters were on the top floor, at a level with the roof. In her arms, she carried a hot-water bottle, a jealously guarded prize that Miss Louisa had given her.

Kindness itself, she had written to David. *Fancy a lady thinking of that!*

She reached the top floor and stood for a moment looking along the corridor. There was no carpet here. None of the luxurious Persian rugs that graced the family quarters downstairs. Just linoleum. Mary had cleaned those rugs many times, scattering tea leaves to absorb the dirt, brushing them outside in dry spring weather, and, more lately, using the new cleaners. They were ridiculous things, in her mind. Little vacuum tubes, like stirrup pumps, that she had to huff and puff over to get any contact with the floor. She preferred the old ways.

She walked to the door of the room that she shared with Jenny. Opening and closing it carefully so as to not disturb the head housemaid, Miss Dodd, next door, she saw that Jenny was already in bed, propped up with a shawl around her shoulders, reading one of her tuppence-halfpenny novels.

"You'll hurt your eyes," she admonished.

Jenny smiled at her. She was a thin, sweet girl who still retained her broad London accent. "You got some hot water then, I see."

Once, it would have been unthinkable for a maid to go down to the kitchens and take anything at all, even water. But since the housekeeper Mrs. Jocelyn had left—been made to leave, thank God, for she was as mad as a box of cats, and Mary had always said so— rules had relaxed a little.

And so much had altered in this last year alone. Mr. Bradfield had taken on many of the housekeeper's duties. He and Miss Dodd split them half and half. The ordering of laundry, the rota of the staff. Even the hiring and firing—such as it was. They had only had one new footman to replace both Harrison and David, and he was parttime. He cycled up from the village on a rusty bicycle three times a week; an eighteen-year-old who had been discharged from the army after Ypres, with a mighty shrapnel scar to one arm, a limb which he favored like a weakling claw in everything he did. A lad of few words and nothing much to recommend him. But you took what you could get these days. And Rutherford was no longer entertaining as it used to.

Miss Louisa and Lord Cavendish were usually quiet in their ways. There had been only a few parties. The Kents—Lord William's friends a few miles away—had organized the shoot last August and there had been a ball afterwards, but it was all very small compared to the years before the war. Christmas also had been a very quiet affair. And Lady Cavendish . . . Well, there was a most difficult thing.

It hadn't exactly been a surprise that Lady Octavia had gone off with the American, for gossip had been rife among the servants when Gould had first been a visitor here. But when Lady Octavia did come back to Rutherford now—as she did from time to time—Mary didn't like to look in her face. And the peculiar thing was, it was she and Jenny who always started blushing as if it was their own fault, their own affair. Lady Octavia, on the other hand, breezed through the house like a young girl, smiling, laughing, bestowing good humor in a way that she had never really done before.

Mary was marginally happy for her—a person couldn't fail to be, when you saw her lovely face lit up, the happiness shining out of her—but, if push came to shove, she didn't approve. It wasn't right. It wasn't . . . well, what Mrs. Jocelyn would have said. It wasn't *godly*. Mary didn't like the Bible being quoted at her, but she believed in being respectable and obeying rules. And she did feel sorry for the master. He kept the scandal quiet, bless the man. And he had such a tragic air of waiting. Waiting, waiting, all the time.

Mary sat down heavily on the bed.

"Is it any better?" Jenny asked.

Mary looked over at her. Jenny was quite different in her opinion of Lady Octavia. She thought it was all *so romantic*, the silly girl. *Mr. Gould is so handsome! Mr. Gould is so smiley, and rich, and glamorous— like a silent picture star!* Heavens, what the world was coming to. Mary grimaced now at her question. "Not so's you'd notice," she replied.

"My mam used to say bicarbonate."

"That makes me heave more." Mary gave Jenny a wan smile. "Eighteen weeks," she murmured. "You'd think it'd be going off."

"Don't come down to Giles's farm tomorrow. Tell Miss Dodd you can't do it."

"I can do it. It's only the butter making."

"It's hard, doing that."

"Well, Mrs. Giles is sick, and their own girl's nearly at her time, and the men are away. We can't sit on our hands up here."

"I don't call twelve hours of cleaning a house that hardly anybody lives in sitting on our hands," Jenny objected. "Look at mine." She held them up by way of explanation. "Coal, that is! April, and still lighting fires."

"You ought to take carbolic to those hands," Mary reproved. "Mrs. Jocelyn would have pulled you out to the laundry room by your ear and scrubbed them herself."

"Well, she ain't here, is she?" Jenny answered. "She'll never be here again. They'll keep her locked up, and good riddance."

Mary couldn't deny this. "Someone will come soon enough," she murmured. "Miss Louisa or Lady Cavendish will bestir themselves and we'll have someone stricter than Miss Dodd mooning about like she does. *She's* not been the same either since her chap wed somebody else."

They looked at each other, and involuntarily burst into laughter.

"Oh, it's not funny," Jenny protested, after a minute.

"Not, it isn't," Mary agreed. "Not after she bought her dress and everything."

They shook their heads. Getting a husband was a task these days. Some other less scrupulous woman had nabbed the local butcher from under Miss Dodd's nose.

Mary got into bed and laid on her side with the hot water bottle in the small of her back. It was bliss. She reached onto the rickety bedside table and took out David's last letter. It lay on the top of a carefully kept pile, bound with a shoelace. She smoothed it out and went over it, reading not so much the words—she knew them by heart—but looking at his handwriting.

It was so cramped, so formal. There were oily patches on the margin of the paper. It had come a long way—all the way from a place called Arras. It looked to her as if David had taken a long time to write it, and the language was bland. The flow, and the descriptions that had always astonished and intrigued her, had gone.

"What does he say?" Jenny asked, closing her book and lying down herself. She looked at Mary from her own pillow. Above them, the rain pattered softly on the skylight.

"He doesn't say anything much," Mary told her. "Not these days. Nothing much at all."

In the fashionable house on Cheyne Walk, Octavia was woken on the morning of the eighth of April by her personal maid. Amelie had been with her for almost ten years, and, as Octavia raised herself in bed while the curtains were opened, she considered her servant with a smile.

There had been a great deal of fuss over Amelie. Ironic, in that the girl herself was so quiet. Amelie, having been born in Paris, was from an allied country, of course; a country in which so much English blood had been spilt. But when war had broken out it had still been necessary to register her residency, and to enter her name as a foreign alien. Octavia had enlisted William's help, as did so many of Octavia's class, to keep her maid with her.

In 1914, there had been frenzied rumors of absolutely anyone who was not British being sent back to their home country—as if Amelie would harbor any thoughts of returning to Paris, a city in which she had been orphaned as a girl of twelve, and farmed out as a lady's helper when she was helpless herself. Octavia had scooped her up from an agency in Paris when they visited the Great Exhibition, and she was very glad to have done so.

She propped herself up on one elbow. "Amelie," she murmured, "would you like to go back to Paris?"

The girl turned to face her. "Paris?" she echoed. "With yourself, madame?"

"No," Octavia replied. "I mean to support your country. If you wish to go there—to be in France, I mean, in its time of crisis, then . . ."

Amelie crossed the room in two or three uncharacteristically ungainly strides. "Madame, you are unhappy with me?"

"No, no, not at all . . ."

"You wish me to leave?"

"No, dear. I simply meant . . . Good Lord, don't cry." She took her own handkerchief from the bedside table. "You must worry so about your home city. That was all I was thinking of."

"Yes," Amelie murmured. "But my home is with you, madame."

There followed a few moments of fluttering smiles. Octavia even offered to share her tea from the tray. The fact was, she worried about her maid. She was a pretty girl, almost thirty now, and barely said two words about herself at any time. When Octavia had once mentioned that Amelie must take more time for herself, and hinted that she might meet someone in doing so, Amelie had rolled her eyes theatrically. "Ah, men," she had said. "This is not worth the time, I think." Although she seemed to be very much in favor of John Gould. Whenever John crossed Amelie's path, the maid would blush scarlet.

As if summoned by her thoughts, the door opened, and John peered around the door. "Awake at last."

"Where on earth have you been?" Octavia asked. "I woke up at five, and you weren't here."

John came into the room, flinging aside his coat. He crossed over to the bed and kissed her. "Miss me? That's a good sign."

Amelie excused herself. John sat down in the chair opposite the bed.

"Let me guess," Octavia murmured. "You've been back to the newspaper offices."

John held out his hands in a gesture to show that he had been found out. "It's all on, darling," he said. He lifted a piece of paper from his pocket. "I'm going on a returning hospital convoy tomorrow morning."

Octavia put her hand to her chest. "So soon."

She'd known it was coming, of course. The reason for John having been on the *Lusitania* last year was that—on the face of it at least—he had been employed to sound out English families about how they felt on the United State's neutrality, and to get himself to France to report on the true reality of the war. John's employer was part of a faction who could not bear the United States to stand by.

But events had moved fast in the last three months. Too fast for her liking, for it meant that John would certainly take up his long-delayed task.

"I rather dislike Zimmermann," she said, naming the German ambassador who had precipitated the United States declaration, and giving an ironic smile.

"President Wilson evidently agrees with you. Congress voted for war two days ago."

She sighed and swung her legs out of bed, drawing her robe around her. "And so you have cooked up your journey, and got your permits. And never breathed a word to me." She shook her head, still smiling, though with less humor. "I knew you would go, darling. You needn't have kept it a secret. All that 'nothing to worry about.' I do wish you'd talk to me honestly. It's not as if I don't understand the war, you know. Every hour I worry about Harry."

John immediately got up, and came to sit beside her. "I didn't want to spoil your enjoyment of the wedding."

He had taken her hand in his, and now she looked down at it and began to smooth the fabric of his sleeve. "The British confirmed it, then."

"Confirmed what?"

"This telegram of Zimmermann's to Mexico."

John let out a short sigh, almost laughter, but not quite. "Arrogant buffoon. Came right out and admitted it. He telegraphed Mexico and promised them half the southern States if they declared war on America."

"And so . . ."

"The whole world is at war," John said.

She turned to him, and buried her face in his shoulder. For a long while they sat on the edge of the bed, holding each other. Her words muffled, Octavia said, "More sons . . . fathers, brothers, husbands." At last, she lifted her face. "I want to tell you to stay here. To order it, John."

"But you won't do that."

"No, I won't." She bit her lip. "William wanted to know what you were doing. He was surprised you were going to France. I expect he thought you wouldn't get permission."

"Ah, I have contacts."

"And you think it so really important. . . ."

"For my countrymen to know what's actually going on, how much we are needed? Yes, I do."

"As if England and France and all our Commonwealth can't cope."

"It isn't that at all," John objected. "We're defending ourselves now, and democracy. We're making a stand against brutality . . ."

Octavia stood up abruptly, dropping his hand and walking to the window. There, she pulled back the heavy damask curtain a little more and looked out at the pretty garden behind the house. There was a lawn, and a little summerhouse, and a paved path bordered by roses. After the downpour of rain the night before, it looked absolutely fresh, newly washed and brightly green. It was spring in London—beautiful, promising spring—and so quiet here by the Thames that one might have thought it was the heart of the country. But she knew that only a few miles away, the armies were struggling with foul weather. It had been a bitterly cold winter in France, and now Flanders was deep in mud through persistent rain.

She heard John get up behind her. He was soon at her back, closing his arms around her. He softly kissed her hair, her cheek. "Dearest. . ."

She looked at him. "I know you must go," she said. "I know they all must go. I know that Harry has to be there, and that Charlotte must be at the hospital. I know that Caitlin is working somewhere, no doubt dreadful . . ." She shook her head. "We had an accident in the mills last week," she murmured absently, thinking aloud. "A letter came last night. They're working flat out, twenty-four hours a day. One of the men injured had been in France. He stumbled somehow. I must go up there and see what's going on. Inefficient overseer, tired workers. It seems one can't escape it. The war reaches in and touches everything. I feel as if greasy hands are enclosing us."

"You're tired," John said. "You must try not to think about it."

She turned on him fully now, eyes flashing. "Not worry about it!" she exclaimed. "Really, John. You sometimes sound so much like William. The mills are my responsibility. My father left them to me. I know those people inside out. I know my son and daughter, I see them going out into the world, and I wonder what kind of world it is that we've gifted to them. I wish it weren't so. I wish we had done more when we could."

"Done more?" he echoed. "What do you mean?"

She sighed, shaking her head. "Not been so smug years ago, John.

When I think of how I sat in Rutherford like a stuffed doll and did nothing but arrange for the color scheme to be altered in the drawing room." She allowed herself a gust of exasperated laughter. "We were so sure of everything. The Empire on every continent. Masters of the sea, all that. Prancing about waving flags and swords at whole countries and taking them under our wing as if they didn't have a mind of their own. We should have learned. Look at Russia. God knows what's happening to the Tsar now. Abdication! We built a world destined to fall apart, John."

"My God," he murmured. "You need to stand for Parliament."

To his surprise, she didn't look shocked. "I heard a whisper the other day," she said. "That if Waldorf Astor is given a peerage, and has to resign his seat, then Nancy might stand for it instead of him." She nodded triumphantly. "Imagine that if you will. And I can."

"Well, well," John murmured. "While I've been busy, you've been plotting insurrection. I expect I'll come back and find you've got a whole lot of suffragettes in here as well as the crowd from the Café Royal."

Now, she laughed with real delight. "But aren't they wonderful!" she said. "Complete bohemians. I would like to have lived that sort of life."

"Why so?"

"Oh, it's so much freer. More abandoned. You know."

"More abandoned?" he said, his voice lowering. "Do you mean more abandoned than you are already, Lady Octavia? How astounding. How impossible." He kissed her, and she wound her arms around his neck, ineffectually seeming to push him away for a moment, and then relaxing into his embrace.

"I really should be getting dressed," she said, as he manoeuvred her backwards towards the bed.

"Let's see," he said. "Do we like that idea?" He made a momentary show of pretending to consider it, then suddenly picked her up, sweeping her off her feet. "I don't think so," he told her. "No, I don't think I like that idea at all."

In Dorset, the rain had swept through during the night, and it was a morning of scattered sunshine.

Just after dawn, Charlotte was standing in the garden behind the house, looking out onto meadows crisscrossed by irrigation channels. Sheep were grazing in the fields. After watching the undulating expanse of green for some time, she drew her coat around her and walked down the long garden path, passing the lawn and the flowerbeds.

Under the three large apple trees farther down, daffodils had flowered through the grass. She paused and looked at them, scuffing her foot among them, lost in thought. Then she noticed the small gate in the fence, and she went through it, finding herself in a wilder patch. Some kind of weed had taken over here; it was a mass of blackberry trailers and straggling shrubs. A large hawthorn hedge now obliterated the view of the fields.

All was perfect silence. She tilted her head and looked at the sky, where the clouds raced. She stood there, quite unmoving, her hands clasped tightly in front of her, for twenty minutes or more.

Cold eventually overwhelmed her; she could feel the damp clay through the thin soles of her shoes. She glanced around in a kind of confusion, wondering if there was some way out in this part of the garden: a path through to the village, perhaps. A road back into town.

Then, frowning, she shook her head; and, wiping the tears from her face, she began to walk back to the house.

Chapter 5

onchy. To Jack Armitage's mind, the name of the French village sounded like a made-up word, something that had been dreamed up by men like him, who labored with the foreign language, shortening and stunting its poetry. He stood, head down in a faint sleeting rain, the reins of a horse in each hand; patient beasts that angled their heads towards him, their flanks trembling against the cold.

He thought about the French names, but on the whole he didn't like to think much. If he allowed his mind to wander, it would always go straight back to Yorkshire, to Rutherford. It would go straight back to Louisa's face, and her arms around him.

No, that would not do. It was too terrible to think of how far away that was, and how much—how very much—he wanted to return to it. He would go in an instant if he could be given the opportunity. He dreamed of her often; he wrote to her almost every day. He poured what he could into the letters, but was always mindful that his parents might open them. He knew, however, that she would read his true feelings behind the banal words. He only wished that he had a better education so that he could eventually write something really poetic. Something that sounded as he really intended. *You are my very soul.* But then, to his mind, that was too much, too extreme, too flowery. Just to put it on a page like that. It would almost be making it ordinary to write such a thing.

But it was what he felt, even so.

Unconsciously, he shook his head. It would do him no earthly good at this moment to think of Louisa. He would rather let his mind stray to the horrors. They would sharpen his concentration. And there had been plenty of them.

And so he concentrated on the cold, and the ground, and the warm breath of the horses.

From this hillside, you could see a flatter plain beneath them. They were on one of the highest points for miles around, a relief from the months of swamp-fringed Somme and railway lines that ran through fens, and canals among coalfields.

Captain Porter swore under his breath as he walked back now towards Jack. Jack liked this man; he was from Derbyshire, a countryside that sounded like his own with its high ground, and a village called Eyam. Little villages, little villages. Jack closed his eyes. Across the valley they could see snow falling, a thick white curtain drifting towards them.

They could hear the artillery in Monchy in the valley below.

The artillery were in Feuchy, taken the evening before by the fifty-sixth division. Feuchy. Monchy. Wancourt. Tilloy-lès-Mofflaines. Words that ought to be in a song because they sounded like pretty pictures.

Jack Armitage stood in the windswept street lost in this dream of words, things he had learned, a little of another language that he had kept in his head. At times like these, in the depths, in the murderous battles, he repeated the words to himself over and over. Green hillsides; he had known those once. Long ago, in another place. It was less than year, but it seemed like centuries. Green grass and meadows full of wild orchids. Wild garlic in Rutherford's woodlands by the river. Moorland high above, blazing yellow in the summer. Home. Ah, he couldn't help it. His mind would race back, the way that the animals raced away from the noise. He allowed it, was drowned in it; he leaned momentarily on the horse and it seemed to him that the beast leaned in towards him, invalids both, each afraid in their own mute way.

He thought about a place up there at Rutherford, a place long forgotten by the Cavendishes, but that he knew very well: a deserted place among the bracken on the edge of the trees. There was a derelict cottage, little more than four bowed walls, and a roof with loose tiles cascading into a space that had once been a garden. He had gone there half a dozen times with Louisa. Just sitting, although none of the men he knew now would have believed that. Sitting while summer rain came and went. And shadows came and went, and sun slowly crept across the floor. In darkness, too.

Hillsides and softly tangled gardens, and orchids. A river running through Rutherford's grounds, blissfully shallow and warm in the heat, raging in winter as the melt came down from the moors. Grey in rain, blue and peaty orange when it ran clear. Granite washed smooth in the riverbed, and iron veining the red stones. In his mind now he saw two images: a little village girl running through the shallows of the river where it turned in the village center, under the bridge—a little girl he'd gone to school with once, whose name he couldn't now remember. Hair flying, and a long sprigged muslin frock dancing around her. He saw her now clearly, this nameless friend, turning back to him and squealing with laughter.

And he saw Louisa resting in the crook of his arm, a strand of fair hair caught across the collar of his jacket. Saying something, murmuring something. He tried to recall the exact words, the tenderness of them.

So much went away even when he tried to summon it. Some weary man, a regular soldier, had said to him when he first came here, "You'll find things go blank. It's the getting used to everything. Bear with it."

And so he had. Borne with it.

In 1916, he had signed up to the veterinary corps. He had gone to Louisa's father and asked if William could use his influence to secure a job for him in the corps. Louisa had only nodded when he had finally made his decision. But she knew what he wanted all along, and said not a word in opposition. Unlike her father.

William Cavendish had looked up at him from his study desk, and shaken his head. "That's not possible. We're low on manpower as it is. So many have gone. You're needed here, Jack."

Jack had been holding his cap in his hands, willing the older man to understand him. "The horses were needed too, sir. They need looking after over there. I can do that." The yeomanry had come and taken Wenceslas in 1915, their big grey Shire, and the farm ponies. My God, that morning had broken his heart. Poor animals that shied away at the least noise. Dumb animals that he owed his care. He'd watched them being loaded into the vans, bound for the railway stations, bound for the coast and the ships—things that they had never seen, and could not understand. He'd lost sleep thinking about them, thinking that he ought to have gone with them and not been a reserved occupation there at Rutherford.

Even so, there had been a lot of reasons given to prevent him enlisting, and a lot of sighing from Lord Cavendish. But eventually his lordship had agreed, and written to a man he knew in London. On the day that Jack had left for the veterinary corps, his mother and father had stood in the stable yard, motionless, silent. He knew that they had everything to say, and no way to say it. His father had eventually shaken his hand, and his mother had looked at him with her eyes brimming with tears. She'd turned her back and gone into the house before he was even out of that yard and walking down the long drive. He'd walked past everything he wanted to keep, and everything he'd known since he was a boy, out of peace and into devastation.

And now it was Easter, 1917.

He had barely listened to the Easter Sunday service. It was not that he wasn't a Christian. He wanted to believe it. He had, after all, believed it all his life. But then being in France had changed his mind about resurrection. None of the dead that he had seen would ever get up and walk like it said in the Bible. Nobody here was Lazarus. And for certain, nobody here was Christ.

"Are you awake?" the captain asked.

"Yes, sir."

"You're swaying about. Stand up."

He did as he was told. All the green images, all the pretty-sounding names vanished as he opened his eyes.

They'd come up with the veterinary station and the third cavalry late last night. Into Feuchy, onto the redoubt. A river lay in the valley ahead of them: la Scarpe. Behind them was The Triangle, where one of the new tanks had taken the area, blasted its way through. Jack had passed it by in the evening light, a monstrous-looking thing, eerily inanimate among the communication lines, the twisted railway, the long column of mules, the heaped wall of corpses.

They had stopped there for a while.

It was strange: this ground that had been so lethal was now silent except for the tramping of men and the sound of artillery getting farther and farther away in the twilight as the Germans were pushed back. Jack glanced over at the dead. Literally pile upon pile that had been stacked at the side of the road like kindling. One man's arm lay in the way, curved like a plea for mercy, or a call into the dead's kingdom. An artillery gun had run over it as he watched, but still the fingers seemed to be beckoning him.

He had looked away.

What had once been a church and a large chateau nearby was now just a mound of ruined brick, with trees grotesquely reduced to split trunks. The village had been evacuated the year before, so at least there were no civilians to haunt them. Shattered winter branches lay in the road, and tumbled walls, and several wagons on their side. A few dead-eyed and exhausted German prisoners passed Jack by, glancing at him only momentarily, too weary to raise their heads, their bodies slumped, their hands hanging by their sides.

Jack had been waiting outside a barn whose roof had miraculously escaped being completely torn away. Inside, they had housed twenty horses. The beasts routinely shook with fright. He had helped to bed them down, although rations were poor. They needed much more feed than was available, but the corps did its best. He'd seen men give their own biscuits, soaked in a bit of tea, to their mount in an effort to soothe them. And he had done that for an hour, going around to each horse, murmuring to them. Nonsense about pastures and soft, quiet bridleways: things they would probably never see again.

He had not been outside for long when a troop of the field artillery came by. High-spirited because of their success. He heard a bitter-sounding laugh: the kind of laugh that a man could give when he'd won over an enemy.

They had stopped suddenly by the German dead.

"Souvenir, mates," one said.

They started looking through the bodies, kicking the dislocated arm away with the tip of their boots. Going through the pockets, they threw away pocketbooks and photographs. Soon pictures of sweethearts and children and parents littered the ground. Out from one tunic came a pocket Bible and a letter written in classic geometric script. It was screwed into a ball and lobbed over the mound of tangled bodies. Then they found a Prussian whose tunic had rolled back and showed a belt. With a lot of tugging, they took it away, and one man slung it over his shoulder with a shout of triumph. Rumor had it that German snipers crawled out of their trenches at night and took the cap badges from their victims, and put them on their belt like so many Indian scalps. The belt that the artillerymen had found was once such, with a dozen or more badges glinting on it like trophies.

The veterinary corps stayed behind the front, having gone through Feuchy in the night shooting horses and mules that could not be helped, and pulling their bodies out of the way. It was a job he abhorred, dreaded. But the suffering of the mortally wounded animals was much worse than that final merciful shot. It was his duty to dispatch them. Sometimes he felt glad, even. Glad they were out of the nightmare, and that he had released them.

Around midnight, Jack and another man dug a trench in a boggy piece of ground where a small stream had once run. They had hoped to bury the horses, but their spades soon struck rock. They tumbled the corpses down and scraped some of the splintered tree branches over them. They knew the burial parties would come up soon for the men, but no one would have cared about the horses.

Captain Porter took the reins of his horse now from Jack's hands. "Where are you from again, Armitage?" he asked.

"Yorkshire, sir."

The officer nodded. "I should have guessed with a name like that. The Yorkshire Regiment attacked Bullecourt yesterday. Know anybody in that?"

"No, sir. I knew a man from my place of work that joined the Borders with his brother. Name of Nash."

"And where is he?"

"I don't know, sir."

"In the July attack last year on the Somme, was he?"

"Yes, sir. Both of them. Side by side. First of July."

"Bloody business. Survive?"

"Yes, sir. He did. His brother didn't."

The officer held the reins of his mount slackly over one arm as he swept the land ahead with his field glasses. Jack looked the horse over. A wonderful animal, a glowing chestnut, seventeen hands, heavy in the body. Not exactly a hunter. But that was a good thing. People had sent over their finest horses in the first weeks of the war, and most of the highly strung horses had to be shot when they got to the front lines. They literally went off their heads, rearing up and screaming. They had voices like wailing children.

When he had first come down to the front, Jack had seen a major pull in a wild-eyed stallion. The officer had run out onto a track and managed to get hold of the reins. The horse was riderless and spattered with blood. The major had tightened the rein, put his face close to its mouth, stroked its nose, and talked to it. The horse had quieted, though it had still rolled its eyes in terror, foaming at the mouth, chewing at the bit. It was shaking like a tree in a storm, completely insane. The major inspected its legs, torn by shrapnel, and shook his head. He asked for a Greener's—the cattle killer that delivered an explosive charge and put an animal out of its misery immediately— but there was not one to be had. Jack had started to run back to find one, but, looking over his shoulder suddenly, he saw the major take his own pistol from his belt, put the muzzle between the stallion's eyes, and pull the trigger. A horse like that—driven crazy, too finely bred, nerves shattered—did more harm than good.

Jack had not always been close to the fighting. His first job had been at a veterinary hospital near the Channel. He had thought then that he would never see the war, only the results of it. It was a well-run place, something he had not really anticipated. He had supposed that he would be made to go straight to the battles, but—at first at least—it wasn't so. The AVC officer that he was first with blessed the "Butterfly Drives" at home—fairs and fetes and suchlike that raised money. It had helped them equip the hospital better. Jack had watched as bullets were extracted from a grey mare, and helped to bed her down afterwards. "Search the straw," the officer had told him. "We find nails and all sorts. Bits of caltrops, the spikes they put down in the roads. Bits of cooking utensils, fences. It all gets in the feed. So go through it with a fine-tooth comb."

He had done so, finding nothing, but standing with the dazed mare until she took some food.

The officer had come back. "What the hell are you doing?"

"Seeing to the mare, sir."

"God in heaven, man! You can't nurse them. Get on to the next one." Seeing Jack's face, he had lowered his voice. "Not like home, Armitage. It's not like home, you understand?"

"Yes, sir."

"We've had fifteen thousand horses and mules through here just this year, in just this station. So get a hurry on. Don't dawdle with any one of them."

Jack had glanced back at the mare as he left, thinking of Wenceslas; the great Shire's doelike eyes, the curve of the huge neck under a collar at harvest time. The way that the horse had trod patiently and slowly, in a dreamlike fashion, never to be hurried. He tried to imagine Wenceslas here; it was said that something that size would have been taken to pull artillery guns. He'd felt his stomach turn over, and that was before he'd even heard a gun firing himself. Not up close. Not in the thick of it, where fire rained down and the earth and sky changed places.

He'd seen all sorts in those first few weeks. A good strong thoroughbred that kept lying down as they tried to get it off the transport. Every now and again, while down, it tried to gnaw at its flank. Colic. That twisted gut that was hard to heal, even in England. He'd seen saddle sores, neck wounds, broken bones, and eviscerated animals who docilely stood in line, turning their heads to Jack with weary and defeated expressions. They'd done their best, followed men wherever they went. Never understanding why. That was the thing that made Jack's blood boil. *He* knew why. His officers knew why. Everybody knew why except the horses, poor obedient creatures.

Bloody war, bloody war.

He said that under his breath a hundred times a day.

The officer lowered his field glasses. "Snow coming."

"Looks like it, sir."

The man sighed. "The Northamptonshire Yeomanry are waiting west of Arras," he said. "They're backing up infantry VI corps. Essex Yeomanry are ready, too." He handed his glasses to Jack. "Have a look."

Surprised—he had never been given field glasses before—Jack took them gingerly.

"Artillery positions in the village," the captain said. "The sixth and eighth cavalry are conforming to the advance of the third dragoon guards."

Jack had been able to see very little. He handed the glasses back. "Cavalry and infantry," he said.

The captain held his gaze. "Cavalry and infantry, to take out the artillery. To take the village. You understand, Jack?"

What was there to understand? What was there to say? He didn't know why his officer would bother to share the information with him. It wasn't his business. They were sending horses into shellfire. What does a man possibly say to that?

The captain stamped the cold from his feet. His horse transferred its weight, and ducked its head. Its warm breath floated in clouds around them.

At eight thirty a.m., the Essex Yeomanry and a squadron of the tenth Hussars passed within a few hundred yards of them, advancing down the slope. At the bottom, Captain Porter had said, was the Highland Light Infantry.

Men from the North Country, men out of mountain country. Jack imagined them down there, in the lull of the snowstorm, turning to see the horses come down the slope that Captain Porter had said was called Orange Hill. It must have been a magnificent, stirring sight.

The cavalry moved in extended order, line upon line of mounted men over the whole hillside. It was a rare moment: Jack's breath caught in his throat. His instinct was to look away, but he followed the lines of horses galloping at breakneck speed. They flung themselves out, racing charcoal lines against the snow, a flying and shifting series of patterns against the white and sepia of the hillside.

There were trenches down there, but crossings had been put down at intervals. The horses took them at speed. Speed, speed. That was why they were wanted. The infantry and artillery were making ground, but the cavalry were thrown like bolts into the furor to forge a quicker passage. Arrows of human and animal flesh and blood to thrust through the defenses. A wild idea, a kind of madness to top all other insanities.

Down the slope, Jack could hear distant cheering from the Highlanders. It was soon obliterated by shellfire and machine gun. Straining to watch, to focus, Jack saw riders falling and their mounts running on into the blasts. The lines and the pictures began to break up, horses suddenly buckling and running head first into the ground, men tossed out of their saddles and dragged under them.

Captain Porter turned away, fretting, cursing. Impotent up there on the top of the hill. A shell burst just below them, sending up a shower of stone and earth. Porter gave Jack the glasses back. "Bastards, bastards," he muttered.

Jack swept the hillside where the cavalry had gone. As he trained the sights, he inadvertently bit his tongue and drew blood, such was the shock of what he could see. A horse, a small horse, was running about in circles, careering over wounded animal and man alike. On its back was a pack saddle, the kind used to carry machine-gun ammunition. As Jack watched, it was raked by gunfire and ran for a while at a curious and sickening angle, dragging its rear until it labored to a halt, front legs propping its body for a moment until it collapsed.

Jack drew the glasses down. There was a lot of noise behind him. They were bringing up reserves for the artillery. Below them, the Highlanders went forward over the top of the trenches towards Monchy. The village looked red in the snow, a scattering of houses and walls. From the center, the German guns fired ceaselessly. Jack heard a bugle sounding down there, the call of the cavalry. Regrouping, or trying to. They were still going forward.

For a village, Jack thought. For a piece of ground. Over the dead and wounded. He had been held in reserve like this scores of times, but this time there were no horses to tend. They were all down there in this morning's version of hell. Captain Porter ran back, and Jack ran after him, feeling the icy windblast in his face. On the very lip of the slope, close to where they had just been standing, a shell bloomed like a black and grey flower, the appearance coming before the sound of the blast. It nearly knocked him off his feet. They ran back through communication lines to wagons loaded with supplies. Porter began checking, rechecking, cursing all the while. He was not a cool man. He was not a calm man. Jack thought him human because of that. He saw in the captain's face what he felt himself: rage and impotence.

But let that go. Let it go you must. Otherwise the anger got the better of you. It distracted you, took the strength out of your legs. You would feel your balance go, your legs begin to buckle, just because your body refused to absorb any more. It could abandon itself under you, become a foreign object that didn't obey your brain.

That had happened to him in the first weeks he was out here. There had been a canal boat loaded with wounded going up the Somme. Seeing them, Jack had felt his stomach turn to water. He had turned away and vomited, and soiled himself like a child. "Never let that happen again," an officer had told him. He remembered, and obeyed. Always, always after that. Remembered that it was his job to stand up and do what he was told, and do it quickly.

And not think.

And not think.

Captain Porter looked at him now, wiping sweat from his face. "Going down now," he told Jack. "Get ready. D'you hear me?"

In Rutherford, the day was almost silent.

Jenny and Mary left the kitchen at eight o'clock, and walked out into the drizzling rain, mackintoshes wrapped around them that had been borrowed from Mr. Bradfield's store. "They're used at the shoots, so I don't want to hear any complaints about the smell," had been his peremptory instruction. "They'll keep you dry."

They had thanked him. Behind his frigid exterior, he had a heart after all. But they knew better than to indulge in any conversation.

Miss Dodd had looked them over just before they went out. "Getting soft in his old age," she whispered to herself. "Never heard of back in the day. Once, he wouldn't have even noticed you."

"I suppose he hasn't got that many of us to notice anymore," Mary pointed out.

"That'll change when the war's over," Miss Dodd replied briskly. "All this is temporary. Remember that, and don't get above your station. If you start being familiar, they'll soon get rid of you no matter how long you've been here."

Mary doubted that, but she said nothing. There were no staff to be had in any of the surrounding villages. Girls didn't go into service so much anymore. There was better money to be in the mills, or in the munitions factories over in Leeds and Bradford and Liverpool, even if it was deadly work. She said as much to Jenny as they walked along the footpath down to the tenant farm.

"It's good you aren't a munitionette," Jenny told her. "Else you'd have a canary baby."

"A what?"

"Canary baby. The babies from munitions girls come out yellow."

"Get away with you."

"They do. Real bright yellow."

"That's jaundice, then."

"It's something in the explosives."

"What, that goes into their bodies?"

"And comes out in the babies."

"Bloody hell," Mary muttered. "Best not think about it, lass. I won't."

They walked briskly, or as briskly as Mary was able. It was a very pretty path down to the farm, crossing the river at the footbridge near the parkland gates. The farm was in the opposite direction to the village, and they turned along the lane. Last autumn, a new surface had been put down, a tarmacadam, obliterating the old dusty track that had wound this way among high hedges. The land rose a little, and, looking back, they could see the village in a dip in the land, and the chimneys and roof of Rutherford just visible above the beech trees on the drive.

Mary caught Jenny's arm. "Stop a minute," she said. "Catch my breath." She propped herself against the dry stone wall, gazing upwards at the scudding clouds in the sky. The two girls listened to the sparrows quarreling in the hedges and the grass of the fields, and in the drooping, rain-sodden cow parsley. "I wonder what David's doing now," Mary murmured.

"He's not in that place anymore?"

"Thiepval? No."

"Did he send you any poems this time?"

"He's sent none since the Ancre last autumn."

"He'd like to be here, I bet."

"That he would."

Mary looked away, over the fields. Half of her wanted to know every detail of David's life in France. Half of her wanted to know none at all. He was such a softhearted man, and his first letters had been one of the reasons that she finally fell in love with him. But the war had changed him. He didn't talk about it. And as far as she knew he didn't write about it.

She could still remember him stealing the books of poetry from the library; finding him there one day, tucked in a chair, a volume of Keats in his lap. How guilty he had looked when she had come into the room, as if he was wolfing down the master's brandy, or pocketing the silver! All that blushing over a book of poems. He was so slight, so narrow-shouldered: you wouldn't have thought that he could have ever made a soldier.

She wasn't even sure if he had. Not the kind of brash, beefy man that you imagined as being a success in the army. She had no idea how he got along, or if the others just tolerated him, like you would a dreamy child.

Ah, but he had that smile. That was what had drawn her to him, and that was what would see him through. He'd still had it—buried, but coming back eventually—when he had last been home. Only when she'd asked him where his brother had been buried did the smile vanish again. "I don't know," he'd told her.

"But you must know!"

He had taken her hand. "Ah, Mary. Don't ask. I don't know, and that's the truth."

The two women resumed their walk, coming to the tenant farm in another ten minutes. This was kept by Mr. Giles—farmer Giles, like the story—a bluff Yorkshireman with a permanent smile on his face. Giles was in his forties and had married late: his wife, Frances, was stout, cheerful, and welcoming as a rule, but she was suffering with influenza now. When they opened the door this morning they found her in a large Windsor chair near the kitchen range, a cushion behind her back. The fire on the range was burning brightly, and a kettle stood on it, beginning to boil.

"Morning, Mrs. Giles."

"Hello, girls." She gave a sudden huffing noise, and shook her head.

"What is it?" Mary asked.

"I'm not right sure," the woman replied. Her accent was almost as broad as she was. "My head's all blocked. Proper miserable, it is."

But, eventually, she waved her hand. "'Tis nowt. Tea's mashing. Shift thisselves, then. Make us a cup, there's good girls."

After they had done so, they sat down at her bidding. "Not long for you," Frances observed to Mary. "Four months?"

"I know."

"Tha's got a long face about it, then."

"No," Mary replied. "I just don't feel right well, that's all."

"Sick?"

"Yes. And . . . more peculiar, like. As if something's not right."

"Well, what can't be right? You look all right to me. Bonny."

Mary shrugged. "I feel heavy."

Frances laughed. "Aye, you'll feel heavier, and that's a fact." She wriggled slightly in her seat to make herself more comfortable. "If you don't want to take more peculiar still, you'd best not go into the yard, then."

"Why?" Jenny asked.

"They brought us help this morning, off the camp."

"The prison camp?"

"Germans, aye. Six of them to get the barn wall repaired. How'd you like that? I said to them guards what's brought them, don't let me look at them. Don't bring them to the house whatever you do. Fancy, if you like. Murdering Germans!"

"Who asked for them? Did Andrew?" asked Jenny, naming Frances's husband.

"He did not!" Frances exclaimed. "It's the land steward. The master's man. Andy told him we was in need of help, next thing we know, the steward's gone to Lord Cavendish and there's a man come from Catterick. But I mean, how can you refuse? We need the help. The barn's lost part of its roof in the snow. We've only got the three men now, and two of them blinkin' half-wits—Jed and Billy Watling.

Neither use nor ornament, those two. So we got to take the prisoners, I suppose. Germans or whatever."

The girls looked at each other. "I suppose they're just people like us," Jenny volunteered hesitantly.

Mary set her face, and got to her feet. "Let's see what they've brought us," she said. As she passed Jenny, she gave her a withering, contemptuous look. "People, is it?" she hissed under her breath. "People what kill other people, like David's brother."

She went out of the door, and Jenny glanced back apologetically at Frances.

The other woman gave a sad, conspiratorial smile. "'Tis David, you see," she murmured. "Don't mind her."

The barn was an ancient building standing at right angles to the yard. Alongside it was the milking parlor, and through the gate the cows were standing close to the yard, sheltering in the lee of a wall while the rain continued to drift down.

The animals stood facing them, intrigued by the presence of the guard dog being held by a soldier who stood under the eaves of the barn roof. He looked as if he was asleep, his head slumped on his chest, until the door slammed behind the two women. Then, hearing their footsteps, he straightened himself up and looked their way.

They hurried across the yard, sidestepping the mud.

When they got alongside him, Mary stopped. "Are they in there?"

"Aye," he told them. "But it's no business of your'n."

"Where did they fight?" she demanded.

"What?"

"Where did they fight?" Mary repeated. "Where in France?"

"How should I know?" he said. "Who the bloody hell cares?"

Jenny tugged on Mary's arm. "Let's go and see to the butter," she murmured. "That's what we're down here for."

But Mary hesitated, staring up at the guard, and her eyes then strayed to the barn door. "It don't much sound like anyone's in there."

"They're having a break," he said. "Tea."

Mary's mouth dropped open. "Tea!" she echoed. "Tea, is it? Why don't you give 'em cake, then? Cucumber sandwiches while you're bloody at it?"

Jenny took hold of Mary's hand. "Come on," she urged. "Mary . . ."

Mary kicked at the door. The guard dog began to bark, and the guard himself stepped in front of her. "Here, missus . . ."

"Mary," Jenny pleaded. She purposefully threaded her arm through Mary's, and pulled her back in the direction of the house, and the dairy building attached to it. "We won't see them," she said, trying to be a comfort. "We'll never see them, Mary, will we? Why should we?"

Chapter 6

At last, the letter came from Caitlin. It was ten days after the wedding, and it seemed that she was already back in France, on duty.

It was a long letter, and Harry's heart had quickened when he saw it. But it turned out that there was nothing in it that he wanted to read.

Dear Harry,

I have tried to write to you so often. You will know it is difficult, but the lack of time is no excuse. It is one in the morning now. I am no longer nursing on the hospital trains, but the convoys. The ship is rolling. It is appalling weather, and I am not a sailor. But never mind—compared to others. You understand. I've been here a week, and I don't know if I shall be here another week, or a day, or if I am to go to England. But that doesn't matter. What I have to say to you is what matters.

Do you remember when you showed me Rutherford after you were first wounded, when you were taken there after the second operation? Do you think of it as a dream? I sometimes wonder if I was ever there at all. Such a lovely place. So utterly quiet. I don't think I have known anything like that. Where I was brought up was never peaceful, and besides London is never asleep. There was certainly not much sleep in the house. Always a drama. The dramas that you described to me of your own home did not seem to mark it at all. I tried to imagine myself back there just recently. The open doors on the terrace, and the candlelight at dinner. Impossible.

Made more impossible by what has happened.

I wonder if you ever remember my talking of Eleanor Brinkley? She was posted with me to Albert when we first came over. We were at the first station back from the front. And then again on the trains. I pointed her out to you. A fair girl, with long hair that she would not cut. A rather gapped smile. You would remember her if you had seen her, no doubt. She is from your part of the world, or close to it. Whitby. I could hear the North Country when she spoke. Such a nice voice, Harry.

You know, some are rather hardened to all this. It's not that they mean to be cruel. But it is so necessary. But Eleanor is different. She is a vicar's daughter, and knows all the Bible texts, but she isn't one to quote them. Not in a lecturing fashion. But I have heard her murmuring a few lines to those that want them, those that ask for them. Faith. Extraordinary, don't you think? I have lost mine. I know as a certainty that I shall never regain it.

We have been at the Channel ports—I am not, I suppose, meant to say where, but you will know more than most. You took the hospital convoy yourself, didn't you? I remember you saying how dreadful it was to wait on that quayside as other wounded were dumped unceremoniously either side of you, and how the ships disgorged the new arrivals, so hale and hearty. You told me that you thought that you had seen one of Rutherford's own horses on that quayside, the great Shire horse you loved, but of course it could not be so, for that would have been a miracle. Have you seen any miracles? No, and nor have I.

Anyhow, Harry, we were posted there; one might have thought it would be a respite from the hospital trains, but it was not so. We were obliged to meet the barges coming up from the Somme. I was taught to drive a lorry. The biggest, you know, the Willys-Overland. Imagine that! I had never been behind a wheel before, and the thing was noisier than the front. The tires were solid; the springs had gone; and the roof was covered with tin. One could not even hear the voices of anyone sitting alongside you. When I got out to crank it up, it regularly slipped out of gear and threatened to run me over.

The lorry was the first and last in one of the rushes; it was the first and last on the field. We took all the blankets and stretchers and officers kit back and forth. When the ambulance trains came down, I was lucky to be in bed before 2 a.m. Alongside us on the quay and in the station were mules and horses, and some of the horses were rather fine, and could be ridden.

I was waiting at 5 a.m. one morning for one of the barges to come in, and we had word that it had been delayed. It was still dark, Harry. Early March, and bitingly cold. We had to wait for the telephone bell to ring: it was that that would tell us if the barge were coming. But the wind was so high that the barge had been stopped somewhere a few miles hence.

Eleanor and I were together that morning. It was said that the casualties were very severe and that both the drivers should be experienced nurses—extra hands, you see. I had been in that *situation before. I have climbed back behind the driver's wheel many a time and had to clean my hands before I could grip it. My shoes, too. One set one's face and scrubbed the stains away, and put the shoes to dry next to the belching brown stove in our dormitory.*

Eleanor liked to ride horses. Or she had done before the war. I told her, standing there in the cold and blowing darkness, that I had never ridden a horse in my life. "You have missed something wonderful," she said. And the next thing, she had run over to the sergeant and asked if she might take two of the horses that waited in line. They are not war-wounded horses, you know, or not very weary at least. Though they stand sometimes with their heads down, patiently absorbing the noises, the cries, the chaos, and turning soft and beseeching eyes to you if you manage to find a scrap of bread or sugar to give them. Poor beasts! I do feel for them.

I have told you that I do not believe in miracles, and yet here I am about to tell you of one, Harry. The sergeant had said that it was all right for Eleanor to take those horses upon the sands. There is a beach right alongside the casino, and lovely flat sands that long ago would have held holiday crowds. I think that Eleanor had spoken to the sergeant before; I don't know if he was a little sweet on her. But he turned a blind eye that morning.

There were no saddles, only the tack to hold on to. My little mule did not know how to canter, but he trotted along with such gusto, as glad to see the sea as I was. Eleanor's horse took off at a gallop, and I lost sight of her. I was simply lumping along, and I began to feel utterly strange. Can you guess why? I had begun to laugh. It was so absurd. The waves were breaking over the mule's feet and making him skip from time to time, and I thought how fantastic it all was—the waves, and the awkward sack of potatoes that I was on the poor animal's back—although he did not seem to mind. *Perhaps I was a good deal lighter than anything else he had carried recently.*

A few stray streaks of light began to show in the sky. And then I saw Eleanor coming back at full tilt. Her hair had come loose and there was a smile of such bliss on her face. She looked about eight years old. She wheeled the horse around us, and they came to a standstill. We all stood there—Eleanor, horse, mule, and me—in the growing dawn while the waves chattered around us, and I realized that I had not laughed—no, nor really smiled at all—for so many weeks. Not an authentic smile. I don't mean the "there, there" smiles one is forced to give. The comforting smiles of the professional. I mean the smile broken out of the soul. It was like fresh water running through me.

We took the animals back, and the sergeant continued to turn a kindly blind eye. The incinerator man—who would have that job, Harry?—had made tea. We all drank out of enamel cups. Nothing had ever tasted so good, not even the brews of perfection that Bradfield delivers to Rutherford's table.

We had on our large coats, and had scraped our hair back into a semblance of neatness. At last the telephone call came and we went to the lorry. Sure enough, as I cranked it, it slipped out of gear and it was Eleanor who called out. She scrambled over to the driver's side as I skipped out of the way, and she saved it from plunging down the road. She was laughing when I got back in.

There is a French battery near the EMO, the Embarkation Medical Officer. Just occasionally we were shelled six weeks ago. A blip in our fortunes, another seemingly relentless push that then is extinguished for no apparent reason. They have long-range shells, the Germans. As do we. But would you think they knew that they shelled the medical offices, the transports, the queues for the convoys that would go up to the port? The gunners probably never knew exactly what they would hit. I like to think so, at any rate. I like to comfort myself with that. That there would be some residue of human feeling in an artilleryman's heart when he saw the damage he wreaked.

We were driving past the French battery. I had a sudden violent premonition that something was about to happen. It was full daylight by then, but there was suddenly a kind of onrushing silence—a moment of calm. Like a still pool in the center of ripples, I suppose. Instinctively, I put my foot on the accelerator. And then the crash happened, and I felt myself torn out of the lorry and being rushed along the ground. My face was rubbed by the gravel and mud. I could feel the skin burning. When it stopped, I felt my nose. I thought it might be broken.

And I looked around for Eleanor. The car that had been coming along behind us was flattened into the road. There was no sign of the people who had been in it. I saw Eleanor then by the roadside ditch. She was sitting up. When I got to my feet my back hurt considerably, but I appeared to be mobile, and so I went over to Eleanor. "You look quite horrible," she told me. "You will need to get that cleaned."

The French came running up. They descended on her, picking her up and cradling her and calling her a poor little pigeon and such. She looked as if she wanted to brush them off. "Gosh, I am winded," she murmured. "I can't catch my breath."

I got down beside her. "Don't speak," I told her.

We got several bootlaces to each leg around the thigh, and then the idiot nearest her put his arm across his eyes like a child and wailed, "Complètement coupé." I could have struck him down. I could have felled him with my fist. What a fool. Eleanor looked up and said, "What is cut?" and I told her that her jacket was in a mess, and she said, "I can always fix a ripped jacket, Caitlin." And she paused, looking intently into my face.

She died just a few minutes later. We couldn't get anyone to her fast enough. Both femoral arteries, you see. Despite our bootlaces and all other efforts. The ambulance came and some sprightly young officer I had never seen danced down as if he were waltzing round the Ritz, as gaily as you like, and gave her morphia. The smile was still on Eleanor's face. I snatched at his arm. "There's no use giving her bloody morphia," I told him as he flourished a hypodermic.

He reported me for swearing at him.

Oh dearest Harry, I can see your face. Concern for me, and horror for Eleanor. Someone whom you only met briefly and I suspect made only a fleeting impression upon you. I wonder how long she will remain in your memory. Will she be obscured gradually by the years, or is she obscure already?

I expect her mother and father and her sister remember her very well indeed, of course. They will have seen in her other times and other years: all the years that she was growing up. They will know things about her that we don't know, and I have known things about her that they will never know. Twenty years is not a very long time into which to cram a lifetime, and so there remain great empty pages of time where something might have been written or experienced. And now what will happen? When her parents go, and her sister goes, she will go. It's like washing away people, my love. Hundreds of thousands, millions. Washed away and only fragments of themselves remaining until at last one day her nieces or nephews will ask who Eleanor was, and her sister might retrieve a memory of something she said. And she'll struggle to conjure up how Eleanor looked, and half of it might be accurate, and half of it might be something fantasized. And the real person . . . by then she will have vanished entirely.

I think I will keep her expression close to me as she rode back that morning as the light was coming up. There was joy in that.

How can I write to her mother and say that she had joy in the last hour of her life? Would it sound empty, or comforting? Would one hold on to that unwitnessed joy until it replaced any other? I don't know what to write to them, and, Harry, it has been six weeks. Things happen, and days run past. . . .

I have become a bad friend in not writing, and I am already a bad nurse. Do you know what I have done, in addition to living when the girl beside me died? I have sat and watched men and not helped them as I should. That impetus, that instinct, seems to have gone. I think I have lost my senses. I fear it. Even now as the ship's pitching about, I wish it would be hit and go down. That is a dreadful thing to wish upon these men. But all I really want is to stop. Just stop.

And so, dear, I am not such a good person to be associated with. I do not think I am decent company at all. I don't know what they intend to do with me, but whatever it is, I feel the need to avoid it. What I would like you to do is to put me to the back of your mind.

It is proof of my selfishness that I have told you all this when you are dealing with . . . whatever the hell is that you're dealing with, Harry.

Caitlin

*I*t was very late in the evening when Octavia arrived at Rutherford.

The Rolls-Royce had been kept in London, and so it was an ordinary taxicab that deposited her on the steps. Bradfield was waiting for her, uncertainly holding an umbrella and glaring from time to time at the threatening sky.

She got out and looked at the house, her gaze swiftly traveling upwards, away from the terracotta Tudor arch and over to the more recent east wing, where one small window close to the roof was still illuminated. It was almost ten o'clock, and so the nursery would be quiet now. But she could hardly wait to see Harry's daughter, Sessy. She might go up despite the hour, she thought to herself. Brave the disapproval of the nursemaid. And then in the morning she would sit down and write to Harry and tell him what she always told him: that Sessy was well, and his image.

Bradfield came hurrying down the steps as best his seventy-year-old legs could carry him. "Welcome home, ma'am."

"Thank you, Bradfield. Everyone well?"

"Yes indeed, ma'am."

"And yourself?"

"Very well."

She walked up the steps and saw that Edward Hardy, their last remaining full-time footman, was holding open the door. She nodded to him: there was no point in trying to hold any kind of conversation. Hardy was a dolt, and that was a fact that had not escaped the recruiting officer in Richmond. That, and his flat feet that even now were turned out at an angle of a-quarter-to-three.

Octavia stood in the hall and breathed in the scent of the house. It was not quite as she would have wanted; the air was musty as if the rooms had not been aired. And, although polished, the reception table had no flowers. She made a mental note to speak to Miss Dodd. Then, down the long Tudor hall with its paneling and ornate ceiling resplendent with the family crest of bluebirds and tropical trees—intricate stucco branches that formed patterns of leaves high above her—she saw William emerge from the direction of his library. He smiled when he saw her. As he walked, his steps echoed.

"Train delayed, I hear."

She held out her cheek, and he gave her a dry and formal kiss.

"Is Louisa home?" she asked.

"Yes, indeed. But she has gone to bed. She has had a slight cold since the wedding."

"Oh dear."

"Shall I call for her to come down?"

"No," she murmured. "Perhaps it's just as well she isn't here."

William seemed not to have heard the last part of the sentence. He was already turning away. "Come into the drawing room and get warm," he said. "A fire is burning."

This room, at least, felt comfortable. Daylight would show that it faced south, and the magnificent view that it afforded gave it breadth. The garden and parkland unrolled before the windows like a carefully manicured green baize, dissected by the great beechwoods on the drive. Very distantly one could see the roof of the lodge at the parkland gates. Octavia went to the window, and her hands brushed the drawn pleats of the blue-and-white curtains in a heavy Liberty upholstery that she had chosen in another lifetime, another world.

It was so strange to come back; and the truth was that she visited more to see Louisa and Sessy than William. She respected her husband—what he had been, what he still was in his advisory capacity to government; she respected his ancestry, the memories of his parents. But in truth, she did not have any sort of warm feeling to him other than that respect. Of course, everywhere in society he was cast as the wronged husband; she had grown used to that. She felt that it was nobody's business but theirs, and they alone knew the troubles of their marriage; but that did not stop all of society having an opinion, and that opinion routinely cast Octavia as the culprit, and William as the victim.

Twenty years ago she might have been called a scarlet woman; fifty years ago she might have been locked up, literally, in Rutherford itself. She knew that had been the fate of many an erring wife in the reign of Victoria. One's husband might dally, might have mistresses—indeed, the wife herself might have a lover. But to fall in love—*that* was the disgrace, the ignominy. Aristocratic women simply did not show their hearts so vividly. In fact, to the upper classes, to have a heart at all was an embarrassment.

But the war had taken away some of those boundaries. England had changed. Women had changed. No one would lock her up now, not even William. No one would snub her. She was still received, albeit coldly. She thought that was partly due to John, for his sunny nature and his astonishing wealth tended to open even the most established of doors.

She wondered what those who gave her their frigid stares at the theatre might think if they could see her and William now. He sat close to her, minutely examining her clothes, her face, and her hands as if to commit the sight of her to memory.

"How are you?" he asked.

"Worried," she told him. "About Harry. And John." She never lied to him, never pretended that things were other than they were. Once she had obeyed him in everything; now, they occupied some kind of foreign country where the truth was spoken and voices were never raised. They were like two lifelong acquaintances whose manner was always excruciatingly polite.

William said nothing. He never did when John Gould's name was mentioned. Instead, he glanced over at Bradfield. "Would you ask Mrs. Carlisle to have a light supper brought in here? Don't bother with the dining room. Here will be more comfortable." He glanced at Octavia; she gave a brief nod of approval.

When the butler had gone, Octavia took a letter from her bag. "William," she asked, "do you think that Louisa is happy here?"

His face showed that he hadn't expected the question. "She seems so."

"Really happy?" Octavia persisted. "Does she go out, see her friends?"

"Quite frequently, yes. She helps on those fund-raising things. What are they called? Butterfly drives. For the horses, y'know. She went to the picture house in Richmond just two days ago—moving pictures. And I believe she went to York the other day, to shop."

"What about the Kents?"

"We had the Kents to dinner a month ago."

"Did you," Octavia mused, tapping her finger on the letter but still not opening it.

William was frowning. "Is there something the matter?"

Octavia pursed her lips. "I just think it's rather odd, you know," she murmured. "Naturally she withdrew a little after the elopement, and Paris. But she's only twenty-two years old. She might be going out a little, but it seems rather dour all the same."

"She seems perfectly happy to me. And she likes to be with Sessy."

"I know, dear. And she is a most devoted aunt. But she's a young woman. She's not mistress of this house. She is the *daughter* of this house. I would like to see some of the old Louisa back, wouldn't you?"

William sat back in his chair. He seemed to be so very old to her now; after all, he was over twenty years her senior. She tried hard not to pity him, for pity was the last thing he would have wanted—but still, she did feel both pity and guilt. Last year's illness had left its mark; his movements were slower. He seemed to take an age to respond. *My God, time,* she thought . . . *time. I gave him so much time once, when he wasn't interested; he broke my heart with his indifference. And now that he has all the time in the world, I am not here, and have none to give.* It was both ironic and sad.

She smiled, and prompted him. "William?"

He was struggling with mixed emotions, she could tell. Louisa had always been his favorite child; to have her here, at his table, in his house, must be of the utmost comfort to him now. Octavia didn't want to rob him of that pleasure, but at the same time she didn't want Louisa being so centered on Rutherford. Especially with what had been revealed to her in the letter.

She held it out to her husband now. "Perhaps you should read this," she said quietly.

While he was doing so, supper was delivered. Bradfield placed it before Octavia on a low table; on another at her left-hand side he put a tea tray. "Thank you," she told him. "I shall manage now, Bradfield. Do go. There's no need to attend."

She watched him leave, poured her own tea, and considered William's face carefully. At last, he put the letter down. "This is preposterous."

"I thought so. But you're here all the time, William. Does she receive such letters from Jack Armitage?"

"I've no idea what Louisa receives. I don't stand over her, you know."

"Has Bradfield mentioned any such thing?" It was Bradfield who brought the post to the breakfast table each morning.

"No, not at all. And how would he know? He's hardly likely to inspect the letters."

Octavia smiled. "Oh, I don't think a single thing escapes him," she observed. "Let alone regular missives from France."

"If they came, he would think they were from Harry."

"Would Jack write in exactly Harry's hand?"

"Ah," William murmured. "I see your point."

Together they sat in silence, then William suddenly slapped his hand on his knee. "I shall go upstairs and wake her and ask her what it means."

"No, you shan't," Octavia retorted. "It will wait until tomorrow. I'll speak to her myself. There's no need to play the heavy-handed patriarch."

William bridled. "I am not heavy-handed with Louisa."

"That is evident," Octavia retorted. "Or even observant."

"What—I'm meant to know if Jack Armitage, nothing more than a stable hand, is writing to her?" he exclaimed. "Who has written such tripe, at any rate? They haven't the decency to sign the letter."

Octavia nodded. "Well, that much is obvious, I think. The postmark is Richmond. The sender knew my London address. The phrasing is very awkward, the penmanship clumsy. . ."

"One of the staff here."

She nodded. "Yes, I rather came to that conclusion."

"Who disapprove as much as we do."

Octavia did not reply. She had had pretty much William's own reaction—minor outrage; annoyance at the anonymity; defense of her own child. Disbelief that quickly followed. Oh, she knew of course how much Louisa had adored Jack when she had been growing up. He was older than her, and had helped to teach her to ride. And Octavia well recalled having to speak to Louisa when she was nine or ten years old to tell her that it was not acceptable for a young lady to sit in the stable yard talking to the grooms, and hanging on stable doors to gape in hero-worship at one in particular.

It had been a childish infatuation. Jack was a sturdy-looking chap, of course; kind-hearted, slow to anger. Reliable. Kind. All the nice virtues that one might admire. But it was not his place to hold conversations with Louisa. Let alone write to her.

"Where is Jack now?" she asked. "Where is his corps posted, do you know?"

"I do not. No news is good news, Octavia."

"Have you spoken to his parents to ask them?"

"I have not."

"And Nash? Mary's David? Have you heard anything about him?"

William stared at her as if she had asked if he had traveled to the moon recently.

"Never mind," she murmured. "I shall see Louisa in the morning." She resolved silently to also speak to Mary and to Jack's father. She folded the letter and put it away. "But for it even to be sent . . . You see now why I think Louisa must be seen to be out, and mixing a great deal more with young people."

"Young men, you mean."

"Well, young men of her own class, naturally. She's been hiding away long enough. I don't want her to become silly, but she needs company of some sort."

Company of some sort. Octavia could almost see a retort rising to William's lips, a reaction that crossed over his face and he quickly extinguished. Octavia had sought out company of "some sort"—entirely the wrong sort, in his eyes. Not just John Gould, but the Bohemian crowd of the Slade and the Café Royal, whom she seemed to find extremely amusing. Octavia could see all that in his eyes, for she knew her husband. And she was grateful that he said none of it.

She finished the cold supper and laid down her knife and fork. "Tell me about this accident," she said.

"The mill?"

"Yes."

William sighed. Here was another source of disagreement. Octavia wanted the rules of employment to be followed as regards children, and conditions; William turned a blind eye, as the overseer did, to regulations in favor of meeting orders. "His name is Netherfield," he replied. "He was working in the spinning shed before he enlisted. He was wounded in Ypres. We took him back."

Octavia nodded. She was feeling tired, and more irritable than she would have liked over this subject. "You might as well say it," she said. "Taken back at my insistence."

"On your insistence, yes. To employ wounded servicemen who are not fit to work."

"As I understand it, Netherfield was quite mobile and he has a family to feed. Five children."

"He is . . . mobile, as you put it. He had a foot injury, which has healed. A *bullet* in the foot, I might add."

"You mean a self-inflicted injury."

"It's impossible to say."

"But you think it."

"However the injury was caused, we took him back. He was difficult. Nervous. A lack of concentration. When one of the looms had a fault, he simply went off his head. Tripped and fell. Fractured his skull."

"Where is he now?"

"The cottage hospital."

"And his family . . . ?"

This was the bone of contention. Octavia had swiftly replied to the original message saying that his family should receive a proportion of Netherfield's wage while he was ill. William had replied that the mill was not a charity, and that it had been foolishness to employ the man in the first place.

"William," Octavia said now, in a low voice. "There are men returning all the time with conditions like Netherfield's."

"The man was of weaker character before he left, and is weaker now. He is unemployable, and a danger to others. There was only an interruption in the loom, a blockage. Hardly a cause for demented behavior."

Octavia narrowed her eyes. "You think he's bluffing."

"I think he is a slacker."

"And all men with that condition?"

"If you're speaking of neurasthenia . . . most probably."

Octavia took a very deep breath. Slowly, she gathered her things together. She stood up. "I shall say good night," she replied wearily.

She walked to the door, where she paused a second with her hand on the latch. Then she turned back and gave her husband a wan smile. "You're wrong to call it neurasthenia," she said. "Neurasthenia is for officers. When it affects a lowly private like Netherfield, it's shell shock."

She went out, and William listened to the sound of footsteps as she made her way upstairs.

Chapter 7

The prisoners were singing.

They sang *Argonnerwald um Mitternacht* just as they used to. A marching song. In the midnight forest of Argonne, a sapper stands on guard; a little star high above in the sky . . . *Ein Sternlein hoch am Himmel stand* . . . So it went. A stamping, striding song about stars.

Frederick understood its sentiment, though. Standing on guard and looking up at a dark sky full of stars in the depths of winter, and wondering why it was—how it could be—that the stars still came out, and the moon filled from a new fingernail crescent to a full face, and how it was that the sun rose again in the morning, and the clouds raced overhead.

It had never seemed right that such things still went implacably on when everything was destroyed underneath those skies. He used to believe that one day the earth would simply stop. There would be no more stars, or clouds, or full moons, or sunlight. One day it would just start to rain fire and carry on until mankind was obliterated.

Like the Bible stories of floods and fire. Man deserved it. And if he didn't deserve it now, when would he?

He never knew that God existed in his soul until then. When others lost their beliefs, he held on to his. He believed in something other than himself, and he believed it because . . . well, *Ein Sternlein hoch am Himmel stand.* Stars stayed in the sky and the world rotated, despite everything. That was proof enough for him.

The rain continued here in England all the way through April. It was very wearing. They went out every day from Catterick and they got off close to the village, and they broke stones and they dug the route of the road. And sang. Someone told him that it was to make a better route through for the milk to be delivered to the station farther up the line: that there were farms around here who suffered in winter trying to get vehicles along the narrow gullies that passed for roads. And so, with all the others, he dug and hammered his way.

This morning, one of the guards had stood, hands on hips, when they were sitting drinking their tea from the glass bottles brought out from the camp.

"You're in England now. Sing English songs," he told them. Did anyone know one, he asked. Nobody did. Frederick sat quietly, watching the guard's loathing gaze, and then he put up his hand. "There is one from the boat," he ventured.

"From the boat? What boat?"

"If you please, from the boat when . . ." Frederick was still struggling with forming tenses in English. It was not a structured language like German. Verbs intruded into the middle of sentences. It was also full of idiosyncrasies. It was illogical. There were *rough* and *bough*, both pronounced differently although the spelling was similar; there was *felt* and not *feeled.* Now and again he could hear the original Germanic root in a phrase, but he wouldn't have known enough to name it. And so he hesitated a little now. "If you please," he repeated, "from the prisoner boat."

"Ah," said the guard. "Go on then. Sing me a British song, bloody Jerry."

Frederick had sung in the choir at school, but for a very long time his voice hadn't sounded as it had done as a young man. He had once had a pleasing baritone—or so he had been told—but chlorine gas from the trenches had got to his throat. It had never been the same since then. He began softly, "Pack up your troubles . . ."

But he faltered. The guard laughed, and carried on at full volume. "Pack up your troubles in your old kit bag and—" He swung one arm around at them all. "Well, what is it?"

"Smile," Frederick whispered.

"Too bloody right. Smile, smile, smile!" They all looked at him, and he yelled back at them. "Can't fucking smile at all, can you? Never seen a German smile, not one of you!"

It wasn't easy to smile. Frederick agreed with that. The guard walked up to Frederick and looked him up and down. He put his head to one side, considering him acutely. Frederick was four or five inches taller, and so he tried to shrink inside his clothes, hunch his shoulders, and make himself smaller.

"What's that wi' yer hands?" the guard asked.

"I am sorry . . ."

"Never mind sorry. What's that holding stuff like you do? What's that for?"

Frederick shrugged. The guard suddenly caught hold of his wrist and pulled one hand high up and shook it, as you would a toy. "Tha's got five fingers, tha's got a thumb."

"Yes, sir."

"So why dost tha hold it like a bloody girl?" And he kicked a spade at the side of the road. "Pick it up."

Frederick did so. There was a stirring in the seated men behind them, a rustling. No one had ever asked him why he clutched at things to get a grip on them, why he had such trouble holding them, why they slithered through his grasp. But the men guessed at the reason even so. He had devised a way of holding any implement with both hands, like a child might do, and using a spade more like a hoe than a shovel. Scraping at earth.

"See?" the guard said. "Hold it proper, why don't you?"

He wondered if the guard had ever been to France. He thought perhaps not. The man was perhaps mid-thirties, but he had a vacant air. He was disinterested and viciously sarcastic by turns. Aimless and disorganized in the head, Frederick thought. When the officers came along he obeyed them like a dog, with his mouth hanging open.

"I try," Frederick murmured.

The guard guffawed. He brought his face close to Frederick's. "Don't think I don't know tha game," he warned. "Lazy Kraut."

Tension swelled the moment. The shuffling behind them increased. Frederick was suddenly afraid that his compatriots might stand up, might rush the guard. "There is another," he ventured. "Another song I know a little. To sing."

"Yeah," the guard responded. "And better you all bloody learn it. I'm bloody sick to death of Argonny or whatever it is."

Frederick had heard this next tune in the docks; the melody had impressed him. "Roses are shining in Picardy . . ." he began. He didn't know the verse, only the refrain with its haunting sound. "In the . . . in the . . ." He didn't know the meaning of this next word, and it was difficult to pronounce. "In the huzz of the silber dew . . ." He corrected himself, his voice failing. "Silver dew . . ."

He stopped. The guard's gaze was fixed somewhere past Frederick. Shadows crossed his face like the flickering of a silent film, black and white, black and white. "The 'ush," he said finally. But it was not that, Frederick knew. It was "hush," like water, like breath, like breeze. Hushing, ssssh, like a mother with a child. Hush. . . .

But it was "'ush," the sibilant "h" removed, the word blunted, in a Yorkshire voice.

Nobody moved. Nobody said anything. Frederick stood with his hands by his sides. They were all, every man of them, defeated by the loveliness of the song.

Finally, the guard stirred himself. "Get up," he told them. "And get on."

On the way back to Catterick, Frederick stood with his shoulder to the side of the truck as it swayed over the narrow gauge. Conversation lapped over him like breaking and receding waves; he was far away.

When he had joined up, three years ago, the corporal in the Saxon regiment had told him that the British would not fight much longer. They had been in a train, like this, traveling to Flanders. It had been night, and many were asleep. He himself had been in a state of nervous excitement. He had watched the towns go by, one after the other. Comfortable and busy towns, then mountains, and stretches of marsh. Glimpses like photographs, quickly erased. The ribbon of a river. The railway crossing where a girl was sitting holding the reins of a wagon, alone. The spires of churches.

"One day none of us will fight," the corporal had told him. "We'll get up like we did in 1914. We climbed over the trench and we met them in no-man's-land." He had reached into his pocket, and brought out a metal tin. "See that? From an Englishman. From London."

It had once held playing cards. Now, the corporal fished out a cigarette and held it, unlit, between his teeth. "We heard them calling, 'Good morning Fritz, good morning Fritz.' Louder and louder. Christmas Day. And then, 'How are you?' We called back. We said, 'All right.' They called us to come over there, and we called back that they would shoot us. And then—" The corporal indicated the cigarette in his mouth by lifting his head. "Come and get some fags, Fritz."

Frederick had heard this story, but not believed it. But then, he had never heard it from anyone who had been there.

"We got over our trench. They did too. It was a bright day. Not snowing, but snow on the ground. As I walked my boot went through ice, and there was something under my boot . . ." He pulled a face. "I carried on, and the British man shook my hand. Imagine that! We shook hands. We had no cigarettes to give them, so we gave them . . . what do you think, what we had plenty of?" He laughed. "Cheese. We gave them cheese. There were about twenty of us out there, and all the others on both sides were standing up and cheering."

"And you think . . ."

"I think one day it will happen again. But nobody will go back in the trenches. We'll all sit down and stay there until the war stops."

Frederick couldn't see that, but he said nothing. At that moment, feeling the battle coming closer to him, he had wanted to get it over with. Fight, shoot. He didn't want to shake hands because he thought that might prolong things. If he could just get a bullet in someone, then . . .

Ah, that was over two years ago, he thought. Two years, and the corporal was long dead.

He had never seen goodness at all in France; he had thought it had been wiped out of mankind. Men, in the frenzy of battle, were capable of treading on their dying mates. Shells tore holes in man and mule and horse and house alike. Nothing was sacred, not even churches. Not even graveyards. The Somme was not pretty; it was a mud bath. He had watched one day as a wagon, pulled by two horses, and carrying six men, had drowned in mud. Tell anyone that and they wouldn't understand you. They wouldn't think it was possible.

Those who had gone to help were sucked down by it, and lucky to escape with their lives. The wagon had vanished into a shell hole deeper than its wheel rims, deeper than its body. The last horse put its head above the mud until only its nostrils remained, and then it too was gone.

That's what he carried in his mind. When he had seen those drownings he had wanted to murder all over again, but afterwards each time that he witnessed a fresh horror the need to kill lasted less time. Eventually, the futility took hold him, and he had felt nothing much.

It had taken this place—this place of trains and the hutted, miserable rain-soaked camp—this place of a new road, this place of a small farm—to make him think that there might be some goodness left in the world.

It had happened on the day, last week, when they had been given a new job. The tarmacadam to surface the new road hadn't come; and anyway, it was raining too hard. Instead, when they got off the train they had been turned to their right, not their left. They had marched for about two miles, never knowing where they were going.

The straggling houses on the outskirts of the village passed first. On one gate two children hung, watching in fascination. One little child was about three years old, he had guessed. She held a bunch of weeds in her hand. Perhaps the children had been playing at gardens, or brides, or whatever it was that little girls played. Their hair was plastered to their heads in the rain, but they seemed not to care. From inside the cottage came the smell of soap and the rattle of a scrubbing board. His mother used to do that, he had considered. Life went on the same everywhere.

Others in the marching line stared at the girls. Not out of any malice, but because it was some time since most of them had seen children. Most of all, their own children. As the line wound to its end, Frederick had heard the mother calling. Afterwards, the men in the last of the line had told him that she had come running out in a panic down the garden path, and snatched the girls up.

They had reached a farm. They were taken inside a large barn, and, once inside, it was immediately obvious what was needed. The vast timber roof was leaking. They were told that tiles had come off in the winter storms. They had hung around for a long time while it was discussed how to get up on the roof, for this had apparently not been thought of. As they stood there, Frederick had realized that this was not necessarily because the English were stupid, but that possibly because there were simply no men to do the job or find any kind of scaffolding.

When the rain had eased, they started to go outside. Frederick was on one side of the yard when he saw a woman come out of the dairy buildings opposite. She was small and dark, and she was holding her hand to her mouth. He had turned his face away because she was obviously going to be sick. They all did so, out of deference to her condition. She ran around the side of the building, and, after a few moments, she reappeared, straightening herself, taking deep breaths, balancing herself against the wall of the dairy. And then she had noticed them, and—just as it had when she'd first glimpsed them all that morning—a dark shadow crossed her face. You would have thought that she had seen a line of devils opposite her by the way that she clenched her fists.

And then another woman had come out. She was the opposite in looks: very thin, and fair, and tall. She was calling, *Mary, Mary.* When she found the first woman, she listened to her, and then, with a jolt of surprise she had turned and looked across the yard.

She reminded him so much of the girls at home. The same coloring. Although German girls, farm girls, were heavier than she. Ruddy-faced for the most part. Hair plaited and swung over their shoulders, like this one. He had gazed with a half smile of recognition. She looked away from him, and the other woman sat down on a stone seat, evidently not caring that it was still wet from the rain. She seemed both angry and embarrassed. The second woman tugged at her hand a little, and then let her go, and looked around her with a kind of despair.

It was the vacant-faced guard who eventually walked across. The fair-haired woman spoke to him; he stared at his feet, then shrugged.

When he came back across, he glared at the line of prisoners.

"Anybody worked on a farm, dairy farm?" he asked.

No one replied.

The guard stamped his foot. "Cows," he shouted. "Anybody worked . . . ?"

"We are a farm," Frederick said. "At home."

The guard came up to him. "You again." He snorted derisively. "You'd be neither use nor ornament," he said. "They want a hand turning the butter churn, else it spoils."

"I can do it."

"You can't hold a fuckin' spade right."

"I can do it. I do before."

He'd done it as a boy, because it was either boy's or woman's work. Tedious work, repetitive. You turned the wooden churn by hand, hearing the milk slop about inside. After a while the sounds changed. When you heard it slop heavier, when the churn itself became slightly unwieldy, it was butter, and the buttermilk was ready to be drained off. But you had to stand for a long time, turning the churn in the same way, at the same speed.

The guard looked over at the first woman, whose eyes were now closed, her hands resting on her stomach. He looked at the anxious fair-haired girl. Then he relented.

"Seein' you try will be an education," he muttered. He took Frederick's arm and marched him over, past the women, in under the low-framed door.

The dairy was a wonderful place. Cool, and very clean, the walls whitewashed, the floor scrubbed flagstone. He had not seen anywhere as white as this for how long? Perhaps never. Their own at home was a much dirtier, rough-and-ready affair. This bore the hallmarks of a wealthy enterprise somewhere, despite the broken roof of the barn. He had wondered what the cottage was like—it was hidden behind these outbuildings. He wondered if it had a fire, or a kitchen smelling of bread or baking. And then he was struck with such awful homesickness for his mother's *kaiserschmarrn*, the pancakes dusted in sugar, the compote she ladled in winter from the glass jars in the pantry that turned a December evening into summer. *Kaiserschmarrn* and strudel, and a fruit marbled cake that she made. It struck him so hard there, and all at once. Songs and *kaiserschmarrn*, who would have guessed that, to make the throat ache, the eyes sting? He had looked at his feet and taken a breath of the air.

It tasted of cream. Then he knew why the first woman had run out. If she was still early in her time, the thick sweet aroma might have not appealed to her at all. As he stood alongside the fair-haired woman came in, hesitantly, almost sidling along the wall to keep away from him.

"Well?" the guard demanded. "Well?"

"It's here," she murmured. She placed one hand on the churn, a barrel with an iron handle. "I've tried and I can't get it right. I can't keep it regular. We've been sent down from the big house. There's nobody else to do it. But Mary . . . Mary is. . . ."

"All right," the guard said. "This one reckons he knows how. So give him room."

She stepped backwards smartly, and behind a table as if for protection.

Frederick walked over to the churn. He took off his coat and began a slow, determined rhythm. Listening to the sound, he stared at the wall, at the ridges of brick under the whitewash. He wondered which "big house" it was that the girl talked about. Another house to the farm? It seemed so. Perhaps that was the wealth that he saw reflected in the way that the dairy was organized. Money enough to make a decent place, even in a tenant farm. Money enough to maintain it. But no one to run it now, he told himself. A countryside leached of manpower, all gone to flounder in the mud of France.

He took both hands and placed his feet apart and persuaded himself that he wasn't holding anything but instead was attached to something that gently rotated, like a water wheel. That was better. Not holding anything. Pretend that, and ignore the tightening in his fingers. Tell himself a story, paint himself a picture; distract himself from the cramps that threatened to etch themselves into his muscles. He imagined himself back at the stream where he used to fish. He laid himself down in long grass. He closed his eyes and traveled, and the drum went with him, clucking and slapping softly inside the barrel. If he didn't think, if he didn't remember. That was the trick of it.

It took a long time, and when it was done he walked away and put on his coat.

The guard was smoking, leaning against the doorway.

Frederick kept his eyes to the floor and the fair girl walked across to him and looked up into his face and whispered, "Thank you."

He saw that she was very thin, and not exactly pretty; but she had a charm to her face, an unexpected innocence and honesty that he hadn't witnessed in anyone for a very long time. He had not meant to be familiar—to be familiar might frighten her, after all—but he couldn't help the gladness that came to his face.

And then a miracle happened. The pale, blond girl smiled back at him.

At the airfield in France, Harry Cavendish had received two letters that week.

One was from his mother. She told him all the details of Charlotte's wedding, and gave him his sister's new address in London. She told him that she herself was going up to Rutherford, and, while there, she would ask the whereabouts of Nash, and of Jack Armitage, because the family had not heard news of them in some time.

He could have told his mother that it was far better not to hear news. News was the kind of thing he had received from Caitlin.

He had read her letter while lying in his bunk. He honestly could not recall Eleanor, but he was heartily sorry for the end she had been dealt. He too was the deliverer of bombs, and had long ago ceased to think about their impact. There had been that time when he and three others had been detailed to bomb the railway station behind German lines, and that was not an incident that he cared to recall; neither the effect of the bomb, witnessed as he pulled away, nor the death afterwards of his fellow pilot in a dressing station.

He held the letter to his chest, and calculated his own odds. Caitlin perhaps was safer than she had been, if she was on her way to England. If she was in a nervous state, it might be that they would give her leave, or some job that was not so exhausting. She had been nursing now for over two years. It would be enough to cut the heart and soul out of any human being, and he hated to think that she felt herself to be of no consequence to him any longer.

He was just about done in himself. Not only did his damaged legs cause him grinding pain, but he was beginning to lose faith in his abilities to advise any pilot. They came over here elated in having passed their training, and God knew that it was a miracle they survived that. One in three never passed their final exam, because they were, to put it quite simply, dead. Smashed into the earth somewhere over jolly old Blighty. And so when they got out here, the light of defiance was in their faces. Defiance and devil-may-care. Wasn't that the badge of the RFC? Three years of war had turned those flying gladiators into screeching Valkyries.

"I'm as wretched as she is," he whispered to himself. "Won't do, won't do."

It was still light, late in the afternoon. He would go out and watch for the last sortie coming back. The RFC had twenty-five squadrons, over three hundred and fifty aircraft. A hundred of those were scouts, the fighters. He wished passionately that they had more SPADs or Sopwith Triplanes; they were the ones that seemed to be doing better against the Albatros of the Germans. The Albatros gave the enemy the upper hand, he was sure; they were more manoeuvrable, and they didn't have the outdated FE8, the lumbering machines that he himself had always disliked. Two days ago, a new plane had arrived, something they called a Bristol F2a. His commanding officer had told him it would be the savior of the squadron. But out of the six that went up, four had been shot down.

Bloody fucking Albatros. It was indeed like its namesake; it would be hung around their own necks as a sign of their inefficiency and disgrace. He wondered how many would be lost as the battle was launched on Arras. And what made it worse was the new red plane up there and the pilot that manned it. It was rumored that his name was Von Richthofen. He was the very devil, and in any other circumstances Harry would have admired him. But he couldn't muster a shred of admiration for whoever the man was who kept smashing his own men out of the sky with his tricks and shows.

What the hell were they going to do about it? he wondered. Keep throwing young men up there? What was he going to say to John Gould when he eventually arrived here? That the RFC was in glorious ascendance, in every sense of the word? He couldn't lie to Gould: the American would see straight through him. The man had an unerring ability to do that.

"Damn it," he muttered. He never left the ground these days, or only rarely. It was his job to come up with tactical solutions and advise on what was needed. But in truth he didn't know what else could be needed other than a fucking miracle.

He turned on his heel, and went back to the mess room. Here, he got a sheet of paper and began to write as if his life depended on it.

Dear Charlotte, he began.

I hear that you had a very nice wedding. Dear girl, I hope that you are happy. You should be with such a fine man as Michael. And so I'm sorry to give you a job while you're in the first throes of marital bliss. But would you do something for your beloved brother? I want you to find somebody for me. A nurse coming back on the convoys. You know Caitlin, don't you? You'll know where she's posted. If you can't find her, perhaps Mother will. . . .

He stopped. He could hear a plane coming back, a fractured noise, its engine misfiring somewhere above the airfield.

It's rather important, he scribbled.

The misfiring stopped. The silence was more shattering than the original sound. He gritted his teeth, and continued.

At least, he wrote, *it is to me. . . .*

Chapter 8

*I*t was ten a.m. on Sunday morning when Charlotte knocked on Christine Nesbitt's narrow door.

It was in a dirty little street between Bloomsbury and Berwick Street Market. If Charlotte had been asked to describe it to her mother, she would have said that it was in Oxford Street to avoid Octavia being worried—she would have described some of the little avenues behind the large shops where sweet little mews houses had been converted from stores or stables. But, in reality, Christine's studio was in Soho, the part of the capital regularly described as a den of iniquity. It would have given William Cavendish forty fits if he had seen his daughter alone there.

It was three weeks since the wedding, but Charlotte did not think about that anymore. It seemed a very long time ago, a place where she still had some of her illusions intact. She looked up at the building, taking a step back on the pavement to stare upwards at what she believed must be Christine's window.

Eventually, she heard a clatter of feet on the stairs. The door was suddenly flung open, and, instead of Christine, Charlotte found herself face-to-face with a man of about thirty: he wore no starched collar, no tie. His hair was uncombed. He stood in the doorway and smiled at her broadly, pulling on a crumpled jacket.

Two things, she knew, would stand in her memory. The first was that his shoes were unpolished. She had never come across anyone who wore unpolished shoes—anyone who was not a workman, that is. And the second was that, with his startlingly blue eyes and thick dark hair, the stranger was incredibly handsome.

"Hello," he said. "Looking for someone?"

"Christine."

He hooked a thumb over his shoulder. "Third floor."

"Which door?"

"There is only one."

He stood to one side; she entered. He disappeared along the street, hands in pockets.

For a while, Charlotte stood at the bottom of the stairs looking at her feet, wondering about the shoes and the uncombed hair. He had spoken like a gentleman. That was the odd thing about it, the thing that made no sense to her.

When she got to the top of the stairs, she found Christine leaning on the landing bannister and grinning down at her.

"Why, if it isn't Mrs. Preston! How perfectly lovely."

"Hello, Christine."

Charlotte was suddenly enveloped by a hug, and Christine took her hand. "Come in, come in," she said. "This is wonderful! I didn't think you'd come at all."

"I sent a letter."

"Did you? Have I forgotten it? What did it say?"

"To make an appointment for today."

Christine smiled at her. "But you don't need to make an appointment. Not for me. Unless . . . oh." Her eyes strayed to the stair, and she began to laugh. "Perhaps you do."

The room was unlike anything Charlotte had ever seen.

It occupied the whole of the top of the house, and had evidently been an attic. The ceiling was merely the roofbeams, looking very rickety and haphazard. One wall was half glass and half brick. In the corner was a partition made with a curtain, behind which Christine immediately disappeared. By the clatter and the sound of water, Charlotte surmised that this was a little kitchen. On either side of the large glass windows were the most astonishing curtains, strung up on a piece of wood balanced on either end of a pile of ordinary bricks, and tied back with something that looked like dressing-gown cord. They looked monstrously heavy—absurd, really, for the room— but such a fabulous color. Orange, with emerald linings and some sort of large circular print in green.

Christine had poked her head out from behind the partition. "Tea?"

"Yes, please."

"Will you take it black? There isn't any milk."

"Oh . . ."

"It's awfully good. Earl Grey. The disapproving aunt sent it. Rather better without milk."

"All right."

While Christine continued to clatter cups, Charlotte turned full circle to gaze at the rest of the room.

There was no carpet on the floor. At one end, there was a kind of chaise longue, quite broad. On it was a single sheet and a pile of pillows and cushions. The sheet was hanging half off the bed, and beside it was a fruit packing case with an oil lamp balanced on top. At various points on the floor and on the windowsill were candles in tin saucers.

But the item that dominated the room was the table. It was enormous; how it had ever made it up the stairs was a mystery, Charlotte thought. Perhaps it had been actually built in the room. It seemed to be made of building planks—the kind used in construction works. She had seen them on scaffolding in the street nearby, close to the market. She wondered if that was where they had come from.

The table was covered in paper and paint. Glass jars smeared with paint and various ones holding water or turpentine. Brushes lay on smeared cloths, or were stuck into pottery jugs. Against the table leg at one side, several canvases were stacked. And at the far end of the table was an easel, with whatever canvas was on it turned away from the room as a whole.

Charlotte couldn't quite describe the smell. It was a mixture of stale cooking, paint, damp, and the peculiar chemical odor of wet newsprint. It ought to have been appalling, but somehow it wasn't. Perhaps because it was so foreign to her, so unusual, so interestingly awful.

Christine emerged from the partition. She was carrying two large cups without saucers. "Here we are," she announced. She put the cups on the table amid the paint and brushes. "Now, I will find us a seat. Only there isn't a seat." She appeared to think, and then picked the cups up again. "We'll have to camp down on the bed," she said.

Charlotte followed her. As Christine put the cups on the floor, and made a scrambled attempt to straighten the sheet and covers, Charlotte found herself blushing. She bit her lip and glanced back at the vast table. "You paint and live and sleep in the same room?"

"There isn't any other, dearest."

"But for . . . washing . . ."

"There's a bathroom two flights down. I share it with a Jewish family and an old lady from . . . where is it? Oh, Genoa. She's a witch, I think. She actually tells fortunes. She's utterly hopeless at it and spits if you tell her she's a fake. The family are nice, though. Four little boys, and they parade them like a set of Russian dolls when they go to synagogue."

"Is it noisy?"

"Not at all. But the fish you can smell . . . that's them. I do apologize for it. Some kind of pickled fish, I think. Do you know the market? They run a stall there. Stockings. We'll go and look at it. Silk stockings, you know."

They sat side by side sipping their tea.

"What do you think of my room?" Christine asked.

Charlotte looked up again at the table, the curtains, and the bare floorboards. "I think it's wonderful," she said.

Christine laughed. "You don't have to be polite."

"Oh, I'm not being polite," Charlotte replied. "It *is* wonderful. It's . . . empty. And full."

"It's empty of Victoriana," Christine said. "And full of me."

"Yes. That's exactly it."

"Didn't you grow up in rooms like that? Full of knickknacks and useless chairs and little tables with horrible little ornaments, and damned great aspidistras?"

Charlotte smiled. "My mother's got a good eye," she said. "But it sounds like how Rutherford was when she married Father."

"Hunting prints, I expect?"

"And stuffed heads."

"Poor beleaguered foxes, and rugs made of dead tigers?"

"Not quite as bad as that."

"Let me imagine. . . . Your father's bedroom has a Landseer print on the wall. *The Stag at Bay.*"

"Yes, it does."

Christine clapped her hands in delight, and they both laughed.

"My God, the seed we sprang from," Christine said. "Shooting beautiful creatures and putting them in glass cases. Macabre. Bizarre."

Charlotte had never thought of this before. Rutherford was just as it was; she felt a need to defend it. In the last three weeks she had longed for her home, wanted so desperately to turn back the clock and be a girl again, running through the grounds, playing in the stream with Harry, or sitting idly in the huge glasshouse where the pineapples grew and which was always scented heavily with exotic lilies, and to have Louisa brushing her hair for minutes on end as she used to do.

Christine was assessing her, watching her face. "That's odd. I thought you'd certainly find it horrible. Are you sure you're not being polite?" she asked. "Because I would really rather you wouldn't. I don't need your approval."

"I don't give it," Charlotte told her. "It's not my business to approve or disapprove."

"How like your father you sound," Christine observed. "I suppose now you're talking about Alexis."

"Alexis?"

"You must have bumped straight into him."

"Yes, I met him. If that's his name."

"His name is Alexis Barrington. He's a fourth son. Of a duke. He paints. And spends his father's money rather rashly. You're a second daughter, aren't you? I shall introduce you if he ever comes back." She finished her tea, and leapt to her feet. "Where is Michael?" she asked, looking down at Charlotte, hands on hips. "I thought you were both coming."

"I wanted to come alone."

"Have you been sent to reconnoiter?"

"Not at all. Michael decided against a portrait for himself, or of the two of us. But I thought . . . well, my mother always had a lovely portrait of herself when she had first been married. It's on the stairs at Rutherford. A Singer Sargent."

"Singer Sargent?" Christine echoed. "Good God above, I hope you're not expecting to come here in an ocean of satin and be turned out looking like one of his."

Charlotte smiled. "I would like to look like myself, that's all."

"You mean, not cubist. Not surreal. Not with four heads or a composition in feet."

"My father wouldn't pay you."

"Don't worry," Christine replied, unoffended. "I don't do that anyway. You saw what I do when I came to Rutherford. I haven't moved away from that much. Less colors, though. A restricted palette." She put her head to one side. "You're awfully pale. Do you want to be represented as pale?"

"I don't know."

"You've never struck me as pale. That's odd. You've always been vibrant."

Charlotte said nothing. She sipped her tea.

"Goodness me," Christine exclaimed suddenly. "You must be pregnant. That must be the cause." She laughed, and came to sit quickly beside Charlotte. She put her hand on Charlotte's arm. "Aren't you well? I can't paint you if you're going to turn green and suddenly run out because of the smell in here. . . ."

"I'm not pregnant."

"But of course, you wouldn't know. Only three weeks. But you *could* be, you see?" She looked closely at Charlotte, and then put both hands on her shoulders and gently turned her body left and right. "There is something different," she said. "Quite definitely."

Charlotte could not bring herself to comment. She sat mutely, allowing herself to be manoeuvred.

"Perhaps it's added something," Christine mused. "A kind of

delicacy." She looked down at Charlotte's clothes. "Are you going to be painted in this?"

"What's the matter with it?"

"A plain wool suit. And grey. And a hat. Surely not?"

"It's a very good suit."

"No, it isn't," Christine decided. "It might be practical, but who wants to be remembered for being practical? Preserved forever as dutiful?"

"I like being dutiful," Charlotte said, thinking of her work at St. Dunstan's.

"Of course you don't!" Christine exclaimed. "You might obey and be very charming. You might even do it with a glint in your eye. But you can't be defined by it, painted as if that's all you were. It might be appropriate for a lady mayoress, or the wife of the master of the local Hunt. But not for you." She jumped again to her feet. Within a pace or two she was at the table, and she came back with a few scraps of paper, on which various colors were splashed.

"Let's see," she murmured, holding up first one and then another. "Pink. Rose. No. What color is your mother's Singer dress? Champagne or rose. I thought so. No, you're much stronger than that. Blue. Sapphire. Ah . . . purple."

She held the piece of paper close to Charlotte's face, and brought her own equally close. "Your skin has quite a coffee tone in there somewhere," she said. "I imagine if you laid in the sun you would go absolutely brown."

"I'm hardly going to lie in the sun."

"Aren't you? Wouldn't you like to?"

"Well, who does?"

"Coco Chanel."

Charlotte frowned. "Who is Coco Chanel?"

"She lives in Biarritz. She designs hats. And these wonderful loose clothes. . . ." She smiled at Charlotte. "Loose clothes, Charlotte. For sporting ladies. Not tweeds. Not wool. You should live there, you know. I bet there's sunshine in your blood."

"Father's ancestors lived in the Caribbean."

"And owned half of it?"

"And owned half of it. Or stole half of it."

They both smiled. Christine's hands dropped from Charlotte's shoulders, and she fleetingly stroked Charlotte's cheek. "Just for a moment there, in that reply, I saw the Charlotte that I used to know not very long ago. What's the matter, sweet one?"

It had been Charlotte's habit, in the last three weeks, to protest to everyone—especially her mother, especially Louisa, who might get close enough, or know her well enough, to know when she was lying—that everything was perfect. But now, looking into Christine's eyes, she found she couldn't do it. Abruptly, she burst into tears.

Aghast, Christine let her cry for a moment. Then, very gently, she patted her leg. "Don't go on too much," she said. "I haven't a clean handkerchief."

Charlotte had plunged her face into her hands; now, she dropped them and stared into space. "I'm sorry."

"What are you sorry about? Crying? I wouldn't be sorry for a little thing like that. I cry all the time."

Charlotte glanced at her. "You do? What about?"

"Money, usually. Not having any. And boiled eggs."

"Not having boiled eggs?"

Christine laughed. "No, you nincompoop. Having to *eat* boiled eggs. It's all I can cook."

"I can't cook either," Charlotte admitted.

"One isn't taught. Or laundry. I've had the devil's own job figuring out how to wash and dry things," Christine said cheerfully. "I heard that one aristocratic gal came to be a Bohemian—she had some wild idea she'd like the freedom because she'd had an argument with her mother over a hat—and she left after a week because no one had picked up her underwear from the floor. She simply couldn't understand it. Mind you, the fact that she was a complete idiot didn't help. Arabella Winsome. Heard of her? Related to the Nettishes?"

Charlotte sighed. "I should never have got married."

"Oh my love, is that all it is? But darling, most women loathe being married. If they're honest. I mean, who wants to be someone's glorified housekeeper for fifty years? Or in charge of housekeepers, and bothering about menus or whatever? Why is it our job, after all? I've seen women artists living with men who tell them quite openly that they mustn't paint anymore because they need to look after the children and put meals on the table. Not one of the men I know would dream of cleaning dishes, or buying food, or cooking it, or washing their socks. It's ghastly. So unfair. I mean, look at someone like Edna Waugh."

"I'm sorry. I don't know who that is."

"Well, quite," Christine replied tartly. "She was at the Slade, and brilliant. Then she got married and *pffft!*" She illustrated the remark by snapping her fingers together. "And Christabel Dennison. Another one you won't know. She told someone I know that she felt she could never be happy again because she had to make meals all day. She used to be so talented." She shook her head in exasperation. "I sometimes think this so-called Bohemian experiment is really just a playground. All the ideals go out of the window when a man wants food, or his shoes polishing. Personally, I find it all quite disgusting, the way men are. But you've got a woman who 'does,' haven't you? A cook?"

"It isn't the cooking, or the house."

"Then it must be living in the house. Is it horrible? His mother's choice? Does she turn up and criticize?"

"No, not at all."

"Does *your* mother turn up and criticize?"

"She wouldn't dream of it."

Christine sighed, then smiled. "One of the reasons that I'm here is that I could never stand the rules. Do you remember, before the war wiped it all away? One wasn't to be vulgar. That was one. Vulgarity was the most dreadful crime. My aunt thinks I'm vulgar now, and she doesn't know the half of it!"

Charlotte nodded slowly. "My mother tells a story that Father once forbade her to walk across the lawn in her bare feet."

"There you are, you see! What on earth would it matter? Would the world grind to a halt? Ludicrous. I was lectured on all kinds of things. That I must never use colored notepaper, for instance. Or wear cheap scent. Or ever wear anything that had dyed fur attached to it. I must wear thick stockings, not thin ones. Never to get in a cab alone. Never to walk alone, never to dine alone. . . ." She threw up her hands. "Stifling!"

"Yes," Charlotte replied quietly. "How awful that must have been. I don't recall anything like that, though. I was a boy-child really. . . ."

Christine fell silent. She saw at once that it wasn't Charlotte's past that stifled her, but her present—her life now. Her married life. She decided that if Charlotte wanted to tell her what the tears were about, she would. But the silence stretched out for some minutes until Christine, losing patience, clapped her hands together. "Enough," she said. "We'll go out."

"I must get home."

"Back to whatever it is that makes you weep?" Christine said archly. "Not before I've taken you to the Café Royal." Abruptly, she reached down, took Charlotte's face in her hands, and kissed her on her forehead. "There! Now wipe your eyes," she instructed. "Nobody feels like crying in the Café Royal, and if Augustus John is there, he'll buy us a drink. Wait while I dress."

*I*t was mid-afternoon by the time that Charlotte returned home.

She put her key in the lock, and called out to the housekeeper that she was back, placing her hat and gloves on the little hall table. There was no reply.

Wonderingly, she walked down the hall as far as she was able; beyond the door in the small entrance was a scullery, a pantry and a kitchen, and a small bedroom in which their cook lived. She was a plain, nice woman who—according to Michael's mother—had never married and was known to his family as a reliable and quiet sort. She would keep regular hours, and was unlikely to entertain men friends. And, although the house was small, it would never have occurred to Charlotte to trespass into the cook's domain. So after knocking softly once or twice, she retreated upstairs.

She would have loved a cup of tea. She was so thirsty. The Café Royal had been an eye-opener, and Christine had been right in that Augustus John had been there at the bar, regaling other customers with his exploits of life in a gypsy caravan on Dartmoor—and, to his credit, he had bought both she and Christine a glass of red wine with the astonishing words, "If you see any little toads running under your feet, pat their heads."

"He means his children," Christine had whispered.

"He brings his children here?"

"No, not really. It's a joke. He always says the same thing. He'll pat any child's head, you see. Because he never knows if it's one of his."

Charlotte had gazed at the great man. He seemed larger than

life, grown more vivid by virtue of his fame. They called him the world's greatest painter. He was like a bull: a sort of vibrant life poured out of him. You could sense it, almost feel it as an electrical charge close to him. He laughed a lot, and spoke in a loud, booming voice. He was puffing on a pipe, and indeed the whole room was full of the smoke of many cigars and cigarettes.

The bar was like a gaudy cavern with green walls and a gilt ceiling, and, at intervals, statues of goddesses. In the mirrors behind the bar an artist's world reminiscent of Manet's *A Bar at the Folies-Bergère* was reflected; domino tables and hardened drinkers, and conversations in full flow. A woman wreathed in a floor-length shawl sat on one chair; a saintly-looking girl on another. "Models," Christine replied, when asked. "And Dorelia."

"Dorelia?"

"John's mistress. His official one, at least."

When they had finally left, Charlotte's head had been reeling. She wasn't used to wine; the outside world seemed peculiar. The afternoon street of people passing in their Sunday clothes seemed suddenly absurdly contained and clean. The sun had come out and the pavements gleamed after the rain; the omnibuses passed up and down, the crowds promenaded. After parting company with Christine, Charlotte had walked for some time rather than taking a cab.

She felt tired now and her head ached as she climbed the stairs. She was on duty at seven tomorrow morning. She would lie down for a while, she thought. She opened the door to the bedroom; the curtains were pulled. The room was nearly dark.

Michael was sitting in the dark in a chair near the window, facing the door. It momentarily unnerved her. "Oh . . . Michael," she murmured. "What are you doing sitting here?"

"Waiting for you."

"Have you had supper?"

"Some time ago." He stood up and walked in the direction of her voice. She was so glad at that moment that he couldn't see her. He might notice the remnants of pleasure in her face. He leaned towards her, and frowned. "You've been drinking."

"Only a glass of wine. Christine took me to the Café Royal."

"The Café . . . ?" His astounded voice trailed away, and then came back with insistent force. "You shall not go there. I forbid it."

"I'm afraid I've been there. I'm sorry, but I don't see how you can tell me where I should go and not go."

"It seems that someone should."

She turned away from him, taking off her rings and laying them quietly on the dressing table. "It's just a café," she murmured. "They are just people."

"People," he repeated, irritated. "I don't want you mixing with them. They are not decent."

She pressed her lips together hard, trying not to respond. He waited a moment, then felt his way around to her. He reached for her arm, and she watched his hand slowly come towards her in the gloom. "Women of a certain type go there, I've heard," he said, as he finally gripped her wrist. "I don't want my wife there."

"Michael, my *mother* goes there." The words hung between them: she saw that he wanted to exclaim—as perhaps he had heard others say—that her mother was no better than the models that draped themselves across the chairs at the Café Royal. But she knew that Michael would not say that. He would observe a formal nicety with her. She felt herself shudder, but it was not because Michael was making an effort to be protective. It was his touch. His careful, dogged, possessive touch.

"If you wish to go there," he said softly. "I shall come with you."

"All right," she whispered.

But you shan't, she was thinking. *You shan't.*

Chapter 9

*I*t was such a blessed dream.

Jack was standing in the last of the afternoon light at Rutherford, and the last year of war had never been. It had never happened at all. He had never walked away from his parents down Rutherford's long drive; he had never glanced back to see the curtains closed across the window of Louisa's bedroom, as if she couldn't bear to see him go. He had never watched the horses taken from Rutherford's yard, or arrived himself at the Remount Center in Sussex.

The year slowly reasserted itself in a series of snatched images.

He saw a fine morning, and the horses exercised. A rolling ship. A single track railway and an open cattle truck, where he stood with a hundred others. The veterinary stations at Albert, and Authuille. It was there that he had first seen men and horses gassed, turning his face as the men staggered past, or were carried retching and coughing into the wagons; and he himself lost for what he could possibly do as the horse he had been assigned to stood half dead, her legs planted far apart as she fought for breath. Please God that it had never happened that they had decided that she was too far gone, too broken, her lungs too full of foam. Please God, let it not be that they had taken her outside and shot her; or that the next horse in the line looked at them with mute accusation, head swaying.

It had never happened. He was somewhere else. The dream came flooding back to him. He was a free man again, wading through the meadows by the river in a line of the other stable hands, looking for ragwort, making sure that there was no invasion of the yellow weed into the pasture. A free man again in the heat of a summer's day, the warmth on the back of his neck, his hands swinging aimlessly among the grass. The war had never come to claim them all; the horses were still in the yard and he was grooming them at first light, and there was no hurry and no fear; he leaned against the sweet-smelling flank of a beast as he brushed it, and they both stood ankle-deep in straw. Across the yard, he saw the wood smoke coming from the chimney of the cottage; his mother would come to the gate and call him. And beyond, the garden wall of the great house, and the gardens.

It was the end of summer three years ago, and Louisa had been rescued from France and the bastard who had tried to break her, and she was once again sitting listlessly at the table at the harvest fair. And his mind took him further back still. It was the year before that, and she had asked him to dance in the orchard, resting her clasped hands behind his neck, looking up into his face. And then it was last year again, and she was bidding him good-bye where no one could see them, and he had kissed her.

Lovely, random, floating images. Mixed up and blissful. Innocent of grief. In his sleep, Jack smiled. One of the veterinary medics passing him, seeing him slumped there on the earth in the corner of the barn that served as a first dressing station for the horses, thought that he would wake him, but decided against it. Jack Armitage had been treating the wounded from Monchy for fourteen hours straight; when ordered to rest, he had fallen almost where he stood, first leaning on the wall and then crumbling to his knees in a crouch. He was almost sitting now, though unconscious. The medic stared at him. Strange how a man could smile in the midst of this, he thought.

But for Jack in his dreams, Monchy had not happened either. The strange scenes he had witnessed were dreams in themselves, apparitions only.

The village had been won after bloody fighting, but pockets of resistance had held out. In the safety of sleep, Jack had never seen the HQ stationed in the cellar and the telephone table surreally set up among boxes of sugar and salt. The place had once been a shop; both armies had ransacked it. Germans had torn open cartons, and the Tommies afterwards. Sugar in the rum, fire in the throat, fuel for the failing heart. Salt for the bully beef stews to make them edible.

And in the dream Jack had never stood by a wall in the darkness, two horses held by their reins, both with injuries. They were gathering them together to take back; there was a veterinary hospital five miles in the rear. A horse that could be treated must be treated. They were needed, and couldn't be thrown away. Repair and reissue, just like uniforms. Like the thirty thousand boots that Jack had seen being made in a place near the coast. Like the makeshift stables that he was required to provide, dragging corrugated iron and bricks from what had once been houses or back gardens. Trying to stop the snow coming in. Trying to clean mud from the leg wounds. Trying to make poultices for mustard gas burns.

In the dream, he had never had his back turned to the building behind him. Two in the morning. The artillery was still pounding. Big bass drums in the blackness. The army had been through here, the Highlanders, and cleared the street. And so it was impossible that when Jack had turned his head that he had seen a German face six feet away, the rifle aimed at his own head. It was strange that he had felt no fear; he was beyond it. He had ploughed through so many dead to find the hysterical horses that he now seemed not to care. His blood ran thinly, liquid ice.

The snow was coming down. The German wavered, wiped his eyes. "Nay, lad," Jack heard himself murmuring. As he would to a horse. A slow soothing murmur. "Nay lad, nay lad." Like that. The man frowned, and then his mouth drew down in a childish-looking grimace. His bottom lip wavered, and he began to cry. There in the snow, there in the dark. He put his rifle on the floor and held up his hands. "It's no use surrendering to me, I can't do nothing with you," Jack had told him. "It's the horses I'm seeing to." He had cocked his head. The soldier nodded. He put out one hesitant hand and placed it on the nearest animal, and stroked it, and began to cry in earnest.

He had looked no more than eighteen at most. A blond boy, alone and afraid and trying to give himself up and get out of this carnage. In the next moment, someone had come out of the shadows, a British sergeant, and caught the boy by the arm, and yelled blue murder. The boy literally screamed in fright; he scrambled for his rifle, in his youth and fear reaching for his gun, cocking it and training it on the sergeant, finger trembling on the trigger. The sergeant shot him at point blank range. The boy dropped to the ground; the patrol moved on. Jack had stood there shaking, looking at the snow gently collecting on the boy's face, dropping on his still-open eyes.

But such things had not happened. Not now that he was safely asleep.

Louisa walked towards him, laughing, holding out something. He stretched to see what it was. A rose from the terrace garden. A new kind that the gardener March had cultivated. She was showing him how pretty it was; yellow, with an apricot center. His mother used to get some of the flowers that were not deemed suitable for the big house; ones that had gone over slightly and were dying. She had always loved them nevertheless, putting them into big jugs on the kitchen windowsill. He remembered them casting their beautiful light into the room, like patches of sunlight, pools of gold.

And then he woke. He couldn't breathe. Someone was crouched down next to him, a fag in hand, blowing smoke in his face. He coughed, and the man laughed. "Get up," he was told. "More coming through, and transport."

He had slept for five hours, and was amazed to find that it was now daylight. Tea was being brewed: a tin cup of it was forced into his hands. His captain came striding across. "Well," he said. "You've slept."

"I'm sorry, sir."

"Long day ahead. Get yourself something to eat. Jump to it."

He went to the table and stared at the food. It seemed incredible, impossible. There was a large straw hamper there, and inside all kinds of extraordinary things. A box with shortbread in it. A flask of whisky wrapped in a straw pouch. Jam and honey and Gentleman's Relish, and cheese and cake. Fruitcake—a Dundee cake with almonds pressed into the thick glaze. He blinked, thinking it was a mirage. Or that he was still dreaming.

Captain Porter clapped him on the shoulder. "Blighty parcel," he said. "Hamper from Fortnum's." It was fantastic. Mail got through, parcels got through. The roads were clogged with a nightmare traffic of men, ammunition, guns, and wagons. Staff cars floundered and had to be abandoned. The wounded were dragged on sleds through the mud. The dead littered the streets. The living drowned in the fields. But the mail got through.

"Fortnum and Mason," Jack muttered, still astounded. He looked at the logo on the basket. "Fortnum and Mason—Piccadilly since 1707." The shop had delivered parcels to the troops fighting Napoleon;

they were delivering now to South Africa and Mesopotamia, and to prisoner-of-war-camps in Germany. But still, it looked so incredible. Both obscene and miraculous. He couldn't decide which.

Slowly, he took a piece of shortbread and cut a slice of cheese. Then he snatched up a piece of the fruitcake and stuffed it, along with some of the cheese and shortbread, into his pocket.

Fortified by the unfamiliar taste of the cake, rolling it around in his mouth with ecstatic delight, he walked the horses down to the barges. In the filthy, mud-banked water that used to be a river, flat-bottomed barges were waiting to take the wounded back behind the lines.

Duckboards had been laid, but even they were submerged now. It was a slither and slide down to the riverbanks. Jack watched as stretcher bearers patiently edged forwards. The snow had turned to sleet. The morning was punctuated by artillery blasts—just a continuous percussion that no one took any notice of. You were either going to be hit or you weren't. The man next to you might take the force of a stray shell. Or the impact would be borne by you.

Jack reasoned that the worst thing that could happen would be if a shell landed, say, twenty feet away. Twenty or thirty feet meant getting sliced by shrapnel as the metal casing shattered into lethal pieces. Twenty or thirty feet away was unlucky. A direct impact was lucky. You would know nothing, he told himself. And so they all worked on: stretcher bearers, men, horses, mules, not knowing if the next crash would have their number on it, a ticket to eternity.

Jack thought that he was luckier than most in having the horses to attend to. It took his mind off himself. It meant that he didn't have to stare down too long at the faces of the injured. He would rather look into the eyes of an animal—patient, unquestioning liquid-brown eyes—than into the frightened gaze of some young lad.

The silence was the strangest thing, and the most admirable. Aside from the hurried orders of those packing the barges, there was not a human sound. The wounded didn't weep or shout. Sometimes Jack could see their lips moving in a prayer, or some kind of instruction to themselves—he had once heard a strong Devon accent whispering, "Don't do that, don't do that," over and over. Occasionally, standing in the line, a hand would be raised and a cigarette given. How often had Jack seen that cigarette fall unsmoked, the grip loosened, the fingers unable to grip, the life running out of the hand that tried to hold it. Others crushed it, fumbled it, gratefully trying to inhale something that didn't smell of cordite or chlorine, bromine or phosgene.

The barges with the men pushed away first. The river was so full of rubbish that progress was very slow. Jack noted how the craft moved like worms threading their way through loose earth, snagging on sunken obstacles. The sky, heavy with sleet, pressed down on the scene like a great wide grey curtain. Color had almost gone from everything around; it was a study in monochrome. Occasionally, when someone spoke, or rolled their eyes, it was a surprise to see the inner red of lips, or the bloodshot rim to an eyelid. Skin was spattered with mud, or grease, or something worse, caked to a brown residue. Hands were knotted on ropes, on rails, on handles, stretcher sides— fists of cold grey flesh.

The next barge was ready for them. Jack made his way down the slope with the mule he had taken from the line. Strange beasts, mules. The most awkward beasts on the planet. He had been told— he had never seen it himself—that the way to subdue one was to take it straight from the ship and walk it round and round a parade ground for two days, until the animal was exhausted. Not to mention the handler. That ironed the kick out of them. Usually. But they got frightened just as the horses did, and when they were terrified they would just stop. Neither shell nor shot would move them then.

He'd seen one looking as if it were carved from stone, absolutely immovable, standing at the side of a road in Étaples. Eventually the pack had been stripped from it and they'd left it there. He'd put a handful of hay at its feet, but it still didn't move. It was caked with so much mud that its coat looked striped—channels and valleys of mud where hair used to be until it seemed to be half mule, half zebra. He'd looked over his shoulder as they had driven on in the veterinary ambulance and it had still been there, a living statue, a monument to defiance.

But this mule was obedient. It staggered because its legs had been impregnated with mustard gas. In addition, it looked to him as if it had windpuffs, the swellings to the deep flexor tendons. He'd seen that on racehorses at Carlisle when Lord Cavendish used to go racing there. Racehorses got a lot of leg injuries, though it was a very long way indeed from the beauties of the racehorse to the stocky, feral-faced little animal that he now tried to manoeuvre into the boat. Poor bloody creature, he thought. It must be like walking on nails, or on enormous blisters. He would spend the night up country, in the light of oil lamps, treating dozens of animals like this. Lancing boils, applying plasters. Cooling the burns, trimming the splintered hooves. Standing in some shadow or other while the veterinary officers did their rounds, dispensing life and death. Sometimes the men—officers and others alike—would kneel by an animal, and a light would come into their faces. The light of other days: as boys, on their first ponies. Or as new recruits discovering the willing partnership of horse and rider. Days of lonely rides through fields or woods. Flying, exciting days of galloping across army rides. Or in his case, days of harvest.

That was what came to Jack most when he felt sorry for a beast. He would think himself back on the board of a wagon, looking between Wenceslas's flicking ears, seeing the lane rolling out in front of them as they took hay down to the barns on the various tenant farms, or came back through the gates of Rutherford. He would remind himself that even the suffering horse in front of him had perhaps had much better times and pleasant days. He would smile when he came to this conclusion, remembering how his own Wenceslas had always listened to him intently. You saw first one white ear and then the other turn back in response to Jack's voice. And the patient, rhythmical plodding: the tenor, the tempo of country life. The speed of a horse's gait: quietly plodding away the years.

The barge was full. The animals and men had to stand all the way, trying to keep their balance as the boat pushed off. At their backs, the artillery still boomed erratically. Trying to find targets. He pitied those artillery horses, pulling such enormous weights. And having to move quickly as orders and targets changed. And being targets themselves. My God, it was horrible. He wondered if he was more horse than human himself, because he always felt more disgust and more grief at seeing part of a horse than part of a human being. A pain went right through him, from solar plexus to the crown of his head. Left him shuddering. *Perhaps this whole bloody circus has turned my brain*, he thought, watching the dark brown water go by. *I'm not sane anymore. But then neither is anyone else.*

They reached a station in the rear in the last light of the afternoon.

The sleet had stopped: now it was merely cold. Rivetingly, breath-takingly cold.

"Nice April, ain't it?" a London voice said to him as they struggled up the slope from the river and towards an abandoned chapel, where faint lights were showing. Jack couldn't see the man's face—there were two horses and two mules between them—but he murmured his agreement. "'Oh, to be in England now that April's there,'" the man quoted, and laughed. "Nice bit of cherry blossom in St. James's Park. That's where my missus'll be. Walking the kids through the park . . ." And on and on he rambled, laughing, talking, cajoling the animals. When they had tied the beasts up, they went back through the growing gloom to the river to get the next lot.

"You from London?" the man asked.

"No. Yorkshire."

"Ah. Whereabouts?"

"Near Richmond."

"Got an aunt in Durham. Near that?"

"Not very far." Jack thought of the exposed high land out Durham way, the isolated farms.

"My nephew's down the mines. Been drafted there, like. Only fourteen years old."

Jack grunted, concentrating on the next animal. It seemed blinded, drooling at the mouth. A mare, piebald. Or perhaps with lost skin. He squinted to see what, exactly.

"RFC flyboys come up round here yesterday. See them?"

Jack had noticed the planes, of course. The word was that they were losing a lot of men and machines. "I know someone in the RFC," he said.

"Is that right? La-di-da. Gunner? Observer?"

"Pilot."

The man laughed again. He didn't believe him.

They worked through the night. At about three in the morning, Jack suddenly remembered the fruitcake and the cheese in his pocket. He went outside—if outside it could be called. It was more accurately simply the other side of the wall of the cemetery to the chapel. He sat down in the dark on the snow-crusted edge of the field and took out the crumbed remains of the cake and ate it. Afterwards, he put his arms around his knees and stared out at the land. It was wide here—wide, open, empty. Just a few hills and a scattering of trees and tiny villages. Or at least, it had been once. Now it was just lost, a space between battles, an echo in the dark where no one lived anymore. He felt like a piece of flotsam on a black ocean: he had once been attached to something that mattered, but he had broken loose, been cast adrift.

He rubbed his hands over his face and got up, and went back through the gate, stepping across graves that someone once had respected and revered.

"Armitage," a voice called.

"Yes, sir."

"See this Ardennes here. You know dray horses, don't you?"

"Not drays exactly, sir. Shires and the like."

"You know what I mean," the officer snapped. "There's a railway siding up the line a mile away. Walk up there with a travois and the Ardennes. He's wanted to pull a truck along the line."

The Ardennes was a magnificent horse. Or had been.

Jack already knew the breed; he'd seen them once in a horse show in the Dales. They had a relatively short head in relation to their body, but they were massively broad with a low center of gravity. The horses that he had seen in the show had tails that trailed to the ground like skeins of rope, and huge balls of combed hair on the hooves; their manes had been plaited into colorful strands as thick as a man's wrist. Like Wenceslas, they were docile when trained, and had relentless stamina. He remembered how their chestnut coats had gleamed like mirrors.

It was a long time since this Ardennes had been fit for a show, however. The head hung low, the nostrils flared; the coat was matted with filth despite a halfhearted attempt to clean it. The tail had been cropped to prevent it trailing in the mud. The hooves, though, even shorn of the great clumps of hair, were still as massive as Wenceslas's had been.

Jack put a hand on the neck and stroked it. The horse gave a low whinny. "There now," he murmured. "We're goin' out o' line, all right? Goin' reet far from the bluddy row." He always seemed to revert to his Yorkshire accent when he talked to the horses, and the rolling, burring tones of the hills seemed to have the right effect. The stallion stopped shuddering, and raised its head a little.

"What're you doin' down t'lines?" Jack asked gently. "Great beast like you. Worth a fortune. Who sent you here, hmmm?" It was cruel and wasteful. This stallion would have fathered a thousand prime foals, aristocratic animals that could pull ten times their own weight. "Ne'er mind," he said, taking up the rein and walking slowly forward. "You're going to pull a right small cart along a little track. Just a cart wi' a couple of men in it, up to the hospital trains. Be safe, old chap. Be a right holiday."

Horse and man trudged forward in the darkness.

The road was slimy and narrow. From time to time they stood aside; not into the gulleys, for fear they would sink—but far enough to let a car pass, or a lorry. Each time that the horse heard an engine, it began to sweat, despite the cold. "Fucking savages, we are," he told it. "Forgive us, eh? We've sunk low, mate. Very low."

It began to get light. Behind them, a long line of other men and single horses were strung out at spaced intervals. Jack knew why. It was so that, if a shell struck, perhaps only one man and one horse would be lost, and not a whole group. He wiped frost from his face, frozen sweat. As the sound of the artillery became more distant, the horse's head raised up.

"What'll I call you?" Jack said. His face was close to the shoulder, a vast muscular machine that towered above him. He wondered if the horse could really hear everything, or just some occasional words. Or if it had been completely deafened. By the way that the stallion only turned its head occasionally, Jack guessed it was shocked. But perhaps only temporarily. My God, how he longed for the day that the horse would walk back to the farm wherever he came from. Be sent out into the fields and set about fathering those foals. He felt his eyes fill with water for a day that would never come.

"I had a horse," he told it as they matched their steps through the mud. As he talked, the first light began to show in the sky. "He were a fine boy. Seen him born. Seen his first steps. Big old fellow, and humored like a great child, he was. He didn't like cars neither. Didn't like the master's car nor young Harry's. Used to dance a bit if they came in the yard. We put the cars in the old stable. . . ."

On and on they went. The tears spilled from Jack's eyes, but he never felt them. He was almost happy in his reminiscences; if he had known that he was weeping, he would have been ashamed of it; he would have said that it wasn't out of pity, but out of a happier time, not the horror of the present. He carried on with his stories, hoping that the mellowness of them could be felt by the Ardennes, if not heard. "We'd sit waiting for the milk delivery at the station. . . . The driver knew to slow down and come in right quiet. . . ."

Words, soft words in the dawn of the day.

Pieces of the past. So faint, so small. So precious.

Chapter 10

In the winding valleys of the Dales, Octavia was driving Harry's Metz. It was a little green sports car; a thing of guttural, grinding speed.

"Should you go alone?" William had asked testily over breakfast, frowning at her over the top of his newspaper. The same William. The same mistrust of the world at large and her own abilities. He never changed, even if the wife sitting with him at breakfast had arrived from her lover's house in London yesterday. He behaved as he always had: straight-backed, polite, critical. Only the slightest tremor in his voice occasionally betrayed another William: a loving man longing to be let out of his prison, who could see his wife coming and going free as a bird. And for that, she tried not to argue with him but be as sweet as she could, for she realized the indescribable delicacy of the situation.

"I shall be perfectly safe," she had reassured him. "The Kents are only twelve miles away."

He had pursed his lips, lowering the *Times* and placing it

methodically to one side. "I saw Hamilton last month in Richmond," he told her. "He has lost weight. And he is—what should I say— distracted. Rather boisterous, outspoken. He struck me as only vaguely resembling the man I knew."

"Rupert's death struck them both down," Octavia replied quietly, naming the Kent's eldest son, who had died in France two years previously. "I wonder at either of them being able to hold a conversation that would make any sense. Elizabeth wrote to me that the world seems terribly bleak to her."

"Hamilton does not behave as if the world were bleak," William responded. "Rather the opposite. Jaunty, if anything. Relentlessly so."

"Two sides of the same coin," Octavia said. "The manic and the unmoving."

William grunted, considering this. "They still have a second son."

"Would the death of Harry be recompensed by the existence of Louisa and Charlotte?" she asked.

They sat for the rest of the meal in silence.

When she had finished, Octavia got up and went to the window, staring out at the rolling parkland and the glimpse of farms and hills beyond. "Everything looked rather untidy when I came from the station," she observed quietly. "Uncut verges, and so on."

"Is it any wonder?" William replied. "We've lost half our work-force to the war. The only ones that we shall see back before the war's over are the wounded. I spoke to Gray last week and he is at his wit's end. Not to mention the problem with the house."

Gray was the land steward, but his observations did not worry Octavia so much as the comment about Rutherford itself. She turned back towards William. "The house?" she echoed. "What is wrong with the house?" She knew that William would not have observed the lack of spit and polish that the interior used to have; it must be something else.

William gave a great, labored sigh and shook his head. "I had March in here last weekend," he told her, naming the gardener. "The coal rationing means he won't keep the temperatures up in the glasshouses this winter. He hasn't the manpower to keep the kitchen garden as large as he has previously. He went into Richmond to get garden tools mended, and almost had to hand them over for the war effort. I had to tell him to sit down while he was speaking to me, he was so distressed."

Octavia came back to the dining table and slowly sat down beside her husband. She was trying to process at least three pieces of information that simply didn't fit her picture of March. Firstly, he was a dour man whom she had never seen in the grip of any emotion except anger. Never distress. Secondly, they had always had the manpower to repair their own tools and equipment at Rutherford; it was a little town unto itself. Or had been. And thirdly . . . She voiced the third. "Surely we have a stock of coal," she murmured.

William gave her a straight look. "We have had it delivered from the merchants," he said. "Who tell us now that it's rationed, like everything else. Like meat and sugar."

She gave him a small smile. "I'm surprised to learn that you know of such household problems. They've never concerned you."

He was still looking very directly at her. Not with rancor; in fact, he dispensed what he had to say with a shrug. "I have been favored with visits from Mrs. Carlisle as well as Mr. March."

Octavia looked down at her hands. She felt a blush rise to her face. Cook should either go to the housekeeper or the lady of the house; there was, of course, neither at Rutherford.

William was continuing in the same sanguine way. "While I was in London I was told that my club would have three meatless days a week on the menu. Meatless!" he exclaimed. "Extraordinary."

"I suppose the meat must go to the fighting men."

"I don't begrudge it," William replied. "And the damned German U-boats are taking out our imports. But as for here . . ."

"What will you do about the glasshouses, the plants, the fruits and flowers?"

"I suspect that we must let them go without heat this winter."

"But that will kill everything."

"Of course it will kill everything," he snapped. Then, seeing her expression, "The coal can't be bought or begged, Octavia. It will be the law before the year's out. And houses like Rutherford must set an example."

She frowned. It would almost be better to have a cottage in the village, she thought. Smaller spaces to keep warm. She thought of William here alone in the depths of winter, and shuddered. She still remembered what a draughty and fearsomely cold place Rutherford had been when she first saw it, before the renovations had been carried out. But the heating and hot water ran on coal boilers. The fires were lit with coal. "Yorkshire has some of the finest coal mines in the country," she murmured. "It seems peculiarly unfair."

"There's the irony of it," William agreed.

An hour later, Octavia had begun the journey in the Metz wrapped in the coat that William had given her eighteen months ago for Christmas—the ankle-length sable. She had thought that in the windy and cold morning she might need it. Then, eight miles away from Rutherford, she had stopped the car, got out, and thrown the sable into the little jump seat at the back.

Their talk of rations had struck at her; she recalled the pages in the magazines saying that it was unseemly to dress in fine fashion now. She looked down at the coat. One didn't register such things in London; women there dressed beautifully, even now. But here in the country it was different. When she returned to Rutherford, perhaps she ought to ask Amelie, her maid, to box up the sable and put it away.

She had stretched her arms and looked around herself at the high and smooth inclines above her, and the drystone walls beneath. It was so good to be alone, she thought. The breadth of the landscape and the sharp, cold wind that was blowing felt cleansing. Freeing. Unconsciously, she frowned. How she had stood all those years at Rutherford, never venturing beyond the gates unless it was with the children in tow, or meekly accompanying William as he drove his lumbering old car—well, it was beyond her now. She felt almost as if, in recalling those times, that she was looking back at another person's life and not her own. Or looking in through a lighted window at a room, a history that she did not recognize.

She saw herself in Rutherford in the year she had been married, listening to the architects and William deciding how her inheritance should be spent in improving the house. Not speaking or venturing an opinion. She saw herself at thirty, at thirty-five: anxious, perplexed, ignored. Rebuffed most of all by William, who showed very little affection for her then. She could hardly credit that she had ever enjoyed a moment of those stifled days, although the children at least had given her happiness. But children grew up, and left one behind. As was quite correct, they lived the lives that she and William had given them, and made their own choices. She would no more dream of telling them how those lives should be conducted than cut off her own right arm . . . and yet. And yet.

She leaned on the wall next to the car, looking down at small stone cottages deep in the valley ahead of her. She must talk to Louisa. Although William was convinced that there must be some mistake, Octavia herself was not so sure. Louisa, with all her reputation for drama and frivolity actually had depth and secrecy in her nature. Look at how she had kept the affair with Charles de Mont-fort hidden from them. Look at how she was with Sessy, playing with the child with such affection that Octavia had begun to fear that Louisa might forget that Sessy belonged to Harry. What on earth was passing through her daughter's mind?

She sighed. She must find a way to the truth, and give Louisa some hope that she would understand. She could hardly occupy the moral high ground if Louisa had developed some sort of relationship with Jack Armitage. After all, wasn't her own with John Gould seen as wholly inappropriate?

"Louisa, Louisa," she murmured quietly.

She returned to the car, started it up, and accelerated away down the narrow lanes. It was the day that she had promised to visit Elizabeth Kent. But this too was not an occasion that she had been looking forward to.

Elizabeth Kent, however, at first surprised her. As Octavia was shown into the morning sitting room at Kent House—their Palladian mansion that always seemed so starkly grand to Octavia—Elizabeth rose to meet her with a smile on her face. Octavia saw that the seats around her friend were covered with embroidery, and, after they had exchanged their greetings, Elizabeth waved her hand at it vaguely. "I do so much of this," she said. "I give it away, you see? To fund-raising raffles. Sales. That kind of thing. It occupies me, and I feel that I'm being useful. The last one we did, Louisa helped me."

"So I understand. I'm pleased to hear it." Octavia examined the nearest piece minutely. "How fine it is, how detailed."

Elizabeth rang for tea. They discussed the weather, the likelihood of a decent summer. Elizabeth inquired of Charlotte and her new husband. After a few more minutes, however, the banality of the conversation seemed to weigh on them both. "You are being very polite to me, Octavia," Elizabeth said, with a faint smile. "But you must know, I'm not china. I have come to terms with my son's death. It is war. He was a serving officer. What can anyone do? I shan't shatter."

There was a pause. "I don't know what I should say to you," Octavia said finally. "I can't imagine your pain. And I have been away in London for so long, and left so quickly."

"Indeed you did."

"Do you despise me for it?"

Elizabeth looked surprised. "Despise?" she echoed. "Not at all. We were shocked, of course. But when you wrote to me and explained . . ."

"It's not an infatuation."

"No, I wouldn't think you were capable of throwing over William for that."

"You make it sound brutal."

"I'm sure to William it is brutal," Elizabeth said. "But I have known your life, Octavia. I have known what it was."

"When you are next in London . . ."

"Hamilton won't go anymore," Elizabeth said, holding up one hand to stem the invitation. "The London house is quite closed. We've not set foot in it since . . . since Rupert." She smiled wanly. "Don't think for a moment I am snubbing you. I'm sure that Mr. Gould is very respectable in his way."

Of course it was a reprimand, but one delivered with grace. Elizabeth was too well brought up to express any outrage as such; and she would, Octavia realized, always receive her. But there would never be any invitations to Kent House for her and John; never a visit to Cheyne Walk by Elizabeth and Hamilton. She took a calming breath, and focused on Elizabeth's family. She asked, "Do you speak of Rupert, you and Hamilton?"

"No."

"Would you . . . would like to speak of him to me, now?"

"Thank you, dear, but can it do any good?" Elizabeth asked. "Hamilton thinks not. He never mentions him. He doesn't mention the war at all. Do you know what has happened to him, how he has changed? He has bought all kinds of things, you know. A gramophone, a camera contraption, a suit of the most absurd clothes. Mechanics for the kitchen that the cook doesn't understand. And a . . ." She gave a gusty sigh that tried to turn itself into a laugh. "A motor bicycle." She shook her head. "He does not use these things. He does not use the camera, or play the gramophone, or ride the bicycle. It is so odd. So ridiculous." She looked down into her lap, and fussed with the embroidery, pulling it into piles. "We are quite mad, each in our own way," she whispered.

Then, suddenly, she sprang to her feet, and grasped Octavia's hand. "Come and walk with me. Is it cold outside? Not really? Then let's walk down to the woodland. To the planted meadow. I want to show you something. It's only a little way."

They went out into the brightness of the day, and it was only then that Octavia realized how cold the house had actually been. The hallway had been uncharacteristically dark, and the atmosphere had lacked something—something vital, something basic. The house was spotlessly clean, the colors of the oil paintings and the upholstered chairs just as always. But some sort of spark had undoubtedly vanished: whatever it was that made one energized. Whatever it was that kept one alive. She shuddered involuntarily, even as she linked Elizabeth's arm around hers. The house did not wear any visible shroud, but it was an empty shrine.

They came to a fenced area beyond the first of the trees.

"Do you see that farm?" Elizabeth asked.

"Yes." There was a farmhouse down a green lane between the trees.

"It is our tenants'. One of tenants, at any rate. They have no children. The husband has come down with some sort of illness. Dropsy, they tell me."

"What is that?" Octavia was utterly perplexed. What business was it of hers what kind of lives Elizabeth and Hamilton's tenants led?

"Renal failure, I believe." Elizabeth's voice was low. "He is not expected to live very long, and his wife is very young. Much younger than he. Hamilton thinks that, when the time comes, she ought to be brought into the main house."

"As what?" Octavia asked, frowning and astonished. "A cook? A maid?"

"As my companion supposedly," Elizabeth answered. "But—" She turned and gave Octavia a wry, haunted smile. "More accurately, as Hamilton's mistress."

Octavia gasped. So this—rather than an extreme and odd reaction to grief—was the source of Hamilton's enlivened behavior. But then—she reached out and took Elizabeth in her arms, despite feeling the rigidity of her friend's body, her unresponsiveness—perhaps Hamilton was reacting to his unhappiness. Perhaps he was yearning for life. She stepped back from Elizabeth. "It is what men are," she said. "They look for comfort."

"And what comfort have I?" Elizabeth demanded. "Just to make myself busy."

"You have Alex," Octavia murmured softly, mentioning their other son.

"He never visits. Or rarely. When he's on leave, he stays in

London and . . ." She paused. "Or in Paris, where I think he's very reckless. As boys will be."

"It is the war."

"Yes. And the example of older men. I hear the jargon and the carelessness in his letters."

"A defense against what they see and hear, perhaps."

"He is not my sweet child anymore, that is evident," Elizabeth remarked bleakly. In the words, Octavia saw with sadness how Elizabeth felt that she had lost both boys. The other woman glanced back at Octavia now. "We are infectious here, you know. In our situation. No doubt you felt it."

"It's wrong to call it an infection."

"Is it?" Elizabeth asked. "But grief is just such a thing. One tries to rally, you know, to shake it off. It comes back all the same."

"They say that time . . ."

Elizabeth waved her hand. "Octavia, I don't expect platitudes from you of all people."

They stood in silence, looking down at the farmhouse.

"You might do me a favor," Elizabeth said, at last.

"Anything."

The other woman turned slowly and looked Octavia in the face, searching her expression intently. "You might take temptation away from him," she said. "You have no housekeeper at Rutherford. The woman is very quick, very able. I might even say that she is reliable and decent. She has an intelligence about her. If I'm to be charitable, I might venture that it is only Hamilton's weakness that has turned her head. It will do her good to leave, to go where she cannot be tempted and my husband can recover his wits."

"I had not considered . . ."

"You have no housekeeper at Rutherford," Elizabeth said. "And you, dear, are not at home in any real sense. I don't think that you will ever come home again, will you, to live?"

Octavia lowered her head. "That is true," she murmured.

She was home again very late, for, after seeing Elizabeth, Octavia had decided to make a long detour via the Blessington mills.

It was some months since she had visited them, although she kept what she hoped was a very keen eye from afar and through her conversations with William.

She parked the Metz in the mill yard just as the day was growing dark; but the windows that were ranged for five stories above her, and stretching on either side for a hundred yards, were brightly lit. From inside came the loud and repetitive noise of the looms, sounding like a thousand heavy sticks clattering against each other. The windows themselves look fogged; she knew it wasn't moisture but the lanolin-coated wool floating in the air, making it thick with fibers.

Ferrow was the manager, and his office was reached from this direction by iron steps that zigzagged down the side of the building, connecting the first floor offices to the ground. On the second flight, Octavia paused, and looked in at the main weaving room. As a child she had done this a hundred times, usually following meekly in her father's footsteps as he stamped up to Ferrow's office. If she really listened now, she might hear his bellowing voice, and feel her own skin prickle with fear. She smiled faintly to herself. Her father was long dead. His fortune was invested in Rutherford. She was quite alone here.

A hundred women, she guessed, were bent over the vast mechanical looms, walking up and down, checking and rechecking, their fingers necessarily accurate. One slip and a worker could lose a hand, or worse. In the old days of her father's ownership, a girl just nine years old had been dragged into a rotating loom by her trailing apron string. Octavia still remembered at how her father had ranted and railed over the lost hours. Little boys at the yard gates, who cornered her one afternoon, had—by contrast—told her gleefully of wiping parts of the child from the machinery, and mopping the blood from the floor. She had been nine or ten years old herself, and had stood there at the mill gates crying until her father's driver had come out from the mill, seen her distress, and bundled her into her father's car to drive her home.

She closed her eyes for a moment. All this sound, all this industry. Octavia was very keenly aware that with every noise—every knock and stamp, every deafening shift of the looms—money flowed into Rutherford. The war had done nothing but good to the Cavendish bank accounts; in fact, William had said quite nonchalantly at the start of the war that it would be a challenge to know how to spend or invest it.

And so their subtle and persistent battle of wills had begun.

She had managed to get a few new houses built for the workers; that had been a victory of sorts. William said that the families wouldn't understand the new places with their indoor sinks, their boilers, their flushing lavatories. She, in turn, had reminded him in a rather forced tone that she knew damned well that some of the very oldest houses of the workers had floorboards laid over bare earth, and where was the use to them in that, with health complaints from the workers every winter? William had frowned at her use of words rather than the issue itself.

And time had proved him completely wrong. Much to her satisfaction. The newly housed workers were more willing, more efficient. "If such a thing can be measured," William had said, when she told him so.

It had been an education watching the families moving into their new accommodations one cool October morning. They had—to a man, to a woman—crept over the thresholds with stunned delight. There were only twenty of the houses at the very top of the hill—she had wanted more, but William had absolutely refused to authorize it, darkly warning her that they would only spread discontent among the workers, with demands for the older houses to be improved. "It is making a rod for our own backs," he had warned her. "And where will it end, do you suppose? When we have renovated the whole town, I suppose, whether or not the property belongs to us? Torn up the roads, relaid the pavements."

"We should put tarmacadam down, and take up the cobbles at least," Octavia had pointed out. "It would make it smoother for the vehicles."

"We have fewer vehicles since the war started," William said with more than a touch of sarcasm. "They have requisitioned our flatbed trucks, and I doubt we shall see them again."

At such times, Octavia deeply desired to shout and scream. She wanted to upend the dining table at which they sat, stamp her feet. But even a tantrum would have done no good at all. Deep in his soul, despite all other relaxations in his attitudes, William was stubborn. He was fixed, and could not help it. It had been bred in him from birth. If confronted, even now, he would simply withdraw. Silence would reign. Nothing would be done. The subject—whatever subject it was—would be closed.

The day of the houses being finished, she recalled a family standing, the children gnawing their knuckles in a mixture of fright and bewilderment, as the parents had come out of the tiny little place laughing at its perceived grandeur. "We shall be like 'un king and queen, right enough," the woman had said to Octavia, bobbing a curtsey.

Octavia had been mortified. Such gratitude for something so easy to do. And the curtsey, as if she were royalty. Oh Lord, how she'd almost dragged the poor woman upright, and heard William's hissing intake of breath at her gesture. But she had felt the blood rushing to her face, imagining these same people in Bentford's Bank in Richmond, casting their eyes over the amounts of money in the account. No working man or woman would believe it; they were, even to Octavia, incomprehensible sums.

And all due to the war, to the provision of woolen cloth. The strands went into the making of puttees and greatcoats. Into blankets and socks. Into horse blankets and officer's uniforms and underwear and mufflers. Into gloves, into bags. It went into seat coverings and saddlecloths and webbing—a few strands here, a few there, multiplied into millions. And still the killing went on, and still the looms rattled, and still the money flowed into the bank.

And from there the very same wealth was transformed; it flowed instead into Rutherford, where the money it had made bought fine linen, and crystal, and flowers, and garden machinery and newfangled ovens and mixers for the kitchen, and oil paintings, and . . . she looked down at herself. It bought Paris fashions, and beautiful leather shoes, and silk.

Such a line she trod. Such a very fine line they *all* trod. She and William. And families like theirs. They and the staff, they and the workers. Such a delicate distinction between the source and the product. Such a very tenuous division, she thought. One that trembled and threatened to break. "An overly active imagination," William would have said. "What is your reason for such negative fancies?" And she could not have told him. She only felt it. Felt they were profiting from misery, in various shapes and forms. Felt that one day it would come back to haunt them.

She thought of Elizabeth's face, and prayed that if retribution was indeed headed for them, it would not take the shape of Elizabeth's loss.

*S*he walked briskly up the stairs and opened the door. The manager's office was open, and Ferrow sat at his desk, illuminated by the harsh overhead electric light. She caught a glimpse of him in an attitude of exhaustion, head resting on hands. His jacket was slung over the back of his chair. Accounts were piled on the desk, and had spilled over onto the floor.

He sprang up as the door clanged shut. "Oh, Lady Cavendish," he said. "This is an honor."

She couldn't ascertain if he were joking or not. "Hardly," she told him. "May I sit?"

"Of course, of course." He shuffled papers out of the way. "Tea, perhaps?" he asked. "Coffee?"

"No thank you," she told him. He sat down opposite her, running a hand over his hair to smooth it. "You look very tired, Mr. Ferrow."

"Oh well," he replied. "The day's end." He glanced up at the clock. "Or it shall be, in two or three hours."

"I've come to talk to you about a scheme I have," she said. "Netherfield's accident made me consider it. Or perhaps it has been in my mind for a while. Since Kessington came back."

"Kessington?" Ferrow asked.

"You wouldn't know the boy, of course," Octavia told him. "One of our stable hands. He is . . . well, he is like Netherfield, I suspect. He's in the village now and not at Rutherford. The absence of the horses seems to distress him more than anything and he . . ." She stopped.

"He has shell shock?"

"Yes."

Ferrow was making what looked like an enormous effort to concentrate on what she was saying. "And . . . and . . . you think . . ."

"I think something must be provided for them, and the others who had been invalided."

"Something here, you mean?"

"Yes. Do you recall the old carding shed? It's empty now. On the moors road."

"Yes, I know it."

"I want to make a workshop up there. We might make ribbon-edged baby blankets, or gloves. Something of that kind. The men would not have to work on the looms, but in finishing. Something quiet and productive. Fancy items. My daughter is at St. Dunstan's in London and the men there make baskets. It is very successful, despite their disabilities."

"And you would like me to organize this?"

Octavia was regarding him closely. It was as if she had launched into some foreign language, it seemed, by the perplexed expression on Ferrow's face. "Mr. Ferrow," she ventured. "You need not worry about bothering Lord Cavendish. This is something that I shall pay for with my own money, as my own project."

But he was merely staring at her. He seemed to have lost the thread of the conversation completely. Her eyes strayed to the papers that had spilled onto the floor, and then back again at Ferrow's face. "Is everything well?" she asked. "With yourself, and your wife?"

"Yes, thank you," he said.

"And the remainder of the family?"

There was silence for some seconds. Then, "It's my sister's boy," he told her. "I don't believe you've ever met Winifred and Edward. Their son Eric is employed by Holt." Seeing her puzzlement, he added, "The company who make tracks. Caterpillar tracks, they call them. For the new tanks. For the war."

"Does he?" Octavia said. "How interesting."

"It is very interesting," Ferrow agreed. "Very bright boy, you know. He went over with the first. It's a patent, the track. A good thing, too. We are losing so many horses, you see. We need mechanized vehicles. Tractors rather than wagons. And they can get through the mud better. . . ." He stopped.

"And he has gone with the tanks?" she prompted. "To France?"

"Yes," he murmured. She saw his gaze descend from her face, and range about among the disarranged papers as if he were searching for something. "He wrote to me," he said. "I have it here. Perhaps in the drawer. . . ." He fumbled with the drawer key, looked in the drawer for a moment or two, and then brought out a letter. "Here it is," he said. He glanced over it, and smiled. "Very good," he murmured, as if to himself. And then he looked up. "He says that he has been driving a tractor, towing a gun barrel. At Arras."

"That does sound useful," Octavia told him, wary now of the distraction in his face.

"I can't help thinking that I encouraged him to go," he murmured.

"That is a positive thing, surely."

He looked up at her. "Is it?" he asked. "Gun barrels, Lady Cavendish. Our artillery doesn't just fire shells without some reaction from the enemy. The death rate in the artillery is almost as bad as that in the Flying Corps." And he suddenly realized what he had said. "Oh, I'm extremely sorry," he stuttered, aghast. "I am very sorry indeed, Lady Cavendish."

"It doesn't matter."

"Indeed it does," he protested. "Please don't think of it. I'm hardly in a position to know the facts."

"I think we all know the facts, Mr. Ferrow," Octavia replied quietly. Slowly, she got to her feet. "I must go. It's rather late. Will you ask someone to look over the old carding shed for me? To assess its suitability?"

"Yes. Certainly."

"And write to me in London with the results. I've sent you my address before."

"Yes, I will." He was hovering close to her, looking desperately anxious still at his tactlessness.

She smiled. "I see it as our duty here to keep optimistic," she said. "Despite everything. To be positive." He gave her an expression mixed with all kinds of feeling: anxiety, cynicism, hope, confusion.

She did something that she had never done before: she reached over to him, and laid her hand briefly on his arm. "Do give my very best wishes to your sister and her husband, and the rest of your family," she murmured. And she patted him gently, as she would a child. "Tell her that I share her feelings, you know. I shall be thinking of her."

*D*arkness had fallen completely by the time that she parked the Metz outside the tithe barn at Rutherford. Octavia got out of the little car slowly, weighed down by the events of the day.

It was perfectly quiet and still. Octavia stood for a while in the dark, glancing around at the deserted yard and the long run of the stables that were now only occupied by the remaining two farm horses and William's own mount. Beyond, at the end of the line, was the five-bar gate that led out into the meadows.

She looked behind her at the magnificent height of Rutherford itself. The rain had passed over at midday, and clouds now scudded across the sky. She could smell grass, and the very faint scent of the flowers in the greenhouses just beyond the kitchen garden wall. She hesitated for a moment, frowning sadly, and then turned away from the house and walked briskly to the gate, and let herself into the field beyond.

This was the meadow where they turned out the horses. The grass was growing strongly and was above ankle height. She walked out into it, aware of the damp clinging to her skirt. She took off her gloves and reached down and touched it. No little crowd of farm ponies to crop it anymore. No Wenceslas. Where was he, she wondered. Was he still alive? She straightened up and crossed her arms over her chest, breathing deeply. She doubted it. The horses keeled over with fright, or were injured, or simply died from exhaustion. She knew that; she was not a fool. After the war they would have to restock here entirely, if that were possible. Or perhaps the horses would be redundant in the future—perhaps they would have a machine to cut the meadows. As always, when alone, Octavia's mind strayed in an anxious fashion to Harry. But tonight it encompassed not only Harry, but Caitlin. Caitlin and Nash, and Harrison, who had died in 1915 at Cinque Rue. My God, it was all too awful. Where was Nash? she wondered. She must see Mary tomorrow and find out. Where was Caitlin, that quiet and self-possessed girl whom Harry so adored? No one had had word of her since the wedding. And where was Jack, for that matter? The Armitages must be sick with worry. Most of all, what was happening with John? He had taken a boat four days ago, and she had had no letter.

She put her hands to her face, a lonely figure out there in the darkness. The despair of losses and hardships were all around her. Rutherford was not the haven it used to be, the luxurious paradise of former years. For all its bulk, it was threatened. What would they do if Harry never returned? Charlotte would never come back here. William was not in the best of health after his heart attack last year, and on his next birthday he would be sixty-four. Eventually, Louisa would be left alone in this great house. Octavia knew that the estate was not entailed to any distant branch of the family with a male heir, and so Louisa would own it if the worst happened.

But alone here . . . How could she bear that for her daughter? Alone in such a vast empty house? Alone to look after Sessy. Octavia's first instinct was that in such a case, Louisa and Sessy must come with her and John Gould. They would go to America together.

She reached the gate, and looked at the walls of the house that rose above the stable yard. They would leave Rutherford.

"Leave you," she murmured. "All of us shall leave you." And realized, in that moment, what an utter impossibility that was.

Chapter 11

The Hotel d'Universe was only a half hour's walk from the front line of the battle, close to the railway station in Arras.

It was now the beginning of June. John Gould had been away from London for five weeks. It was a balmy night with a strong, warm breeze blowing. It was dark, and he had to feel his way along the street that ran behind the hotel, tripping occasionally on the uneven stones and into the gutters. His hands brushed against door pillars that had stood for centuries; over handwriting scrawled on the walls; over bullet-scarred brick and the miraculously clean glass of a few shop windows that showed faint pools of light cast by candles and oil lamps.

Alongside him was the ever-cheerful adjutant who had been detailed to accompany him; a brisk man with a strong Scottish accent. He came from a place called Wanlockhead, a village on the Borders. "High place," he'd told John. "Tae beautiful for words." Alan MacKay was a stocky man, a regular, and he propelled John now with a guiding hand under his arm. When he had heard that John was from New York, he had expressed no surprise, but John was getting used to that. No one seemed surprised by anything; by histories, or horror, or coincidences. Reactions had been ironed out in men: flattened, crushed, their sensitivity removed. Some, John thought, were automatons; there was nothing behind their eyes. MacKay was not like that, however: he strode along with a gaze that missed nothing, a permanent grin on his face, and a turn of phrase that would have been unforgiveable in Chelsea. It was fookin' this and fookin' that. "You'll have a mind to that fookin' major," had been his first warning. "He's a fookin' maniac." And he'd slapped John heartily on the back, while glancing behind him at the top brass.

He was whistling very softly to himself now as the two men progressed. When they had passed the second little shop, he muttered an instruction in John's ear. "Din'ae feel in the next fookin' doorway," he said. Then, in the next moment, exclaiming, "There now! Did I nae warn ye? Excuse us, mamselle," he said to the overpainted woman who grinned at them like a surrealistic head, and who had dipped forward into the half light to breathe brandy fumes into John's face. "Ach, he's nae one for you," MacKay laughed, elbowing the woman out of the way. "He's a man bewitched by a lady elsewhere."

They paused when they had gone a few steps farther. "I never knew there would be so many civilians left here," John said.

"Shocking, right enough," MacKay agreed. "But there's men to feed and service, and Arras has been behind the lines awhile. They deem theirselves safe, so much as anyone can be."

"But so near the front."

"Aye, sae near."

John had been traveling along that front in the last two weeks, only marginally tolerated by an army who grudgingly admitted the need to convince their new ally of the need of America's support.

Coming down on the overloaded train from Albert, he had passed through eerily tended fields with the crops growing in them, bordered by makeshift sidings, ammunition dumps, and shattered villages. He had found himself in a landscape that had been tossed about, shifting from one perilously close shift in the front lines to another.

He had thought to himself, as he had descended from the train, his permits clutched in his hand and his press pass buttoned into his coat, that the countryside hummed with an unusual vibration. It was not the guns, though they could easily be heard: it was something else, a tension that hung over the place. He thought he could feel it stretching away in all directions, as if France were seized in a permanent expectation of horror.

And yet France had also surprised him, even delighted him: the children holding makeshift gifts on the station forecourt had touched his heart. "Souvenirs," they said, running up to him. They held out pieces of shrapnel, uniform, ribbon, bullets; posies of flowers, greetings cards, and even old postcards of what France had been before the war. He had looked down into their faces, amazed at the resilience of the human spirit. They grinned back at him as he handed them American candy that his mother had somehow managed to ship over to him. It had come through submarine blockades and now it landed in the sticky palm of a little girl who pushed the brass button of an English uniform into his hand by way of payment. "No," he had said to her gently. "You keep that, okay?" And under his breath muttered, "Try not to sell it at all."

"*Give us the real world out there,*" had been Bellstock's instruction to John by telegram before he had left London. He was the man who had first suggested the job to John two years ago; now the newspaper editor was anxious to wade in with the best firsthand reports that he could muster. "*Give us the muck and bullets. Full picture.*"

And so yesterday he had written about the children with their pieces of shrapnel, and the girl's face. She was seven or eight, incredibly thin, with eyes that ought to have been bright and alive, but which were not. She looked wizened and old, wearing some other's child once-pretty frock. "They've come from out there," MacKay had told him, nodding his head towards the front line. "Maybe two years ago. Maybe they've traveled all over, who knows? And they've come back to the biggest town near where their home used to be."

Over the next twenty-four hours John had walked where he wasn't wanted, sometimes with MacKay in tow and sometimes not. He had started out thinking quite cynically that stories about children would wring the hearts of the reading public in the States and get their attention; but now it just wrung his own heart. He sat down in the few little cafés that were left and watched the cooks trying to make bread out of ground-down straw and husks. He watched refugees go by; women, mostly, towing silent children, walking behind scraggy-looking mules hitched to farm wagons, past piles of jealously guarded splintered wood. More often than not, though, they walked alone, heads down.

He had been near Monchy yesterday. The army had brought in a pile of bodies and laid them in a trench dug at the side of the road. MacKay had been at his side. "They're the lucky ones," the soldier had muttered.

"Lucky?" John had asked. "How do you figure that?"

"They've got a grave," MacKay said. "Wi' their own name over it. When this is over, someone will come and stand over them. So they're lucky, because someone will come and shed a tear over them. And there'll be a place to put their mammy's tears. But there's hundreds and thousands, they that hae disappeared."

"How so?"

"Drowned, or pulled to fookin' pieces that can't be identified.

Nobody picks up the pieces. There's no time for that." And he shrugged.

"So when the family do come—if they ever come—they'll wander around, not knowing where to mourn."

"Aye. About right, laddie."

John had looked at the tank tracks in the slush: snow had given way to rain. "I believe that somebody I know is serving near here," he murmured.

"The flying officer that you're hoping tae see tonight?"

"No, someone else from Yorkshire. He was a groom in—in the large house there that I visited."

"Which regiment?"

"The veterinary corps. His name is John Armitage. They call him Jack."

MacKay had shrugged. "Ach, they're all over. He could be here today and move tomorrow. Go where they're needed."

"But weren't they needed here? Wasn't there a cavalry charge?" John knew full well that there had been.

"Aye, well. Fookin' madness, ye see? We'll ask about, sir. I've got his name, and we'll ask." But he'd given John a sideways look of exasperation. John thought that he probably wouldn't ask at all. He couldn't blame him. It would be like looking for a needle in a haystack.

*Y*esterday evening John had laid down on a bunk bed in MacKay's own billet, and he had written his diary. He began with the idea that had bothered him all day.

Where are the dead to be honored? he wrote.

Where are the places to be? I can't imagine a wife who has nowhere to mourn, no place to go. She may get a letter, a telegram; it may tell her that her husband is missing or dead. And missing is just another word for dead, a word that plumbs the depths of cruelty. She has handed over her man to the war, and the war has obliterated him. The war has somewhere lost him. How can that be? How can a man be simply "lost" or "missing" in this great avalanche of bureaucracy? How can they have done this to him, she'll think. Sent him out and marked him "missing." Where did he go, what did he do? Questions that simply no one, not even the commanding officer, and sometimes not even the men who were alongside him, have an answer to.

How wrenching that feeling must be. There won't be a ship coming home carrying his remains, because there are no remains. He has been smashed to pieces, to shreds, to less than that. She'll pass some cemetery or churchyard during most of her days and see the stones with their inscriptions. But there's no inscription for her. She can't go to a stonemason and ask for his name to be put on the grave, with the words she's chosen. She can't ask for whatever the family wants—an angel, perhaps, or a scroll, or a laurel wreath carved. She can't take her children anywhere to show them, to reflect, to sit and stare. There is no grave and there is no stone.

He paused then and stared into the dark. Would there be memorials in France eventually? he wondered. Would there be proper cemeteries? Would they be tended? He cast his mind back to the ditch at the side of the road, and the sight of bodies being rolled from the trucks, or manhandled hastily by the exhausted soldiers who tried not to look at the faces of the dead. Would someone come back for these? Would someone record where they were? Who knew them for certain, who had recorded them? Who wrote to what department— to some safe office somewhere in London, saying who had died where and for what? At what time, in what circumstances . . . He thought not. The office would exist, and the records no doubt. But a piece of paper with a hundred names on it has lost the savagery of the roadside ditch and forgotten the terror of the day. There was perhaps a blessing in that, but also an indignity.

He lay thinking of the dead turned to paper. If there were eventually some kind of memorial, he hoped to God that there would be no differentiation in the graves—no "them and us" between religions or nationalities. There were plenty of Sikhs and Hindus and Jews fighting for the British; he hoped that they wouldn't be put somewhere else. And that the officers wouldn't lie in somewhere more appealing than their men. He lay for a long time thinking about this, about how the world could be altered when the carnage was all gone. If only it could be a world where equality came—like the memorials. Where the world was all done with rank and favor.

And then he thought of Octavia, how she sometimes said the same thing and sometimes forgot entirely how fortunate she was. How fortunate they both were, in fact. A guilty flush rose to his face. Fortunate bloody beings in a world of wrong. Soon he would leave here and go back to Octavia, and he'd leave behind the men struggling in the mud, and weeping and praying in the hospitals.

What the hell would Octavia do, he thought, if Harry were killed? If he were one of the thousands, the millions? It didn't bear thinking about. He could imagine her pacing about in their house. She would pace forever, because there was nowhere to direct her. "My God," he murmured. "What a shit-infested mess."

Sighing heavily, he at last turned his attention to his impressions of the last few days: the things that had struck him most, and began to write again in a hasty scrawl, squinting in the half light of the lamp.

Most of the movement of the army is at night; hours when the enemy can't see you. Hours when the horses' hooves are muffled to stop the sound of them on the road; when the wagons that need to go fast instead go slow at the cross-sections of roads for fear of their rattle being heard by the enemy.

Those cross-sections have names that the locals never gave them. They've been newly christened Hellfire Corner and Clapham Junction, among many; words that describe the mayhem they see, and the havoc of passing along them. The trenches get named, too. Crump and Crete; Gordon Alley and Iberia and Malt and Ibex and Ice. There's a trench line near Ypres called Caliban, never a name more aptly given, christened for the monster in Shakespeare's play. The land changes likes waves on the sea here, and Caliban fits right in: a thing cast up on an unimaginable shore.

They name their craters, too. On 9 April, the King's Own Scottish Borderers went forward from two mine craters in no-man's-land. One was larger than the other, so they nicknamed them Claude and Clarence, like cartoon characters. But there were no real funnies on what came after. Not unless your humor's blacker than the Devil himself.

I ask names a lot. It's a way to put down a marker in the sea of faces. I ask an Australian where he comes from, and what he's called, and he tells me he's from a place right up on Australia's right-hand corner, where the sea is edged by mangroves and his father is always absent, because he's in the opal mines in the burning center of the continent. That the whole family went to Australia from Bristol in England five years ago, to find a better life. And that now he's come back by volunteering. I shake his hands fiercely several times, full of admiration. "Better here than the opal mines, you reckon?" I ask him. "Yeah, mate." He grins.

No one really tells the truth. Scrape a man's smile off his face and he still stares back at you; he won't say what he's seen. There's gallantry in that silence. He won't tell his sweetheart, either. He won't tell his mother. He'll just say that he went up to see what games were playing outside Arras.

And he'll go on marching, singing "Rule Britannia, marmalade or jam, Chinese firecrackers up your arseholes, bang bang bang" at the top of his voice.

Before he went to sleep—just a short while in the early hours—John imagined all those million dead men wandering the fields of France, ghosts without anywhere to go.

*J*ohn and MacKay emerged at the front of the hotel, and a surreal sight met their eyes.

In daylight, Arras was a ghost town, an apparently deserted place, bombarded by the Germans. But at night, under the cover of darkness that protected it from the strafing of enemy aircraft, it came alive. The military emerged from the cellars that ran under the town: catacombs and corridors dug by the Romans two thousand years ago. MacKay told him that there were hospitals down there, but John said he would save that for another day. He wasn't quite ready for that.

They stood on the battered street corner and watched the men go by like fluttering frames in a celluloid film, caught for brief moments by the few lights cast by bedraggled shops and cafés. They were like Charlie Chaplin walking with his uneven gait. But these men, and these mules, and these cars weren't trying to be Charlie Chaplin. Everyone was struggling with some load or other, and the staff cars that occasionally went past weren't trying to be funny as they manoeuvred quietly between the lines of men, or lumped over the potholes in the road, shaking their occupants. It was a kind of hushed mime of speed, all broken up in places as someone staggered or turned around. Lines came to a halt and restarted. Horses shook their heads to dislodge the flies that flew even at night, so fat and gorged were they with the day's rations on the battlefields. And in and out of the feet of both men and mules and horses ran rats, bloated from the same feed. They got a severe kicking whenever anyone had time to notice them; and then they went rolling away, and picked themselves up squealing, and ran on.

MacKay was standing at the door to L'Universe, and smiling his usual smile. "Funny old world going by," he commented, as if reading John's thoughts. "But nae one to mull over, Mr. Gould."

They opened the door.

L'Universe was also a very curious place. It looked like a restaurant, it sounded like a restaurant. It had tables and waiters and food; it had stairs leading up to rooms. Loitering on the stairs, John noticed a few women, and there was a large fat Frenchwoman who seemed to be lording it over a till, and gesturing and shouting as she pointed at the bar. But the customers were all men, and most were in groups that were singing or shouting or talking at full volume. The place was a nightmare of noise, and the sound had a frenzied, manic quality. It was pitched high, and it was sometimes punctuated by a rumble under their feet, or a distant crash that made the framed prints on the wall tremble. But nobody took any notice. It was a feast on the edge of the Styx, John thought.

They saw Harry Cavendish almost at once.

In the noise and movement, he was remarkably still, sitting at a table by himself and nursing a glass of Calvados. He had evidently seen them before they saw him, and he was looking steadily at John. They walked over, edging between tables.

"It's damned good to see you, Harry," John said.

Harry Cavendish smiled. "Sit down," he said, gesturing to two empty chairs next to him. "I've kept these at cost of life and limb, let me tell you." He pulled the Calvados bottle over to himself, and poured.

John was looking him over. By God, the boy he remembered from the photographs in the family drawing room was all gone. Here was a man. What was he, twenty-two? He looked much older. He was tall, but very slight under the uniform. One leg rested on another chair. Harry nodded at it now. "Thing's playing up again," he said. "Blasted fucking thing's seized up entirely. Had notice of leave today. I'm Blighty bound, and another operation." He banged his fist on the leg. "I wish they'd cut the bugger off," he told them. "Fucking thing."

"Blighty bound? When?"

"Whenever I take myself out of here. Now. Yesterday. Tomorrow. Whenever."

John smiled. "Harry, that's great news. Your mother will be overjoyed."

Harry gave him a curious look. "I daresay."

"Not at the operation. At your coming home."

"I understood you. There's no need to labor the point."

As Harry drained his glass, John glanced over at MacKay. The adjutant was sitting very upright, the drink untouched. He raised an eyebrow but said nothing.

"This is Captain MacKay, Harry."

Harry leaned forward. "Mr. Gould," he muttered. "I would appreciate it if you call me by rank."

It was like a slap in the face. John nodded, though. He could see something very brittle, very ragged, in Harry's expression; hear it in his voice. "I'm sorry," he replied.

MacKay got to his feet. "Gentlemen, I'm away if you don't have objections."

"No objection," Harry drawled. "Guess you've got things to see to, you and your regiment. Flash bang wallop, and all that."

MacKay frowned. He dipped his head by way of good-bye, and looked at John. "You've all you need?"

"I'll come back and find you."

"Aye. Good luck if I'm not about."

John got up and shook his hand. "Good luck yourself."

When he had gone, John sat down again. Harry was drawing circles in the spilt liquid on the tabletop. "You'll excuse me, too," he muttered. "Awful day. Lost another beer boy." He glanced up. "New boy. Eighteen years old. Straight from Eton." John was opening his mouth to commiserate when Harry's glare stopped him. "Don't apologize," he said quietly. "You heard how it went out here in April? If you hadn't, write it fucking down, will you? The loss of one man is nothing, you know. Write it for your American friends. In April we lost two hundred and forty-five aircraft. Two hundred-odd crew. Over a hundred were taken as prisoners of war. And what did we do in return? We shot down just sixty-six. Sixty fucking six."

He was slurring his words slightly. "Flight commander," John said, drawing his chair closer so that they wouldn't be overheard. "There's a show on tonight, they tell me. Biggest show there's ever been."

"You know it." Harry brought his index finger to his lips. "Top secret, old man."

"Yes, I know it. But I've been there. To the tunnels under Messines."

Harry at last showed a minor spark of interest. Humor gave a dry luster to his eye, a sardonic squint. "They took you down, did they?" he asked. "Lucky chap. I should like to see them."

"Yes," John said. "They took me down just a short way last evening. Strange down there. Under the clay, the ground's white. So white it gives you snow blindness."

Harry looked away momentarily, fiddling with his glass, then pouring himself another drink. "I should like to see them," he repeated softly. "We reconnoitered it all. Over and over. Messines."

Behind them, someone started bellowing to the tune of "If You Were the Only Girl in the World." John listened a second, then turned his head. Instead of the song's usual words, they were singing, "If you were the only Boche in the trench and I had the only bomb . . ."

"Nothing else would matter in the world today, I would still blow you to eternity," Harry yelled. He laughed, and the men singing on the other side of the room raised their glasses to him.

John turned back to watch him. Harry slammed his glass onto the table. "Won't do, won't do," he said. "Shouldn't be here. Should be keeping an eye."

"An eye? A watch, you mean?"

"I should be keeping a watch," Harry confirmed. "It's all I do. Don't you know that? All I can do."

John realized that Harry was very drunk indeed. But he held it well. He was rigid in his seat, with a small sad grin on his face. "Got signed off," he said. And for the first time he looked like the teenager in his mother's photograph, wide-eyed, innocent, and surprised.

"You did?" John prompted.

"Bastard," Harry responded. "Medico . . . medical . . . signed off. Bastard. Been here two hundred years longer than him. Up from Oxford on an officer cadet scholarship. Jumped up little office boy. Frustrated horse doctor is what he is. Should be operating on nags. Nags and dogs. You see? Knows it all. Thinks he does. 'Pulmonary disorder,' he says. 'Heart dysfunction.' As if that's a proper word. It's something he made up to bloody annoy me. Think I don't know? Something made up to trot me off. They must reckon I'm getting in the way. No use to them. So they make something up. . . ." He winced, and shifted his leg. "He was a bloody bastard with a long face. Like . . ." He gave a great gust of ironic laughter. "Match his customers, he would. Face like a horse."

"Is that what he told you?"

"That's what he told me. I'm useless. Infected leg and . . . this."
He thumped his own chest. "Idiots. Idiots. Medical board." And
Harry hung his head.

John had felt his stomach plummet, just as if something icy had
gripped it. Harry had a heart disorder and an infection. He ought to
have been on a train out of here tonight, not sitting by himself getting
drunk. And John could see that Octavia's son was nursing something
even worse than the losses of his squadron and the news of his own
illness. He wondered what it was. "Tell you what," John said, leaning
forward. "Let's take a turn outside. It's noisy in here. I can hardly
hear you. Why don't you lean on me a little way? Let's go look see
what the world's doing. Fresh air."

Harry gave a twisted smile. "Fresh air?" he repeated sarcastically.
Then he seemed to change his mind. He swung his leg from the chair
and pushed himself awkwardly upright.

"Hang on," John said, holding out his arm.

Harry hesitated, and then put his arm round John's shoulder.
"Lead on there then, if you like," he said. They threaded their way
unsteadily through the tables towards the door, and as they walked
Harry muttered to himself. "Cannon to right of them, Cannon to
left of them, Cannon in front of them volley'd and thunder'd. . . ."

John pushed open the door with one shoulder. The cooler night
air rushed in on them, but Harry had been right. It was not fresh at
all. The wind had changed direction. It suddenly reeked of decay and
cordite. "Into the valley of death," he agreed, "rode the six hundred."

They went out down the road, and sat down some way off from
it, at the side of a large house that would have looked reason-
ably normal had it not been lacking an upper floor. Only the gable
ends stood up in the night air. Through the open windows in the half

light, John glimpsed a surreal set piece, as if the occupants had just gone away for a moment, or into a back room. There was a large dining table, and a fireplace set for a fire. A tablecloth was still on the table, set with plates. But most of the books had scattered from the large mahogany bookcase, and lay on the floor. He looked upwards and saw a fringe of curtain draped over the brickwork as if for decoration. He and Harry trudged onwards into what had been the garden.

There was no such strange order here. The place was a tangle of bricks and lopsided trees, shattered at the top and looking for all the world as if some giant animal had been gnawing at them. John let go of Harry, and the younger man slumped down on the ground. John sat next to him.

"Do you think the world is hollow?" Harry asked, after a minute or two of strained silence.

John looked at him, perplexed. "That's a strange idea."

"Isn't it, though, Harry agreed. "I get a lot of strange notions. I think . . . So we make the tunnels. All these tunnels that we're going to surprise the Boche within the next twenty-four hours. They say that there's twenty-two mine shafts and tunnels all the way along Messines Ridge. All full of bloody explosive. And you know, we've tunneled, and they've tunneled, and sometimes they've met."

"Yes," John agreed. "They fished someone out the other day. His party had been caught, and the enemy exploded a bomb down there. He'd been there with thirteen other men, and it took four days to reach them, and he was the only one who came out alive." He paused. "Four days in the dark."

"I should have liked to see the shafts all the same, before they blow the buggers up."

"It's the top act in the whole circus, all right," John agreed. "A real death-defying seat-of-the-pants. Twenty-two corridors thirty feet down, packed with ammonal."

Harry nodded. "And you know what they'd do with us, if they heard us talking about it?"

"Shoot us."

"Correct." Harry laid back in the rubble of the lawn and stared at the sky. "Stars and a hollow earth," he murmured. "You see, we'll break through, and there'll be another world. We're rats at the moment, running about in the filth, and digging down through the clay and chalk. But once we break through. . . ."

John realized that it was an allegory for heaven. For passing through something. Or perhaps not heaven, but death.

Harry laughed, and crooked his arm across his face. "You mustn't mind me," he said. "I feel bloody rotten, if you must know."

"I'll get you some transport."

"Will you?" Harry murmured. "And take me away and deliver me home. To a hospital in London. To retirement in Yorkshire. I'll be like my father. I suppose you know of my father."

"Harry . . ."

"Like a dumb beast now," Harry said. "But fine sort in his day." John said nothing at all.

"I don't blame you necessarily," Harry continued, still with his face obscured. "Very difficult to deal with. Hardly spoke to me as a child, except to reprimand me. But he was a breed, you see?"

"Yes, I know."

"I suppose Mother told you." Harry let down his arm at last, and propped himself up on one elbow. "You ran a blade through the old man by turning up alive after the *Lusitania*. It would have been kinder to kill him straight off."

"I can't help being alive."

"You could have stayed away. It was a bloody shock to us. Not just Father. Neither Louisa nor I nor Charlotte knew what . . . what you were to Mother."

"I'm sorry," John said quietly. "But I couldn't have stayed away. That was impossible."

And then it occurred to him, in a sudden rush of realization, what it was that was really destroying the young man in front of him. It was the same thing that would have destroyed him if, after surviving, he had not found Octavia waiting for him. Harry Cavendish was in love, and he needed the woman. "Your sister is looking for Caitlin," he said. "If anyone can find her, Charlotte can."

Harry Cavendish stared at him a second. Then, very grudgingly, he smiled. "It's the only bloody thing that stops me putting a gun to my head, Mr. Gould." There was a prolonged silence while John watched him and tried to decipher the truth in the remark. He couldn't. "What time is it?" Harry asked.

John looked at his watch, angling towards the faint light from the road. "It's eleven o'clock."

"Four hours to go," Harry said.

"Yes," John told him. "Four hours until we prize the lid off the world, and see what's underneath. We'll see if you're right."

"Hollow," Harry said. "Just an eggshell world. It'll fall in on itself and there'll be nothing left of us."

John frowned. He stood up slowly, and held out his hand. "Come on," he said. "Nobody is going to fall through the world." He paused. "Not on this side of the fence, anyway."

Chapter 12

Christine pushed open the door at St. Dunstan's and stood in the narrow green-tiled porch, the entrance to the convalescent ward. It had been pouring with rain all day and her feet were soaked. She tried to shake the moisture from her coat and hair. "Wouldn't think it was June," she muttered. All the same, she couldn't repress a smile. She had had wonderful news this morning, and couldn't wait to share it with Charlotte.

"France, France, France," she whispered to herself, grinning.

She leaned against the wall and tried to compose her face. Not for the men; they wouldn't care, even if they could see her. But for the nurses. Because not everyone was like Charlotte, blithe and welcoming. The VADs were all right; most of them were upper class—notoriously frivolous—rushing from the bedsides to dinner at the Twenty-One Club or curtained rooms at the Ritz. She'd seen them peeling off their uniforms, dead on their feet but determinedly bright as they wedged their feet into satin shoes and begged the porters to run out into Regent's Park for them and hail a taxi. Christine adored such behavior. There was one here—Amanda de Cholmondeley-Row, or Rowbotham or something—the daughter of a knight of the realm anyway, father an industrialist and in the House of Commons—who went home after serving meals all day in the wards, and had her dinner served at home by a butler.

But not everyone was an aristocratic VAD. There was one sister here—one of the old school, nursing long before war broke out—who frightened the hell out of her. She always looked at Christine as if the younger girl had crawled out from under a stone. Of course, Sister disapproved of the hair, shorn so short. "I can see the lobes of your ears," she had observed coldly last week, as if this were the height of depravity.

"I can see the lobes of every nurse's ears in here."

"That is because their hair is properly pinned up."

"I can't pin my hair up," Christine pointed out. She had trembled despite herself: the woman reminded her of a hated governess who had used to make her stand on a chair to repeat her times tables. Sickly old Stevens, who had smelled of mothballs. The sister looked just like her, rotten old trout.

"I'm here to draw the men. I shan't get near them."

"You had better not," Sister had replied. "I should think you are most unsanitary."

Christine pushed herself away from the wall now, having caught her breath, and—after peering through the glass panel to make sure that Sister was not in this ward—pushed against the door, and went in.

Out in the grounds here, they had erected temporary shelter for the vast numbers of men who were relentlessly appearing. Most stayed just a short time; others went into the main houses where they recuperated. It could take a long time for a man to adjust to being blind, she knew. Others—like Michael Preston—seemed to accept it with calm, even resignation. "Just glad to be out of it," one officer had told her as she was preoccupied with drawing his scarred face. "Blind or not. Whatever it takes. Glad it's over for me."

She had laid her pencil down. The men very rarely spoke of what had happened to them. "What did you feel like, before?" she prompted him. She'd forgotten his name long ago, though she recalled the conversation clearly. This was last winter, and they had been sitting out on the lawn in the depths of the snow; they had had to clear it from the bench seat, but he had told her that he liked the cleanness of the frosty day. "Was it fearful? Were *you*?" she'd asked.

He had kept very still as he spoke. "You're afraid when you're going up to the lines," he murmured. "There's these far-off noises. You feel the ground shake. You think, maybe we're going into that. What'll happen to us? Of course, you don't say that. You whistle instead. You joke. Rag each other, make fun. And there's excitement of course. But after a while, after the months go by, you just have no feelings for yourself."

"No feelings? No fear at all?"

"I don't mean in the way of courage, of having no fear. You don't have a choice about that anyway. Fear just sits with you. It's like daylight or the dark. Always there. Disgust and despair the same. They're like another skin. They sit with you and they're in everything you taste. In the food. In the air and in the tea you drink." He smiled. "If you get any tea."

"But that must be sickening."

"You don't think of it. You're past being sick or having a thought. Artillery can go on for days, weeks. If you've got that endlessly happening, you've got to let it. I mean you can't resist it, else you'd go crazy. People do." He turned his head in the direction of her voice. "There was one officer, he'd tap a little drumbeat on the fire step, or his belt, or on his other hand. If the barrage is heavy, you've maybe got thirty seconds between shells. There's an instant when it's silent after a shell has dropped. But only an instant. Then you hear another, and you start counting. While he counted under his breath, he tapped whatever came to hand." The man laughed. "Funny thing. It wasn't the shells that nearly drove me mad. It was his tapping."

"What happened to him?"

There was an infinitesimal shrug. "The one that got me got him. Shrapnel. We were stuck in a shell hole. Couldn't go forward, nor back. Thirty-six hours. The funny thing was, they told me that when it came down twenty yards away, this officer—he was a fine man, don't misunderstand me—but he just broke. He dived for cover." He sighed slowly. "You don't do that, you see? Bad example. But he dived, and he went forward into the blast. It was the last thing I ever saw. Just a second. That's all it took."

Christine was sitting forward very close to him watching the fragments of memory chase across his face. She wondered if he was aware how much his face twitched and creased; perhaps he didn't. He couldn't see himself in the mirror anymore, and so he had possibly lost a sense of his looks or the way that his face behaved. She found that interesting, poignant. Faces told so much that voices could not.

"May I carry on drawing you?" she asked.

"Aye, why not?"

She smiled a little at the "aye." He had told her that he came from Cumberland, and she heard it in him. Promotion to an officer class had not removed the lilt of the North Country. He would be going on soon, up to Liverpool and then on to home.

"Where is it that you live?" she asked, taking up the pencil again.

"Ah, a place called Longsleddale. Narrow valley. Lovely big mountains."

"And what will you do?"

"We've got a farm. Father and I. I shall go back." He nodded to himself. "I've a younger sister. She'll walk with me."

"Along the paths in the village?"

"There's no village," he told her. "I mean mountains. We'll walk the fells."

"As you used to?"

"Just the same."

*I*t was men like that who kept bringing her back to St. Dunstan's. Men who'd managed to somehow put the past to one side. Not behind them, but to the side. It was a soft, silent piece of courage—one entirely without words—to put such demons away, to deny them attention. They said that fighting took courage, but it wasn't anything to the courage that was needed to come back.

She glanced round the ward quickly now: there were many new patients. She hurried between the beds, and out to the little galley kitchen. A nurse was in here making tea.

"Is Charlotte on duty?" Christine asked. "Charlotte Cavendish? Oh—I mean, Preston."

"No," the girl replied. "I haven't seen her in a week."

"Is she on another ward?"

The girl shrugged. She looked very weary, almost sullen, splashing the contents of the big white enamel teapot, which she held with both hands, along the rows of waiting cups. "She might be."

Christine gave her a sympathetic grin. "Bloody awful day?"

"Bloody awful," the girl replied, not glancing up. "Two gone. Changing dressings on the rest. Blind eyes cry." At last she put the pot down and looked at Christine, hand on hip. "Did you know that?"

"It's miraculous."

"Is it?" She shrugged. "It's sad. That's what it is."

"But miraculous," Christine insisted, as she turned to leave. "Think of that."

"I don't need lessons from you in what to think," the girl told her. "What are you? The drawing girl. Hardly an expert."

"Chin up. It can only get worse."

The nurse relented at the black humor, and smiled back. "Oh, do be a dear child and kindly bugger off."

Christine obeyed. Instead of going back through the ward, she let herself out of the back, and ran over the grassy yard to the main building. Here, up two flights of stairs, she found Michael Preston's office. The door was open, and two assistants were typing. In one corner, Michael Preston sat half propped on the windowsill. He was talking in a brisk fashion to the nearest girl.

"There's another place," he was saying. "On Farringdon Road. Turning out bicycles. Tell them I'd like to come. We want a stationary cycle, on a ramp, for exercise. They've already told me they're busy, but I want to talk to the organ grinder, not the monkey. Find out the top man there, would you? Address it to him. And the usual, Maisie, if you'd be so kind. 'I should be so deeply obliged, etc.'"

Christine gave a short knock on the doorframe. "Captain Preston."

"Yes? Who is it?"

She walked forward. "It's Christine Nesbitt. Charlotte's friend. How are you?"

"Well enough. We haven't had the pleasure of your company in a while, have we?"

"No," she said. "I've been gadding about rather. Garsington Manor for one."

"Should I know the place?"

"No," she admitted. "Lady Ottoline Morrell? She's awfully nice to people. Artists, anyway."

"Is she?" Michael said coolly. "How kind of her."

"I expect you wouldn't approve. She likes guests. She has a swimming pool. People paint there, and she feeds everybody and puts them up and there are charades in the evening. I'm not quite sure if she's grotesque or superb, but it's great fun. I went with a friend. He gets invited, and I tag along." She was embarrassedly aware of how much she was gabbling, and that the typists had stopped work and were staring at her. She cleared her throat. "I was working," she mumbled. "Preparing an exhibition." She was intensely aware of how flat this sounded. She felt like a complete alien, a timewaster. She hastily changed the subject. "I was wondering if you knew if Charlotte was on duty today, and which ward it was."

"She isn't in," Michael said.

"Oh?" Christine couldn't keep the disappointment out of her voice. "I had such news to tell her."

Michael Preston got to his feet. He made his way across the room. "Shall we step out into the hall?" he asked.

They walked some distance from the office, into a cream-painted corridor lit at intervals by plain, high windows. Here, he stopped. "Charlotte's at home," he said. "What was your news? I can relay it."

"That's awfully kind. But I wanted to tell her myself. I'm going to France."

He frowned. "France? Why in heaven's name are you going there?"

"War artist," she said. "Female war artist. Isn't it thrilling? My exhibition that was in The Strand did it. You didn't come. I sent an invitation. Last month. I was shown with Fry and Gertler. Imagine!"

"I'm afraid I don't know them."

"Oh . . . no, of course." She paused. "But, anyway. That's not important. What I wanted to tell Charlotte is that I shall be going soon. Perhaps next month. And I'd like to finish the portrait of her before I go. I've only got preliminary drawings so far."

"She's not terribly well at the moment," he said. And he suddenly shuffled his feet and moved his head back and forth like a bird pecking at the air. "She has a broken wrist."

She looked at him. Unlike the other man that she had been thinking about, Michael Preston's face betrayed no emotion at all. It was the bobbing movement, however—that entirely involuntary movement—that gave his unease away. "How did that happen?" she asked.

"She missed her footing coming down the stairs, apparently."

"You weren't there?"

"It was early in the morning. She had an early shift."

"I see," Christine murmured. "How annoying for her. And painful. It stops her nursing, of course."

"Yes. Although she has come in a little. There's some things that she can still do, and being Charlotte . . ."

"She comes to do them, yes." There was a pause. Michael began to turn towards his office. "I'll go and see her," Christine said.

"She may be resting this afternoon."

"Or she may not. She may be quite bored," Christine replied. "I shall take her something. A treat? I know an Italian café in St. Martin's Lane. Where they get their butter from I don't know. One doesn't ask, after all. But the cake is quite scrumptious."

She could see that he was wrestling with his reply. Then he smiled. "She'd adore it." Graciously, he held out his hand, and Christine shook it. She could feel that despite the hesitation and that restlessly bobbing head, Michael Preston was actually quite calm. His hand was steady and dry. "How kind of you to seek her out," he said. "And how brave of you to go to France."

My goodness, she thought. *Aren't you absolutely charming?*

"Thank you, Captain," she said evenly. "And good-bye."

*L*ondon was still humid despite the rain. She got a bus to Trafalgar Square and dodged across the lanes of traffic, holding the precious cargo of cake in her hands. Before the war, the café had wrapped everything in deliciously crisp striped paper, with a chic black-and-white ribbon neatly tied on top. Now, the wrapping was brown and there was no fabric tie. "I am sorry," the Italian owner had said to her. "It is the war."

"I know," she replied. "Never mind. It doesn't alter the cake."

It took half an hour to get to the mews house, even walking at Christine's brisk pace. But that was preferable to another journey among the dripping mackintoshes of a public bus. One of the paintings that she had done for the exhibition had been of the inside of an omnibus—a pastiche on Alfred Morgan's *An Omnibus Ride to Piccadilly*, which had showed the prime minister in 1885, Gladstone, traveling with ordinary people. The passengers shown in that painting had been a tradesman, a young mother, and an older woman shepherding two children; a boy had been seated with his back to the viewer dressed in a sailor suit with a toy boat on his knee. Christine had painted a similar-looking bus, but the occupants now were young women in munitions uniforms, and the little boy had been replaced with a real sailor slumped over his kit bag, asleep. Instead of Gladstone, Lloyd George now looked out straight at the viewer, his face half his own, and half that of the Kaiser. The hands in his lap were red with blood.

The painting had caused a sensation, almost a riot. Mark Gertler, whose own painting of a fantastical carousel of mechanically grinning occupants she so admired, had warned her that the public might try to lynch her. She'd smiled up at him; he was rather attractive. "An artist should always tell the truth," she had remarked.

"Ah, it's the truth you want?" he had said, returning the smile. "Good luck with that."

She reached Charlotte and Michael's home in mid-afternoon. She rang the doorbell and waited for the sound of the housekeeper's feet along the hallway. The door was opened and the woman looked out. Christine remembered Charlotte saying that the housekeeper had been chosen by Michael's mother and her immediate reaction was, *Gosh, I would hate to look at that sulky face every day.* She summoned her smile again. "Is Mrs. Preston home?" she asked.

"I'm afraid not." The woman's gaze strayed down to the now-soggy brown paper parcel.

"Do you know where she might have gone?"

"I do not."

"Or when she'll be back?"

"No, I don't."

Christine steeled herself. She often got this kind of reaction. People could see that she wasn't working class, but she didn't dress as a lady either. She had no hat, no gloves; her coat was a workman's, and she wore it over a bright green dress that she had fashioned from a much older garment. Her stitching wasn't exactly professional, but she had partly hidden it with a yellow scarf. A horrendous sight to most people, and a paean of eccentricity to herself. No corset either, and no stockings. She loved it, but she could see how much the housekeeper hated it. She stood across the doorway and evidently was not letting her in.

Christine held out the parcel. "Would you be so kind as to give this to Mrs. Preston when she comes back?" she said. "It's a little delicacy for her. I know she must be feeling rotten."

The housekeeper took it, holding it away from her as if it might explode.

"Do you have a piece of paper?" Christine asked. "May I leave a note?"

The paper was found; the note was left. Christine had no alternative but to turn and go, leaving her name. The housekeeper repeated it, and added, "Most visitors leave a calling card."

"I don't have a calling card," Christine said. "I'm awfully sorry."

When the door had been shut, and Christine was walking along the narrow cobbled street, she inwardly cursed herself. When would she get over this horrible little middle-class habit of apologizing? As she walked, she kicked at the stones underfoot. "So sorry, so sorry," she muttered. "For heaven's sake!"

The truth was that she was not sorry about a calling card; but she was desperately sorry that she had not seen Charlotte. It was selfish, she supposed, to gad about the country and just write to Charlotte occasionally. She ought to have made more of an effort to visit. But then, she considered, reaching Oxford Street, Charlotte hadn't contacted *her*. Why was that?

She stood on the pavement looking down the long street towards the Oxford Theatre with all its gaudy trappings of music hall and variety shows. Vaudeville had been her father's weakness; after her mother died when she was a teenager, he used to go out to the clubs and theaters all the time. "Oh, it's a little bit of fun," he would tell her. "There's not enough fun in the world." For a respected gentleman, he could be a lecherous old goat all the same. After his death she'd been shocked to find that all his money had apparently been spent on the painted chorus girls of Shaftesbury Avenue. His sister had rallied to Christine's side and bestowed the necessary but oh-so-hated annuity that enforced the ritual visits to her aunt.

"Where the bloody hell are you, Charlotte?" she muttered, as people brushed past her. She wanted to take Charlotte somewhere, to entertain her. Her father had been right in one respect at least: you needed fun. The theaters were packed every night in London. She would like to take Charlotte out to see Bessie Bellwood or Vesta Tilley, into the bright and bellowing world with its tiller girls and jazz and silly costumes and bright lights. If anyone needed cheering up, it must be Charlotte, she thought.

But there was something else. Christine looked at the crowds and at the passing traffic of horse and bus and van and the occasional absurd-seeming carriage, and she saw nothing at all of it. She only saw Charlotte's face. "Oh Christ," she whispered. "I'm going to France." And it suddenly struck her that it wasn't an adventure at all. Because she was going to France and she wouldn't see Charlotte. Michael Preston would keep his wife close. That nodding, pecking head kept coming back to her, that rigidity of pose and expression. She was going away, and would miss the opportunity to paint Charlotte's portrait. And suddenly that seemed to matter very much.

The rain came down harder, and, at last registering it, she began to run.

She got back to her studio and walked up the stairs at a slow pace, taking off her coat and trailing it behind her. She was thoroughly wet from the rain, and sticky and hot from the temperature outside.

"What a wasted day," she muttered, trying to find her key in the pocket of her dress. "Bloody rain. Bloody everything."

She was almost at her own landing at the top of the house. She found the key and looked up.

"Bloody everything," Charlotte said.

Christine gave a little yelp of triumph. She started to rush up the last few steps, and then stopped. Charlotte was sitting on the floor, under a skylight to the roof. She wore a terracotta-colored linen coat, something with a great deal of material. It rippled around her like a tawny wave; her hair was drawn back severely. What had stopped Christine, however, was the expression on Charlotte's face.

It was both hard to read and extraordinary. Or perhaps it was extraordinary *because* it was hard to read. Charlotte looked much older, but her face was unlined, as smooth as a child's; it was the expression in her eyes that was strange. It was full of irony and a kind of sad humor. She was incredibly pale.

"Something has happened," Christine murmured. "Please don't tell me it's Harry."

"No, it's not Harry."

"Caitlin? Louisa? Is your father all right?"

Charlotte smiled. "They're fine. Everyone is fine."

Christine took another few steps, and then lowered herself onto the top step so that she was level with Charlotte. "It's you, then."

Charlotte held up her injured hand. She looked at it objectively for a moment.

"I've been to the hospital," Christine said. "I spoke to Michael."

"I've not been in work this week. I doubt that I can really be of any use until this is healed."

"How long will that be?"

"Four weeks? Five?" Charlotte lowered her hand. "Why did you go to the hospital?"

"Why do you think? Looking for you."

There was a silence. "Shall I be in the way if I come in for a while?" Charlotte asked.

"I almost wish you could stay there. I'd love to paint you just as you are, under that light. Summer afternoon light."

"I don't want to be in the way if Alexis Barrington will be here."

Christine jumped to her feet and held out her hand. "He isn't here and isn't likely to be. We were at Garsington a fortnight ago and he left with a very sweet girl from Hampshire who knows his mother. So I think that is probably that." She pulled such a face that Charlotte gave a glimmer of a smile. "He was rather beginning to grate on me, actually," Christine informed her, unlocking the door. "His work was so much more important than mine. He said that if we lived together I should have to stop painting."

"He said *what*!"

"Apparently the talent of women is a short-lived thing."

"He's jealous of you," Charlotte murmured.

"Yes, I thought the same."

They stood looking at each other. Christine threw the wet coat onto a chair. "Are you hungry? I've just delivered a most delicious cake to your house, by the way."

"Have you? Why?"

"Because someone should be looking after you. What kind of question is that?"

Charlotte stood perfectly still. Then she dropped her head, and began to cry.

"Oh, darling, not again!" Christine exclaimed, going to her and putting her hand on her shoulder. "What is it?"

Charlotte didn't answer. The tears convulsed her; she put one hand to her face and half-turned away. "Don't look at me."

"Don't *look* at you? What on earth are you talking about? I like to look at you more than anything." She enveloped Charlotte in her arms, felt her thin frame, her awkwardness, the way she curled in on herself. "You must tell me," Christine said. She stroked Charlotte's hair. "Tell me."

But nothing came out except the tears. After another few

moments Christine guided Charlotte to the makeshift bed, and sat her down. "I expect you hate the damned stuff after doling it out to half of Kitchener's army, but would you like some of my usual milk-free tea?"

Charlotte wiped her face with the heel of her hand. "No. Thank you."

"You're awfully polite these days, aren't you?" Christine observed softly. "There's no kicking and screaming like there used to be."

"I've never kicked and screamed."

"Metaphorically, I mean."

"Oh . . . well."

Christine slammed the flat of her hand onto her knee. "This is exactly what I mean. 'Oh well.' What a simpering little person you've become."

"You don't understand."

"Quite right. I don't. Suppose you tell me."

There was a prolonged silence. Christine sighed. "Look, I went to the hospital to tell you some news. I had no idea that you'd had this injury. I supposed that you'd be working there. And after Michael told me what had happened, I went to your house to be met by Mrs. Cow-Face. And then I came back here. And it was all because I want to paint you before I go to France."

Charlotte's head snapped up. "What?"

"I'm going to France as a war artist. I shall be gone in a little while and I want to paint you before I go. I've been thinking of it. I have ideas. I want a portrait of you, a large one, just by these windows. I want it to be all light, because that's what you are in my mind. A creature of light. And now I'm looking at you and I see the light's been turned off. I don't want 'oh well.' I don't want 'thank you.' I don't want that person. I want you."

She placed a hand on Charlotte's chin, and turned her to face her.

She scrutinized Charlotte's face. "You have such a wonderful look to you. I think it might have deepened, altered. Improved you somehow."

"Oh," Charlotte said, her eyes brimming. "Something's improved anyway."

"And what has not?"

Charlotte looked away, and moved so that Christine's hand dropped from her. She got to her feet, walking slowly over to the big attic window. "You can see such a lot of London," she whispered. "So much space."

Christine was watching her. "When are you going home?"

"In an hour or so."

"Then can I start the painting?"

"If you like."

Christine sprang up. She almost ran over to Charlotte's side, and grabbed her by the shoulder. "No," she exclaimed. "*Not* 'if I like.' *Not* that! My God. That's another one. What's got into you? Wake up. Look at me. *Not* 'if I like.' But because you want to. Because you'd want it more than anything. Because you'd want to be painted by me. Because you want to have the evidence of what I see in you. Don't you understand?"

Charlotte was staring at her.

"Look . . ." Christine turned on her heel, looked about the room as if for inspiration. She put both fists to her temples, and then started laughing. "You really make me despair," she muttered, glaring at the long table opposite where her paints were spread about. In a stride, she was over to the window, brushing past Charlotte. She looked up for just a second at the purple curtains with their lurid green lining, and then she reached for the nearest, clenched her hands around it, and pulled.

"Oh," said Charlotte, with a gasp. "What are you doing?"

Christine wrenched until the pole that had been precariously holding the curtain came away. "I'm getting a blazing color for you," she muttered. The pole clattered to the ground; at the other end of it, the opposing curtain slithered to the floor. Christine gathered up the nearest and dragged it over to Charlotte. She pulled a corner of it and put it against Charlotte's face. "I want you to have this draped around you. I want the bottom half of the painting to be this. As if you're rising from it. I want you to sit in the light over there. On the end of the table, and look out of the windows."

"But . . ."

Christine waved her hand. "Don't object, please. I want to see your neck and shoulders. I'll arrange the fabric. I want you to look away from me, half profile. And I just want you to have one hand holding the material and the other in your lap. Don't worry about the dressing on it. I shan't paint that." She stood in front of Charlotte, grasping the material and smiling at her. "It will be fantastic, I promise."

Charlotte got to her feet slowly. "All right," she said, and started to walk.

"Just a minute." Christine laid a hand on her shoulder. "You must undress."

"What? But I can't do that."

"Your shoulders and neck."

"No, Christine. Michael wouldn't like it."

Christine frowned. "I don't mean you to be entirely naked," she said. "Pull down the straps on your underthings if you must. And I'm sorry, but damn Michael! What's it to do with him?"

"But . . . in the painting . . . I will look naked. Naked, and just covered up with a piece of material."

"Yes, darling. You will."

Charlotte hung her head. "No, that's impossible. I'm sorry." And she took a couple of steps backward towards the door.

"I promise you . . ."

"No," Charlotte repeated. "You can't promise me anything. I simply can't pose for you."

"But of course you can!" Christine sighed in exasperation. "I've wanted to do this painting. I *must* do it."

"I don't care what you want or what you must do," Charlotte said.

To Christine's horror, she made for the door and had her hand on the handle. Christine dropped the curtain and rushed over, stopping her from opening it at the last moment. They stood face to face, a foot apart. It seemed to Christine that time then became extremely slow, stretched thin. They were just reflections on its surface, like the reflections on water as it passed. She could almost see them from another perspective, as if they were two separate beings that she was drawing: ethereal things, just whispers. It was the most surreal feeling. She thought of the phrase about angels dancing on the head of a pin, but they were not angels, just approximations of what they were, or how they used to be once. Two changelings, two phantoms.

"Please," Charlotte murmured, hand on the door itself now. But she made no effort to move.

"Don't beg me for anything. Tell me what it is. You can trust me. Why did you cry on your wedding day?"

Charlotte shook her head slowly. "That was a different reason to now," she said. "I was afraid of being trapped."

"And are you now?"

"Oh yes," she replied, and smiled, as if to say this was humorous, or at least ironic. "But not in the way I'd anticipated."

"In what way, then?"

Charlotte closed her eyes momentarily. "I can't remember very clearly what I was afraid of," she said. "He was a good man. He still is. Charming and attractive. Intelligent. He seemed to be an understanding person to everyone else. He is understanding with the men he works with. He is patient with them. I hoped that he would be the same with me. I had no reason to think otherwise. Mother and Father were so pleased when we were engaged. I think Father always thought that I was a loose cannon, and . . ." Her voice faded. "Perhaps he felt I needed control of some kind. I didn't want to spoil it all. And I hoped for adventures. I wanted to be out in a different kind of world, experiencing something new. Marriage itself was an adventure. Even a gamble."

"One that hasn't paid off, it seems," Christine said bluntly, but not without kindness. "But tell me why your painting, the way I see it, is so wrong. It's an adventure of sorts, isn't it?"

"It's not that I don't trust you, Christine. It's that I don't trust myself."

"I don't understand."

"I don't know what I've become," she murmured. "A coward, perhaps. Less than I was."

"But that is ridiculous!"

Charlotte looked at her steadily.

And she walked away, back into the room. Standing where the curtain was still pooled on the floor, she took off the great tawny-colored coat, easing her hand out of the wide sleeve. Underneath, she was wearing another loose-sleeved garment: a black crepe de chine dress with a long skirt and a large square neckline. It had a drawstring waist, and Christine watched as Charlotte undid the knot with her free hand. The dress became a loose oblong shape. She reached down and pulled it up and over her head.

She was wearing just a slip underneath; nothing else. Through it—to Christine's horror she could count every rib—Charlotte was painfully thin. The bones of her shoulders stood out in sharp relief. Even her hipbones could be made out: there were no curves at all. Charlotte looked like a starvation victim, a fact that had been hidden by the voluminous coat. Christine walked slowly towards her; then stopped, her hand to her mouth. The upper part of Charlotte's chest was not in such dark relief only because of her thinness, but because she was bruised. It looked as if she had been pressed against something ridged or paneled; the bruise had a definite suggestion of a fretwork.

"My God," Christine breathed. "What's this?"

Charlotte held her gaze for a second, and then she slowly turned around. "We had an argument," she said quietly. "A disagreement. I don't think that he meant to push so hard."

"Not *so hard*? He oughtn't to push you at all."

"I try his patience. And he is a very patient man."

"Are you serious? Are you *sane*? You're bruised. What was it, a piece of metal of some kind?"

"There's a radiator grille in the wall. From the boiler in the basement. It heats the upper landing."

"And he pushed you against this?" Christine considered. "Were you not wearing anything? This looks like direct contact with the skin."

Charlotte crossed her arms across her breasts as if to cover herself. "I had got up in the night."

"Why? Were you ill?"

"No," Charlotte replied, still not meeting her friend's gaze. "I was . . ." She couldn't finish the sentence. Christine put her arm around her. "You see, I don't like him," Charlotte murmured. "To touch me. And after all, it's what a husband wants, isn't it? I thought it would be all right. I've steeled myself to it. I *want* to be kind. It's just that, when he . . ." She seemed to set her teeth, as if the very memory sickened her. "He says that I am not natural."

"Oh, poor love," Christine said softly. "Who have you told about this?"

"No one."

"Not your mother, or sister?"

"No."

"But why?"

Charlotte hung her head. "I feel ashamed."

Christine had to literally bite her tongue to prevent the immediate response, the furious denial that sprang automatically to her lips. She tried instead to keep her voice low and level, to hold her temper in check. "Your hand, your wrist . . . ?" she prompted. "It wasn't a fall."

"I was trying to get out the door to the street," Charlotte said. "It was very early in the morning. I know it was madness, because I only had my nightdress. But I thought I might be able to run away, and . . ."

"He found you," Christine guessed. "He held you by the wrist as you tried to get out."

"I couldn't open the door. He had hidden the key. He came down the stairs. He said I must be quiet. That I mustn't make a scene. What was I doing, trying to go into the street? How would that seem to anyone? He said that I must appreciate . . ."

She had stopped. She was shivering. Christine ran to pick up the curtain, and she put it around Charlotte's shoulders. She stepped around to the front, and wrapped it across Charlotte's body, and held it there, looking closely into Charlotte's face. "You are never going back."

Charlotte paused a long time before replying. "I wanted to be like other women," she whispered finally. "I thought I could make myself like other women, but I can't. He says that I am . . . badly formed. I don't . . . want to do what I should with him. What he says I must do as my duty." She glanced momentarily up at Christine, and then back at the floor. A slow, dull blush of color was flooding her face. "He said that I am made wrong in some way."

"And do you believe him?" Christine asked softly. "When he tells you that you are unnatural?"

"I don't know what to believe anymore," Charlotte said. Her voice was so quiet that Christine had to strain to hear it. She put her face very close to Charlotte; felt the other woman's breath mingling with her own.

"Let me tell you something," Christine told her. She smoothed her hand over Charlotte's hair, brushing it gently over her cheek. She put her hand below Charlotte's chin and turned her face towards her. "Look at me," she said. "And listen to me. You *are* like other women. A great number of other women. Do you know why?"

Charlotte shook her head.

Christine smiled. "Because, my dearest, you are exactly like me."

Chapter 13

Finally, the summer had come.

It seemed to Frederick that he had been living in the thick wool coat for years, and it stank to high heaven. Sometimes, in the camp, the guards would come and take their clothes to the laundry and issue them with others: ill-fitting underclothes and shirts and strangely shaped boxlike jackets of canvas. Frederick was wearing the boots that had brought him from France, from Munster, from home. He didn't mind. They were good boots. He wanted new socks, but he took care to wash out the pair that he had.

Not to complain. Others did; it was their entertainment. He simply didn't like the feeling it left in him: sour and scratched inside, hungering for home. He tried to think of other and more immediate things. The pattern of plaster cracks on the wall nearest his bed and a funny kind of map that they made, almost like the Mosel. He imagined vineyards growing on each side, and the terraced restaurants where his uncle had once taken him on his only holiday as a child. He tried to think of pleasant scenes. Of a music festival in their

village where someone had played a violin, and there had been dancing, kicking up summer dust under the linden trees. He would like
to dance again, and be happy. He didn't want to lose the knack of
being happy. He didn't want to go home with his soul scoured out,
grim-faced, resentful, pained. He had to keep something of himself
clean. Still be able to stand up straight. That was how he thought
of it.

And now, at last, the sun. He liked the light in the morning. So
much light after the rain. It got light at five thirty, pale rims of apricot and pink outside the window. He would get up and look at it. It
was important to remember that God still gave you summer morn-
ings, and that it was man who had taken away the pleasure of them
and made war on the green earth, churning it up and soaking it with
slaughter. He looked at the sunlight and imagined it flowing over
the battlefields. Grant them grace to stop, he thought. He was sure
that for all the armies with their priests calling on God—and God
was unerringly on the side of whatever priest was speaking, German
or Turkish, Indian or French—he felt that God had no particular
side at all. He just kept giving them summer and spring and winter;
rain and harvest and darkness; water and sand and sea. It was man
that made a mess of it all, and for that God's heart must ache.

And so he looked hard at the dawns and tried to note them in his
head. If he had a notebook he would keep a record, he thought. A
record of pleasant days. He held them close in his head and ran his
mind over them repeatedly to keep the memory fresh. He wished he
could write things down. He hadn't seen paper or a pencil in three
years. Not to hold. Not to write with.

They had left their greatcoats behind this week, and went out to
work in their trousers and jackets. By noon the jackets would be
discarded and the shirts clung to their backs. But they were not
allowed to take off the shirts. He didn't know why. Offense to the

female population, perhaps. Although they didn't see many. An occasional woman in one of the villages. A child sitting on a wall by a church.

This morning, they stood by the bridge near to where they had built the road. They could see it now snaking away between the green hedges that had grown much taller, fringed by what the English called "cow parsley." Like frothy wedding flowers on a church aisle. Like the head of cream on new milk. Here and there, a chestnut tree rippled in the summer wind. Where they were standing he could hear the river water flowing under the village bridge.

"Listen to me," the guard said.

It was a new man. The shouting one had gone. They were all pleased with that. This was an older soldier, very quiet in his ways. He had a long scar on one side of his neck that looked raw, a lilac edge. Frederick wondered where the guard had picked that up; the Western Front, or Mesopotamia or Gallipoli. He looked at him idly, wondering what his name was, and if he lived near here. If he got to go home in the evening. Or if his wife came to see him. He noticed that as he walked up and down, he limped slightly. His gaze, when he turned it on them, was not aggressive, but soft. Even sympathetic.

"The fields up at Rutherford need to be cut for hay." He paused. "Understand? Cutting hay."

No one said anything, but there was a slight shuffling as a long blade was brought from the covered van at the roadside. The guard held it up. "You know what this is?"

Frederick didn't know if the men from the cities knew it, but he did. He tentatively raised his hand.

"Yes. You then. What is it?"

"If you please . . . *sense.*" Inadvertently, he had said the German word. He was thinking of the phrase, *menschen nedermahen.* To scythe people down. To scythe down men. To cut them down, like armies, like the British coming across the rotted ground towards them. "I think . . . sighing," he stuttered.

"Scything," the guard corrected, watching Frederick's face as if he'd seen the fleeting images reflected there. Wary of him. Narrowing his own eyes. "A scythe," he repeated twice, for the benefit of those at the back.

"We know," a voice among them muttered. It was ignored.

"It's for cutting hay," the guard was continuing. He demonstrated. "An art to it, mind. But the meadows slope near the house. They go right to the river. They want it brought in, made into stacks. You understand? Haystacks in the fields, near the barns you mended."

Fredrick was nudged in the back by two or three of the prisoners. He translated as best he could. Some of the Germans didn't ever listen, didn't ever try to pick up any English. They had begun to look to Frederick as a mouthpiece. "You must not be lazy," he had told them all one night last winter. "You must use your brains. Learn something. We are here. We may as well get along."

"Get along with the enemy. Learn something." A man sitting on his bunk had spat on the ground. "What are you, a schoolteacher now?"

"I am done with war," Frederick had told him.

The guard came walking towards Frederick now. "You're the man who helped in the dairy once or twice."

"Help. Yes. The butter."

"You know what Rutherford is?"

"No, sir."

The guard walked back to the front of the prisoners. "Rutherford Park is the big house. The estate. Owned by Lord Cavendish. All this around you, all you can see. Village, too. Right up to Catterick's gates. Now, Lord Cavendish is at home now. So if you see . . ." He thought a moment. "Never mind. You're not going to see him. He's not interested in you. But he's lost a lot of his men. His workers. No workers, understand? So you cut the hay."

He looked back and forth among them, and finally indicated a third of them, the third where Frederick was standing. "You lot over here, hay cutting. The rest, laying a wall. Drystone walls here." When they didn't respond, he gave a great sigh. "Never mind," he said. And he actually smiled. "It's a good job. Easy. Nice to do today. You'll pick it up."

The two-thirds shuffled off, led by two very young-looking guards in uniforms that looked far too big for them. Frederick watched the boys sadly, seeing the pink skin rubbing at the back of their collars, and the red tips of their ears. Like schoolboys. Fodder for guns very soon.

"Ey up," the older guard urged the prisoners. "Move on."

They followed him.

"Ey up," Frederick repeated softly to himself, smiling, and unconsciously echoing the broad Yorkshire accent. "Ey up, ey up."

*I*n the kitchens at Rutherford, breakfast had been a lengthier affair than usual.

Just as they were finishing, Mr. Bradfield held up his hand to prevent them all leaving. "Stay where you are a moment," he said. He handed out their letters, looking for some time at one from the front, which was passed to Mary.

There was nothing for Jenny, for Jenny knew no one at all. She'd been a lucky one, taken up by a local Methodist church in London who had helped her find work because she regularly attended. She was the pastor's walking good deed. But neither the pastor nor the rest of the church wrote to her at Rutherford. "I guess they've got others to look after," she had told Mary once.

Mrs. Carlisle took a handful of letters with a smile. She had a vast family in Bradford, a whole host of nieces and nephews. Despite her traditional title, she had never married; but the nieces and nephews and cousins kept her supplied with news. Bradford mill workers, for the most part. She was handed two letters this morning.

Nothing for Miss Dodd. Mary stole a glance at her out of the corner of her eye. Miss Dodd was fast becoming a dyed-in-the-wool spinster, devoted to Rutherford. Mary could see her dying here, duster in hand, her starched uniform apron in place to her last breath. When her sweetheart had run off and married another woman, it was obvious that she'd probably lost her last chance. Men were so few and far between. She was married to Rutherford instead, Mary thought. Miss Dodd already had that look: a bit petulant, a bit prim and proper. Disappointed and determined at the same time.

"There's something you need to know," Mr. Bradfield announced. "A new housekeeper has been appointed. A Mrs. Nicholson."

A murmur went around the table, except from Edward Hardy, who was pushing the breadcrumbs around his plate in the usual vacant way. He didn't care if Rutherford had a housekeeper or not. He might care if Mrs. Carlisle left and there was no cook, Mary thought. He'd register *that* departure all right.

"Can we know where she's come from?" Miss Dodd asked.

"From the Kent's estate near York."

"Is she the housekeeper there?"

"No. She's the wife of one of the tenants, I believe."

A ripple of dismay went round the table. "No experience?" Miss Dodd said huffily. "I should think that I have more knowledge of here than a farmer's wife."

"I'm told that she was in service before she married, and also had a nursing post in a hospital."

"A nurse and a housemaid?" Mrs. Carlisle said. "Hardly a recommendation for a house like Rutherford."

"You'd think she'd be needed in some hospital or other now, with all the wounded coming back," Mary observed. "If she's qualified." She leaned forward. "Did Lady Cavendish interview her when she was here, Mr. Bradfield?"

"I understand so."

"I never saw anyone come to the house."

"It'll be an agreement between Lady Kent and the mistress," Mrs. Carlisle opined. "She'll have spoken to her over at the Kents', I expect." She put her head to one side, a new idea occurring to her. "Perhaps the woman's a bother. Perhaps Lady Kent wants to put her here to be rid of her."

This was more accurate than anyone knew, but Mr. Bradfield frowned. "It's not for us to speculate. I doubt that Lady Cavendish would employ anyone who wasn't very good indeed. And her ladyship is very aware of how much a housekeeper is needed."

Miss Dodd seemed to bridle at this, straightening her shoulders and setting her mouth in a disapproving line.

"How old is she?" Jenny asked.

This time, Bradfield stared at the maid until she blushed. "Quite an inappropriate question."

"What Jenny means," Mary ventured, "is . . . is she senior?"

"I cannot say."

"If she's married, does she have children?"

"I understand not. Her husband recently died."

A slight *oh* sound went round the table, a note of sympathy. But still the general air of disapproval remained. Mrs. Carlisle was looking around at the kitchen itself, muttering, "I shall have to give this place a thorough going-over before she comes." She looked at Mr.

Bradfield. "Will his lordship allow me another girl up from the village?" she asked. "I've only a scullery maid, you know."

"I shall ask, if you think it's needed."

"Needed?" Mrs. Carlisle said. "I should think it is. I can't struggle on forever. We used to have six in this kitchen, when his lordship was first married. Six! And far more on the night of a formal dinner!"

"They've all gone off to the mills, the fools," Mary murmured. "Even Cynthia."

"She was plain lazy," Mrs. Carlisle retorted. "I don't want no more like that."

"When is Mrs. Nicholson coming, Mr. Bradfield?" Miss Dodd asked.

"On Monday."

"Oh Lord above," Mrs. Carlisle muttered.

Bradfield got up, took up the newspapers, and, after casting another glance around the room that warned them that they soon must be about their business, he went out. They listened to his footsteps along the stone corridor, and then on the steps that led up to the green baize door that admitted him to the main house.

They waited until they heard the door close.

"Well!" Miss Dodd exclaimed. "Husband's died and Lady Kent doesn't want her."

"There must be something about her to recommend her," Mrs. Carlisle mused.

"I could have done the job, given half a chance," Miss Dodd complained. "I've been more or less doing it so far."

"'More or less' isn't in charge though, is it?" Mrs. Carlisle replied. "You're very good, dear, but this woman will have . . . well, something else to recommend her. Education or experience. And we don't know what kind of tenant we're talking about. Her husband might have farmed one of the big affairs they've got over at York. One of those rambling ones that the Kents own. When your husband does that, you become quite adept at helping him. Accounts and staff, all that."

"I hope she's not a horrible old dragon like Mrs. Jocelyn," Jenny muttered. "Thumping her Bible and warning us we'll all be damned."

Mrs. Carlisle raised an eyebrow. "We won't have bad talk about staff, whatever or whoever." She looked at Mary. "Letter from David?"

"Yes." Mary was turning it over and over in her hands, unopened.

"Well, then. Tell us what he says."

Mary ran her finger along the gummed edge of the envelope with trepidation. David had always used to write such nice things, but he rarely said much at all now. Hello and good-bye, and "I am well." And "are you well." Nothing with any heart in it. "Hoping this finds you as it leaves me," he would write. Just like everyone else. The poet in him seemed to have been lost somewhere. She'd given him a book of poems to take with him when he had left at the beginning of December last year, and he'd received it without a word. A week's leave he'd had because of an infected foot. A week's leave, and three days of it spent getting here and going back.

She thought of this as she opened the letter, and laid her hand on her stomach as the baby moved. At least he'd given her the child: a miracle, considering how very little time they had ever spent together. Married almost two years, and with barely a fortnight spent together in all that time.

They all waited while she read. They all knew from what he had told them in December that he had been at a place called Albert. It was a little town, he had said. Or at least, it had once been a town and now it was. . . He had stopped in his description. "Something else," he had ended.

They'd all seen Albert mentioned in the obituaries that appeared in the local newspapers. They were starting to recognize the names: Albert, Bapaume, and Ypres.

"Master Harry is at a place near Arras," Miss Dodd murmured. She'd heard the master say so.

"Mrs. Armitage said that Jack was near there," Mrs. Carlisle added. "There's a big push on."

They all sat in silence a few moments more. None of them really knew what a "big push" meant. It sounded like jostling in a queue.

"I don't think David is there anymore," Mary murmured. She was frowning as she read. "That's funny."

"What's funny?" Jenny asked.

Mary read a portion of the letter out loud. "Moving about a bit," she said slowly. "Like we talked about the day after we got married."

"It's the censors," Mrs. Carlisle told her. "You're not allowed to write down where you are."

"I know that," Mary said. "But I don't know what he means."

"Well, what did you talk about the day after you got married?"

"I can't remember that!" Mary exclaimed. "How am I supposed to?"

"Holidays," Mrs. Carlisle suggested. "The future. A family. A place to live. Plans. That's what you'll have talked about."

"Plans . . ." Mary mused. "I remember saying it was a pity we couldn't have a proper honeymoon, if that's what you mean by a holiday." She sighed. "I'd have liked to go to the seaside. I've never been."

"Well, that's what it is then!" Mrs. Carlisle said, beaming triumphantly. "He's been posted somewhere by the sea."

"But . . ." Mary put the letter down in exasperation. "They're not anywhere near the sea, are they? He said it was miles and miles in a train to get to Albert."

"The trenches don't go to the sea," Jenny agreed.

Mrs. Carlisle got to her feet. "Well, I've got no time to sit here figuring it out," she told them. "His lordship has several people coming to lunch, and it won't make itself. Besides," she added darkly, "I've got orders to make fodder for them Germans."

"What Germans?" Mary demanded.

"Them that's helping take in the grass on the meadows."

"What, up here, near the house?"

"So I'm told." She paused. "You might have to help Alfred take it out to them, if he can't manage."

Mary knew that the hall boy wouldn't manage, of course. He'd be more likely to drop everything. Still her face was set. "I shan't take them a single thing," she said. "Not a bite. I'm not a maid to *them*."

Mrs. Carlisle and Miss Dodd looked at each other significantly.

"I'll take it, if I have to," Jenny offered. "Mary doesn't need to . . . I'll do it. It don't matter to me."

*I*t was a pure pleasure to work in the meadows.

And Frederick had been astounded by the estate as the work party had approached the large house. They entered through a lodge gate. On the gateposts were little statues—birds perched on what looked like sugarcane. Ahead of them—they were sitting in an open-backed wagon—they saw a long line of beech trees. Enormous trees, probably more than a hundred years old, making a lovely arched cover over the road. In the distance he could glimpse barley-twist chimneys and a terracotta-colored wall, hidden by a rise in the land. His eyes scanned it; he guessed that it must be an enormous place. But they were not allowed to see it now; the wagon turned abruptly left, and the track skirted a slow-flowing river. Beyond the river, a woodland. And above the woodland, a stretch of moorland, glowing pale yellow in the morning sun.

They passed a bridge, and a small shingle-and-sand beach at a curve in the river. And then more gates were opened—big five-bar gates each with the same insignia of sugarcane topped by a little bird. It looked like a bluebird to him, so frail and delicate. Bluebirds and sugar . . . what did that mean? Sugar barons, from long ago?

The track began to rise a little, skirted a hill, and then they saw the meadows. They were small fields, one after the other, each separated by a gate. In them, the grass was knee-high and full of wild flowers. The wagon stopped, and they got off; they were walked up the rise, and as they ascended, suddenly the west wing of the house came into view. It stopped Frederick dead. So lovely, so huge. Roof upon roof with windows set between; a large, mellow-colored kitchen garden wall. To the side, the roofs of smaller cottages.

"It must be paradise to work here," he murmured to the man alongside him.

"Heaven to live here, more like," the man replied.

Yes indeed, he thought. Very like heaven.

They set to work, each holding the long-handled blade with the separate grip that stuck out at right angles to the stave. Frederick did the best he could. Some days he could hold a spade or a hammer quite well; on others, the ability was sporadic. Today was one such day; he started off at the bottom of the field, working in a line with ten others, gripping the handle of the scythe, but occasionally finding it slithering through his fingers. Although they knew the reason, the other men still found him frustrating to work alongside.

A bull-necked man from Dortmund began ridiculing him. "Getting very fancy, want to be English. They run about like that. Don't you know? Like that." And he mimed a limp-wristed boy. The others laughed, watching to see what Frederick would do.

"I don't want to be English."

"Don't you, though? All you ever talk about is being peaceable."

"I don't want to fight."

The Dortmund man gave a snarl-like smile. "Don't want to kill an Englishman. Got no guts at all." And he prodded Frederick in the back.

Frederick looked up, past the man. The guard was at the far end of the field. "Don't touch me," he muttered.

Another prod. "Don't touch you? Why would I want to touch you, bloody traitor?"

Frederick stopped, and straightened up. "I'm no traitor."

"Like it here, you do. Paradise. You just said that. I call the Fatherland paradise."

"I'm a good German."

"You're bullshit." And the man pushed him on the shoulder, making him stumble. "Hear me? Delicate flower, aren't you?"

He couldn't have that. His brother had tried that with him more than once, and, if he wouldn't stand it from his brother, he wouldn't stand it from this dirty idiot. He let himself be pushed just once or twice more and then he balled his better fist and struck out. It wasn't a good shot, but it took the other man by surprise. He reeled back, holding his face, and tripped over his feet, landing in the dirt.

"You don't call me names," Frederick said. "You, nor nobody else." And he glared balefully around the group. One or two of them were smiling; others looked at him deadpan.

The sergeant came striding up. By that time, the Dortmund man was on his feet. "What's going on here?" the sergeant demanded.

"He is not working," the prisoner said.

The sergeant stared at Frederick. "Feeling pretty handy with your fists now, are you?" he asked.

"No, sir."

"I saw different. Able to punch a man but not to work. Offense, mate. You'll get a work detail tougher than this, all right?" And he looked at the others. "Don't stand there," he said loudly. "This isn't a music hall. It ain't a show. Rake it up, what you've done," he told them.

He motioned for Frederick to step away from the others. They stood together in the hot sunlight, almost overpowered by the sweet smell of the cut grass. The guard pointed at Frederick's hands. "All right, tell me the story, and make it good."

"Story?"

"Your hands. You took an injury?"

"No, sir."

The guard appraised him. He lost his temper as others had done. "What, then? You can't hold the scythe properly."

"I will do my best."

"I can see that," the older man replied. He thought a moment. "Where did you serve?"

"Serve?"

"Fight."

Frederick wondered where this was leading: if something he said would make the guard angry. "I was with Kriegsfreiwillige. Kinder corps."

"Boy soldiers," the guard said.

"Ah . . . yes. What you call 'children army.'"

"How come?"

"I don't understand."

"Why was it you were in the division, the kinder corps?"

"I volunteer."

"What age?"

"Sixteen."

The guard nodded. "For mud and glory."

"It was said. Yes. For glory."

The older man smiled slowly at him. He took a cigarette out of his jacket and lit it, drawing in the smoke and looking over the field.

"You know what a scythe is, even if you claim you can't hold it," he observed.

"Yes, sir. We have farm at home."

"Like this?"

"Not big like this."

The sergeant nodded. "And what battles was you at, in France?"

Frederick didn't want to name them, but he did. "Houthulst forest. Langemarck. Yser canal."

The man's head suddenly turned sharply towards him. "Ypres."

"Yes, we try to take Ypres." There was a silence. "When the war started, the army move into Ypres. We march in. Ten thousand men. And then we march out again, and. . ."

"*We* marched in."

"Yes."

"Strange, eh? Stupid."

Frederick's eyes narrowed. Was he being asked to agree that the Germans were stupid, or the British? "Yes," he murmured.

"And this . . ." The guard indicated Frederick's hands. "From when?"

"I am captured. From then."

"Someone did it to you?"

"No, sir. They . . ." He knew the exact moment when his hands began to fail him, become objects that seemed hardly attached to him. But he was not going to tell this British man. "I do not know why."

The guard nodded. He tapped the side of his neck. "The hill at Zillebeke. April 1915. Hill sixty. We exploded five mines, and blew the top off the hill. And a piece of metal from the German entrenchment on the top of the hill . . ." He gave a twisted, disarming grin. "I saw a horse go up in the air. A flying horse and flying men. I never forgot that."

The sun beat down on them. High above they could hear the larks soaring up into the sky, just as they had in France.

"Ah well," the guard said, grinding out his cigarette under his heel. "No mines here and no shells. You just try and hold that scythe, all right? Looks like you're not working. Even your mates think so."

"I try, sir."

"My name's Vickers. Like the planes. Like the flying school."

"Sergeant Vickers."

"That's right, mate."

He pointed back to the other prisoners and Frederick went off, digging the nails of his fingers into his palms. "Work," he muttered to himself. "Work."

Chapter 14

They were going north, and into Poperinghe.

Harry had told John that the hospital train was just like the one that he had been transported in when he was injured in 1915. Same atmosphere. Same color, same crowding. It was the sort of train where he had first seen Caitlin, Harry had added, with a mournful tone in his voice.

They'd stood on the platform in the dark, and watched the wounded being loaded. So much cargo, the air thick with the smell of dirt and gas; fetid and bloody. Inside the train, the stench was of antiseptic. Antiseptic and stewed tea. Mingled over it all, smoke and oil and sweat. How many of these trains had gone from here, John wondered sadly. And how many more would there be? He watched the men go by, very young in most cases; shattered beyond belief, some of them.

"This is nothing," Harry had told John, when he saw his face.

"I appreciate that," John replied.

"I doubt that you do."

John tried not to say much; he was on a short leash with Harry, he considered. Added to being his mother's lover, he was now the man who had compromised Harry's ability to move about as he wished. He'd been ordered to accompany John to the Channel ports, as Harry's own squadron was being posted as part of a new coastal operation near Nieuwpoort and Harry was being sent back to Blighty anyway. John respected Harry's frustration with him, and was sorry that they could not, apparently, be real friends. He knew that Harry would have liked to slope home by himself, alone with his depression and cynicism. More than once in the last two days he had seen Harry look at him with something like disgust as John tried to take a happy line with those around him.

He couldn't exactly blame him. For what was he, Gould, anyway? He wasn't a fighting man. He wasn't an expert on anything. He wasn't a veterinarian or economist or tactician or industrialist. He did nothing, really. That was undoubtedly Harry's unspoken opinion. The most he ever was was good company. John looked around himself as they settled in the cramped quarters on the train and smiled grimly.

But Harry was still Octavia's boy.

John looked now at him, and envied his ability to sleep. *Octavia's boy*, he thought to himself. He wondered if he should describe Harry to Octavia: she would want to know the details of her son. But he couldn't think how he could phrase it. *"There's someone else in Harry's place"* might be accurate.

She'd told him often of how it used to be at Rutherford when Harry was growing up. William had been pleased that their first child was male: the heir, a necessity. John tried to imagine William Cavendish as a new father. He would have been well over forty. By all accounts, the earl had been on the brink of being a lifelong bachelor, moldering away with his dogs and damp rooms until Octavia had come into his life. He must have been so proud of his firstborn, and of his new wife, even if he never showed it in any great depth. Where on earth had it gone wrong—how could a man let a woman like Octavia slowly slip away from him?

Octavia always maintained that it was the appeal of her money that had made William Cavendish propose to her, but John wondered at that. The painting on the staircase at Rutherford showed Octavia when she was still not thirty, dark-haired and vivacious-looking, her head dropped slightly and looking out at the painter with a slightly rebellious air. Who could not be attracted to such a face?

William must have loved her. He loved her still. Who could not love a beautiful, intelligent woman like Octavia? Ever since John had first seen her, she had possessed him, and he had never looked at another woman. He never would again. She was perfection. Momentarily, he closed his eyes and thought of her in his arms, like a girl, her parted lips, her soft, smooth skin. In the last three years, William Cavendish had been robbed of what he wanted to keep near him: first Harry had been taken by the war, and then Octavia had been taken by John himself last year. He couldn't help feeling sorry for the man, even if he truly didn't understand him. He didn't understand this English reserve of simply standing by and watching his wife walk away.

That night when John Gould had returned to Rutherford, he had glimpsed an expression first of disbelief and then utter disappointment on William Cavendish's face. Octavia had hesitated at first, struck dumb by John's sudden appearance, but then—in front of the staff, the villagers, the family, no less—she had run to John and flung her arms around him. You could have cut the silence in that room, at the wedding of Mary and David, with a knife. The color had drained from William's face, and he had sat down, staring at John, his mouth set in a rigid line.

"William," Octavia had said, suddenly dropping John from her embrace embarrassedly. "Look who it is."

The room had waited for William's reply. "I see very well who it is," he had murmured.

Poor William. Yes, he could say that. Not to anyone else, of course, for it would sound condescending. The smug opinion of the victor. But he really felt it in his heart. If William Cavendish hadn't responded as he himself would respond—God help him, he would knock down any man that his wife flung her arms around—well then, John had to give him admiration in one respect. William Cavendish had dignity. He had composure. In fact, he had so much dignity and composure that he had dignified and composed himself straight out of his marriage.

John glanced again at Harry. There was no noise now on the railway track; the train had been stalled here for almost an hour. It was now eight in the morning, full daylight. They had been traveling since three a.m. Night manoeuvres of a kind. The train had no windows, no seats as such; as a moving ambulance it had no room to speak of for hitchhikers like themselves. They were in what had once been the guards' van, which was now stacked high with stores. Once on board—sidestepping the stretchers, the nurses, the piles of ammunition at Albert—they had commandeered a tiny corner and stared out at the dark.

"Rum do," Harry had commented. "Traveling with you. Press pass gets you into some strange places."

"You'd rather be with the corps," John replied.

"Sir, you are bloody correct. But when a man is told to do a thing, he does it."

"Accompanying me."

"Accompanying the honored representative of the United States on his Royal progress."

"Is that what your commanding officer suggested to you?"

"It was not a suggestion," Harry replied sulkily, and had crossed his arms, sunk his head on his chest, and slept almost immediately.

He felt sorry for Harry, too. Sorry in more ways than one. All that Harry Cavendish had wanted at the beginning of the war was to fly. John recalled that conversation at Rutherford's dining table, when he himself had been banished from the room while Harry's parents argued about his signing up at all. He remembered the dawning horror on Octavia's face, the tenor of her voice. William, in frustration, calling his son an idiot, and Octavia's pathetic attempt to broker a peace between father and son. "Harry, you don't need to fight in a war," she had said plaintively. "Your father really doesn't mind you flying . . ." And Harry's reply. "Mother, I don't need your permission."

He had told them, while they stared at him aghast, that he was going to Upavon, in Wiltshire, to train. Octavia had immediately suggested that John himself could go with him.

John had known then, of course, what her motive had been in saying that. She couldn't go, and neither could William. But John, as a free agent—merely then a visitor from the States—might find an excuse to wander through England and end up wherever Harry was. He would be her eyes and ears. Harry had remonstrated against the idea at once. "I don't need a nursemaid, for God's sake. I'm nineteen years old, Mother."

My God, John thought now. It was only three years ago. Not even that. Not quite. It was the wonderful summer before war was declared. He and Octavia had become lovers not a month before; the air in that dining room had sung with tension of one kind and another. He could still see Harry's handsome and youthful face, and the idealism and excitement in his expression. Still see the way that his hands had clenched and unclenched in an effort to keep calm and stop himself running out of the room. And he could still see Octavia's pleading smile.

Harry had finally turned on his heel, and, on his way out of the door, had stopped next to Harrison, the footman. He had looked back at his father. "I'm bloody fed up of people opening doors for me," he had exclaimed. "Why should Mr. Gould open a door for me at Upavon? Why should Harrison here open any door?"

John Gould sighed heavily. Harrison had been killed in 1915 at a place called Cinque Rue nears Aubers Ridge. On the ninth of May, there had been eleven thousand casualties among the British; many fell within a few yards of their trench, because the artillery bombardment had left the enemy largely unscathed. Brave men, and Harrison among them. He survived hours of shellfire out in no-man's-land, and was picked up conscious, talking about going home to Rutherford. By the time that they got him back to his own trench, however, Harrison had been dead.

As Harry slept on, John got up and edged his way slowly down the train, stepping aside frequently for the nurses who bustled back and forth. Now and again he stopped by a bed, looking down at eyes looking beseechingly back at him. "What can I do for you?" he asked more than once.

He got out his notepad and pen and squatted down beside them. He could feel the temperature inside the train starting to rise, and the sweat began to trickle down his back. "I'm listening," he kept saying. He took down addresses, and names. "To Eva Marshall . . ." "To Adelaide Blake . . ." "To my dearest father . . ." "Dear Mother . . ." John didn't know if he would be allowed to send these messages, and he certainly wouldn't send them for print. But he kept on listening and writing.

"I've come through all right," one boy told him, watching John write. "Tell her I . . . tell her . . ." He had gripped John's wrist. "Tell her . . ." John had looked about him for a drink of water, a cool cloth. Anything. "I got a boy I never seen," the lad said. "We was eighteen when we were wed. I've got a boy . . ."

"That's a fine thing to look forward to," John murmured. The lad's face was unaccountably livid, bright as a poppy, and his eyes tinged a jaundiced yellow. The fingertips on his own wrist pressed yellow, too: yellow knuckles and lilac-colored nails. "I've got a boy . . ."

John stood up after a while and closed the notebook. The lad had given him no address; instead, he took the number and name scrawled on the rail of the bunk. Private Anderson, King's Own Rifles. John looked away, out of the window. There were busy sidings out there, and beyond it a marshaling yard. Coming into Poperinghe. He wondered if Private Anderson's wife would ever know exactly where and how her husband died. Just outside Poperinghe, at eight o'clock in the morning, talking about his son.

John walked to the end of the carriage, and then saw Harry at the other end of it, signaling to him that he was about to descend the steps, and get off.

John nodded, and followed him.

*H*e had not known quite what to expect of a town so close to the German front line in West Flanders, and to the coast, but it existed as if it were nowhere near a war. Unless, of course, you stopped to look about you, and realized that nine out of every ten people who passed you were in uniform.

The town was positively heaving. They stopped at the town hall, a miraculously new building, built only six years before, and sparkling white in the sunshine. It appeared to have given up its civic status entirely, however: the flags outside it showed it to be a divisional HQ. Harry wrinkled his nose. "Too many brass hats," he said to John. "Sitting it out in comfort while the young go by. I bet they come out on the steps and wave. Bastards."

John said nothing. Harry glanced at him. "How many do you suppose are here?"

"What, you mean the armies, the men?"

"Yes. How many?"

"I don't know. It looked like we passed a lot of billets and camps on the way in."

"Quarter of a million," Harry said. "All to be fed and watered. Imagine the logistics of it. You ought to write about that."

"I have," John replied. "One of the first articles five weeks ago, about the quartermaster's stores in Albert."

"Hmm," Harry mumbled. He inclined his head towards the town hall again. "Know what else is there?" he asked. "Execution cells. Have you written about those?"

"Military execution cells?"

"Too rich for your readers' blood, I should think. Guess you won't chance it. We had a man a year ago. Stories like these go through the place like wildfire. Been wounded. Was on his way back. Fight broke out in The Doll. Bloody idiot took out his pistol and shot someone. Local. Over the price of a bottle of champagne."

"Good God! What happened to him?"

"Detained over there for a week. Medical assessment. Men with him said he was do-lally. Pretty shocked, you know. Had come down in his Strutter, the one with the backward-facing Lewis gun. Prized asset. His gunner bought it, the man fired through the propeller—you can, if you want, with a Strutter—and got himself in a complete fug. Plane came down much like my own, next to British lines. But they said that ever since he came back he was, you know, not right in the head." He paused, staring across the square. "Just an argument about a bottle of champagne."

"Did they execute him?"

"They did. Will you write about it?"

"Perhaps one day."

"Not now?"

"Bad for morale. As you say, the average reader wouldn't stomach it. They want reassurance and glory. Nobility. Strength of purpose."

"Not to hear of their bright knights breaking down."

"No. Not that."

Harry's eyes narrowed. He leaned forward a little. "But you will, one day? You'll say how it was? What happened here. What they all did. Heroes and madmen the same?"

"I will, Harry. Yes."

"No banging of jingoistic drums?"

"No, Harry. Just how it was. I give you my word."

Harry had been leaning against a wall; now he pushed himself away from it and sighed, straightening up. "Want to visit Petit Paris?" he asked abruptly. "They told me it's on the other side of the town. MPs and the provost marshall turn a blind eye to that." He smiled sardonically. "Not to gambling, though. It's much worse to have a flutter on the dice than take advantage of some poor bloody girl whose misfortune it is to be a refugee." He looked John up and down. "You in need of a girl?"

"No, no."

Harry smiled. "Me neither. Let's have a drink, though. Coffee and a glass of wine. Too early for wine?"

John thought of the lad on the train and the grip of the yellow-tinged fingers. "No," he said. "Not too early."

They passed café after café: places where French and Algerian and British and Sikh flocked together. John heard New Zealand voices; saw the unmistakable features of Maori faces among the crowds. New Zealand. Australian. Indian. Chinese. And soon the Americans would come. Very soon indeed. He wondered if the German army could resist it all; he doubted that it would. Privately, he estimated that the war might be over by this Christmas. Christmas 1917. He imagined Poperinghe cleared of its troops, vehicles, mixed races, the rattle and drone of trains and aircraft.

They passed Cyril's, Skindles, and the Savoy restaurant. Harry smiled at him. "Not quite the Savoy we know," he commented. There were fish and chips on the menu, written exactly like that. No "frites." No "poisson." Fish and chips and beer. Scrambled egg and tea. Now and again they would glimpse somewhere that was trying to be more homely, with cloths and bunches of flowers on the tables. *The irrepressibility of the human spirit*, John thought.

"Here it is," Harry said. "Right where I was told it would be. La Poupée. The Doll."

They entered a pretty little place, under an OFFICERS ONLY signboard hung over the doorway. There was a small garden at the rear, under a glass canopy. Harry pulled out a chair, seated himself, and propped his leg on the seat opposite.

"Hurting much?" John asked.

Harry waved the question away. A girl came out to serve them. They watched her wipe down the table, smile at them, take their order, and disappear back into the recesses of the kitchen.

"Red hair," Harry murmured. "Like Caitlin." He drummed his fingers on the table.

"Harry," John said. "I shall be back in England in a week or so, like you. I expect they'll operate again pretty quick on that leg, so you'll be out of it for a while. Would you like me to try to find her?"

"You'd do that?"

"It'll be my pleasure."

"She ought to be with the same setup. However . . ." Harry paused while their coffee was brought to them. "I don't know, truly. I don't know why she's cut herself off from me. I think she must be suffering."

"I shall look for her, Harry. While you're in hospital." He paused, looking at the young man in front of him. "You *will* be in England in hospital, Harry?"

"I might," Harry agreed vaguely. John frowned. Wasn't it understood that Harry would cross the Channel very soon, as he was about to do? "Harry," he said. "You are coming back to England, aren't you?"

"I have my orders," Harry replied.

John knew that counted for nothing very much. Octavia had confided in him that she feared Harry didn't listen very much even to his commanding officers. He was still the devil-may-care boy deep in his heart. He would do a thing—including taking up an aircraft—if he felt it had to be done. "You aren't thinking of flying at Nieuwpoort?" he asked.

It looked as if he had hit a nerve. "I'd be a fool to do that," Harry murmured, holding his gaze. "Wouldn't I?"

"New area. Very tempting. Just to reconnoiter?"

Harry at last gave him a grim smile. "What does 'Operation Hush' mean to you?"

"Nothing. Why?"

Harry raised his eyebrows once, then glanced away. The girl was bringing their wine. "Doesn't matter," he said. The carafe was placed in front of him, with two glasses. Harry lifted the carafe, sniffed at it, and called the girl back. "Do you have Burgundy?"

"We have a vintage, m'sieur. It is expensive."

"Bring it, please. And take this away." She did as she was told. Harry closed his eyes.

John leaned forward, pulling his chair close to Harry's so that there was no chance they would be overheard. "Is this operation what I've been sent here for?" he asked.

"If they haven't told you, it isn't my job to."

"Come on, Harry."

Harry opened his eyes. "I suppose you'll learn in twenty-four hours," he said. "We'll be in Nieuwpoort by then."

"I know that the area round there was flooded. Belgium opened the sluice gates, didn't they? The sea flooded in over the polder. Germans thought it was natural—some sort of tide coming in, some sort of spring flood or something. They fought till the water came up to their knees, then retreated."

Harry nodded. "That's it."

"And this is . . . We're pushing forward from Nieuwpoort," John guessed. "Into Belgium."

Harry smiled. "You didn't hear it from me."

"That'll need a lot more men up here," John mused. "Where are they coming from? Farther south?" He knew that, in February, the Germans had suddenly retreated back to what they called the Hindenburg line, giving up miles of the Western front that had cost so many lives. They had dug in there, built up huge defenses. But it released a lot of land and therefore, possibly, regiments that could be moved elsewhere for a while.

The Burgundy was brought to them. They filled their glasses, watched the girl go again. Outside, the sun was still streaming, the birds in the little garden gently singing. It was so hard it believe that they were discussing more bloodshed.

"We must be going all the way to the sea," John considered, thinking aloud in little more than a whisper. "That'll mean the navy involved."

Harry said nothing. It was evident that he felt he had said more than enough. He was staring out into the garden; his glass was already almost empty. "Mr. Gould," he murmured. "What does my Mother expect of me?"

"In what way?"

Harry shifted, and looked up at him. Weariness was written all over him. "Does she expect me to go back to Rutherford?"

"I should think so. Isn't that what the only son and heir does, inherit?"

"Of course I inherit," Harry retorted. "Whether I want to or not."

"And you don't want to?" This was news to John, and no doubt would be to his parents.

Harry stared into space. "It isn't that I don't want to look after the place, or see that it is cared for," he murmured. "But after this, I'd like to see something of the world. Like yourself."

"And take Caitlin with you?"

"If I could."

John paused. "Have you asked her?"

"No. How does one ask such a thing in a war like this?"

John topped up Harry's glass and his own. They gave each other a brief salute. "Your health, Harry."

Harry shifted his leg, and bent down to rub at it, massaging his calf muscle with a wince of pain. "They've told me that there's to be a training camp for American pilots," he said. "It was mentioned that I might like to go there."

"Oh? Where is it?"

"Texas. Somewhere called Camp Taliaferro."

John gave a low whistle. "Yes, I heard of that too, in London some time back. Pretty darn far." He immediately thought how grateful Octavia would be that Harry was out of France, even if her son had to cross the Atlantic. And then he thought how much Harry could heal there and feel free. He smiled broadly.

"Good place, is it?" Harry asked.

"Different. Big open landscape. Plenty of room. Different to London. Different to Yorkshire as can be. I imagine that flying there would be pretty exciting. In a good way."

"No clever fucking Hun on my tail," Harry agreed. "Is Texas desert?"

"In parts."

Harry nodded slowly. "I'd like to go somewhere where the sun burned down to my bones. Breathe empty clean air. A wide, wide country."

"But what about home? England?"

"Oh, I suppose I would come back eventually. It's what I've been defending these last three years."

"But not to Rutherford?"

"If Caitlin were with me, it would depend on what she wanted."

"And you don't think she'd like to be chatelaine of Rutherford?"

"Did my mother?" Harry asked.

"Well, gosh . . ." John paused to consider. "If circumstances had been different."

"You mean, if she'd been loved." John didn't answer; he thought it was not his place. Harry tapped the table. "I don't want to fence her in," he said. "Rutherford is a giant responsibility." He paused. "I want peace."

"Everyone wants peace," John observed. "Rutherford is the place to get it."

"Peace without worries. Without duty."

"You mean that Rutherford would be a worry, perhaps a confine to Caitlin?"

"Maybe. I don't know, Mr. Gould. All I do know is that I want Caitlin more than I want Rutherford." He slammed his glass back down on the table. "I wish to hell I knew what had happened to her. The last thing she wrote to me was that she was on a hospital ship."

"Which ship?"

"She didn't say. But an RMC officer told me that his brother was on *HS Salta*, and saw a red-haired nurse there called Kate. It's a straw in the wind. I know that. I thought she might be compulsorily rested, you know? But then, I wondered if . . . experienced nurses are gold dust . . . she wouldn't walk away." He put his hands to his face, pressed them there, and then let them fall into his lap. "I can't think where she is. It won't leave my head."

"Did Charlotte find out anything?"

"She hasn't said. I've only had a note or two from her. The last one was from her husband, saying she'd broken her wrist. A fall, he said."

"So perhaps she hasn't been at the hospital."

"All the same," Harry replied savagely. "You'd think she'd make an effort for me."

John could see his frustration boiling, however much Harry tried to disguise it. "I shall find Caitlin," John said, adding it to other promises that he made that morning and intended to keep. He looked up through the glass cover of the little terrace and thought of the sun streaming through the glass roof of Rutherford's orangery. "Rutherford's a wonderful place," he said finally. "You really think you might not take it on? You are the son."

"I am the son," Harry murmured. And then he laughed shortly. "But you know we have a habit of running away. Me, my mother, Louisa. I hear Louisa's back now, but for how long? And there's someone else to consider. My daughter, Sessy."

John regarded him: saw the light of affection light up Harry's face. "Sweet child," he murmured.

"And what's the future for her if I take Rutherford on?" Harry said. "It always used to smother me somewhat, you know. What if we never have another child? What if she's like Charlotte, fretting at its confines? Sessy will be twenty-one in 1936. Do I give her Rutherford then, or in 1940 when she's twenty-five? How will she get income, how will she run it? The world's falling apart. You can hardly get servants now, or staff. Who wants to come back from a war like this and take orders?"

"Seems to me that you're getting a bit ahead of yourself there, Harry."

"Am I?" Harry demanded. "I've had a while to think about it, especially when I was having my bloody leg operations one after the other. The world's changed. Do you know how many staff we had in the year I was born? Thirty! We had four undergardeners for a start." He started ticking the names off on his fingers. "We had an underbutler as well as Mr. Bradfield. Housemaids, laundry maids, kitchen maids, scullery maids. I hear from Father that Miss Dodd and Mrs. Carlisle are struggling to run the show by themselves now, though. Do you know why? Because people want more. They want independence."

"Rutherford can afford its staff because of the mills. That's where the income will come from."

"Mills," Harry said. "You suppose England will always corner the cotton and wool-weaving market? Maybe somewhere else in the world will do it cheaper. Maybe other empires. Think about it. We get our raw materials from our empire. But what if there's no empire? What then? What happens to the mills?"

"Whoa," John remonstrated. "That's going too far."

"Really?" Harry asked. "England's a very small country, Mr. Gould. Very small." He stopped, and glanced back towards the inner rooms of the café, where they could hear Indian voices now. "By contrast, India's very big. Australia's very big. Vast places, like America. We're an old order here in our little island. Old orders fall and decompose. And I'll tell you something else. We're here and fighting this hell because of empires. Borders. Territorialism. It's all such . . . bunkum. Such petty bunkum."

John sat back in his chair, looking at him in astonishment. "You've thought it through all right," he said.

"I want to be part of the new, not the old," Harry replied.

"And abandon Rutherford."

Harry gave a great sigh, and ran a hand through his hair. "Oh, who the hell knows," he muttered. "I don't, actually. I just feel it's all coming crashing down. The only thing I know for sure is that I must find Caitlin. I must see her, talk to her. She's the only good thing to come out of this whole war for me."

"And get her to marry you."

Harry said nothing. But he raised his glass, and then, in one swallow, drained it.

Chapter 15

*I*t was a beautiful bright morning in London.

Octavia was standing at her bedroom window, looking out at what could be glimpsed of the Thames through the trees on the Embankment. The garden was in full bloom: swathes of white and cream roses framed the gate to the road, and sunlight barred the patch of lawn. The herringbone path reminded Octavia of Rutherford's around their own rose terrace. How miniature Cheyne Walk was to Rutherford, Octavia thought. A small paradise.

When she and John had first fled to London, they had taken a suite in Claridge's. Every day she had expected to wake to find that his remarkable appearance had been a dream: that she would be back at Rutherford trying to make the best of the rest of her life without him. They had both been afraid to sleep for exactly the same reason: that, among the finery of their room, they were each nothing more than ghosts of the other's imagination. A strange concept, but it was the unreality of it all. To find that he was back, literally, from the dead. That he had wandered, alone, for so long, disoriented and racked with guilt from his experience. "So many died around me," he had told her in those first few days.

They had laid together and talked right through the night. She had kept kissing his hands when he talked of having been frozen with cold; wept when he said he had been half blinded by oil in the water. His image of having been dragged down in the ocean, and seeing the bulk of the *Lusitania* pass within inches of him—of him actually having put out his hand and felt the brush of the hull against his palm—had shocked her to the core. He had been so close to dying. So close. "We looked for you," she whispered, again and again. "Even William sent a man to Ireland to look for you."

John had listened with head bowed. "Did he?" he had murmured. "That was very good of him. Much more than I deserve."

She supposed that she had never lost the thrill of those first days alone, shut away from the world. The feeling was still the same now. John erased every unhappiness, every moment of loneliness. She was almost drunk in his company; drunk with the very thought of him, like a child grown besotted with too many good things. She wanted to leap and dance. To run out in the street and shout. To take hold of the nearest unsuspecting passerby and shake them and say, "He is here. Isn't it a miracle? Isn't it impossibly good?" She would look in the mirror and see that she was endlessly smiling, and could not stop. And she thought—my God, how many times she had thought—*so this is what real happiness is like. This is what it's like to be loved, to feel wild with joy. And to have that sensation returned.*

They were each other's new worlds.

She thought again of this now, and whispered a fervent, brief prayer that he would once more be returned to her unharmed from France. Still, the fact that Louisa had come back with her to London had partly eased the agony of waiting. It had given her a small pang of guilt to take Louisa away from Sessy and William, but she considered that Louisa needed London, just for a while. It had been a wrench nevertheless to leave little Sessy, so appealing in her little canvas pinafore with her starched ringlets escaping their curls; Octavia saw how much Louisa looked back to catch a last sight of her niece.

It made her think that it was time Louisa had a family of her own. Octavia adored Sessy—she was such an image of Harry—but she looked forward to a time when Louisa would be a mother herself. There was such affection in her daughter, and nowhere to lavish it but on her brother's child, and on her father. William too looked a lonely figure as they had departed. Octavia had patted his arm. "I shall send her back to you very soon," she promised. "And Mrs. Nicholson will be here shortly. I've introduced her to you all. Louisa likes her. And I take it you approve?"

William had shrugged eloquently. "Not my business, hiring staff. She seems a nice woman, however."

Mrs. Nicholson was indeed a pleasant surprise. Octavia supposed that, in the back of her mind, she had half expected some sort of sluttish harpy—it was hard to remove Elizabeth Kent's sadly despairing face from her memory—but Mrs. Nicholson had turned out to be small, fair and neat, and rather well-educated. Hardly the image of a farmer's wife, nor of a potential mistress to some self-deluding husband. Softly spoken, she had arrived at her interview with Octavia ahead of time. She had not curtseyed nor fawned in any way, but met Octavia's eye with utter calm. *She'll do*, Octavia had decided, almost at once.

Octavia had smiled at William again on the day of departure, pulling on her gloves, and glancing down Rutherford's long driveway. "I've asked for the building plans for the old carding shop to be copied to me in London," she said. "When you've cast an eye on them . . ."

"I shall tell you my opinion. I shall go over there myself and talk to Ferrow, and look at the site."

They smiled briefly at one another as Octavia got into the motor cab, and Louisa followed. William had held his head up, his spine straight, his face then stripped of expression. Impassive. He had turned and gone back into the house before the car had pulled away.

*B*ehind her now, Amelie was taking up her nightclothes from the bed. "It is a sunshine at last, madame."

"It is, Amelie. I think that the girls and I will walk to Tower Bridge today. It will do us good."

"Mrs. Preston is coming to see you, madame?"

"Yes, to see us both." Octavia smiled and out of sheer pleasure clapped her hands together like a girl. "My goodness. We were last all together at Christmas. At least Charlotte's broken wrist has got her out of the hospital drudgery."

"She came here while you were away, madame."

Octavia gave a start of surprise. "She did? I didn't know that. You mean she called here unannounced? Did she say what for?"

"No, madame. I am sorry. I am thinking that perhaps you knew this?"

"No, I didn't know at all. She didn't write to say so." Octavia frowned. "How odd. Did she say anything? There was no note left, was there?"

"No, madame. I am called down to speak to her. She is with her friend . . . I don't know the name. . . ."

"A woman friend?"

"Yes, Madame. Christa . . ."

"Christine Nesbitt, the artist?"

Amelie's face lit up with humor. "Yes indeed, madame. She is dressed like an artist."

"And they said nothing at all, simply visited and went away again?"

"That is so, madame."

Octavia sat staring down at the things on her dressing table. It was rather odd that Charlotte had not written or telephoned to say so. But Christine would have been helping Charlotte, no doubt. Taking her out of her listless mood. And there would certainly be no one better than Christine to do that. Although . . . Octavia sighed. Christine was a little fast; a little outré. Charming for a while, but not a constant companion. Not for a married woman of Charlotte's class.

"Oh well," she murmured. "She is getting about, at least. And we shall have such a nice walk today. We shall go to Simpson's-in-the-Strand for luncheon. Lord Cavendish and I always went to Simpson's at one time. It will be interesting to see how much has changed."

"Very traditional, madame." Amelie nodded approvingly. She was a very old-fashioned girl in some respects; Octavia thought that the developments of the last year or so—her own personal developments, that is—were not really to Amelie's taste. Still, as Octavia's personal maid, it was not her place to say. Octavia watched Amelie bustle around for another moment or two. "Is Miss Louisa up, do you know?"

"Since some time, madame."

"Really?" Octavia was surprised. It had never been Louisa's habit to rise early when at Rutherford. Of course, that was when she was still very young, Octavia supposed. Still in the time before Charles de Montfort. Still in the rose-colored heyday of balls and flirtations. A great deal had altered since then.

"I'll go down," Octavia murmured.

The housemaid Milly was just in the act of closing the French doors to the garden when Octavia entered the dining room. "Good morning, ma'am. Miss Louisa has gone out to the summerhouse. . . ."

"Leave the doors then, Milly. Let the fresh air in. I'll join her. Bring out our tea, would you?"

"Yes m'm. I'll bring fresh. That one has been made a while." The girl left the room, china teapot in hand.

Octavia glanced at the table. The morning mail had been delivered. She sorted through it, and gave a gasp. Harry's handwriting. She tore it open at once.

My dearest Mother,

I am instructed by an extraordinarily irritating fellow called John Gould here to inform you that we are on our way to port. He has a painful habit of smiling twenty-four hours a day. How on earth do you stomach it?

We are stopped en route in a place that I am not permitted to mention; and we have, of course, been in a place that I am again not permitted to mention. Except to say that it was rather hot there and—shall we say—sky-high. This letter shall be handed in at the next station. I hope it finds you.

I have instructions to come to England to repair this leg once more. Don't concern yourself that it is serious as I certainly find it more of a nuisance than anything else. But more so than the blasted leg I am concerned over Caitlin, Mother. I have had no news from yourself or Charlotte; I wonder if you have found anything out? It seems very strange that she should go to ground unless she were very ill. I feel sure she would not do you the disservice of ignoring you should you contact her. Would you have any news for me? I will probably be back before the week is out.

Mr. Gould has been a decent companion. He instructs me to send the regards that he was not able to make in person to you on

account of my commandeering the only piece of writing paper on
the Western front.

    Would you please inform Father of my intended return?

Harry

She smiled, and walked out into the garden, holding the letter in
her hand. She couldn't wait for Harry to be home. Part of her felt a
childish selfishness and greed to get her boy on the next boat; there
was a little voice in her mind, *don't keep him from me.* But he wasn't
her possession. He was a man in the service of her country. Nevertheless in her deepest heart she didn't believe it. He was still her son,
her child. He belonged with her. She thought of his small hands
resisting hers when he was a little boy, and there was something of
that feeling in this apprehension now. Fighting to protect him, when
nothing she could do would alter his will. She knew that her worry
for him was threatening to overcome her, and she wondered at it.
Wondered why now, just as he was coming back, that she should feel
this so strongly. This shattering frustration.

    They'll both be back this week, she told herself firmly. *You'll have*
them here in England, both of them, Harry and John. Just a few days.
Be thankful. Don't be ridiculous. Don't be weak. She closed her eyes,
and there in the warmth of the sun she pressed the letter to her
mouth. "Please Lord," she murmured.

    When she opened her eyes again, she saw that Louisa was sitting
at the far end of the garden in the summerhouse; she was in profile
and staring rather vacantly into space. Octavia walked down to her.

    "Hello, darling."

    Her daughter gave a jolt, as if she had not heard her coming. "Oh,
hello, Mother."

    "A wonderful day."

"Yes." Louisa shuffled a little on the bench seat, tucking her skirt underneath her. "There's room for two."

"Thank you." Octavia sat down. She held up the letter. "Look. From Harry. He's coming home."

Louisa took it. She read it carefully—very slowly, in fact. At last, she put it down, and smiled. "What a relief."

Octavia looked closely at her daughter. "What is it?" she asked. "Surely you've not been crying."

"No, not at all." Louisa brushed her face. "But I ought to cry over this. Perhaps we both should. Tears of relief." She smiled. "What does he mean, 'sky high'?"

"There was something in the paper, wasn't there, a day or two ago? A great triumph at Messines."

"Oh, that."

"Ten thousand men killed in ten seconds," Octavia murmured sadly. "By countless tons of bombs put into tunnels underneath the German line. Perhaps Harry heard it. They say it was the largest explosion ever heard on earth. Harry must have felt it. Or even seen it." Involuntarily, she shuddered.

"Yes, I suppose so," Louisa replied. "I don't know. It seems a cowardly thing to me."

"We can't call it cowardice, darling. The Germans do the same. It's battle."

"It's hardly British."

"I don't know if the army can afford to have fair play. War isn't a cricket match."

Louisa put her hand briefly to her face. "No, it isn't. How bloody and how ghastly."

Octavia heard the breaking note in her daughter's voice, but could say nothing to her for a moment, as Milly arrived with the fresh tea. Assuming an air of calm, Octavia poured her daughter and herself a cup. Then she sat back and surveyed Louisa's face. "You might as well tell me," she said.

"What do you mean?" Louisa asked, still not meeting her mother's eye.

"Darling, you ought to know something," Octavia began. "Someone has written to me about you. About letters received at Rutherford."

"Letters?" Louisa said. "What letters?"

Octavia stirred her tea, and gave Louisa a lingering, appraising smile. "The conversation really won't be helped by your trying to lie to me," she observed mildly.

"Lying!" Louisa exclaimed. At last, she turned and looked at her mother. "I haven't lied to you. What a thing to say!"

"I think you were about to," Octavia commented evenly. "So we might as well be perfectly honest with one another. Has Jack Armitage been writing to you from France?"

Louisa opened her mouth to object, but evidently changed her mind when she saw her mother's face. "There's no harm in Jack writing to me, surely," she murmured. A slow flush of color spread over her face. "I can't think who would tell you such a thing," she added. "As if it is anyone's business."

"I don't know myself," Octavia replied. "The message wasn't signed. But it was evidently from someone who thought the correspondence improper. Or more accurately, your keeping it secret."

"That's unfair."

"It *is* rather unfair, I grant you," Octavia said. "And impertinent. I don't like it, darling, especially as I suspect it must be one of the staff."

"Then it's doubly not their business."

Octavia drank her tea, and replaced her cup slowly on the table in front of them. "You must understand," she said, "that the idea of propriety isn't peculiar to our class. It matters just as much to the servants and tradesmen. They see the dangers in familiarity just as much as we do."

Louisa looked back up. "Do we?"

"Do we what?"

"See the dangers of . . . familiarity," Louisa said. "In an innocent friendship."

"Is that what it is?"

"Yes."

"I see. Then may I see his letters to you?"

Louisa looked shocked. "I don't see that letters I write or letters I receive are anyone's business but mine."

"Since you're my daughter, I don't share your perceptions, and neither does your father."

"You've discussed this with Father?" Louisa gasped.

"Of course I have. We're your parents, darling. We do care what is happening with you."

Louisa appeared lost for words. Her color was still high with embarrassment and irritation. "I've done nothing wrong," she insisted. And she stole a glance at her mother from under her lashes. "If that's what you're thinking. And Jack has done nothing wrong."

Octavia tried a different tack. "Where is he?"

"Oh . . ." She sighed. "Like Harry. Unable to say. And . . ." She stopped, her sadness getting the better of her. "He is having such a terrible time. So terrible."

"Have you received a letter this morning?"

"What makes you think that?"

Octavia sighed. "One doesn't cry over nothing at all."

Louisa's mouth pressed into a firm line.

Octavia shook her head. "It's simply that I want the best for you," she said. "After Charles de Montfort . . ."

"Oh, I know what you must think," Louisa burst out. "That I don't have any sense."

"I don't think that at all," Octavia told her. "I think de Montfort made you see the world as it really can be, and I also think that you've conducted yourself very well since. I know you've always been fond of Jack, but if there's gossip about Rutherford, it must have some sort of foundation. Why is it that your father has never seen these letters come to the house?"

"I really don't know."

"Come, Louisa."

"Oh, all right. They come to Jack's father. And Josiah delivers them to me."

"Good heavens!" Octavia exclaimed. "How grossly unfair of you to put Mr. Armitage in such a position. How difficult for him." She paused, trying to work it out. "I wouldn't be surprised if it were Mrs. Armitage who has sent me the message. She'd be awfully uncomfortable. If the letters are as innocent as you say, why doesn't Jack address them to you in the normal way, to the house itself?"

Louisa put her hands to her face. "Because we knew exactly how it would seem. We knew it would cause some sort of needless and ridiculous comment just like this."

"But you've made it so much worse by hiding it," Octavia said, exasperated. "My dear, do think of your position and his."

Louisa's hands dropped. "Position?" she echoed. Now the flush on her face was different: from anger rather than embarrassment. "Well, I like that."

"Louisa!"

"Well I do, Mother. Here you are living with a man who isn't my father and you lecture me on impropriety."

"I am not lecturing you," Octavia retorted. "I am advising you."

"Oh, rather sound advice. But not your example. A case of 'do as I say and not as I do'?"

"You will apologize to me for that, Louisa."

"I will not," Louisa snapped. The tone of her daughter's voice shocked Octavia as never before. "You have chosen to live in a scandalous way. Don't think people in London don't talk about it, because they do. And in Rutherford, too. I was in Richmond the other week, and I heard two women speak your name as I passed them in the street. I looked back at them and they were quite audaciously looking back at me. In a not very nice way at all."

Octavia's heart was beating fast. "I'm sorry if it has caused you embarrassment," she said.

"I am not embarrassed," Louisa said. "I have a very fine mother, and I challenge anyone to say otherwise. I love you very much and I admire you for your bravery. And, incidentally, I think Mr. Gould is rather nice. But you are quite the topic, the pair of you. And my father's heart seems to have been broken. I can't pretend otherwise."

Octavia and Louisa sat looking at one another, caught in an impasse: two women each in the same predicament. Octavia suddenly saw in Louisa's eyes all that she herself felt about John: the same determination to grasp at happiness. She willed herself to be calm. "I really am thinking only of your future well-being," she murmured. "The family is weathering scandal that would make us social pariahs if it weren't for this war. We must emerge intact. It doesn't matter about me, but you girls must make lasting and sensible marriages. Your father and I have made a great many mistakes. Please don't repeat them in your own life."

Louisa was very still, her hands folded in her lap. The height of color was draining away; she seemed composed now. "Mother," she said quietly. "Will you choose a husband for me, arrange a marriage?"

"Certainly not."

"You admit that I have some choice in the matter?"

"Well of course, darling. But . . ."

Louisa held up her hand. "That's all I needed to know," she said. "Thank you."

They were interrupted suddenly by Milly standing at the French doors to the house. "Lady Cavendish, a visitor for you." She dipped a faint curtsey and stepped back.

Charlotte was standing in the room behind her, wreathed in smiles. As Octavia got to her feet, she had a moment to think that her youngest daughter looked better. The greyness that Octavia had noticed in her face since the wedding had vanished, together with that unnerving look of listless apathy. She stepped forward, and, smiling, took Charlotte in her arms.

They walked along the Embankment together.

As the girls walked ahead of her, Octavia reflected on her daughters: how unlike each other they were. Louisa was still so fair and rounded, and Charlotte dark-haired, thin, and spare. William had used to call Charlotte "his little Indian," and, when she was out of earshot, "the dumpling." Louisa had always been his favorite—his "flower," his "rose." More than once Octavia had admonished him over his frequent inadvertent revelations that Louisa was his favorite. As for her, she had no favorite. Each girl had her own appeal.

The two of them paused now and leaned on the Embankment wall and looked down at the river.

The Thames was a streaming landscape of boats; farther downstream the water was packed almost side to side with cargoes and lighters. Ferries, dredgers, pleasure boats, steamers, and even small sailboats plied their way along one of the busiest waterways in the world.

Since the war had begun there were many naval vessels, and alongside some of the bridges were the earthworks and stone platforms for searchlights. If one walked Regent Street or Mayfair the war was a world away, but here it was very close at hand. Octavia looked back at Victoria Bridge and wondered too at the amount of traffic that passed over it. They said that soon the bridge would come down and all its gothic ironmongery taken away. She hoped the new bridge would retain a little romance, though. It was on it that John Gould had first told her of the house he had bought for them, as they stood looking down the river towards the lights of Westminster.

She glanced again at her daughters. Charlotte was in the act of saying something to Louisa, something that had made her sister turn to her, putting one arm around Charlotte's waist, and gazing at her in an attitude of horrified astonishment. Charlotte's face was serious; she shook her head from side to side several times. And then, in an impromptu gesture that surprised Octavia, Louisa threw both her arms around Charlotte's neck.

She walked quickly up to them, having to pause to sidestep several bustling pedestrians. "What is it?" she asked.

"Oh, Mumma," Louisa breathed.

It was a word that Octavia hadn't heard in years. It had always been "Mumma" when they were tiny. The softly lisped baby word had been replaced by "Mama" as they grew up, and, more lately still, by "Mother."

Octavia looked from Louisa to Charlotte. "What is it?" she repeated.

Charlotte glanced from left to right. "Shall we sit somewhere?"

They ended up in Ranelagh Gardens. Octavia felt as if she were being propelled like an invalid across the road, with a daughter on each arm. She was at a loss to know what had prompted such a move; Louisa seemed agitated, but Charlotte—who at first she had thought had imparted some terrible piece of news to her sister—looked relaxed, even happy.

They sat down in the shade of a tree on a municipal bench. Walkers went by them towards the hospital grounds, or paused to take in the view of the river. Here and there small boys ran, squawking like untidy birds, chasing dogs and each other across the grass.

"Do tell me," Octavia said. And, with a jolt, she realized. She looked at Charlotte with an enormous smile. "You're expecting a child," she said.

"I am not expecting a child," Charlotte said quickly, patting her arm. "I doubt that I ever shall." She was sitting side on to her mother, with Louisa at the far end of the bench. Octavia noticed that Louisa was unconsciously, and quietly, wringing her hands.

"What, then?"

"I have left Michael."

There was a moment of silence. "Left him?" Octavia echoed, baffled. "To come out today, you mean?"

"No, Mother. I have left the house. I have left my husband. For good. Forever. And . . . if it matters to you . . . I am very happy."

"But you can't have done," Octavia exclaimed. If she sounded ridiculous, she thought, it was because the very idea *was* ridiculous. Charlotte had been married for less than three months.

"I'm sorry," Charlotte said, evidently taking pity on her mother's astonishment, and suddenly holding her hand. "But I shan't go back to him."

"It is an argument," Octavia decided. "A disagreement. All married people disagree."

"It isn't a disagreement."

"The first year of marriage is difficult," Octavia insisted. "There have to be adjustments to one another. . . ."

"It's not a matter of adjustment."

Octavia closed her eyes temporarily, and took a deep breath. When she opened them she saw the determination in Charlotte's face. "You've been ill and feeling low," she said. "No doubt sitting at home finding fault." She smiled encouragingly.

Charlotte glanced at Louisa, and back again at her mother. "It isn't a case of finding fault with Michael," she said slowly. "Michael has found fault with me. He's tried to correct that fault. But if fault it is, it can't be corrected. I've fallen in love with someone else."

Octavia burst out laughing. "What nonsense!"

"It isn't nonsense."

"But for shame, darling! You can't love anyone else. You have just got married. You *wanted* to be married."

"Actually," Charlotte murmured, looking down now at their hands, and then gently disengaging hers, "I didn't want to marry at all. I was afraid of it. I was trying to make myself . . . as I thought you'd want me to be. But I'm not. And that's all there is to it."

Octavia stared in disbelief. One of the ragged boys wheeled across the grass close to them, pointing his fingers in their direction and miming gunfire. "Go away, you little brute," Louisa told him.

"Lady lady, la-de-da!" he yelled, pulling a face. He made one more gesture at shooting the three of them, and continued his mad gallop.

"Charlotte," Octavia said. "You must go home. I don't know who this other man is, and I don't wish to know. Your duty is to Michael. He needs you, and you are his wife."

"I shan't go home again." Octavia heard the old Charlotte in her daughter's voice: the truculent, obstinate child. "I've come to tell you what has happened, not to be told that I am wrong."

"But of course you are wrong," Octavia exclaimed. "Nothing could be more wrong!"

"Mumma," Louisa breathed. "Don't."

Octavia stared from one daughter to the other. "Don't?" she asked, amazed. *"Don't?"*

*S*he always wondered, afterwards, where exactly the conversation would have gone if there had been time to pursue it. She might have found out a great deal more, even if the revelation of it was something she could never understand.

But there was no time.

There was suddenly the most enormous and strange sensation. It was as if the city had somehow imploded; a crushing silence that seemed interminable, but lasted a fraction of a second, and then a ground-shaking thud. All three of them felt the air press on their eardrums, and then release. They looked instinctively towards the sound, or lack of it. There was a distant roar, and then another. A series of repeated thunderous impacts, as if giants were patrolling the city and slamming their feet into the ground with each step.

They saw smoke rising then—a fast upward-circling stream—out of central London. Again came the crushing, plunging sense of impact. Octavia could feel the shuddering repeated in her chest like an echo chamber. Her heart seemed to repeat the sound, hitching and staggering for a moment. Everyone around them had stopped what they were doing: everyone looked towards the smoke.

"What is it?" Louisa whispered. There had been an explosion in a munitions factory at Silvertown earlier in the year, and Octavia had heard something distant at the time, some vast rocking disturbance; but this was different. It was much closer, for one thing.

She gasped as they heard a line of explosions stitched in a line from Liverpool Street eastwards. Then, and only then, they heard the aircraft above them. The crowd in the Gardens began to run towards the river. And, for what reason they couldn't explain,

Octavia and the girls ran too, crossing the grass, running through the gates. Traffic on the Embankment had slowed. A horse-drawn cart was slewed across the road, with the driver climbing down from his seat and rushing forward, trying to catch the reins that had been pulled out of his hands by the frightened horse.

All at once, Octavia thought of their own Rutherford horses that had been taken from them. She thought of Wenceslas, imagined him in some miry battle, petrified. She thought of Jack Armitage who, in another place, had probably tried to calm many horses like this. She thought of Harrison, and John. And she thought of Harry.

"Oh please," she whispered, unaware that she was saying anything at all out loud.

They looked up towards Tower Bridge and saw six ungainly shapes in the sky: Gotha bombers, with their seventy-foot wingspan. "They've come down in height," Charlotte said. "They want to see what they've done."

Or what they're about to do, Octavia thought.

The crowd watched in strained silence, the women clutching their children. All traffic had now stopped; everyone looked towards the bridge in the distance. Farther out, they heard more explosions, still heavy but more distant drumbeats. "That's not in the city," Louisa said.

"It's going east," Charlotte answered. "Poplar . . . Rotherhithe . . ."

The six Gothas were rapidly going out of sight, but the rumble of their engines shook the road. They seemed to be flying slowly, almost in a leisurely fashion. Taunting the city underneath them.

Octavia wondered if they were following the river or railway lines. What was farther east from here? She tried to think. St. Paul's, Fleet Street. The Wren churches. St. Clement Danes, founded eleven centuries before. The art collections of the Tate; the Tower of London. A fierce patriotism overwhelmed her. They could not be touched. Not destroyed. Not these precious things. The heart of England.

"The docks," Louisa breathed. "That's where they're going. They'll bomb the docks."

The Port of London and the West India docks were certainly in the direction that the Gothas took, but after a while they heard nothing more, only the faintest drumming of the engines, until that too was eclipsed.

It was as if the whole of London was standing still, holding its breath.

Chapter 16

There was a village called Vlamertinghe to the west of Ypres.
Jack Armitage was standing ready. A railway line here
among the dozens of scattered camps, and beside the muddy ruin of
a road. Strange how roads kept coming back to him, their even sur-
faces and the hedges at the side of the banks beside the church. Roads
within dreams, roads that seemed like extraordinary other worlds.

It was impossible to think that roads ran quietly somewhere on
earth. Vlamertinghe had been a quiet place once. Now a thousand
men walked back to the front, and a thousand walked away from it.
Jack waited by the side of the line with the travois, waiting to get
onto the single-gauge railway track, and he watched them go by.
Those that came from Ypres sang, some of them. Those that were
going to Ypres looked at them stony-faced.

There was a veterinary station at Vlamertinghe, as well as the
dressing stations and hospitals. His officer had been taken to one
such hospital three days ago; a hut with bleached sheets for walls.

The road to Messines was still shelled by a long-range gun. Like a grim circus it provided explosions that hurt no one—no one, that is, until one landed among the men and horses. Trying to crowd out of the makeshift lines, untying the hysterical geldings he had only just attended to, Jack had elbowed his officer by mistake in the smoke. "Get on," he had said, bumping the man behind the knees so that he stumbled. He hadn't seen that it was his CO until then. The man grabbed his arm. "I'm blinded," he said.

So he was. So he was. They took him up to the dressing station and then on to the bleached white walls and Jack had stood outside. A piece of the shell had almost taken the top from the officer's head. They struggled with him, but it was all for nothing. An Eton man and Oxford man, he had volunteered when he was nineteen, had no brothers, had no sisters. A brilliant only child. Jack had liked him. He had replaced his CO from near Arras, who had been taken away to Paris for some high secret position.

Jack didn't care much for secrets, nor for the thought of Paris, nor for Eton or Oxford. But he had liked his officer very much. He had a sense of humor. He was liberal with the whisky that most officers kept for themselves. And so when the nurse had come out and had shaken her head, Jack had felt exhaustion wash over him. "He's for Vlamertinghe, I'm afraid," she said.

As it turned out, she had been wrong. The vast cemetery in the village was being closed to make way for another railway line big enough to carry heavier trains, and to make sidings. Instead, his officer's body was taken up the line to Brandhoek. Only yesterday, Jack had learned that the man had been mentioned in dispatches. For bravery under fire. For men. For horses. For England. For taking the troop through the blood of Messines and bringing back German horses that had survived the explosions. Bloodied and wild-eyed beasts solid with shock.

As he waited, Jack thought he might sing a little song. It was ridiculous, perhaps a kind of madness; but he had to do something. Something to disengage his mind, to step outside what he was doing, what he had seen. His officer's face or half a face; the hemlock growing at the side of the road. Sing a little song. That was the ticket. His mind wandered, as loose as the wind that shuffled the dust. Loose and grey. Like fog or shadows. Or was it hemlock? Perhaps it was fool's parsley. It grew here like it grew at home. You had to know what it was, it was so like ordinary cow parsley. It could burn the throat. The flowers were irregular. You had to know that. If you didn't know that, you were poisoned. Perhaps they were all poisoned and that was what the trouble was. Blinded, poisoned, and all by some horrible sort of accident. He would sing a little song.

But he couldn't remember any.

"What's the matter with you?" asked a voice.

He looked up. There was a sergeant standing at his side. "They don't load themselves, you know."

Jack saw the wounded being handed down. Some were going in the open truck that was being pulled by a broken-down Clydesdale. Another was on his way to Jack, holding up his thumb, the universal symbol of going home. "All right, mate?"

Yes, all right.

"My knee," the man said. He huffed as he was put into the travois. A contraption made by force of circumstance to accommodate the many: two poles slotted into a pair of wheels that fitted the track, and a mule hitched up to the poles. "Going to bounce me all the way there?" the man asked, grinning. He laid his head down. "Fucking bounce me then, mate. I don't care. Just get me out, all right?"

"All right. Are you Australian?"

"Aussie, yeah." He raised his head now that they were walking, snail's pace, along the single gauge line. "What's the story with your bloody generals? Bloody officers? Fuckers don't know what they're doing." And head down and asleep within seconds.

No more they don't, Jack thought. He's right about that.

Take me back to dear old Blighty. Put me on a train to London town. That was a song, he thought. He was sure it was. It had just come into his head. Unless he had written it because of the trains and the road. But he didn't write songs. He would sing a little song.

No songs. Just the rail.

He could see the Clydesdale up ahead. The horse wasn't long for this world, he guessed. One day soon it would lie down. He'd seen it happen. They laid down, and they didn't get up. It wasn't a wound, unless it was the kind of wound that doesn't leave a mark. It was deeper than flesh. It was just weariness with being alive. Something went out, flickered, and was gone. The horse would lie down. They would haul on the reins. Kick it perhaps. But it would be immobile. They sank to their knees, buckled over like wet clay. And they went away, went out like a light, went back to their fields and lanes and the warm seclusion of some stable on some farm. High in the hills perhaps. Or down by the sea. Lungs full of salty air instead of the brackish remains of chlorine.

They just went out, you see? Like songs.

He would sing something.

But you had them in your head, and then they were gone.

It isn't the girl I saw you with at Brighton.

That was one. About a girl in Brighton.

Who, who, who's your lady friend?

He had been brought close to a line where it was thought there'd be no action. The Germans had withdrawn behind a new front line. They named the pieces of it after Wagner, the opera man. So his officer had told him. Siegfried and Wotan. The Wotan part of this line—the Hindenburg Line, the captain said—ran from the coast to

Cambrai. The Siegfried part ran from Cambrai to St. Quentin. And so on. The fighting still remained, though. The shelling still went on. One night, they had been near a line of trenches and the grass was growing fast there. What had been a quagmire in the winter and spring now looked innocuous. Weeds and rats. White bones. Pieces of rusted equipment. They still had trenches, though.

At night, at dusk, the men would get up and walk about. There was never much shelling at dusk just there. They stood and watched the evening performances over Bullecourt. Rumbling guns, and hundreds of Very lights shooting skywards, mixing with flares of white and green and red. The lines of color wriggled about in the sky and lit up the ground underneath.

And then as they were dragging shelters and making temporary operating theaters for mules—half a dozen or more; and a kind of water tunnel for the ones that had mange—one of the companies were told that they had to go out and capture an enemy outpost at a crossroads. It was causing trouble to the passage of supplies. From somewhere behind at the appointed hour, British 18-pounder guns suddenly started up. It was all over then for the makeshift theater; they dismantled it, cursing all the while. A stream of shells passed over their heads while they worked.

Jack glanced up now. The line of travois and trucks had come to a halt. Across the track and half a churned-up field, now dry and rutted with dust and stones, there was a barbed-wire camp. It was full of Germans. In the sunshine they stood and looked out at the humble little line of wounded. They hung on the wire, some of them. He remembered his latest officer telling him that he had been haunted by one corpse that he had seen where the war was hot, out east of Ypres. A man on his back, two hands gripping a strand of barbed wire, and the hands awfully grey. Gripping the wire for all he was worth. Which wasn't much. Not anymore.

The German prisoners said something. Waved and said something in the sunshine, laughing. They were scratching and holding out their jackets. Alive with lice. Like everyone.

He would sing a little song.

What would we want with eggs and ham?

When we've got plum and apple jam. . . .

"You!" someone shouted. "You!"

He wouldn't look. There were 18-pounder guns, and a man hanging on the wire.

His arms were grabbed from both sides. He woke up then, focused on the hands, looked down at his feet. He'd dropped the rein of the mule that he was supposed to be leading, and he was standing at the side of the track and the mule and the travois were going on without him. A captain from the Staffordshires was staring at him while his soldiers held him upright. "What day is it?" the captain asked.

He would sing a little song.

If he could remember any songs.

If the road got smooth and the grass grew higher.

It grew high in the fields just around June.

*W*hen he came to, it was nearly dark.

There was a padre sitting next to his wire bed. Jack gave a great start; he had been dreaming about dropping the reins of the mule. He sat up immediately. He could see the paleness of the road beyond the door, and the endless passing to and fro of men.

My God, I'm dead, he thought. Padre sitting at my side; men passing along a white road in the summer dusk. Hundreds and hundreds of weary men.

"Private Armitage. Good evening." The padre held out his hand. "Carlyon."

Jack took the proffered hand gently, expecting it to be merely air. But the man was real. He looked all over his surroundings and decided he was still alive. In some place he couldn't recognize.

The padre picked up on his confusion. "You're in number ten clearing station at Poperinghe. You've been unconscious for ten hours."

"Clearing station," Jack repeated. He felt dull, confused. "But I'm not wounded."

"Battle fatigue."

Jack struggled then to get to his feet. Battle fatigue was something not right; it was for slackers, those who couldn't cope. "I'm all right."

"Lie still. It's an order."

He did as he was told, fuming with resentment.

"It is a real condition," the padre told him. "The body shuts down."

Jack thought then of the Clydesdale that he had considered was dying on its feet. He had looked at the horse and pitied it without knowing it was him, not the horse, that was about to crumple into the road. Still, he felt ashamed. "I can stand," he said.

"Let's see if you can."

Jack averted his eyes from those around him. They lay silent, row upon row. They ought to bring those that can't breathe nearer the door like me, he thought. The padre offered his arm. He shook his head to refuse it, then felt the ground swimming up towards him. The padre tightened his grip, and the two of them staggered into the field beyond. After only a few steps, Jack came to a halt. He tried to keep himself still, though he felt himself swaying like a tree in a storm. "Bugger me," he muttered.

The padre brought out a packet of small cigars. "Do you?"

"No, sir."

"A man who doesn't smoke. A rarity."

"Never liked it, sir."

The padre smiled, lit his own. "Alcohol and tobacco keep many a man standing," he observed.

"I shan't start it even so, sir."

"Congregationalist, are you? Teetotal? Methodist?"

"Church of England."

"And from where?"

Ah, that he couldn't say. He tried to, but the name of the village and of Rutherford stopped in his throat and choked him.

The padre looked away again, affecting not to notice. "I come from the inner city myself," he said. "Birmingham. New Street." He went on talking about his parish. Slums and poverty and kindheartedness. It was what kept the average man going, he said. Not God but kindheartedness. Decency, that sort of thing. Not bravery so much. He wondered if anyone were truly brave.

"I don't know if I care so much about men as I care about horses," Jack admitted. "They never let you down."

"Indeed they don't," the padre acknowledged. "But they have what some would call human instincts, wouldn't you say? To be afraid, and so on?"

"Being afraid isn't humanity," Jack replied. "Not what I'd rightly call humanity. Tis just reaction. Can't help it. Neither can men. But to slog on. That's a human trait, maybe."

"Yes . . ."

"Endurance, like."

"Yes indeed . . . and faith. Faith in their owners." He paused. The sky above them was a subtle duck-egg blue streaked with lazy streamers of high clouds. It was lovely. "And have you a faith?" the padre asked.

"Not no more," Jack said. It took a lot to admit it. He was not sure that he ought to, and especially not to a man of the cloth. But it came out anyway. He felt it so much, so deeply. The conviction of it. "I always went to church, every Sunday."

"Do you think you might again?"

"I don't know, sir. After what you see here. What we do."

"But God's love remains the same, whatever is done."

Jack shook his head. The sensation of swaying and rocking was subsiding a little. "There's no love here. And no humanity either."

They walked on a little way, arm in arm. Jack became embarrassed at this and asked to sit down. They slumped together on a stone platform. It was some time before Jack realized what it was. He looked behind them at the tented camp, and from side to side.

"Looking for something?"

"A gate. A farm."

"I'm afraid if there was a farm, it has long gone," the padre said. "But there is what remains of a chateau along the road. Pretty blasted, but standing."

"They will have had farms."

"Will they? Yes, I suppose so."

"Cattle. Dairy farm."

"What makes you say that?"

Jack patted the long oblong stone. "Tis for the milk," he said. "Churns on the side of the road, stood here for the carts to take to dairy." He gazed upwards, into the distance. "Must have been a dairy around here, too. Be a house with cool floors. Next a railway track. Milk for Paris, maybe."

"How interesting," the padre murmured. "I can tell you are of country stock."

"Yes," Jack murmured. "Country."

"I expect you believe in that."

"How do you mean, believe?"

"You believe in that life. A country life. The turn of the seasons. The dependency of it. That the year comes around. Harvest, and such like."

"That I do."

"Then there's your belief, your faith."

"Hard not to believe in what's before your eyes."

"And in your blood, your upbringing."

"Aye."

The padre smiled. It was getting much darker now. The evening light was almost gone. "Are you hungry?"

"I am, I think." It hadn't occurred to him until that moment, and then his stomach growled. He couldn't think when he had last eaten. Yesterday? Or two days? He had had maconochie—pork and beans, he thought. Filthy horrible pork and beans, the one dish he disliked. And milk biscuit pudding. He had no idea what was in that. Raisins or biscuits that had been boiled down to a pulp.

There had been cooks just behind the lines, and one of them a poor squawking boy with a high-pitched voice who was scared to death. He would have regular hysterics. He'd seen the boy being slapped. Slapped, tripped up. Facedown in the dirt, with a ladle in his hand. He would throw himself down whenever he heard a shell come too close. The opinion was that he would get used to it, and be like the rest of them, laboring on trying not to flinch, trying not to listen, trying not to watch.

"Let me get you something."

"I can't have you do that, sir."

"I'm getting some for myself," the padre said. "When I come back, you can tell me more about the place you come from."

Jack watched him go. He considered getting up and hiding himself. He couldn't be seen here being waited on by an officer. Droves of men still passed, and they would see. Although he watched a few lads passing now, and he saw something strange in their faces. They glanced at him, and then looked away. A few of them gave him a pitying smile.

What was the matter with them? he wondered. He was all right.
Just the jittering. Just the swaying. He was all right.

*P*adre Carlyon went to his own mess.

As he went in at the door of the shell-spattered
outhouse—for this was what his mess was now—he flung down his
hat. "I say, Portman," he asked the nearest man. "What's the supper?"

"Stew, sir."

"Bully beef stew?"

"No, sir. Braised beef and potatoes."

"Pudding?"

"Peaches."

Carlyon smiled. "Peaches, eh," he murmured. "What a feast."

"We found a tree in the garden, sir."

"Did you? That's excellent. Bring me two portions of both, there's
a good fellow."

"*Two* portions?"

"That's right. Two portions."

The orderly hurried out. In the ruin of a garden behind, the cook
was producing miracles on a single stove pitched among the bricks and
weeds. The steam and smoke drifted in at the door. There was a young
officer fast asleep on the floor, wrapped in his greatcoat. Poor show,
some would say. But Carlyon had no such presumption; he guessed at
what the man had been through. He moved quietly back to the
entrance and leaned against the doorpost and stared at the landscape.

He'd been talking to the wounded at the clearing station all day.
They blurred into one seamless scene in his mind. Hands that reached
for cigarettes. Silences that masked the agony of the wound. The only
one he recalled clearly was the man coming in from the St. Julien
road, an officer of the Worcesters. He'd asked Carlyon if he could

reach under the stretcher and move the gas helmet wedged underneath him. Carlyon had been horrified—and it wasn't easy to horrify him anymore—to find that the gas helmet had been pushed into the man's spine by a molten piece of shrapnel. The two were sealed together in the shattered back.

"I can't remove it just now," he had told the man kindly. "Ah," the officer had replied. "Thank you, at any rate." His voice was a solid, monotonous line. As discreetly as he could, Carlyon had given him a blessing, and the man smiled at him, knowing what it might mean. A small pained smile, a whisper of gratitude.

Soon after someone else had come in, another man whom the officer had known since their early days of training, it seemed. Carlyon had stood at the end of the stretcher while they clasped hands. It had been hard to tell what was life and what was death; perhaps the grip on the hands had slackened. In any case, in less than a minute, the friend laid the hand on the blanket, and closed the officer's eyes with a gentle brush of his fingers. Standing up, he had caught Carlyon's eye. "Known him some time," he whispered. And Carlyon saw something else in that face that he himself knew only too well. Love deeper than words. Perhaps a love that could never have been spoken about at all at any time. The other man went out: Carlyon watched him wander about for a moment or two, as if disoriented. Then he disappeared into the foot traffic of the road.

As Jack sat looking out into the growing dusk and the interminable movement on the road—slow and staggering, he thought—he narrowed his eyes to focus, and Louisa came into his line of sight. A pale glimpse of her weaving between the trucks, the men. She seemed very careless of the place, smiling as she always did.

He straightened up, leaned forward. "No," he murmured.

Her hair was loose down her back, tied with a spare bit of ribbon. She reached up and brushed it back. Her hands moved lightly. She was so white in the gloom. So white.

The last time that he had seen her, he asked her if she intended to cut her hair. She had looked up at him. "What would you say if I did?"

"Nay, it's not my business."

She'd touched his face. "I'm your business, Jack."

He had stroked the fine, fair strands away from her face. "And you're mine."

It had been last summer. The last time that he had had leave. She was at Rutherford, and he had come home. The first night he had spent with his parents in Grooms Cottage. His mother had kept looking at him as if he might dissolve in front of her; as if she wanted to grab hold of him and not let him go, or to try and feel that he was real. She had sat for quite a while just holding his hand in hers and turning it over repeatedly as his father spoke. It had been as if she'd been trying to convince herself that he was still real flesh and blood.

"Are you hurt at all?" she'd asked him, when his father had got up to go into the garden to smoke.

"No, Ma. I'm very well."

She'd gazed at him. "You're different somehow."

Aye, well. They were all different. He'd heard some men say that they would never be able to look at living people the same way again, never be able to just take them the way they were, clothed and fit and clean—not without seeing the other figures. Those that were dirty and cold. Those left out in the otherworld of no-man's-land where they rotted. Or cried. Or simply drifted away, leaving sagging uniforms where bodies had been.

One man had told him that he'd never be able to look at his wife's body again, or those of his children. He was afraid that when he got home he would have to turn aside from the thing that he used to love and look forward to: bathing the littlest ones and wrapping them in a towel by the fire, and telling them stories while they smelled so sweet and fresh.

The scent of pure innocence. The men longed for it, hungered for it, but doubted they'd be able to stomach it. Not without the memory intruding of the smell of muddy weeks, of the stink of other men, and the indescribable stench of the dead.

"You know what?" the man had said. Just an anonymous soldier whose troop had stopped near the horses, and who had come over to pat the head of the horse that Jack was holding. "I'm afraid to go home at all."

"You'll feel different when you get there," Jack said.

"I couldn't lay a hand on my wife," the man told him. "I keep thinking of it. I'm mired in all this muck. I look at my hands and think, I can't touch her ever again. I can't put my hand on her at all."

"It'll be different," Jack had told him.

But he thought afterwards that it was just something to say. Something reassuring. He knew what the man meant. You didn't want to take it back home. You didn't want to infect them with this suffering; you didn't want to open your mouth and tell them what you'd heard. You didn't want to look at them for fear your eyes would communicate the horrors.

And so when his mother had stroked his hand and asked him if he was hurt, he had said, "No, Ma. I'm very well."

Ah, he watched Louisa now come picking her way across the dust.

Pretty girl, but she was more than that. She was sweet to the bottom of her soul.

The second day that he was home, he had told his parents that he was going for a walk.

"We've told your aunt Annie we'll be along for tea," his mother had said.

"I'll be back in time," he answered.

And he'd gone out across the yard, and through the gate. The same gate where he and Louisa had led Wenceslas two years before, to put him on the transport for Remount in Wiltshire. The guilt he had felt at it came rushing back to him as he put his hand on the latch, and the five-bar wooden gate swung back. He remembered how Louisa had helped him then, put the lightest touch on his arm and, later, her hand on the small of his back as they stood side by side to see the transport go.

God gave you things to do. That's what everyone said. "God doesn't give you more than you can carry." But it wasn't true. Every day he saw men carrying more than they could bear, walking into the ground, grinding to their knees. This padre who wanted to talk to him also wanted him to believe there was something good left in the world. But it wasn't here, if it existed at all.

There was one thing that he kept trying to lay aside. If it was a burden that God had given him, he wished that same God would take it back. Because he didn't want it anymore. In the name of all that was clean in the world, he didn't want it.

They'd been close to Zillebeke. It was only two weeks ago. It was this same part of the line that the officers kept telling them had been abandoned, but by Christ the Germans didn't let it go easily. What they had left behind they had booby-trapped, and what was left after that, they shelled. Especially wherever they thought they might have left stores or ammunition.

The corps had been asked to try to clear up. Troops were tired and decimated, too long without real rest. Some got careless. They were the ones that decided the Hun had left them alone. They went down into old Boche trenches, and they forgot. Forgot the war was still in those deep and efficient-looking lanes under the ground. Electric light, some of them had. Pumps that took away water. Stoves still warm to the touch.

"Help us with a burial party," Jack and the other troops had been told as soon as they got there. He had wanted to say no. But of course you couldn't say no. It was your duty, even if you had only ever enlisted to see to the mules and horses.

The Yser Canal was close by. There was a bridge too, but as soon as he got close to it, the smell made his stomach heave. The earth looked like a dark green swamp, a horrible pool in which they could see the bodies of both men and horses, and shafts of wagons and gun wheels. The towpath had formed part of the front line and had once been a tidy row of dugouts. Jerry had found the line since then, however. The shells had penetrated one such dugout where half a dozen British Tommies had been sheltering.

It was necessary to go down into the hole, feeling their way down a ladder covered with the slime that had once been living men. They brought out what they could, and, at the bottom, they found a man who had evidently been sitting with his gun across his knees when the shell had struck. The gun had speared him through the chest as neatly as a spike. His face had been only mildly surprised.

It was that, Jack thought, that had got inside his head somehow. It had unlocked something, unwound all the tightly rolled balls of memory. The things that he wanted very much to forget. He had thought that he had overcome them. He had thought that he had succeeded: that they were gone.

But after the man at the bottom of the ladder of the dugout, the images came back. Back like the wildly hurtling horses at Monchy,

flinging themselves in front of him, throwing themselves into his
path.

*L*ouisa was closer. He had an idea that he must get up and
warn her.

Don't come here, don't come here.

He never wanted her to see what measures men took against each
other. He wanted her to stay where she was, safe and gentle in the
arms of a place that had never hurt her.

He rubbed his eyes, feeling the way that his hands flagged and
waved and felt as if they rippled, like the way wind touches water
and makes it move. It was very odd. Mystifying. He frowned, and
put them back into his lap, watching them because they were quite
different to the hands he knew. They looked so different: pale, flaccid,
colorless.

That second day last summer, he had walked through the fields
and down to the river, and crossed the bridge where the water was
shallow and the stones underneath it glowed. Sandstone and iron
and granite in the stones. Bright pools. When he got across the
bridge, he had begun to run. Behind him was all other life: ahead of
him, the only life that mattered. He ran up the path between the
trees, through the woodland where the sun streamed through the
high branches.

He came out where the woodland met the moor, and an old drystone wall ringed Rutherford's outer boundary. It was probably two
hundred years old, overgrown in places, tended in others. He saw how
the lack of groundsmen at the house had resulted in the land looking
wilder, as if it wanted to run away from the attention of men and was
going back to how it used to be before Rutherford was ever built.

After another mile, he came to the cottage.

It was their place. Two more summers had made the roof bow further, the neglected garden more like a woodland itself with just a few blazing colors of wild perennials dotted in the grass. The door, bleached by endless seasons, had been open.

He stepped across the threshold and she got up to meet him.

Two years before, he had barely kissed her. Only sat with her, glad to do so, glad that she was here at all. Glad to listen to her, and glad to be silent. Now they held each other for a very long time.

"Jack," she had said. "Don't let's talk about now. Let's talk about how it will be."

Oh, they made up such a nice story together.

It was all about having their own place, a place like this, out in the country somewhere. And it would have fields, and it would have horses. They would get another horse like Wenceslas. More than one. They would have a smallholding. He told her that he wouldn't have her washing and cleaning like other women. She must live as she was used to, he said. They would have a maid, a cook. She had begun to laugh. "And how would we afford that?"

They'd let it go. Details weren't important in their fantasy. They would have a big featherbed. They would have a wood floor. They would have a kitchen range and a fire. It would roar in winter, warming the house, warming them. He could see exactly how she would look sitting in front of that fire, or by the bedroom window where the clematis curled on the sill.

My God, it was a lovely picture.

And they never trespassed over it; never tried to make the future into the present. They would wait, they agreed. They would wait for it to happen.

If he told any man here that, they would probably ridicule him. "There's no lead in tha' pencil, lad. There's nowt for her." He smiled to himself. One day he'd have Louisa for his wife. He kept telling himself that.

It was just a story, a made-up fairy tale.

But it was all he wanted to believe.

*S*he had stopped walking.

She was looking at him, and raised her arm, and beckoned.

Jack got up, putting one foot in front of the other as best he could. Louisa was going towards the railway line, looking back over her shoulder to make sure that he was with her. He tried to hurry, but it was not much good. The ground pitched and rolled as if he were on the deck of a ship.

She got to the place where the horses were standing in line, waiting. Patient statues all in a row. In front of them, a small open-trucked train was shunting carefully. It was empty, going back for more. In front of the horses was another row: men, this time. Not so bad, some of them.

One was hitched onto his elbow, calling out for the RMC officer. He was laughing about something. Happy to be going. Almost giddily hysterical with it. Got a Blighty one. Never mind the blood congealed on his face, the uniform peeled back on his shoulder over a grimy bandage.

He noticed Jack coming towards him. "Hey, mate," he shouted. "Look where you put your feet."

Jack tried. He stared down, just avoiding others stacked around him. He could see, just in the corner of his vision, the pale edge of Louisa's dress as she moved between the men.

"Don't go on," he muttered. "'Tis too much."

He came to a stop. Looked up at the horses.

Poor bloody beasts. Poor bloody boys.

He looked for Louisa and saw her standing at the farthest end, her back to him. She was in front of the last horse. He got closer to her—it felt, incredibly, as if he must be swimming. Like he used to swim as a boy with Master Harry, in the river. Catching dragonflies. Feeling little fish wriggle between their fingers. Going out into the murkier depths where the river curled away from the house.

Louisa looked back at him, and then stepped aside.

It was then that he knew that it was all a dream. He would wake up, and he would find that there was no Louisa, no river, no line of men, no horses. He would wake up and find himself in the clearing station with the kindly padre looking down at him, holding out his supper.

But for now, it was beautiful. It was all he had wanted from the moment that he set foot in France. He went up to the great grey Shire, and he examined it carefully all over, running his hands along its back and down its flanks. It had been hurt more than once; he could feel the pitted scarring, the shrinking of the flesh. The ribs protruded: the horse was slowly starving. As he touched it, a terrible shuddering began. And it seemed that once it had started, it could not stop. "There now, lad," he muttered. "Don't tek' on, there now, there now." It turned down its head and looked at him: the brown eyes still full of their old docility.

"Hello, old friend," he said.

And he put his face into Wenceslas's neck, and held on tightly, feeling the warm breath of the horse on his own skin.

Chapter 17

They said that it was going to start to rain in August, but it was hard to believe it. Jenny stood on the steps outside the dining room of Rutherford; the French doors were open and it was mid-morning. Heat baked up from the herringbone brick path; the trees of the woodland across the river, a half mile away, seemed to float in a glorious haze.

If she looked down past the terrace she could see the parkland and the edge of the beech drive, now a vast slumbering landscape of green and gold. If you stepped just outside, as she had done a half hour ago to clean the glass, you were engulfed in the scents of the roses. Just by the doors here, the hydrangeas were almost past their best, their pinks becoming cloudy, their leaves red.

But it was not the view that Jenny favored at the moment. She liked to go to the little writing room that belonged to Lady Cavendish, just beyond here, tucked into the end of the corridor and opposite Lord Cavendish's study. From here, Mary had told her, Lady Octavia would sit sometimes through the morning, answering her letters, with the door open so that she might see the green baize door that led to the stairs.

"She liked to keep an eye on things once," Mary said. "Not just us—though she was always properly fair and nice. But the children, too. Miss Dodd told me that when Master Harry was smaller, her ladyship would let him run about in the Tudor hall. They were forever cleaning the marks from the paneling. Playing soldiers, you know? Strange to think of it after all that's happened—him being in the war and everything."

Lady Octavia's room was, of course, shut now. The maids polished the little French desk with its beautiful inlay, and they shook the rugs and dusted the ornaments. Meissen, they were. Delicate and pale shepherdesses and shepherds that had once belonged to Lord William's mother. The staff had decided now that Lady Octavia must have only tolerated them; she had not taken them with her, and the house in London—so they had heard Miss Louisa say—was very modern. All the painters that her ladyship liked, the French ones, had been bought for the house in Chelsea. Cubists, Miss Louisa had said. There was apparently a large blue and red painting by a man called Picasso on Lady Octavia's bedroom wall.

"Foreigners," Mary had sniffed. Still, Jenny made the room her special project, even if her ladyship was unlikely to come back to it. And Mrs. Nicholson had found her there later that morning, staring out of the window.

"Something to see?" the new housekeeper had asked.

Jenny had almost jumped out of her skin. "No, nothing, Mrs. Nicholson."

The woman had walked over to Jenny's side and looked out. "Just the garden wall over towards the greenhouses," she observed. "The cottages beyond. The stable yard. The meadows down to the river."

Jenny felt herself blushing.

"Are they finished?" Mrs. Nicholson asked.

"Is what finished, ma'am?"

Mrs. Nicholson had smiled. "Not 'what,' Jenny," she said. "A 'who.'"

Jenny didn't quite know yet if she ought to respond when Mrs. Nicholson smiled. She still remembered how Mrs. Jocelyn had used to respond to a smile—a pause, and then the amiability would drop from her face, and she would inevitably shout. But Mrs. Nicholson was a softly spoken woman with a keen eye. An accent that Jenny couldn't quite catch: not gentrified but then again not a working-woman. No trace of Yorkshire or Durham. They had been told that she came from the borders of both counties, but she had an even, slow way of speaking. And always the humorous glint in her eye that so unnerved the staff.

"Jenny," she said now. "Have you taken a shine to one of the prisoners' guards?"

"No, ma'am." She felt a guilty prickle of sweat break out on her back.

"They seem very young."

"Yes, ma'am. They are."

Mrs. Nicholson put her head on one side. "How long since you were in London, Jenny?" she asked.

"Oh . . . almost three years, ma'am."

"No family there?"

"No, ma'am."

"You wouldn't like to be down there with her ladyship? If so, I can perhaps arrange it."

Jenny stared at her. "If I've given offense I'm very sorry. . . ."

Mrs. Nicholson astonished her by laying a hand on her arm. "Don't jump like a startled deer, Jenny," she said. "I'm very pleased with you. You and Mary both. I simply want you to be happy. I was wondering if staring out of the window indicated that you weren't."

"Oh, no, ma'am." And Jenny felt herself blushing even deeper. She folded her hands in front of her and stared at her feet. "I'm sorry."

"Go along, then. You may help the hall boy take the baskets out to the field for lunch." She smiled and turned away, needlessly rearranging the books on the desk. "That is, if you *must* catch a last glimpse of someone. Mr. March has told me that the fields are all done. They will be taking the hay to the tithe barn later."

*J*enny ran out into the hall, opened the green baize door, and waited until it had closed behind her. There in the cooler shadows of the stone stairs that led to the quarters below she stopped, her heart beating fast.

Dear God, I am useless, she thought. She put her hands to her face. She'd never been able to hide her feelings. She looked down at herself, at the fingers reddened by work. At the nails bitten to the quick. It was all right for Mary and Miss Dodd, she thought. Mary took no nonsense, and resisted help; Miss Dodd seemed to know what to do instinctively. But she . . . she always had to be pointed in the right direction. She couldn't help her nervousness; she'd tried often to hide it. Mary thought she was funny. "What're you worried about?" she had chided her more than once. "Time enough to get worried if someone bawls you out. What's the point of worrying before then? Stand up straight and stop faffing about."

Faffing about. It was one of Mary's favorite phrases. She loathed anyone who *faffed* like Jenny did. She tut-tutted to herself if Jenny clattered a plate or dropped a duster. "What *is* the matter with you?" she'd demand. *Like a startled deer,* Mrs. Nicholson had said just now.

But if only they knew.

When she'd first come here, she'd already been anxious. Anxious and hesitant: thin, tall. "Not a scrap of meat on you," Mrs. Carlisle had said at the very first breakfast table. She had promptly buttered a piece of bread as thick as a doorstep. "Get that down you, and fatten yourself up. You'll need your strength."

But Jenny never had fattened up. She was just as thin now as she had been on the first day, despite eating everything that Mrs. Carlisle foisted on her. She never would be a well-rounded girl. She'd looked at herself in the piece of speckled glass that passed for a mirror in her and Mary's room, and she knew that she would always have those jutting bones, the pale skin, the pale hair that she knotted into the tightest of plaits. Next to little feisty Mary, she was like a lamppost, she knew. She would never be attractive.

A man in London had told her that. She had had a job given her by the church, to take the pennies that ended in the collection plate to the post office. Just the copper: the farthings and halfpennies. The postmaster would kindly change them into shillings, and then Jenny had to take them back to the church, where the minister put them into a locked box that he kept in his room.

The postmaster had a boy who worked for him, a lad as tall as Jenny. But not thin at all. He was bulky, and always looked her over like a butcher assessing a carcass, wondering how to take his knife to it. He frightened her, and she'd avoid his eye; but one day he had caught her as she hurried up the lane, and he had bundled her into a side alley and pressed her against the wall. She'd prayed that someone would come, but no one did. He had pawed her while she wriggled in panic, and then he had laughed. "You're nothing but a bag of bones," he'd muttered. She had pushed him away, and he'd let her go, and called after her, "No bloke with any sense would want you." She'd run, hot with shame, to the church, the bag of silver clutched in her hand, slamming the door behind her, gasping for breath.

Harrison had been something like the boy from the post office. Groping and patronizing; unreadable, surly. She had never been able to figure him out; neither him, nor his letters from France. When they had told her that he was killed, she had felt nothing but confusion. She'd gone up to her room that night and tried to cry, but no tears had come. She'd thought again, then, that she must be a strange person. Unloving, and unlovable.

And then . . . and then. Her hands sprang again to her face.

Now, a man that no woman should notice had noticed *her*.

"Oh Lord," she whispered to herself. "What am I going to do?"

She and Albert took the food out to the fields.

Mrs. Carlisle had packed it into two wooden boxes. The boxes were lined with hay, and Mr. Armitage had packed it in tightly, muttering to himself all the while. "Fresh hay wasted on bloody Germans," he'd told her, while she waited alongside with the tureens of stew balanced on a nearby mounting block. "And what's she made stew for on a day like this?"

"It's just what's left over," Jenny had explained. "Vegetables. No meat to speak of. Just bacon rind. It's more gravy than anything. Mrs. Carlisle was glad to be rid of it."

"And yet still we've got to keep it hot," he retorted, and spat on the ground to show his disgust. "Waste of time cooking it, waste of hay packing it, waste of your effort carrying it."

"We've only got to go as far as the gate, or just inside it," Jenny said. "The men will come up and get it then."

"Men?" Mr. Armitage had straightened himself up and looked her up and down. "They're prisoners, not men."

"I should think anyone is a man and not a beast," she blurted out. "Prisoner or not."

He stared at her, and put his hands on his hips. "They killed more than one from here. Have you forgotten that?"

"Not these men."

"Ones just like them."

She didn't feel able to argue. She knew what she wanted to say—that none of them had any say in the matter, that terrible things were done by both sides. But she knew what it would sound like. Conshie stuff. Cowardly stuff. Bad, unpatriotic. Wicked, even. And so she kept her mouth shut.

Albert brought a trolley—a long flatbed affair with four little wheels—and they put the packed boxes onto it, and walked to the stable yard gate. Out of the corner of her eye, she saw Mr. Armitage turn on his heel and stamp back towards his cottage. Albert stopped the trolley, and climbed on the gate and leaned over, shouting. "Grub's up, grub's up!" She ssshed him; he was a witless kind of boy, ham-fisted, always smeared with coal dust or dirt. "I'm only hallooing them," he told her.

The prisoners were right at the bottom of the field, close to the river. They were all standing in a patch of shade under an oak tree and Jenny could see that the guard was talking to them. Another stood to one side, leaning against the fence, his rifle held across his chest. Mary had said that you should never go near them, never speak to them; but she had spoken to Frederick when he had come to the dairy to help with the cream. Not on the first two occasions but on the third. He had asked her name, and told her his. He had seemed to fill the room, but there was nothing about him that was threatening. Rather, he reminded her of the coal wagon horses in London: soft, lumbering animals with sad expressions.

And when he had left the farm on that third time, he had turned back to look at her, and smiled.

Was it a sin to think about a man like that? A German? The fourth time that a message had come to the house to help with the butter and cream making, to her immense disappointment the footman

Hardy had been sent, protesting that it was not his job at all. Jenny had gazed at Mr. Bradfield and seen his sharply raised eyebrow as she was about to object.

"Hal-looo!" Albert shouted again.

"They've heard you," Jenny said. "Be quiet." And, sure enough, she saw the sergeant turn his head, and hold up his hand by way of acknowledgment. She waited a moment longer, heart in her mouth, willing and *willing* that they would send Frederick up to get the food. She'd be able to see him again just for a moment, and he might say something to her. But no one down in the field moved again; and, after a while, disappointed, Jenny turned back for the house.

She trailed through the yard and into the cool corridors that led through the laundry rooms.

As she got close to the kitchen, she could hear voices; and was surprised to see that the room was crowded with Mrs. Carlisle, Miss Dodd, and Mrs. Nicholson standing around Mary, who was seated at the table.

"Mrs. March has got children," Mrs. Carlisle was saying. "She'll know what to do."

"I don't want the old crone," Mary snapped. "She was no use when . . ." She stopped herself. "No use with Emily." And she put her face in her hands.

"What's the matter?" Jenny asked.

Mrs. Carlisle looked up at her, hands on hips. "Mary thinks the baby is coming."

"What!" Jenny rushed to Mary's side.

"Don't fuss," Mary muttered.

Jenny looked up at the three women, and realied that none of them there had ever had children themselves. "What shall we do?" she asked them.

"I'll ask his lordship if we may send for the doctor," said Mrs. Nicholson, moving towards the door.

"I don't know if we should," Mary said, from behind her hands. "It might only be a false alarm."

"It's no false alarm if . . ." Miss Dodd blushed. "If your waters have broke," she added.

"And that's the case, is it?" Mrs. Nicholson asked.

"Yes," mumbled Mary, still with her face in her hands. And she gave a low, hitched groan.

"There's a proper state-registered midwife that the doctor uses," Mrs. Carlisle offered. "But I think she's in Richmond." She spread her hands. "Well, they all used Mrs. Mercer in the village once. She's still allowed to practice. Doctor Evans gave her a proper certificate when the law changed a couple of years back. But she isn't a trained nurse or anything."

Mrs. Nicholson hesitated a second, then seemed to make up her mind. "Better safe than sorry. I'll get one of the garden lads to run down to the village, or at least to the land steward's cottage at the bottom of the drive. He has a motor car. Perhaps he'll go for us."

Miss Dodd put her hand to her mouth. "The whole family's gone to Scarborough, Mrs. Nicholson," she whispered. "It's their summer holiday. One week, every year. His sister is there." She dropped her eyes. "If you don't mind me saying, ma'am."

Mrs. Nicholson sighed in exasperation. "Mary, who has been looking after you through the pregnancy?"

"Doctor Evans saw me twice. When he came to see his lordship about his heart."

"I see. Twice in eight months? Well." Mrs. Nicholson stood hands on hips. "Roll on the day when women are treated better than dogs," she exclaimed. "The veterinarian has been twice to my knowledge to his lordship's spaniel in the last week." They all looked at her, astounded. It had been said without anger, but with absolute conviction. "Proper Bolshevik, it was," Mrs. Carlisle would confide to her cousin when she next saw her. Then the housekeeper came to a decision. She patted Mary's shoulder. "I'll ask Mr. Bradfield to send the boy. And I'll ask his lordship at once if we may telephone the doctor. Jenny, help Mary into my own room while we're waiting."

She went briskly out of the door, and immediately she had done so, Mary dropped her hands and stared wildly at them all. "Don't take me to her room," she said. "I don't want to be there."

"But it has a nice little bed," Mrs. Carlisle pointed out kindly. "And a chaise longue, unless Mrs. Nicholson's got rid of it."

"No," Mary cried, wild-eyed. "Not there."

Mrs. Carlisle came round the table, and gently began to lift Mary up. "Now now," she murmured. "You must lie down."

"Not there, please not there," Mary moaned. But she was unable to resist the women as they led her out of the kitchen and along the corridor to Mrs. Nicholson's room.

As luck would have it, as Mrs. Nicholson emerged into the main house from the stairs, William Cavendish was standing in the hall. He had evidently stopped while reading the morning newspaper, and glanced up as she opened the green baize door.

"Oh . . . your lordship. Good morning." William nodded, raising his eyebrows at her in inquiry. "I wonder if it might be possible to have Dr. Evans to the house, sir?"

"Are you ill?"

"Not at all. But Mary Nash, the maid . . ." She smiled. He

apparently had no idea whom she might mean. "Mary Nash, who was married two years ago . . ."

"Ah, yes."

"I think at the very least we shall need a midwife."

He lowered the newspaper. "I'm sorry, Mrs. Nicholson," he said slowly. "But is this my business?"

"Might I use the telephone to call the doctor? Affairs seem already to be too far on to have just the village woman here."

William waved his hand, frowning. "Do whatever is necessary."

"Thank you, sir." She half turned to go.

"And . . . Mrs. Nicholson."

"Yes?"

"In the event of Lady Cavendish or Miss Louisa not being in the house, such matters should be settled between Mr. Bradfield and yourself. I expect to meet the doctor's bill, but I don't expect chapter and verse for the reason he's required."

She paused a moment, then bowed her head to acknowledge him, and walked quickly again to the door.

The room was exactly as Mary remembered it.

Except for the picture of *Elisha Raising the Shunammite's Son*. That horrible thing was gone. Mary laid on the chaise longue, feeling the cretonne edging with superstitious horror. Emily Maitland had been lying here just under three years ago. It had been Christmastime. There had been snow outside. Oh dear God, it was a picture that she would never get out of her head. The coal fire roaring too hot in the grate; the picture above the mantelpiece; the clock that ticked so loudly.

Her eye ran around the room as if she were looking for somewhere to escape. Mrs. Nicholson had not only taken down the picture, but all the embroidered cloths from the chair back. The antimacassars that Mrs. Jocelyn had kept starched as hard as boards. That had never had a guest laying his head on them. But she hadn't made enough difference to dispel the ghost that lay here, frightened and hollow-eyed—Sessy's mother. Just a young girl; the housemaid that Master Harry had seen fit to seduce. Poor Emily.

"I must get up," she said.

Jenny sprang to her feet. "Oh no," she whispered. "Mrs. Carlisle has gone for tea. They're sending for the lady in the village. You mustn't move."

Something terrible washed through Mary then. It was as if time was replaying itself. Three years ago, she had been where Jenny was now: it had been her who had been pleading for Emily to keep still. It had been her who had grasped Emily's hand just like this, and Emily had told her about a box that had been left in the greenhouse, a present that Master Harry had given her. It was a little bracelet of sapphires, and Mary still had it, a guilty secret tainted with grief that she had not dared to show anyone, hidden in a locked box where she kept David's letters and pressed flowers from her wedding day.

"I must get up," she repeated. And seeing Jenny's panic-stricken face, she managed a smile. "I'm all right," she reassured her. "I just want air. I want to walk outside."

Fretting at her movement, nevertheless Jenny helped her. They passed the kitchen, but Mrs. Carlisle was nowhere to be seen. They got to the laundry, and then through to the yard. Sunlight splashed the stones, and the heat baked up.

"It's too hot for you," Jenny protested.

"No it isn't," Mary told her. She couldn't put into words what a relief it was to be away from the housekeeper's room. All kinds of random images were playing through her mind. David on their wedding day, and David as they had shaken Mr. Gould's hand. The sight of him walking briskly up the drive to the main house, while the two of them gripped each other in astonishment. "Come back from the dead," David had muttered.

Oh, Jesus Christ. There it was again. The dead, the dying. Her own sister in the diphtheria ward. Her own father weeping. The news of Harrison, and pushing away the imaginings of what might be happening in France. She felt both hot and cold. The air seemed brittle with both sun and frost. Sun and ice, snow and the yellow blindness of the moors scorched dry by the summer. She'd ridden behind Jack Armitage once on a little pony, going over those moors to see her sister. Memories fought in her head for purchase in a slippery, shifting consciousness.

She stopped, feeling the pain recede. Watching it almost. She gasped, sighed, breathed slowly. That was so much better. "Hold my arm," she told Jenny. "And come with me."

They got to the kitchen garden, and the gate in the wall to the stable yard. Just there at the little gate, a wave of pain gripped her again, and the sensation of immense, unbearable pressure. "I've got to get away," she muttered, through gritted teeth. "Just away for a while."

She heard Jenny's sharp intake of breath. "But you can't move anywhere, Mary," she protested. "Oh please. Come back to the house. You can't be out here."

But she could be out here. She could be anywhere, Mary thought. Anywhere to run from it, to step aside from what was coming. Just for a few hours. She would come back when she was more ready. She felt the irrepressible urgency and her only instinct was to turn away from it. The baby wasn't due for another month, after all. She had plenty of time. She had another month.

"I want to walk," she said.

And she hauled Jenny with her, despite the pain.

*I*t was half past six when the prisoners finished in the field.

Frederick was sorry that it was over; they had cleared four large meadows, and for several days now they had taken the hay to the large medieval barn far behind the house. He had marveled when he had seen it, a huge barrel-roofed affair with a flagstone floor. Looking up into the roof was like looking into the depths of some great ship. At the very far end, there was a fenced-off area, and in it stood a little green two-seater sports car, a Metz.

He supposed that no garages had been built yet for the cars. Perhaps that was something that would come after the war. As they brought in the hay, the barn began to fill with the sweet smell of the summer, and they baled it and stacked it up like a large straw castle. Each night they pulled the huge wooden doors shut, and each morning they opened them again and felt that same sweetness rolling out towards them.

He longed to lie down in the mown grass, and sleep. It would be so much better than sleeping at the camp. He wouldn't mind if there were rats; he had grown used to them at the front. But he couldn't help thinking that it would be so peaceful here. No noise of men. No noise of machines. Just the age-old building—centuries of stone and timber. He wondered if they ever had parties here, harvest dances, or anything at Christmas. He would have liked to see that; it must be very fine.

More than anything else, he had loved this place deep in the green parkland, and yet commanding such a view of distant hills. A city called York was out there somewhere, old as the Vikings. Older. So he had been told. This country reminded him of home with its open spaces and magnificent buildings, but it was prettier by far. It felt enclosed and secure. Certainly the weather was more temperate. In Germany now the summer would be fiercer, the workmen slumped at midday in the shadows if they could steal a few moments; he remembered how his mother would sweat and curse at her work. And they had a hill or two out on the farm at home, but nothing like the grand sweeps of the hills here.

Frederick was thinking of this as they rode on the back of the cart bringing in a mountainous, swaying load of hay. The younger guard walked behind them, glowering at them as they smiled down at him. He felt the cart coming to a halt, and then he heard the women's voices.

He climbed down, a few of the other prisoners with him, and looked towards the gate. The girl Jenny was there, trying to undo the latch. Behind her he could see another women who wore a white apron, a striped dress, a lace cap. A housemaid, he thought, like Jenny. But much older. Both of them looked distraught.

"Stay there," the sergeant said. He went striding up the field and the women opened the gate at last. Frederick could see that Jenny was wringing her hands; something had frightened her. She glanced once in his direction, and then she gripped the sergeant's arm. Frederick saw him shake his head; shrug. Jenny gripped him even harder, and with her free hand wiped her eyes.

"What is it?" the man next to him asked. "What are they saying?"

"Nobody in the house," Frederick murmured. "They need a doctor."

"For who?"

"I don't know."

They all waited, straining to hear the conversation. The young guard was uninterested, picking his teeth with a sliver of wood. Then, from inside the stable yard they heard a scream. Jenny clapped her hands to her ears; the older woman clutched her, and then backed away, towards the sound.

Frederick took a step forward.

"All right, you," the guard said. "Just try it."

"I am not running away."

"And not moving at all," the boy warned, pleased at this unexpected opportunity for authority. He waved his rifle at them all. "Just see what happens."

"You think we want to run anywhere?" Frederick said. "We are tired. We can't run."

"Try it," the young boy grinned.

Frederick looked from him to Jenny. Then he walked up the slope towards the gate.

"Hey, you!"

"Shoot me," Frederick muttered.

The sergeant glanced over his shoulder. "Get back," he warned. "None of your business."

Jenny was staring at him; then she dropped her grip on the sergeant's arm, and ran. She rushed up to Frederick, out of breath, tears running down her face. "A gardener's boy went for the midwife in the village, but she's not come. The doctor isn't home. We can't find anyone, and Mary's in . . . she's in the stable yard. We can't raise her up, and when we try to, she says . . . she won't go in the house. There's something wrong. . . ."

"Who is this?" Frederick asked.

"Mary. Don't you remember? You saw her once."

"The lady who is . . ." He didn't know the English word. He had tried very hard to understand what she was saying. But the words were so rushed, so garbled. "You speak slow, please," he said.

She gazed at him in misery. "The baby."

The sergeant was at their side. "I am sorry to speak to this lady," Frederick explained. "But she is the lady I help with the work."

The sergeant was frowning. "You're a farmer, aren't you?" he asked.

"We have a farm, yes."

"Livestock?"

"We have. . ."

"Cattle. You have cattle, animals?"

"Yes, sir."

"Calves then?"

"I don't know. . ."

"Births, man! You've had births."

All at once, Frederick got the sense of what he was saying. "Oh no, I don't do this."

"You *don't*?"

"I cannot." Frederick glanced towards the stables, where a devastating cry of agony was ripping through the air. "With persons, sir. With women."

The sergeant stared at him, and then at Jenny. "Show us," he said.

To everyone's horror, Mary was now on her hands and knees close to the door of one of the empty stables. She was crawling, and Miss Dodd was behind her, the very image of fright. "She won't listen to me," she wailed, as Jenny and the two men advanced. "Mrs. March has been out here, and Mary did so curse at her. She's gone away for blankets, but they shouted at each other. . . ."

"Do something," Jenny pleaded to the men. She got down at Mary's side. "What is it you want to do?" she asked gently. "Mary, you are out in the yard. Talk to me. What is it you're trying to do?"

Mary put her head down, and let out an almost inhuman sound of pain that rose to an almighty scream.

"Oh my God, dear God in heaven!" Miss Dodd wailed.

Frederick turned away from the scene and spoke in a soft voice to the sergeant. "Maybe the woman goes for soap and water. To give her . . . make her with something to do."

The sergeant, agreeing, told Miss Dodd to fetch water. "Unless someone else is bringing it?"

"I'll go," Miss Dodd said, and ran.

The two men looked down at Mary and Jenny. "You have children?" Frederick asked the sergeant. "You know all this?"

The older man blanched. "I never seen them born," he said. "That's not a man's job."

"But you think this is my job?" Frederick asked.

"Better than nothing."

"I am better than nothing, yes?"

Jenny suddenly sprang to her feet. "Stop arguing!" she screamed at them. "Help me get her inside the stable at least."

Like a great clumsy six-handed beast, they managed to get Mary out of the sun and into the stable. There was a sprinkling of sand and hay on the floor. They heard Mrs. March come running across the yard. Behind her, her husband was struggling with a large enamel bowl and a tin flask, with towels hung over his arm. As the two of them got to the stable door, Mr. March looked at Mary. "'Ere's a right to-do," he observed laconically.

"Give me those," Mrs. March snapped. She gave the sergeant and Frederick a stare that would have frozen the Devil in his tracks. "You needn't be here, neither," she said.

"We was called, missus," the sergeant protested. He and Frederick stepped back out into the sunshine, each man turning his face away from the door. For his part, Mr. March simply shrugged. "Allus an awkward lass, that one," he told them, and walked back across the yard.

The two raised an eyebrow at each other, but said nothing. Inside the door, they could hear Mrs. March remonstrating with both Mary and Jenny, instructing Jenny to hold this, hold that—and accompanied by Mary's moans and protests. Then came a desperate scream. "Take her away!" Mary shouted, her voice sounding strangled. "She killed Emily, she killed her!"

A minute passed. More groans and curses—the latter from Mrs. March. And then the old woman came out into the yard, red in the face and sweating. "I've had five children," she told the men. She wiped her face with her apron. "And nivver a fuss like that."

"What's the matter?" the sergeant asked.

Mrs. March shrugged. "Tis a breech, I suppose." She shuffled her shoulders, crossed her arms. "Killed Emily," she sniffed. "I like that! Baby was premature, girl was bleeding. We couldn't stop it. She was nubbut skin and bone, poor child. Nobody could have done more than we did that night."

Since neither of the men knew what she was talking about, they didn't answer, until the sergeant said quietly, "Breech. What's that mean?"

"Wrong way round. The doctor must come."

"There's a woman coming from the village."

"Mercer, you mean? Neither use nor ornament. She's over seventy. She'll nivver do it."

"Well, can't you?"

"I might if she let me near her." And the woman stared at her own feet. "Though it feels like summat not right," she murmured.

"With this baby?" Frederick asked. He could hardly translate the sentences to himself, but he could see the expression on her face well enough.

"Probably big," Mrs. March said. And, gratuitously, she spread her hands wide. "Seems very big to me."

Inside the stable, Mary's cries had descended into sobs.

"What'll we do?" the sergeant asked.

"Nothing no one can do. Wait for the doctor."

"Move her to the house?"

Mrs. March smiled grimly. "Good luck, boys," she said, turned her back on them, and went back inside the stable.

They waited.

They waited while the sun sank slowly, and the shadows crept across the yard. The other prisoners had been marshaled into the tithe barn, guarded there by the young soldier, Mr. March, and his sole remaining boy—all staring at their languid captives as if they expected to be overpowered at any moment. At one point, having checked on them and seen the faces of the unwilling makeshift crew, the sergeant returned to say that all of them must leave. "Got to get them back to camp," he explained. "It's nearly seven o'clock. Orders is orders."

Jenny rushed out, pleading with them to stay. "We could still carry her inside if it let up a moment," she begged.

The sergeant pulled her gently to one side. "Listen, my love," he told her. "I've got thirty men here, and yon bloody fellows look like they'll have proper hysterics if one of the Boche as much as scratched his arse. If you'll pardon me. We'll have to get back to camp."

"Can't you leave Frederick here, with us?" Jenny said. "You said that you thought he'd be some help."

"Well he isn't, though, is he? Even if I could."

"But the midwife hasn't come, and the doctor hasn't come, and I don't know what we shall do," Jenny whispered, and burst into tears so pitiful, so heartrending, that the sergeant sighed. He looked at Frederick. "You tell me what you think."

"I think?"

"Yes. Bloody hell, man, what—you—think." He cocked his head towards the stable.

Frederick looked from the sergeant to Jenny. She stared at him blank-faced, lost.

He walked slowly to the door.

Mrs. March was squatting on the floor next to Mary, with the girl's head cradled in her lap. Blankets had been put under Mary's back, and one covered her stomach. "It's no use," Mrs. March said. She was past shouting or cursing; she looked as if every atom of energy had been drained out of her. Miss Dodd and Mrs. Nicholson stood to one side, hands clasped, the bowls of water and soap on the floor beside them.

Frederick was reminded of his father then. A very distant memory. Perhaps a year or two before his father died. He was a small boy, and it had been summer then, just as this was summer; that same mellow light colored the pictures in his head. He had run to find his father, who had been out all night in the cow byre. It had been very early, and an opaque pink and gold flooded the sky, and was reflected on the ground. In his mind he saw his own small feet trotting along between the light and the shadow.

The byre had been a shed just like this—larger perhaps, enough for a milking stand. They had not had many animals; to his certain knowledge they had never been able to afford them. But they had enough to milk to make the cream and, occasionally, butter and cheese. The cheese house was a cool little place half dug into the shallow bank behind the sheds, where a small stream ran. Even though he had been so small, he had known the cows by name. He remembered their immense-seeming bodies, their gusts of breath, and the searching of their faces lowered to his own.

That morning, his father had been propped, exhausted, against the shed wall, and at his feet lay a lifeless calf. Frederick had been helping him at midnight, until his mother had come and insisted that he go to bed. He had been so sure and so excited that he was running to see a new live calf—after all, hadn't he followed his father's instructions and felt in the mother animal, and actually felt the miraculously slim outline of a hoof, and a soft-nosed face beyond it? But there had been no live animal now. Instead, there was a dead body of a calf lying in the straw. It had been pulled from the mother roughly, to save the cow, and its legs were broken.

"I wasn't in time," his father told them. "I wasn't quick enough."

Frederick kneeled down now. He recalled the horror of it all so vividly, and it came rushing back to him now. If only these people knew. He had seen many a live birth, helped at many such a one, but it was the dead calf that inhabited his mind now. He breathed deeply, trying to banish the image; and just for a second—a very fleeting second—Jenny's hand brushed his own as she stood up to get out of his way.

Mary's gaze was unfocused, her eyes brimming with tears, her face a ghostly color.

"Mary," he said quietly. "Hello."

There was a beat or two of perfect silence.

"Mary," he prompted. "May I see? Will you allow, please?"

Mrs. March at once stiffened with outrage. He looked at her, and the reaction faded as quickly as it had come. She turned her face away.

He picked up the soap, and washed his hands. He looked from one woman to the other. The one in the black dress met his eye. "Please," he said. "You help me."

She did as he asked, and he felt their eyes on him, everyone in that stable, and the ones outside. He tried to concentrate, to be calm. Most of all he tried to steady his hands. He looked at the poor woman lying in front of him, and he had a ghastly flashback to others lying in pain, and especially to the boy with the broken back. Where had that been?

Near Pilckem.

The officer had been drinking that night. Frederick could see it in his eyes, and smell it on his breath. He had staggered to Frederick at three in the morning while Frederick was on sentry duty.

"I want you to go out there," he had said.

"There?" Frederick echoed. He couldn't understand.

The officer had waved his hand towards the British front line. "Go and find them," he said. "Tell me where they are."

"But they are just here, sir. They are forty yards away. We have seen them yesterday."

"And are they still there?" the officer demanded, with a horrible grin on his face. "How do you know that? Are you telling me lies?"

"No, sir. They must be there."

"But you don't know, do you? You can't see them. Go out and find them for me."

"Out there?" Frederick had repeated, fear prickling through every nerve in his body. "But what shall I do, sir? How can I go?"

"You go because you are ordered," the man replied. "As we are all ordered."

"But it is impossible, is it not?"

"That's right," the officer confirmed. And still the horrible grin remained. "Entertain me. Do the impossible."

And when Frederick hesitated still, a gun was brought to his forehead. "Do you disobey a direct order?"

"No, sir." He had taken a handful of the filthy soil and rubbed it over his face for some sort of camouflage. "No, sir."

The British line was very quiet, but he could feel their eyes on him. He got over the trench, walking up the short wooden steps. At first he crouched and crawled. And then he heard a dreadful thing—the sound of the gun being cocked at his back. He was not moving fast enough, it said. He started to run, doubled over almost, slipping and sliding. In truth, he was looking for a shell hole. Anything that would hide him from the imminent death that both faced him and was at his back. And all the time he was guessing where the British were exactly. It was hard to run in the dark, tripping over the remains of dead men. He prayed for a shell hole. God in heaven, there ought to be enough. But he found himself on a slight ridge and was suddenly sure that he was visible. He heard voices ahead of him. And he froze.

"Fritz!" the voice called. "Fritz!"

He couldn't reply. He thought of his mother and what she would do when she read the letter. He doubted that the officer behind him would ever order for his body to be recovered, and so he would simply disappear.

"Fritz!" Nothing but the stars. He looked up, waiting. A lot of stars up there in the heavens.

More voices. It sounded as if they might be discussing him. He was half expecting a shot in the back from his own officer, but nothing came. Perhaps he had already forgotten him and the insane order. Frederick heard the British calling again. More voices now. He felt their attention fixed on him. And then they began to shoot.

Bullets sprang up from the ground. They were raking the soil directly in front of him, deliberately not killing him. Trying to make him move. Trying to see his intention. Well, he thought, it was intention to die quickly and without fuss. And so he remained standing.

The firing increased, but always missing him. And then, for some reason he could never understand afterwards, his body began to dance, to sway, to jitter as he stood. He staggered, stumbled, waved. Let it be over, he thought. The voices rose to shouts, and then to jeering. And then he dropped his gun, and as it left his hands he knew that he would never hold anything again.

He was taken prisoner that morning. He ran straight on. Or, rather, his body ran straight on into the British trench. Someone grabbed him, and he fell, and he was stamped on and then bundled back under guard. They talked about him a lot, and laughed. But he did not mind the laughing. The humor of his awkward and puppet-like dancing in no-man's-land had saved him. He had made them laugh with his shambling terror.

*H*e looked again at the woman on the floor in front of him. *This is not Pilckem. This is not Pilckem . . . .*

He put his hand gently on Mary's stomach.

"I am sorry," he murmured. "Please to excuse. But . . ."

As softly as he was able, he soaped his hand again. Very gently, very slowly, he felt for the child. Sure enough, in a moment or two, he could feel a tiny arm, a shoulder. Mary barely stirred. The head of the child was there, the birth was not breech, but there was something beyond the small body.

He breathed in deeply, afraid of hurting the woman, afraid of hurting the child, afraid of his own clumsiness. Afraid of his traitorous, clumsy hands with a will of their own. *Very quiet*, he told himself. *Don't think about your hands. This is not the place, nor the time.*

"Mein Gott," he murmured.

"What is it?" Mrs. Nicholson asked him softly.

He frowned, but didn't reply. He closed his eyes. Here was another arm, another foot. He felt tiny fingers: slack, unresponsive.

The chest so fragile. He ran a fingertip over a rib cage that felt as small as a bird's. This child was not large, he thought. This child was not too big. He hooked his fingertip around the twisted cable that was the umbilical cord, and beyond that. And beyond that . . .

"We have two," he said. "There is two."

"There is not," Mrs. March protested.

He didn't hear her.

They were both there, frozen in their battle to be born, lodged in the too-small space. A terrible shudder went through the body of the woman, and he felt it—he *felt* it in his own body and blood—that ancient imperative, that crushing need. To live and breathe. He laid himself down almost to the floor, and worked his fingers past the first child. Mary moved. "Please hold her so she stay the same," he said.

Another child. Another cord, and the whole tangled together like a ball of twine. Very gently, he eased the shape of a small arm, and a hand curled in a fist, back. The second cord shifted and he felt a thrash, a resistance. "Come now," he murmured. "You come and see the world."

Mary suddenly woke, yelling, heaving. Her breath flowed over him as hot as fire. He could hear Mrs. March speaking, but the woman at his side was silent. Thank God. Silence was what was needed. Peace. Peace in the wide world, dear God. Just peace. "Come, little child," he whispered. "Kommen jetzt mit mir, kleiner lieber ein. . . ."

It happened in a rush. The cord slithered; the second tiny body retreated for a moment, the first crushed his hand. He tried to extract it, straighten his fingers, pull his own flesh as far back as he could, and then in one fantastic movement, his fingers and the child rushed into the light together. Before he knew what was happening, he was holding a tiny body in his hands and the hands of the woman next to him, and several voices rose up, and he lifted the child up, and he was gasping and laughing, and he tapped it gently, and it let out a cry. Such a cry. Such a great, thunderous, piercing, blessed cry. And moments later—perhaps forty seconds, thirty seconds, not even that—came the second miracle. Mary's second son was born.

Frederick sat back, overwhelmed, crowded out by the women, by the sudden storm of towels, wrappings, by Jenny's long hair brushing his face, by a slap on his back from someone. He looked at Jenny, and in the confusion she flung her arms around his neck, and kissed the side of his face; he didn't know if anyone saw them, and he didn't care. "Don't leave here," she whispered to him urgently. "Promise you will never leave here." She drew back fractionally, dropped her hands, and gazed at him.

"I promise you," he told her. "Yes, I promise."

Then he suddenly realized that his legs were in cramp and in an almost comic sudden reaction, he fell backwards. Jenny jumped up, smiled, and ran to help the other women. He found himself on his back, sweat stained, looking up at the ceiling, and into the face of the sergeant.

"Well, mate," the sergeant said, smiling broadly. "Doctor's here now. He's right behind you. Better late than never, eh? Shall we send him home again?"

It was almost dark by the time that Mrs. Nicholson gently tapped on the drawing room door.

Hearing a muted reply, she went in to find William Cavendish in one of the large armchairs by the window. He was reading a book. He looked up at her, smiling. "One of my father's relics," he said quietly.

She moved forward. "I've heard his lordship was a naturalist, a botanist."

"Yes, he was," William murmured. "A fine person. I miss him greatly."

She waited until, smiling still, he closed the book and looked up at her. On the table next to him was a tumbler of whisky, and a letter.

"You asked to see me, sir."

"I hear that the drama is over."

"We have taken mother and children up to the nursery for the time being. I hope that is in order."

He raised a hand and beckoned her to come, indicating another armchair by his side.

"Do you find Rutherford to your satisfaction?" he asked, when she was seated.

"Very much so."

"Affairs in order, belowstairs?"

"There are some things to be remedied," she told him.

"Yes," William murmured. "Do as you think fit. That was what I meant earlier today. A free rein. It is pointless, on the whole, to consult me. I have never been involved in the arrangements."

"No, of course," she said. "But if I may say . . . it's the staffing. We're perilously low."

"I realize that."

"I may go to see an agency. There is one in Richmond. The house needs a certain sort of servant—trained, I mean—and they are scarce. But we may have more hope with the scullery maids and plain cook maids. There may be girls in the village. Poor Mrs. Carlisle is struggling."

"You must do as you wish. Hire whom you please. Don't concern yourself as to cost, if that is your worry."

"Thank you, sir."

"As for the footman. . ." He stopped. He lifted the letter and looked dolefully at it. "As for the footman and gardeners," he repeated. "I estimate we shall probably lose Hardy to conscription in a few weeks. I have asked Mr. Bradfield to approach the larger hospitals to inquire about men seeking employment on discharge. There are various large houses that have let themselves out for convalescents; I trust that there will be men of a certain decent class who cannot conduct very hard manual labor or accurate office or factory work, but who might be trained in a capacity here."

"That is very kind," Mrs. Nicholson commented. "War wounded, you mean?"

"Exactly." He glanced away temporarily. "Her ladyship is employing that type of person at Blessington, in a new workshop. I thought we might apply the same principle here."

She smiled. "A practical solution, if they are mobile and willing to work."

He looked back at her. "Do you have relations serving in the army?"

"No, sir."

"No children, nephews, nieces?"

"None. I was an only child of only children."

"Unusual."

She gave an infinitesimal shrug.

"And you trained as a nurse . . . ?"

"For a short while. My father had actually left an annuity for me to have an education. It rather worked against me, I'm afraid. Unless one is really academic, and even then . . ." She saw that William's attention was not on what she was saying.

As she stopped speaking, he looked up at her. "Our boy is with the RFC, you know."

"So I understand."

"He will be coming home shortly. Within a few days."

"Oh, that's very good news," she replied. "I shall make sure everything is ready."

"Yes, yes . . ." William's voice trailed away. He nodded slowly. And then he held up the letter. "This came an hour ago. Not a telegram, you see. So not the worst of news, thank God. But the postmaster recognized it as pertaining to us in its way. Nash's mother, in the village, has seen it."

"Nash?" Mrs. Nicholson echoed. "You don't mean . . . not Mary's husband?"

"I do." He gave her the letter, and she read it. When she was finished, she looked back at him. The fire burned through the very last of its embers, and the light faded from the room. "It doesn't say where he is," she murmured. "'Wounded.' It isn't very informative."

"No, indeed."

She offered him the letter again, but he shook his head. "No, keep it," he told her. "And when you think that Mary is ready to read it, let her see it."

She nodded, and folded it away. "I wonder if he is able to come home," she ventured. "I wonder if he is able to."

"Indeed," William said, almost in a whisper. "Indeed."

Chapter 18

The Channel crossing had been remarkably smooth; something for which John Gould was grateful. Every time that he saw a ship, a dock, or the ocean itself he was brought back to an Irish town and a crowd of soaked and hollow-eyed survivors. The *Lusitania* was a garbled and recurring dream.

As the troop ship, full of wounded, traveled slowly out from Le Havre, he watched France disappear into the evening mist with trepidation. He watched the wake, a broad line in the dark sea, and prayed that no U-boats were following them. To either side were accompanying ships, smudges of grey merely, but their presence gave him no peace. He was determined to stand there all night, pacing the decks when he could; to go below was too close to the nightmare that he always carried with him.

He remembered the awful sensation of dropping in that other mirrorlike sea; he remembered the body that had floated past him and dragged him. He remembered climbing onto the rail with twelve-year-old Joseph Petheridge and instructing him to swim for his life. Oddly enough, he even remembered the first of the water swirling about his feet as they prepared to jump, and how cold it had been, filling his shoes. From ordinary life to imminent death in a matter of seconds.

But, after that, he only remembered the faces on the dockside and the green-painted walls of a boarding house where he could do nothing but stare and shake. Words had felt heavy in his mouth: he had been literally struck dumb. Soldiers out here in France had told him the same, many times—that a man could go rigid with shock, and become an automaton in his movements afterwards. That the world became a plastic, artificial thing, a kind of grubby theater where it was possible to see, to watch, to feel hot and cold upon one's skin. But not to really feel. And not to speak at all, just tremble. For days. For weeks.

The night passed with interminable slowness. John went to the prow and narrowed his eyes, searching for the lights of England. It was only a few miles, but it felt like a thousand. He knew that he would probably go to France again, but he hoped that he would not be asked to do so while the war raged. He had already promised himself that he would do something to drum up financial aid in England and America, despite rationing having descended on England. He kept thinking of the children and their ragged souvenirs, and how glad they had been to have a few candies. He thought of the men and their blank faces. And the horses. Something, he thought, should be done about the horses.

"It's not just horses," Harry had told him as they had approached Le Havre in an officers' staff car the day before. "There's all sorts of animals, you know. One of the squadrons had a little fox cub as their mascot. It loved going up, it really did. Used to stand with its feet on the dashboard and prick up its ears. There was a chap riding courier who had a collie dog—a French farm dog, I suppose—on his pillion, front legs balanced on his shoulders. Then there's the messenger dogs . . ."

"Yes, I know," John had replied. But he didn't like to think of the messenger dogs leaping across the trenches, or those laying telephone wires. Or the dog he'd seen in a reserve camp, its bandaged feet the result of mustard gas lying on the ground. Or, stranger still and somehow so poignant in their fragility, the carrier pigeons strapped with diagonal webbing in their boxes, ready to take news much faster than man could manage. "It's a crazy world," he'd said, and patted Harry absently on the shoulder. Harry had looked out at the fields, waterlogged in the summer rain, and said nothing more.

And then, as they approached the port, Harry had suddenly said that he would not be going on board with John. "I've been called to IV corps," he said.

"You have? When was this?"

"I received a message."

"But when? Did I miss something?"

"I have received a message," Harry repeated with dogged, raised-voice insistence. "One doesn't question."

"To go to Nieuwpoort?" John asked softly.

Harry merely raised a finger to his lips, and smiled.

"Well then, I guess we must part," John had said as they got off the train. "You've got some sort of transport, I expect?"

"Yes."

John held out his hand. "Good luck. Don't be long, will you? Your parents will be expecting you."

"I shall be as long as it takes." And Harry had touched the brim of his cap, and promptly disappeared among the crowds.

Finally, the night was over. The dawn came up over the sea, and Dover came into view. "Dearest God, thank you with all my heart,"

John murmured, turning up the collar of his coat and speaking the words under his breath, self-conscious to feel so relieved.

It was a melee of men and machinery on the dock. He stood in line, carried his gabardine holdall, and showed his passport. "American, eh?" said the police officer who was shepherding civilians out of the way of the army trucks.

"Train to London?" he asked, by way of reply.

He got to the station, forced his way into a train, stood in the corridor, and gave his seat to a major who looked grey with fatigue. The man slumped after only a minute, even before the train started to make its way out of the station. In sleep, John could see anger etched in the man's face. *Angry even when asleep*, John thought. And wondered what made the man angriest of all. Himself, or others. Impatience or fear. Or even stepping onto English soil. Yes, there was a curious anger in that: finding England so usual, so ordinary, and so peaceful. A strange sort of frustrated, unreasonable anger.

It took many hours to get to London. In that time, John, too, fell asleep, sitting finally on the floor. Now and then he felt the nudging or tripping of passing feet; now and again, the train lurched or came to a full stop, and he vaguely registered the smell of oil and heard the rolling, echoing, and jumbled conversation of others. He didn't dream at all now; just felt grateful for the dirty floor and the stumbling feet and the patchwork of voices. It meant that he was going home. He curled up in his greatcoat with his holdall underneath him, and occasionally he would check that his notebooks were still there, feeling their outline through the holdall sides.

By the time that the train pulled into Charing Cross it was eight in the morning. John emerged into the light, rubbing his face wearily. He looked up at the Eleanor cross memorial, reconstructed by the Victorians; a copy of the thirteenth-century wooden one that had been taken down during the civil war. The white stone copy had been here now for just over fifty years; Octavia had told him that on one of their first walking days in London together. A cross raised to a queen, a wife. "Imagine raising a gift like that, and it standing here for eight hundred years," Octavia had mused. He had smiled, and kissed her gloved hand. They had paused, looking into each other's eyes. "I wonder who will remember us in eight hundred years?" she had mused.

"Rutherford will remember you."

"Oh, I doubt it."

"Why not? What do you English call a wandering wife? The Bolter. That's how you'll be remembered."

"Oh my God," she'd laughed. "How terrible." She'd put her head on one side, looking thoughtfully at him. "No one will know you," she'd murmured. "No one would guess why."

"You know me," he'd told her. "That's all that matters." He'd glanced up again at the cross. "Shall I raise a great monument to you?" he'd asked. "Commission a sculptor, buy a piece of land and put you on it? Men could come and worship you."

"Oh, John," she'd said, and laughed. But, as they'd walked away, she had looked again over her shoulder. "He must have loved her very much," she'd whispered.

John was suddenly consumed by his desire to see her.

He stood on the pavement across from the main square and the fountains, and then gave up on hailing any sort of cab. The road was packed, even at this early hour, crammed with the average Londoner going about his hurried business, and with military vehicles threading their own way through the chaos. Horses, vans, motorized buses, and pedestrians all jostled for position in the wide road.

He thought of turning back and going into the depths of the earth on the Tube, but he couldn't face it. It was only two miles to the house: he would walk. He began at an ordinary pace, going in the direction of Buckingham Palace Road, down The Mall. The Palace shone in early sunlight at the far end; halfway down, he cut across the welcome green expanse of St. James's Park, across the bridge. Across the bridge to peace, and to the only thing that really mattered to him in the world. He picked up his pace, and passed by Grosvenor Gardens, Eton Square, and Sloane Square. The opulence struck at him, unnerved him. It didn't seem right. The world was somehow out of kilter. How the Londoners loved their greens and gardens, he thought. How precious it was, and how bizarre compared to the countryside across the Channel.

He caught himself shuddering, and closed off the thoughts purposefully in his head. A sort of panic, a sense of loss, was now clutching at him. He started to run. Before he knew it he was charging down Royal Hospital Road like a man possessed, oblivious to the looks of passersby. He passed the redbrick hospital chapel—he registered a flash of arched windows and cherry trees seemingly overburdened with the dark green leaves of late summer; it all whirled past while the breath burned in his chest.

The handles of the bag grew slippery in his hand. His legs ached. He felt a cold stream of panic-induced sweat course down his neck. She would not be there, he kept thinking. For some reason, she would not be there. Something had happened to take her away. As he came out on the street of Chelsea Physic Garden, he was suddenly utterly convinced that he would never see her again; that she had been spirited away while he was looking in another direction, absorbed by another place.

His feet pounded on the quiet pavements, past the delicate pale brownstone brick of the houses. Then all at once he could see the river, and the trees by the river. He was almost there, and when he at last saw the house, he had to stop. He couldn't breathe anymore. His heart banged inside him and the blood pounded in his ears. At last he got himself together and walked quickly to the gate of the house, up to the door, and knocked hard on it, after trying to find his keys and failing.

Milly answered, and broke into a smile. "Oh, sir! Welcome home."

"Thank you, Milly." He dropped the bag, shrugged off his coat, and stood at the foot of the stairs. He hardly dared ask the question. "Is Lady Cavendish here?"

"Yes, sir, of course," the maid said, giving him a puzzled frown. "She . . ."

But he didn't hear the rest. He bounded up the stairs two at a time, ran along the landing, and threw open the bedroom door.

Octavia was sitting up in bed, a cup of tea in her hand, the newspaper open on the coverlet next to her.

He stood there for a moment gazing at her, then reached for the nearest chair and fell into it, never taking his eyes off her. She stared for a moment, put down the cup, and then jumped out of bed and ran over to him. "Why, John," she said. "Darling, what is it? Whatever's the matter?"

He started to laugh uncontrollably, shaking with relief. "Nothing at all," he told her. "My love, absolutely nothing at all."

At Rutherford, Louisa made her way to the nursery before breakfast.

At the end of the gallery—the long room that linked all the bedrooms—she stopped to look down at the portrait of her mother. Octavia's image hung on the wide stairwell; it was impossible to enter or leave the house without looking up at her, dressed in a voluminous satin gown with the Rutherford estate behind her. Louisa often thought lately that her mother's gaze had a distant quality. Growing up, she had always assumed that it showed a lack of confidence; but now she wondered if Octavia was really gazing towards a future that she longed for, or to a place that she couldn't go. The hands clutching the intricate carved rail of the seat were gripping it rather than resting on it. Strange. She hadn't really noticed that before.

She turned and continued along the gallery. There was no sound from her father's room, and, of course, all the others were empty. It was more a mausoleum than a house, she considered. A shrine, anyway. Every now and again she would go into Harry's bedroom and walk slowly around it, looking at his boyhood models of ships, and his silly comic books. In his wardrobe hung a suit of school clothes that her mother had never been able to bring herself to throw away. And there was his Oxford gown, a testimony to a few short months at university. Louisa smiled to herself. Anyone less like a scholar than Harry was hard to imagine. He had been trying to fit the shape made for him, of course. But sooner or later he would have broken free, whether the war had come along or not.

She left Harry's room and opened the door to the narrow stairs that led up to the third floor. Once here, the house was more alive. Especially since Mary and her two sons had been brought here. They had been allocated a side-nursery that dated back to the times when the house needed both a nurse and a governess. Louisa went in there now, tiptoeing in case she should disturb the occupants.

Mary was asleep, but it was evident by the shawl draped on the nursing chair that she had been up at least once during the night. Louisa smiled, and crept to the cots underneath the large fireplace picture of Queen Victoria. The twins each lay in their cribs looking like angels, all tousled dark hair and both the very image of Mary. They looked so sweet that it was hard to believe that they constantly screamed and bellowed. "What voices! What pairs of lungs!" Sessy's nurse had exclaimed the last time that Louisa had spoken to her.

And, with a hint of reproof, "Miss Cecilia might not sleep as well with that going on next door."

Louisa had dismissed the comment. She knew that Sessy was wildly intrigued by the new arrivals. And besides, she herself had had such fun fixing up the room to suit Mary. She had gone straight out and bought the curtains and carpets herself; the vivid red rug, the fireguard, the bowls and little tea service, the changing cabinet, the linens and towels. In fact, she had bought up half the children's shop in Richmond. She knew that it had caused a stir downstairs—that she had bought things more suited to a real child of the family. But she didn't care. Her father didn't either. "Do whatever you must," was his mantra these days. And so she had done just that.

She left the room as quietly as she could and went in to the larger nursery. To her delight, Sessy was awake, standing up in her cot and testing its wooden barrier by gently shaking it, even inspecting the latches that led down the sides. Louisa picked her up. "You're a minx," she told her. "Come with me." She left a note for the still-sleeping nurse and snatched up a set of clothes; in her own room, she dressed the child in her rompers and woolen coat and little leather shoes.

"Beff-fast," Sessy demanded, suddenly seeming to wake up.

"In a minute," Louisa told her. "There's a surprise waiting downstairs."

Sessy gazed at her in rapt attention, turning up the face that looked so much like Harry's: fair-skinned, even featured, but with a pout of stubbornness to the mouth that so easily and so often turned into a smile.

Down through the great house they went, out through the French doors of the dining room, and along the path to the walled garden. The sun was just touching the top of the walls, rimming them in gold; down in the raised beds the plants were a mass of dark green, heavy with dew. They went out through the gate and got to the stable yard. All was quiet, even here. Louisa stood a moment, breathing in the fresh morning air. She closed her eyes and imagined Jack walking towards her. *Come home*, she thought. *Please come home.*

Sessy began to struggle in her arms. Opening her eyes, she let the little girl down and gripped her hand tightly. "Don't run off," she said. "You must come with me. Come and look."

They went across the yard to the stable closest to William's hunter. Louisa could hear the stallion stirring slightly inside, but she ignored him. It was the next door that was so important. Softly, she opened the upper part, and then hitched Sessy up again onto her hip. "Look," she whispered. "It's for you. Just yours."

Two years before, Louisa had sent Jack out on a mission to find a little pony for Sessy to ride. Her niece had only been seventeen months old then, and Jack had not been in favor. "She's only a bairn," he had pointed out. But Louisa had insisted, and he had gone to look for a pony over at Mrs. Hallett's livery yard. But the horses had been all gone, requisitioned that very day. And there had been nothing left for Sessy at all.

Since Jack had left, he had written to her about the fate of other horses caught up in the war. He had hinted at their suffering, but he did not dwell on it. It was up to Louisa to read between the lines, and she did so acutely, hearing his distress in every written and unwritten word. And she decided that if there was ever to be a future for Rutherford and for men like Jack, there had to be something rekindled, something to look forward to, to nurture. A sort of beginning, at least. And so she had hit upon her own plan. She had found a horse for Sessy that would never be taken away.

Inside the stable stall was a miniature version of the horse that Jack loved most. Granted, it was hardly the size of the Shire—how could it be?—but it was very reminiscent of Wenceslas all the same. The coloring was exact—a grey, with white hooves and a placid, intelligent

eye, and a fine head, for all its minute stature. It was a miniature
Shetland, and on the racks in the tack room hung an equally small set
of bridle and reins, and a most charming miniature saddle.

"Small," Sessy observed, seemingly not impressed.

"Yes, darling, he's very small," Louisa agreed. "But he's exactly
the right size for you. See? He's looking at you. Shall we feed him?
Shall we see if you might be friends?"

Sessy struggled to get down; Louisa opened the door. The horse
stamped once or twice. "Don't crowd him, don't frighten him," Louisa warned. But she need not have bothered. The Shetland dipped its
head, and Sessy immediately hung from its neck, kissing it wildly.
"Small!" she crooned.

"What shall we call him?"

"Baby!"

"No, not Baby. That's quite insulting. He's fully grown, you
know."

"Poppet."

"Rather a girl's name."

"Tom Thumb."

Louisa smiled. "Perfect," she agreed. "I knew you should come
up with something. Tom Thumb it shall be."

There, Jack, she thought. *Not quite Wenceslas. Just a very minor
addition in more ways than one. But I hope you like him, all the same.*

*I*t was some fifteen minutes later that she saw Jack's father
come out into the yard.

He was walking very slowly and was in his shirtsleeves. She
glanced over at him, and then looked again. Josiah was an archetypal
Yorkshireman. He said very little, and he usually moved determinedly,
head down; slow to speak, slow to anger. Hardened outwardly,

softhearted within, he hated to be questioned. But he stood now as if lost. He had come to a halt and was looking at the ground.

"Josiah," she called. There was no reply. "Mr. Armitage."

He heard her then; looked up, but did not move. She pulled Sessy away from the Shetland, and closed the door despite the child's protests. They hurried across the yard.

"Mr. Armitage," she repeated. "Is everything all right?"

"I don't rightly know," he said, "I can't guess it."

This in itself was a surprise. Josiah knew everything. It was not some kind of arrogant act at all; he had a wealth of experience in what he did. He didn't pretend to know the world outside Rutherford, but he didn't need to. And so what he had acquired was faultless, exact. He was master of his small world. But the face that he turned up to her this morning was that of a lost boy.

"Can I help?" she asked. "What's the matter?"

"That I don't rightly know, miss." And he ran a hand through his hair distractedly. "It's the letter."

The letter. Suddenly, an icy cold blast ran through her. A cold tide of dread. "A letter . . . from France?" she asked. "Is it Jack?"

It seemed to Louisa as if a century passed while Josiah Armitage searched in first one pocket and then another. At last, he withdrew a familiar-looking pale-fawn-colored envelope. He handed it to her. But, to her overwhelming relief, it was not the terrible and formal announcement from the war office that she had expected. Inside the envelope was a folded and flimsy page. Her eyes ran down the script to the signature. "It's an army chaplain," she murmured. "About Jack."

"He can't come back," Josiah suddenly exclaimed. "Not like that."

"I'm sorry . . . like what?"

"What he says there. Fatigue."

"I don't know what that means, Josiah."

"It means he's a bad'un, warped in th'eed." The old man knuckled his eyes, actually resting his fists on his face. Louisa had never seen him express an emotion, much less cry.

"It can't mean that. Only that he must be exhausted."

"I know what that yon means," Josiah retorted savagely, dropping his hands. "Addled, like the rest! Come back weak in the knees, falling over hiss'en. Like Kessington were. Him that we had to send back to his mother."

"Oh no," she breathed. "It can't mean that at all."

"They don't send them back fer less. They'd have to be fallin' down, useless like. Else they don't send 'em back."

Louisa tried to read the letter. But the words swam in front of her eyes. Eventually, she looked back up at Josiah. Seeing the grief there, she gently put her hand on his arm. "May I take it to show Father?" she asked. "Would you mind awfully? Perhaps there's something that Father can do. You know . . . to find out a little more. To help in some way."

The man held her gaze for a second, evidently struggling with the idea that his shame should be revealed. Then he muttered, "He'll know sooner or later, I suppose." And with that, he turned away.

He looked back at his cottage, and then absently at the yard. And then he began to walk towards the fields, dragging his feet as if he had aged fifty years.

Chapter 19

The afternoon light came through the curtains, highlighting the bed.

Octavia was not asleep, but she lay with her head propped against the soft deep pillows, cradling John's body in her arms. He began to stir, and finally opened his eyes. For just a moment she saw an unusual expression—a mixture of resignation and grief—in his face. And then he smiled.

"Have I been asleep for long?"

"Six hours."

He frowned, wriggling to a sitting position. "I'm sorry, love."

"It doesn't matter," she told him. He looked away, although he held her hand. "Are you hungry?" she asked.

He ran a hand through his hair. "Not so much. Tell me what has been going on here with you."

"Not before I ring for something to eat. Or tea, at least."

It was a full half hour before he finished the tray of food that was brought to them, though he picked at it more than eating it whole-heartedly, sitting at the small table and gazing out into the street.

"I can see in your face that it was terrible in France," she said.

He didn't answer.

She got up, wrapped her dressing gown around her, and took the chair opposite him. "I have news," she said. "I have had a letter from Harry. And Louisa rang this afternoon. I do wish that Harry had come with you. I've something so pleasant to tell him. Something he would want to hear."

"Harry," he echoed.

"Yes, the letter came from a place called Poperinghe." Smiling, she took the letter from the pocket of the gown. "It's postmarked three days ago."

"That's right," he said. "We were in Poperinghe then."

"He says that he has been ordered to go to the Belgian border," she told him quietly. "I was so hoping that he would come home with you. That was what you led me to believe."

John pushed away the plate and the tray. "That's what he told me himself. It was only when we got close to Le Havre thirty-six hours ago that he said he would come back to England later."

"How much later?"

"Darling, I don't know." He frowned. "He said nothing to me at Poperinghe at all. The implication was that he was returning with me."

"But how can they keep him there?" Octavia asked, her voice rising. "He is not well. Your letter a week ago said as much."

"I don't know," he replied. "But when a man is ordered . . . disobedience is a court martial."

"They have no right at all to order him!" Octavia exclaimed. She put the letter into her lap, exasperated. "Oh, it's not your fault, John,

I know. Of course it isn't." She sighed. "But I wrote back at once. Because Hetty de Ray has worked her usual wonders. You remember Hetty—yes, you do," she exclaimed, seeing his doubtful expression. "Large woman, loud voice, husband in Whitehall?"

"Ah yes. How could I forget the redoubtable Hetty."

"Indeed. She has had word of Caitlin de Souza. Harry was so insistent that I try to find her. And Hetty's husband has a friend—oh gosh, I can hear her now over Harry—'A man who knows a man who knows a man, darling!'" Octavia gave a broad smile. "She's in Harrogate, of all places. I could have screamed when I got back here and found Hetty's telegram. I would have been only a few miles from Caitlin when I was at Rutherford."

"Thank God. Harry will be very happy indeed. Why Harrogate? That's a heck of a way from London."

"Recuperation. A country house turned over to nursing staff who've been injured."

"Injured? How?"

"There's no details. Hetty's abilities only run so far. When Harry's back we can go up there together. And I wrote to tell him. At Poperinghe. Of course I knew that the letter might miss him, but it was such good news that I sent it anyway. I've been imagining telling him for days now." She gave a great labored sigh. "I do so wish he had come back with you. How did he seem?"

It was the question that John had been dreading. "Just the same old Harry."

"Happy? That is, as happy as one can be?"

"Yes, darling. Comfortable in himself. Resigned, perhaps."

"Oh well," she sighed. "That is something, I suppose." She considered. "Resigned to what?"

"Oh, you know. The war. The frustration of it all."

"Just that?"

"Yes, just that."

"He says that it's a reconnaissance matter. Is it a new area for the troops?"

"I think so."

She lifted her head. "Let me tell you something more joyful. Mary Nash has had twin boys, at the house. At Rutherford."

"Good heavens!"

"Isn't it extraordinary? Louisa has put them in the next room to Sessy's nursery. They are making the devil of a noise, apparently."

John smiled. "David will be so pleased."

"William phoned me to say that David has been wounded. He'll be home to see his sons. Isn't that wonderful? The news is quite flying to and fro. Thank God for the efficiency of army mail." She sat back, wrapping the gown tightly around her. "Mary has told Mrs. Carlisle that he said he was near the sea. Do you think it's near to Harry? How many battles can there be on the coast?"

"It's a special operation, I think," John murmured absently. "At a place called Nieuwpoort."

"An operation? A true battle, you mean? An advance of some kind? You don't mean that Harry is involved in the same thing?"

"No, I don't mean that," John said hurriedly, although he could almost hear the lie in his own voice. He knew that Harry had been drawn to Nieuwpoort. He had been unable to resist the siren call. There might have been an order, or there might not have been an order. *Damn the boy*, he thought involuntarily. He looked at Octavia. "There are a great many events in all sorts of places, darling. Harry doesn't have to be even at the front line. He is an advisor."

She didn't answer. She looked hard in his face, seemed on the verge of questioning him further, and then let it go.

"Tell me what you've been doing," he prompted.

"I went up to Rutherford to see William," she replied. "I went to the mills, and saw Ferrow, and we have come up with a scheme to make a workshop for finished goods. Fancy goods, small things. For war wounded to work in. It's coming on apace. I've asked Louisa if she will supervise when I'm not there."

"And will she?"

"I hope so. She's . . . well, she has an issue. One that I don't quite know how to deal with. But never mind that."

"Is William well?"

"He seems so. I arranged for a new housekeeper. She came over from the Kents. William has taken a liking to her, at least."

"That's good. And Louisa . . ."

"Yes." She furrowed her brow, put a hand to her head momentarily, and the smiled. "Both my girls have been . . . I don't know the word for it. Secretive. Odd."

"In what way?"

"Darling, this is astonishing, I grant you. But I hope just a temporary thing. Charlotte has left Michael."

"You don't say."

She raised an eyebrow. "You're not surprised? Shocked?"

"I was never completely convinced. You know that."

"You don't suggest that I forced her into something?"

He smiled a little. "Did I say that?" he asked. "Ever? Or is that something you've said to yourself?"

She opened her mouth to speak, then thought about it. "Did I force her? No," she murmured. "But I was glad about it. He seemed such a nice sort of person."

"Where has she gone to?"

"Not very far. She's living with a friend. Christine. The artist."

"The one who came to your art fair at Rutherford?"

"Yes, the one who was going to paint Charlotte and Michael's portrait."

"And has she?"

"Not that I know of."

He leaned across, and took hold of her hand. "This is awful," he said. "Would you like me to go and see Michael?"

"What good will it do? She is absolutely determined that she will not go back to him. I'm at a loss. I've written to William and told him, and he hasn't replied. I daresay he feels just the same."

They sat looking at one another. In his own mind, John was thinking of Christine. He remembered her look, the directness of her gaze. "They have the same spirit," he murmured. "Christine and Charlotte."

"The same outlandishness," Octavia agreed. "It can't be countenanced in a married woman, John. It really can't. Not if they want to live any kind of decent life, an untroubled life, in the future."

He was still holding her hand. "I wonder what constitutes a decent life these days," he murmured. "Life of any kind should be sacrosanct to us now."

"That doesn't mean we sacrifice our standards, our ideals."

He glanced up at her. "And what is your ideal, Octavia?"

"That everyone should be happy."

"And how is that to be achieved?"

"By having . . ." She stopped. "By having freedom."

"To choose?"

She frowned. "But not by throwing good things away."

"Society's good things?"

"You mean us."

"You chose love over society."

"But Charlotte isn't running to find love or companionship. She's running away from it. Or a promise she made for it, at least." She hung her head. "I want Charlotte to be happy above anything else."

"And does she seem happy now?"

"Very much."

"With Christine."

"Yes." She began clearing the tray a little absentmindedly. Then she paused. "Happier than I've seen her in a very long time."

"Happier than her wedding day?"

"Well, one is always very nervous then."

"And have you seen Christine?"

"They came here together while I was away, apparently." And she smiled. "Now that I know you're safely back, I shall go over to Christine's studio, and talk to them both. Perhaps Christine might encourage Michael and Charlotte to speak to one another."

"Octavia," he said quietly.

She smiled brightly at him, leaned forward, took his hand, and gazed into his face. "What is it?"

"Perhaps Christine's friendship is more important to Charlotte than her marriage."

She didn't take his point. "But that's absurd!" she said. "Oh, I don't mean that it isn't very nice to have a friend, but one's husband . . ."

"She doesn't want this husband. And actually, darling, we're not in a position to lecture her about the sanctity and rightness of marriage."

"No, all right," she conceded. "But she was very close to Michael. She admired him."

"Octavia," he murmured. "Did you admire William? Do you still?"

"I respect him, yes. I admire the work he has done for his country."

"Like Michael."

"Yes."

"And why did you leave William?"

"But, John. You know the answer to that."

"Tell me."

She stared at him, puzzled. "Because I loved you."

"And that overrides anything else, doesn't it?" he said gently. "Convention. Institutions. What other people say. It overrides the respect or admiration that one might have for a husband, doesn't it? Perhaps it shouldn't. But I'm afraid that it does."

"Yes."

"Because one must be with this person. Because there is no conceivable choice but to be with them. Because they make you so happy."

"Yes . . ."

"Radiantly happy, darling."

"But . . ." She was still continuing to stare at him. And then suddenly, the truth dawned on her face, and she caught the inference entirely. "Oh, but you can't mean . . . !"

"Do you remember their talking together at the art fair? You told me that they couldn't be prised apart all the time that Christine was there. That Charlotte talked about her incessantly after she had gone. You told me yourself that Charlotte seemed besotted with this woman. Your words, darling. *Besotted*."

"I meant impressed. Charmed. I'm sure that it was . . ." He could see that she was on the verge of saying "nothing more," but she didn't. She hesitated, perplexed.

"And you told me that Christine had gone to Charlotte's room after the wedding ceremony."

"But it can't be. It's a friendship. Nothing more than that. Surely . . ."

"Radiantly happy, darling. You said so yourself. Happier than her wedding day."

"But to accept Michael's marriage proposal, if she felt that way!"

"Well, I don't know the answer there," he admitted. "But perhaps it was a last attempt to try to feel what society would call normal. To go through the motions, to *make* herself as others. But against her nature. Against her true feelings."

He watched as her mouth dropped open in surprise. She was not very deeply shocked, he could see: nor morally outraged, or even disapproving. None of the things that other people might be; none of the things that the previous generation might have been. Octavia was not a woman like that, he knew. She was not narrow-minded or self-righteous or demanding. But this was nevertheless outside her remit, her experience.

He got up, and pulled her gently to her feet, and embraced her. "Darling," he said, kissing her cheek, inhaling the wonderful scent of her hair, and closing his eyes against all the images of the last few weeks that threatened to invade his mind. "There are so many worse things in the world than falling in love with the wrong person. We should know that more than anyone else."

T he day ended quietly.
They ate a dinner at home, much preferring their own company to the noise of the city. After dinner they walked in the garden, and sat beside each other as the evening drew slowly on. For some time they said nothing at all, as the shadows lengthened and all around them the trees became dark outlines through which the first stars began to show.

At last, Octavia laid her head on John's shoulder. "What's the subject of your article for the newspaper this week?" she asked.

"My God," he murmured. "There are so many. There's so much I hesitate to write about for fear of hurting the families here."

"What, then? Something personal to yourself?"

"I was thinking a great deal about memorials, graves. How that would be organized. When it's over. Tracing the dead is actually a logistical nightmare. Many have simply disappeared."

"A memorial to the missing, then?"

"That would be appropriate, yes. Then—and this would strike a chord with Jack Armitage, I'm sure—there's the horses. The rations are low. I've seen horses that are plainly starving. One feels impotent, furious about it . . ."

Octavia suddenly sat up, and clapped her hand to her forehead. "Oh, but I forgot to tell you!"

"What?"

"Louisa phoned me to tell me that Jack is coming home. His father is very distressed because Jack has some sort of battle fatigue. Louisa spoke to William today. They're trying to contact the padre again who wrote the letter to Josiah. Apparently he said that Jack had been working with transporting the wounded, and he suffered some sort of breakdown. . . ."

"I'm very sorry to hear that. Jack is a good man."

"Yes, but darling. He couldn't be parted from the horses he was working with. He simply wouldn't leave them. There is your story. A man's loyalty to the horses, and how we should support them." She was gripping his arm. "I have rather a lot more to tell you about Louisa, but it'll wait until tomorrow. But I was thinking after her call . . . couldn't we raise money, start some sort of fund? For rations for the warhorses. When Jack comes home, perhaps he would like to be part of that."

John raised her hand to his lips, and smiled. "Shall you walk down Piccadilly, banging a drum and holding a collection plate?"

"Yes, of course. Some of those million horses were ours, you know. Rutherford's."

"I can see you now. You will be very charming."

"I don't want to be charming, John. I want to do something."

He stood up, stretched, and helped her to her feet. They walked up the path and reached the house, and stopped for a moment to look at the lights inside: the soft colors, the shine of the silver, the rich colors of the paintings, the bright reds and pinks of the roses in their vase by the fireplace.

"Where was the letter from?" John asked. "The padre's letter?"

"I don't think Louisa told me."

"And what about the horses, the ones that he wouldn't be parted from?"

"Some sort of heavy horses. The ones too broken down to be used on the artillery guns anymore."

"Perhaps one might be brought back. To use in the campaign. I wonder if it could be done."

"It would be wonderful," Octavia mused. And then, in little more than a whisper, "I keep thinking of Jack refusing to leave them."

"How sad," John observed.

"Yes, it is sad," Octavia agreed, slowly opening the door to the house. "But how like Jack."

Chapter 20

*I*t was a glorious day.

The motorcycle was tearing up the track, and it registered every bump of earth, every stone in their way; the vibration felt like the very devil to Harry, like the repeated prodding of a sharp blade in his right leg. But he didn't much care. The ride was a free one and the courier a wild character, roaring and cursing in a broad Glaswegian accent. He had given Harry a lift, an against-all-regulations lift, and for that Harry was grateful. They sang an RFC mess song at the tops of their voices. "*So stand your glasses steady, this world is a web of lies, here's to the dead already, and hurrah for the next man who dies.*"

The Glaswegian liked that. Harry put an arm around him when the leg got worse, and the courier grunted in complaint. "It's this or falling off," Harry had yelled in his ear.

"Fall off, then. You're a dead weight, sir," had come the reply.

They saw the coast before the airfield. A beautiful steel grey and blue line glimpsed over the flatness of the land; a haze out over the Channel. Harry knew that kind of sky. A man could take off in perfect sun and rise above the haze, and there could be a brown layer above that instead of the expected blue. He'd often wondered if it was the miasma from the millions of exploded shells. Somebody in the last station had talked darkly of a host of dark souls watching the world below. Been cuffed, of course for his bloody talk. Dark souls, indeed. Absolute tosser.

Although, in dreams . . . He'd dreamed a lot since leaving John Gould. Anxious that he had told a lie, when everyone was expecting his return, images came to him while asleep of empty railway stations, empty tracks. A sense of being uninhabited. And then he had seen that the image was always of the railway station nearest Rutherford. The track unused, with grass growing up between the sleepers. Weeds between the paving slabs on the platform. Moss hanging from the ticket barrier and the roof. Nature reclaiming the whole scene, obliterating even the road beyond. And he would wake in a sweat, wondering why he could imagine such a thing.

The track now became, quite suddenly, a decent but narrow road running right alongside the sea. Now and again a little shingle beach would appear, a rim of stones merely between the water and the flat, still-waterlogged fields beyond. Stunted poplars and willows passed them; trees that had been shaped almost to horizontal lines by the prevailing winds. *Good flying country*, Harry thought to himself.

Harry closed his eyes, inhaling the salt on the wind, and hearing the rumble of waves on the shingle. He thought of the Matthew Arnold poem had been taught at school. Something about a beach. Something about shingles, and the sound that it made as the waves came in. Was it Dover beach? He'd always thought of that being perplexing, because he had never seen a beach at Dover. He supposed that there must be one, of course. A beach like the ones in Sussex, deeply shelving shingle running down to the water. Like the one in Pevensey, where William the Conqueror was supposed to have come ashore. *On the French coast the light gleams and is gone, the cliffs of England stand. . . .*

He was suddenly struck with a piercing homesickness. *The cliffs of England stand. . . .* He ought to have gone home as commanded. As ordered. They seemed to have lost track of him now; perhaps when he arrived at Nieuwpoort they would have caught up with him. Perhaps he would walk into this air station and the commanding officer would say, "Cavendish? *Cavendish?* You bastard, you're not meant to be here. Get the fuck away with you. Go home. Quite plainly says here to go home. . . ."

But men did all kinds of strange and ungovernable things. Take the man Churchill, for instance. Yesterday Harry had seen a newspaper—the first in many days—and there had been an article about the previous First Lord of the Admiralty. Booted out of his government post, Churchill had been made lieutenant-colonel of the sixth Royal Scots Fusiliers. But it hadn't been for long: he was back in Parliament now, spouting off all the usual blarney. He'd got permission to go back to London because he'd said that his public duties had become urgent. Harry thought that was very funny, and the courier shared his opinion when Harry told him. "I read something about Churchill . . ." he had begun, when they had stopped to get water for the steaming, smoke-wreathed motorcycle. "Och aye, the Butcher of Gallipoli," had been the reply. "There's a real lot of urgent duties in a tart's knickers."

Harry couldn't help laughing. "He didn't go back for that. He's a good chap."

"That right?" the courier snarled. "He can come back and have some urgent business here, then. The Royal Scots lost half their battalion at Plug Street."

"He flies aircraft," Harry murmured.

"Aye, does he, now?"

"He used to take kites back to England for his leave. So this article said. Said the ships took too long."

"And he'd be a bloody lot safer up there," the courier said. "Only my opinion, mind. Only my opinion."

The words in the newspaper article had struck something in Harry's mind, and once the thought had arrived, he couldn't shake it loose. Churchill had taken a plane to go back to England. A needed plane. If he, Harry, went to Nieuwpoort against orders, then he might as well compound his misbehavior. He might as well fly back to Blighty.

Maybe he'd take a kite that was under maintenance. Nothing much wrong with an aircraft that was being trimmed; usually just a few bullet holes. If it started, if it was intact, he could take it from the maintenance engineers. Take it up. Then find a hapless Fritz, and knock up his number of hits while he was at it. Harry had nineteen kills to his name. He'd always thought that was an ugly, uneven number. He'd make it twenty as a kind of farewell. Then, and only then, would he take the plane home. After all, if it was good enough for Churchill . . .

It was just before nine when they reached the temporary airstrip.

It looked like a poor campsite, tents billowing in the wind where pegs had shaken loose. It was like washing day, sheets cracking in the sharp wind. Men were running round trying to repair them; Harry could smell breakfast being cooked. Dew was thick on the grass, and the kites were lined up in three long rows, like girls waiting to be asked to dance. Harry got off the motorcycle, thanked the courier, apologized for being a burden. The courier had grinned at him. "Can't really tell an officer to go to hell," he had said, and shaken Harry's hand.

Harry had watched him running towards the nearest building: a farm had been here once, and part of the farmhouse remained. To one side, a wall had been exposed, and it was painted bright yellow. His mother's sitting room in London was that color. It was the same color as the drawing room in Grosvenor Square. He liked his mother's eye; so much more cheerful than the dour preferences of his father. He always thought of William in tones of earth: brown, dark green. His mother was more like him. Bright blue. Summer colors. Yellow and pink. Apricot and rose. The cheerfulness of the memory made him smile. He would salvage something out of this mess, he thought. He would make a pretty little home with Caitlin somewhere. Perhaps he would actually go to Texas. Everything would be better there. Quiet and less complicated.

He saw himself by another ocean, another stretch of beach. They said that the beaches were fantastic in California. He would like to see them. He would like to see that whole coast. Swim in the warm water, perhaps. That would do a power of good to his aching legs. San Francisco was being rebuilt now: that was an optimistic city. He could breathe fresh air there. None of the grinding and oppressive business of aristocracy, the crushing sense of responsibility.

He would take a few years out of it all, he decided. Out of the old country and into the new. John Gould would advise him of what was best to do. How to be an American. He stood in the sunshine and laughed to himself. He could be a boy for a while, he considered. He'd never had much of a chance; just those wild days in London after Emily's death, when he had been consumed by guilt of his treatment of her.

No. He would start again. That was what war and peace was all about, surely. One fought for a fresh start, a different perspective. One fought to do away with all that was old and outdated. He could do that; forge something better, take up challenges. In time, he could bring them back to Rutherford. Churchill's example, if it showed him anything, was that one mustn't be bound in by rules that others wrote down for you. It was possible to rewrite one's own history, surely. Start afresh. Fly.

Watching almost absentmindedly, he saw the courier come out of the farmhouse and gesture towards him. The RFC officer alongside put his hands on his hips. He made a kind of pantomime exaggeration of shaking his head. Then he lifted his arm, and beckoned Harry.

On the way, the courier passed him.

"You're not going straight back?" Harry asked.

"I am," the man replied. "But at least I'm not in your shoes, sir. Good bloody luck."

The squadron leader was very young; perhaps younger than himself. It was hard to tell these days. He was, at least, extremely tidy and clean, unlike Harry. This was made quite explicit as the officer's eyes ranged up and down Harry's disheveled figure. "You had better come with me," he said at last.

They walked through the house and into a sitting room that might have been in Sussex. An overstuffed sofa; a Victorian glass case with taxidermy inside. Hummingbirds. Harry stared at it in wonder. That it had survived; that it was the most vivid and most poignant picture. Forty or fifty hummingbirds sealed forever against a watercolor sky, their wings outstretched. And alongside the domed glass, a round farmhouse table with a cloth. A white cloth. Harry looked further around the room. Curtains. A windup phonograph. A bookcase. A pile of magazines. A framed photograph of a handsome man and two small sons, and their mother looking modest in a Breton headdress. He wondered where she was now; where they all were. They might have merely stepped outside.

"Sit down," the officer said.

Harry did so, in the nearest armchair. Such unaccustomed luxury made him feel immediately sleepy.

"You must be very pleased with yourself."

"Pleased?" Harry replied laconically. "Not at all."

"I had a call yesterday to say that I might expect you."

This was a genuine surprise. "Oh really?"

"Last station you passed through."

"Ah."

Well, yes. He had told the captain there that he didn't want an escort through what was a very hot area, *minenwerfers* pounding away a few miles to the east. Harry lowered his eyes to the carpet.

"Acting very much like desertion, rattling around the country with no rhyme or reason."

That made Harry sit up. "You will retract that," he retorted. "I cannot be deserting a post from which I've been relieved. I might be deserting a hospital ship, but I doubt they'll take a head count. It's not a holiday cruise. They don't have a passenger list."

"That's what you're relying on, I suppose."

"I'm not relying on anything."

"God in heaven, Cavendish, what do you think this is?" the officer suddenly demanded, red in the face. "You treat it *exactly* as one would a holiday! You are ordered to go back to England and instead you jaunt around the countryside. Why the devil have you come here?"

"I heard of the operation."

"And you thought you might come along and gawp at it."

"I came to observe."

"You've no bloody business observing anything. Nobody asked for you."

Harry stared at his feet for a while. Then, very slowly, he leaned forward. "I daresay I am a thorn in the side of the Flying Corps," he said, enunciating each word precisely. "But I have not commandeered any transport to arrive here. I am on my way to port, via a strange diversion, I grant you. If my advice is not needed, I shall go on my merry way."

"Advice!" The man looked at him. His face bore every evidence of trying to add up the sum parts of Harry's case, and finding that none of it came to a satisfactory total.

"I am following orders to Le Havre," Harry added. "If you do not want me here, so be it."

"You are a bloody fool," the officer remarked.

"And you are impertinent," Harry exclaimed suddenly. "You don't outrank me any more than I outrank you, so I shall be obliged if you keep your fatuous remarks to yourself."

"I am making a report to HQ."

"Make it in triplicate," Harry said. "You bloody pen pusher." He struggled out of the chair, and went out of the room, ignoring the calls for him to come back.

Once outside, he walked over to the planes.

The man was right, of course. Harry didn't like to admit it, but it was true. If everyone did as he had done, the war would be lost. A fighting force had to keep track of its men, and the men themselves had to keep together and act as a unit. He supposed that the word was that he was ill, and for that he had been given some leeway; leeway which meant that, for all the bluff and bluster, he might be allowed to remain in the RFC.

If the truth were known, that was what worried him most. That—either due to illness or subordination—he would be forced to leave. He reasoned with himself they wouldn't lose an experienced man—for after all, how many were left?—but all the same the tirade just now convinced him that he ought to toe the line.

He looked longingly at the line of Bristol fighters, the BF.2s. New

babies brought in at Arras and most of the first ones downed in what
they now called "bloody April." They'd learned lessons from that;
learned how to use them properly. Harry didn't know how many men
had died in learning those lessons. He guessed that the lifespan of a
pilot in that month—judging by his own unit's losses—at something
like twenty hours. Twenty hours, for God's sake. It wasn't right. But
then nothing was quite right anymore. He sighed to himself.

He ran his eye up the line of machines and spotted the new
Sopwith biplanes at the far end. He had never been in one. It was
rumored that it took three months to get used to them; they were
touchy machines with a strong right-hand list. He wondered now
what it would be like to soar to the nineteen thousand feet and 110
miles an hour that they were reputed to achieve. Nineteen thousand
feet! Close to heaven. Unshackled. Faster than the birds, cracking
the sky in two.

Looking at them now, he recalled the rakish innocence of the
early days. In the summer of 1914, no one had guessed that these
glorious toys would be used in war. The early pilots—before 1912—
had flown over a million miles and only 140 had been killed. And
usually that was from what the boffins called "preventable causes"—
putting a plane into too deep a dive, or fuel exploding, or poor maintenance. Or simple devilry—showboating for the gaping crowds
below.

But, by God, it had been enormous fun. Even when he had flown
across the Channel for the first time, the hair-raising nature of it had
merely been an excess of adrenaline, not fear for one's very life. He
had always had an absolute confidence in his own ability and—his
father would be surprised to hear it—he was capable of being stone-
cold calm once he was airborne. In the early days of the war it had
got him out of many a scrape. Now, he merely watched from the
ground, having told the pilots to employ the same care. "Sit tight and

don't sleep," he told them, meaning to keep aware, keep an even temper. No triumphalism. No coarse language to the observer, or contempt of the enemy. No stunts. Not now. Not anymore.

He approached the nearest plane, and put his hand on the fuselage. He could see that it had been repaired. The circles were freshly painted on the underside of the wings.

"Help you, sir?"

He looked around. One of the ground crew had come alongside him and was staring at him inquiringly. He introduced himself. "She been up today?"

"Yesterday, sir."

"Over Nieuwpoort?"

"That's right, sir. You've been out here long, sir?"

Harry wondered if he would be believed if he told the man he had been one of the first three years ago. He and Harvey-Kelly. Hubert Harvey-Kelly, who was now the commanding officer at Vert Galant. Harry put a hand to his head. No, that was not right, he thought. Hubert was no longer there. He had gone up in battle over Douai in April—"bloody April." The top man, Trenchard, had arrived to speak to him—he shouldn't have been up, and a meeting was scheduled—and Trenchard had waited for Hubert to return. But Harvey-Kelly never came back. He'd been shot down by that well-named harbinger of doom, the Albatross.

Harvey-Kelly dead. Leefe Robinson VC, captured. Albert Ball—that pinup boy—had died on the seventh of May. Gone the way of so many. Harry glanced again at the man alongside him. "Been here a lifetime or two. But you mustn't mind me," he said brightly. "Off home shortly. Fix me up."

"Fix you, sir?"

"Knee injury."

"Ah. Then good luck, sir." They both paused, listening to a sudden artillery bombardment somewhere to the east. It started up like growling thunder, the sound rolling in their direction. "Shore batteries and naval guns," the mechanic said. "Australians are up on the Yser line."

"Sounds bloody fierce."

The mechanic nodded. "Catching a ship out of where, sir?"

"Le Havre."

"I came in that way," the man said. "Port is mined now. Tricky business since the *Salta*."

Harry was just in the act of turning back for the farmhouse. He stopped and stared, frowning. "The *Salta*?" he echoed. "The hospital ship?"

"That's right. Got to be right careful. She's sunk in the shipping lane. April. Struck a mine. She went down in ten minutes and the boat that came alongside struck another, and that was lost, too. Can you credit it? Bastard Krauts."

"She went down?" Harry repeated.

"About a mile and a half outside, in the Channel."

"What happened to those on board?"

"Lot of crew gone. Eighty, they said. People on the dock were still talking about the row it made. All gone up in a second. It weren't full, though. It were coming back loaded with medicals."

"Nurses?"

"And RAMC."

"Nurses . . ."

"A lot got off. Nine drowned. There's a memorial to the RAMC and nurses in the field station near the port. I saw it when I visited a mate. Stuck in my memory, like. Nurses and doctors and supplies. Not even fighting men. Turns your stomach. It properly does."

Harry was looking at him silently. He couldn't frame a single word. Eventually, the man pulled on his cap by way of salute. "You'll excuse me, sir," he said.

"Yes. Yes, of course. . . ."

He watched him walk away.

He closed his eyes, and listened to the thunder in the east.

*I*n London, Charlotte and Christine had been awake for several hours.

There was a bag packed by the door; a leather doctor's bag that they had found in a market stall, much creased and battered, but with a good strong lock. Just before dawn, Charlotte had got up and walked to the door and stood over the luggage—the bag, and Christine's sketchpads and portfolio tied together with a webbing strap. She had stood with her hands pressed to her face, until she had heard Christine padding across the room behind her, barefooted. In a moment, the other woman's arms had encircled her.

"I shan't be gone long."

"But how long is 'not long'?"

"Darling, I don't know. It's a job of work."

"I shall miss you." She had turned to Christine, and held her hand. "I'm sorry," she murmured. "I sound so utterly maudlin."

"You *are* maudlin. It's very boring," Christine replied, smiling. "Such a disappointment to me. I had you down as being much more interesting."

They had gone back to bed, but neither of them had slept. They'd lain and watched the sun rise over London. There were no curtains at all now at the window, and the bed was nothing more than a mattress laid on the floor. But it didn't matter to them. Nothing did. Nothing and no one.

"I'll write to you," Christine told her. "I'll send you sketches, too."

"Have they told you where you're going?"

"Not a word. But you shall know, if I'm allowed to say."

"You won't go to the front, though."

Christine had kissed her gently. "Do you think *Paths of Glory* or *La Mitrailleuse* were painted after taking afternoon tea?"

There was no answer to that.

Eventually, Christine got up and held out her hand. "Come with me," she said.

Together, they walked over to the easel. It still stood at the far end of the table, and was draped with a cloth. Standing in front of it, Christine eased the cloth away and let it fall to the floor. They looked at the portrait that had been finished yesterday.

Charlotte sat half in shadow and half in light. The division struck diagonally across the painting; in the bottom half, the purple and emerald of the material glowed with supernatural brilliance. In the upper half, Charlotte's bare shoulders were chalk-white. She looked away from the viewer, out past the window, where the rooftops of London were depicted in shades of steel grey and blue under a blazing sky. In the top left-hand corner, a mirror reflection showed her back, arched to one side, as if she were about to spring from her sitting position.

The face on the canvas was brilliantly alive, the mouth parted, the hair cut short and straight, dark with shades of copper. The one visible hand that lay in the lap was not relaxed, but had the fingers defined and spread, the material rippled between them. It was as if Charlotte were clutching at color and life. There was more than a hint of a smile in the eyes, in the tilt of the head, in the energy of that hand and those fingers.

They did not discuss it, even now. There was no need. It was perfect.

In years to come, it would be called *La Fille Vert* on gallery cata-
logues. But the real title was more personal.

Christine would always call it *L'Evasion*. The escape.

*W*ithout thinking, without looking back, without listening
to any sound, Harry walked down the line and climbed
up into the Sopwith Camel. He sat for a few seconds acclimating
himself to the controls, the layout inside. It might have been minutes,
it might have been half an hour, it might have been a day for all he
knew or cared. Until the mechanic came running back.

"I'm taking her up," he said. "Tell them it's Commander
Cavendish."

The mechanic looked doubtful, but he was outranked. Together
they started her; the mechanic got down and watched Harry take
her out of the line.

If anyone then wanted to stop him, he knew that they couldn't.
He was airborne in a few seconds, and wheeling over the airfield, and
the world became a grainy map underneath him, and he was alone.

Harry wondered absently how the distance would feel, to go back
all the way to England and Rutherford. And he wondered about his
father; if William might be able to teach him to live alone for the
rest of his life.

He knew that Caitlin was no longer living. She was either lying
in a grave in Le Havre, in one of those cement lines that they tried
so much to keep orderly, or she was lying in cold water a mile out
from France, or something much worse had happened. She was deaf
and dumb and dead in her soul. He'd seen it. He'd seen the face of
the poor bloody infantry in train sidings and in field stations. He'd
listened to them, but watching them was much harder. And he'd
seen it a thousand times in his own crews.

A man came out to serve. Young man, hardly able to grow a moustache, so young was he, so baby-faced, so eager. Little children in men's clothes. They came out and he'd meet them, give them the pep talk, see the enthusiasm, and watch the vibrancy in them. And he'd say, *Don't take the buggers for granted. Watch your sky. Question the observer if you have a moment's doubt. Don't be a hero; just get the job done.*

And they would listen. They really would. For the first half dozen times. And then the light would go in their faces. That fresh and eager light. It would be replaced with something harder. A grim determination. And then fatigue. They were brave men, but they knew nothing. Getting in a plane was the steepest climb out of consciousness; it was a dreamlike state; it was like nothing else. When they came back to earth they were silent, or they snapped replies stuttering like trails of bullets. Grey washed their faces, and puzzlement. A perplexity of the shattering of ideals, and a sense of the utter strangeness of flight.

It was another world at fifteen thousand feet. Among the gods and elements, with no boundary markers but the scribbled lines in the ground underneath them. Puffs of smoke below might mean a hundred men slaughtered; traces of dark air the only evidence that a team of men below were trying to end one's own life. Air currents plucked at the wings, and thermal currents buoyed one up or tore one down.

The days would wear on, punctuated by triumphs, scarred by losses. And then the faces would change again. Sometimes a man would come down and appear quite unscathed, and then—it might be an hour later, it might be days—he would begin to shake. One couldn't control those nervous reactions. Shame and embarrassment clouded the eyes. What had been a smiling recruit only a month ago became withdrawn.

And then the worst of all. The broken psyche. What was the saying? *The butterfly broken on the wheel*. It was not done to remark on it of course: if a commanding officer saw such an expression, he might wisely advise a month in Blighty, a spell in hospital. Craiglockhart or somewhere of the sort. The place for mending men. Sometimes those who had been sent away came back, apparently healed. But Harry doubted that healing was possible. It was a plastering-over of invisible wounds, and once back in service that man would reveal his anguish. He would—sooner or later—be Icarus flying too close to the sun. He would come back to earth with wings burning.

Harry couldn't bear to see anything resembling that in Caitlin's face. He couldn't cope with it in his men—could hardly cope with it. It was what had driven something essential out of his own character, he knew. Hardened to necessity. He couldn't bear to look in her face and know she'd lost that crucial piece of humanity. Or was pretending at life.

The plane roared upwards, and he tried to stop thinking.

Sensitive and unpredictable, the Camel had to be kept strictly in a flying position to stop it rearing up. He tried to recall all he knew about the new Sopwith. Hold the nose steady. Resist the powerful torque of the rotary engine that wanted to haul the machine to the right. Balance the left rudder to prevent a spinning nosedive.

He was flying a knife-edge in more ways than one. Flying a machine he was unused to; flying without permission towards the English coast. Flying without sense of himself.

Ah, love, let us be true to one another! For the world, which seems to lie before us like a land of dreams . . .

That was the ending of the Arnold poem. For a moment, the verse became alarmingly clear; he was nine years old again, and reciting it for his tutor. Funny how things came back to you. Funny what was lodged there in the back of your mind.

He glanced to his right; he had seen a sudden glassy reflection out of the corner of his eye. But there was nothing there now, only a bank of clouds below. The coast of Belgium looked terribly messed beyond Nieuwpoort and around the Yser, God help them.

Swept with confused alarms of struggle and flight . . .

He'd seen most of it, he thought. Most of what a plane could do. He wondered what else they would dream up for them, in time. He pulled the Sopwith higher, above a trail of smoke, a thin drift of cloud. He felt very tired; so tired that he could sleep. In a slow, rolling cadence other flights came back to him.

Going very low over Passchendaele. Ordered to fly in the tunnel created by the trajectory of British shells. To come out of the fire, as it were, to take the enemy by surprise. Flying in pairs. He'd watched his colleague go into the tunnel and followed him from the other side, and passed into a hell on earth. He was so low that he could see the wreckage of men and machines on the ground; even see the barbed wire. So low that he passed over a German machine-gun post and saw them diving for cover.

Flying towards a church tower . . . Where had that been? He'd had a juvenile idea that he could use the tower for target practice, and God had rewarded him by putting a sniper in the tower. A bullet came straight through the windshield. Missed him by a fraction of an inch.

Of course, some men had an aura of invincibility about them. Hardly human, he considered. Naturally one felt like that on first flying. The invincibility part. The feeling of eternity in an empty sky. One absorbed it. But only for a while. Sooner or later the look came to one's eyes, the "thousand yard stare" that the men on the ground talked about. The infantry got it after bombardments; numbness and shock. But the air crews got it when heaven came crashing down. When one realized there was a limit.

The flash again. He turned his head.

There was a Hun above him, and in the same moment that Harry realized what it was, there came a burst of machine gun fire. He felt the bullets hit his plane. *Good God, I'm done for*, he thought. He was utterly calm. He knew that his seat was positioned right over the fuel tank, and that if a bullet hit the petrol vapor, it would explode. But nothing happened. The bullet must have gone through the fuel.

He tried to swerve, to dive. But the tank was finished. He only had the gravity tank on the wing. But you couldn't climb, achieve height, with just the gravity tank.

He saw the German plane come back, rear up like a horse just yards away. For a second of absolute clarity, Harry admired the skill. He relaxed his hands on the controls. He looked down the silhouette of his enemy, the lines of the wings, the fragility of the machine, the arc that the plane was describing.

The sky was so clear, and the earth so small.

*T*he German pilot landed behind Peronne an hour later, after chasing other Sopwiths up and down the Yser.

He was spattered with oil, and had run out of ammunition. The plane grumbled as he landed—there was a wheel fixed, hit by shrapnel from below. It brought the machine to a grinding half circle, and he scrambled to disengage the controls and jump free.

He ran back across the grass, pulled off his helmet, and stood there in the field, in the sunshine of the late afternoon, gasping for breath.

When he made his report, he told them about the Sopwith kill. They slapped him on the back to congratulate him, and he walked to his camp bed, and laid down on it, and closed his eyes.

But he knew that he wouldn't sleep again. Not the kind of sleep he needed. Not the oblivion he wanted. He wouldn't sleep because he wouldn't forget that Sopwith pilot. They had been only feet from each other, and he had looked into the other man's eyes. The Englishman had been handsome, not very old. He had been headed, strangely, towards the coast, alone. Quite alone. And he had taken no real action. Once he had at last noticed him, he had not really evaded him.

The strangest thing of all—the thing that he could not forget—was how that Englishman had looked at him. So directly. He had looked at him and actually smiled. And, as the Sopwith had begun to fall, the pilot had held up his hand in an eerily leisurely fashion. The Sopwith had begun to spiral; he had watched it go down, vanish in the line of brown smoke for a moment, and emerge almost immediately, tipped on its end.

He had circled over the spot, and saw how suddenly, not a hundred feet from the ground, the plane had exploded. An orange bloom of fire; petals of dust and smoke as the impact came. Black stems of burning fuel. A ghastly drawing of a burning flower in the middle of a waterlogged field by the sea.

He would never get it out of his mind.

Because of the smile. The Englishman's smile.

And his casual wave of farewell.

Epilogue

It was snowing heavily when the train pulled into the station. It was early in the morning, and the week before Christmas. The mail train serviced the villages all along the river valley right up to Rutherford, and on most days there would be other freight; the usual deliveries to the farms—feed or small machinery. But this morning the cargo was very different.

The stationmaster and his men had spent an hour in the early morning darkness shoveling the snow from the platform. Ice hung from the roof, and they worked in pools of bright light reflected from the waiting room windows. Then, as the morning finally dawned, and they heard the steam train coming along the line, the ramp was ready to put alongside the guard's van.

A small crowd from the village stood waiting. There was an air of expectancy because of the fame of the Shire horse; because it had been in the London and Yorkshire newspapers, and because an unheard-of species—several newspaper reporters—had come to the houses grouped around the green and the church and asked what they knew of Rutherford.

No one liked to say very much. In any normal circumstances, they might have celebrated—brought out the bunting and flags. Perhaps had a little meeting at the village hall before the horse was taken up to the Park. But it didn't seem right anymore. They were glad that the Shire was back—who could not be glad at such a miracle?—but the return was mixed with grief. There were so many men who had not returned, and here was a horse, simply a horse, rescued out of the mire of France.

And so it was with mixed feelings that the crowd at the station watched the ramp taken to the train, and the doors open. A kind of sigh went around in the freezing air as the great grey Shire stumbled, feeling its way uncertainly down the short slope. Those that had known it before it had left over two years ago let a ripple of shock escape them. Its sides were scarred, and the ribs showed, even now. For a moment it hung its head at an odd angle. And then they realized that its sight was poor; that the movement of the head was an attempt to see clearly at all.

They murmured among themselves. Here and there a name. Here and there a word of admiration. They watched the American emerge from the van, and a photographer stepped forward. They posed, until the flashlight sent a violent tremble along the horse's flanks. John Gould took hold of the leading rein, and the horse followed like a child.

The crowd formed a line behind them both, and they crossed the station yard. Seen from above, they resembled a long dark thread among the whiteness of the snow, slipping on the wet ridges made by wheel tracks, walking the two miles out of the village, and at last turning in at the gates of Rutherford under the statues of the bluebirds, and the bare branches of the trees.

Far behind the followers, a man walked alone. He had waited until the station yard was empty before he had got off the train, and, when he did so, the stationmaster had stepped forward and shaken his hand. The station men watched him go, seeing the difference in him. They half expected him to falter or fall. But he kept upright, slinging his bag over his shoulder and walking with slow and concentrated determination.

It was only when he was out of their sight that Jack Armitage stopped to steady himself, to take a breath, and look around him. He had reached the village church, and ran his hand gratefully along the stone wall that skirted the graveyard. He waited while the clock in the church tower chimed eight.

And so he was the last to come down the long beech drive to the great house. Far ahead, he could see the head of the horse visible above the crowd. He finally smiled to himself, remembering the summers that he had walked behind Wenceslas, and the winters like these that had named him. The horse had been born in snow, a harsh and unexpected spring snow that had wreathed the parkland for weeks. His first steps had been taken out in the unmarked sweep of white that was the river pasture, and the name had been given to mark those memorable imprints on the ground, the line of hoofprints across the sleeping grass.

Jack slowed his pace as he got closer to the house.

The crowd had stopped at a respectful distance; there was no sound now. No talking as there had been as they walked the lanes. Just the soft hush of the rolling grounds, the snow-silenced hill, the frozen trees.

On the steps of the house, a group had been waiting to meet them.

Jack searched the figures, looking for only one. She was not there, it seemed. He glanced over at the house, seeing how the blinds were still down. It had been more than three months now, but the mark of mourning—the drawing of blinds—would not leave Rutherford until the following year was out. Until the shock became a little muted, a fraction bearable. Until another summer had come and gone.

Lord and Lady Cavendish stood side by side, watching the procession. His lordship leaned heavily on a walking stick; his wife—for she was still his wife, Jack knew, if only in name—was wrapped in a deep-collared coat pulled so high around her face that only her eyes were visible, and her mouth was obscured. But he saw the same expression in both faces; even today, grief had disfigured her ladyship's beauty and his lordship's stoicism. They looked, Jack thought, like two mystified children. Helplessly human, diminished in size somehow. He pitied them, and hung back, guilty to be the one who was coming home. He was quite sure that it was not him whom they wanted to see.

Then the silence was broken. The door behind them opened, and a slight figure walked forward. It was Louisa, and she was holding Harry's daughter's hand. It took the child to do what the adults seemingly could not do, at least at first: breaking free of Louisa's grip, Sessy rushed down the steps and flung herself at Wenceslas, holding up her hands so that the horse lowered its head to perceive her. Streams of the horse's breath surrounded her; the warmth of life in a cold world. The little girl began to dance around, and the crowd watched her, and, like sunlight breaking through the gloom, there were smiles. Others grew close, stroked the flank of the Shire. Voices rose on the air.

John Gould walked up the steps, but stopped halfway up. He looked up at those above him, staff and family alike. "We've brought them home," he said. And something about it working well—something that Jack could not catch. He was not concentrating. He was looking at Louisa.

She stopped next to her parents for a while, her arms crossed in front of her as if she were very cold. She and Jack regarded each other without a smile, without a hand raised in recognition. It was a stare deeper than all else. Deeper than words. And then, out of the corner of his eye, Jack saw his own mother and father walking towards him. At the last moment, his mother rushed forward. He hadn't known that he was falling, or even that he was so cold to the touch. He heard his mother exclaiming, felt a coat being wrapped around his shoulders. "I wanted to walk," he told them.

Then down the house steps came Bradfield, marshaling Hardy and the hallboy Albert behind him. They were carrying hot drinks. On the trays were branches of holly and red ribbons. Jack saw one such raised to Wenceslas's head, and pinned to his bridle. Ribbons of red, he thought, in confusion. Red against soil and snow and hands and faces. He looked at his feet, took a breath. Felt his father's arm around his waist. It was nearly Christmas, that was all. That was all it signified. He was given brandy, and coffee that smelled incredibly sweet and rich. The household had made all kinds of little cakes and biscuits; he put one to his mouth, but couldn't stomach it. The brandy was scoring a white-hot circle in his stomach. He was unused to spirits. His vision swam.

And so it might have been a dream that Louisa came down the steps. It might have been a dream that she went to the horse and smoothed his neck, and whispered, "Good boy," in that familiarly soft voice. The same voice she had used when they had cajoled Wenceslas towards the trucks that had carried him away. Sweet persuasion. He watched her hands.

And it might have been a dream, so much later. Later in the day as the afternoon light drained away. It might have been a dream because it was what had been in Jack's mind and what he had hoped for for so long. He had visualized her all the way from France and all the way to the north of England, and all the way on the slow mail train weaving its way across the hills.

But he knew when he saw her come across the yard; saw her running despite the snow.

He knew when he opened the door of the stable, and she rushed into his arms and held him so tightly, and turned her face up to him, smiling, laughing, and taking his hands in her own. And then she buried her face in his shoulder and he felt a kind of shaking run through her. And he heard her say, "It's all right now, Jack. It's all right now."

No, it was not a dream. Never a need to dream again.

For this was the real world at last.

READERS GUIDE

FOR

*The Gates
of Rutherford*

BY

ELIZABETH COOKE

Discussion Questions

1. Octavia is in a loving, happy relationship with a man who is not her husband, yet she objects to Louisa's relationship with Jack, and also encourages Charlotte to go back to her husband out of "duty." She even says, "It doesn't matter about me, but you girls must make lasting and sensible marriages." Why do you think Octavia advocates for "sensible marriages" for her daughters when it's not what she wants for herself?

2. William stays at Rutherford, clinging to what remains of its grandeur and reputation. However, when he is speaking with Octavia, she notices signs of "a loving man longing to be let out of his prison, who could see his wife coming and going free as a bird." Do you feel sorry for William? What exactly is this prison he wants to break free from? Is it simply Rutherford or something else?

3. What do you think Rutherford signifies, especially considering the novel's title? Is it a safe haven, a place for Louisa and William to live in peace, or does it imprison its inhabitants?

4. At the very beginning of the novel, Charlotte recalls longing for "the old untouched days at Rutherford . . . the innocence of it all, the feeling that England would never change." Which characters do you think embrace the changing times, and which seem to be

trapped in the past? Going further, how do you think their willingness to embrace change affects their happiness?

5. In the epilogue, Jack Armitage returns home from the war with Wenceslas, the Cavendishes' great Shire. Do you think that this ending is hopeful, or does it represent defeat as both Jack and Wenceslas show signs of psychological and physical breakdowns? Further, why do you think Wenceslas is such a presence throughout the novel?

6. The German pilot who shoots down Harry's plane will never forget the "Englishman's smile. And his casual wave of farewell." Why do you think Harry is so content to meet his end? Do you think he is at peace with his life, or has he given up?

7. Octavia is a woman of the upper class, but often feels uncomfortable or even guilty, especially when she wears the latest fashions in Yorkshire or when those of a lower class treat her as if she were royalty. To what extent does Octavia shun society's expectations of what a woman of her class should be, and to what extent does she comply? What does this say about her character?

8. Do you think Louisa is truly happy at Rutherford, caring for Sessy and Mary's twins while waiting for Jack? Or do you think she's scared after being left at the altar, too intimidated to leave Rutherford again?

9. Jenny and Frederick are instantly drawn to each other, yet their countries are at war. Why do you think they feel such a strong connection, even though they have barely spoken a word?

10. Mary is terrified that she will suffer the same fate as Emily, who died during childbirth. However, with Frederick's help, she gives birth to twins. Why do you think the author chose Frederick to deliver the twins, ensuring that history did not repeat itself?

11. Frederick is able to momentarily create peace among his fellow prisoners and the British guard when he sings: "They were all, every man of them, defeated by the loveliness of the song." Why do you think the author paints Frederick the German as such a gentle, kind man? What does this scene in particular show about war's impact on one's sense of humanity?

12. Before she gets married, Charlotte considers the house her mother and John Gould share, and "could see a kind of correctness, a way of holding on to life." Do you think Louisa and Charlotte would have had the courage to be with the ones they truly love if Octavia had not set the example?

13. Patriotism is a central theme throughout the novel, as the women do what they can to support the war effort and the men are eager to enlist. If you were in the same situation as Jenny and Mary, who are asked to bring their enemies food, would you do as you were told or would you consider that to be unpatriotic? What, to you, does it mean to be truly patriotic?

14. How would you describe the relationship between William and John? Do you think that on some level they respect each other, or are they simply rivals?

15. Christine is an artist, helping others to see what they cannot. She not only paints what blind soldiers cannot physically see, but also desperately wants to paint Charlotte so she can see her true self. Do you think Christine represents a sense of truth? If so, what does this say about the novel's message, considering her character and status?

Read on for a preview of
the first novel of Rutherford Park

Rutherford Park

Available now from Berkley Books

*S*now had fallen in the night, and now the great house, standing at the head of the valley, seemed like a five-hundred-year-old ship sailing in a white ocean. Around it spread the parkland, the woods, terraces and gardens; beyond it and high above was the massive slope of the woodlands and the moor. To the south and the east, the river described a wide loop; to the west, the nine-acre lake was a grey mirror fringed with ice.

Although it was early, Rutherford was not asleep. It was never truly asleep, for everywhere in that white landscape there was hard labor to keep the estate functioning. Power and influence had raised Rutherford; power and influence trailed in its wake. Just as the late Victorian additions to the house spread outwards from the Tudor hall where the first brick had been laid in 1530, so Rutherford spread outwards from the house itself, radiating through the tenant farms, the villages, the long sweep of the valley down towards York, touching and altering everything in its path: commanding lives, changing landscapes.

On the first floor now, above the terrace, a light was shining, and the heavy curtains of the largest room in the west wing were drawn back. It was barely seven, but Octavia Cavendish had been awake for some time. She sat swathed in the Poiret dressing gown, full-length black-and-white satin, lined in sable, that William had bought her in London eighteen months ago. A fire glowed in the limestone-framed fireplace; Octavia's morning tea was laid to one side.

Around her fussed Amelie, her maid, laying out the first changes of clothes of the day: four alternatives. The lavender, perhaps, for luncheon, or the morning dress of grey velvet. A tea gown for the afternoon. And the elaborate white tulle with green appliqué for the evening. Past the gowns, on the dressing table, Amelie had already spread out the jewels that had once belonged to Octavia's husband's mother: heavyweight emeralds set in gold, and the opals, which she particularly loathed. In a room awash with silks and gauzes, Octavia looked, and felt, like some overblown rose wilting before the fire. "The lavender," she decided eventually. Amelie dipped her head in agreement, bundled up the grey velvet over her arm, and retreated to the dressing room.

Octavia got up and looked out at the snow. It was more than an hour since she had first noticed the great beech tree lying on its side at the top of the drive, and she gazed at it now, watching the men gathering below the curved steps: monochrome silhouettes against the branches and the burned-out color of last year's leaves.

She had an overwhelming feeling that she might go outside; she might go and listen to their conversations. She might run in the snow as the children used to. She remembered running across this perfect lawn, this perfect terrace, when she had first come here with William, a bride of nineteen, alive with a happiness that had been rapidly extinguished, brimming with an enthusiasm that was not required. She remembered passing the North Lodge in the old landau on the very first day, the large carriage dipping and rolling as it turned the corner of the drive, and Rutherford had come into view, with its towers, mullioned windows, and barley-twist chimneys looking so ravishingly pretty in the afternoon sunshine.

Octavia unconsciously straightened her shoulders. Of course, it was impossible to go outside. One would hardly be expected to, unless there were a shooting party or one was dressed to walk, as she sometimes did in the spring or summer. Besides which, it would not be seemly for the wife of the eighth earl to run. And she certainly could not go to listen to the talk among the servants. Still, it was unreal: the huge tree lying broken-backed. The silence of the snow for miles beyond. The ghostly atmosphere of the day. She had once dreamed, not long after Harry had been born, that all of Rutherford had vanished. She had dreamed that the grounds had fluttered for a brief second and were suddenly gone: the glasshouses, the lake, the long drive to the edge of the hills, gone in an instant, shut up in a breath, eclipsed in one long, suffocating sigh.

She wondered why she thought of that now. It was Christmas Eve, 1913; the house was entertaining for the next four days; as the mistress of the house, she ought to be too busy for such fantasies. She turned back and looked at the room, frowning and calculating. There were sixteen guests coming in all: a rather small house party, but she preferred to have simply friends at Christmas, for there were too many formal parties to host during the rest of the year.

She had no doubt that the stoical little steam train would run from Wasthwaite along the valley; but she wondered about the horses struggling along the country road to the house. There was no possibility, surely, of the Napier or the Metz going out in this weather? The Napier was temperamental at best; the wheels would slither down the incline to the gates—and as for the Metz, it had been a whim to occupy Harry, to distract the boy from his perpetual obsession with air flight. The Metz was a little green roadster hardly capable of battling through snow. However, no doubt William would insist upon his Napier, for, to the horror of the staff, he enjoyed driving it himself, and had an enormous fur driving coat, a boxlike monument of a coat, that he would wrap himself in today. The drive would be cleared, the lane, the hill—four miles of snow. William would set the ground staff to it. Four miles. Eight more guests to add to those already here. Two more trains, Charlotte and Louisa returning on the same afternoon train and Helene de Montfort before luncheon.

"Oh, Lord," she murmured.

There was a knock on the door. Amelie ran to answer it, but Octavia already knew who it would be. There was no mistaking the thunderous three raps.

"M'lord," Amelie murmured, as Octavia's husband was admitted.

William Cavendish looked uncomfortable in the yellow-and-white upholstered sanctum that was Octavia's room, but then, he always did. He walked stiffly over to her and gave his wife a small dry kiss on the cheek. He smelled of shaving soap and—rather more distantly—of dog: His spaniel, Heggarty, slept in his room. William's suite was far more spartan than hers, and Octavia rarely trespassed upon it; painted blue, with plain furnishings, it was startlingly male, with its hunting prints on the wall and the costly Landseer that he had told her was far too sentimental, but which he had bought all the same. Leaning towards her now, William seemed almost loath to bend. He was a tall, broad man.

"Will you come to breakfast?" he asked.

She raised an eyebrow. "Have you come to ask me? Dearest, how romantic."

William did not return her smile. He merely indicated the presence of Amelie with a glance.

"Leave us," Octavia instructed. The maid vanished, carrying the unwanted tea tray, closing the bedroom door behind her.

"Are you ill?"

"No, not at all," she said. "Why?"

He pursed his lips, rocked on his heels. He was twenty years older than she, and sometimes the way he stood, hands locked behind his back, was reminiscent of her own father building himself up to one of his storms of temper.

"Cooper has told me that you were downstairs this morning," he said, naming his valet.

"Cooper?" she echoed, amused. "And why would Cooper be in the least interested in that?"

William let the mild joke hang ominously in the air for a second. "Cooper is not *interested*," he told her. "Cooper has been told by Mrs. Jocelyn."

Octavia sighed. "Lord, how they gossip."

"Octavia," William said. "You were seen by a housemaid. You spoke to her."

She flung out a hand carelessly, as if to swat his inquiry away. "The heavens shall open, I expect."

"What were you thinking?"

She met his gaze. "Thank you for supposing I was thinking at all," she murmured with a smile. "But I had seen the tree. I wanted to look at it."

"Look at it? What for?"

She wondered for a second whether she ought to explain the childlike impulse to run out in the snow, and suppressed it. "I have no idea," she said finally. "I was simply awake."

"You have perplexed the staff," he told her.

"I'm dreadfully sorry for it."

He looked at her for a while, shaking his head. She deliberately puzzled him sometimes; she rather thought that it was good for him. Besides, somewhere down in her soul, a little light still burned. It was a sense of humor. Something that neither he nor her brute of a father had ever been successful in removing.

"I shall expect you for luncheon," he said, turning away. "I am going to fetch Helene de Montfort."

"I haven't forgotten," she said. And, turning back to her mirror, she grimaced at the very thought.

In the corridors below the house, Emily Maitland had begun work that morning while it was still dark.

Her day began at five thirty, long before dawn in winter. She had woken, as always, cold in the iron-frame bed in the top-floor room that she shared with the two other chambermaids, Cynthia and Mary. In the dark, she had struggled into her clothes, feeling with her eyes shut for the fastenings of the long navy wool dress, and tying the white calico apron around her waist. The room under the eaves was icy: Even her face flannel had frozen to the side of the water in the washing bowl. She poked her finger through the thin layer of ice in the jug and rubbed a few drops over her face. It would have to do.

For the last two months she had got up first, dressing quickly, and holding on to the nightstand when she needed. She had never known what it was like to be drunk, but she thought that this must feel something like it; to combat it, she had learned to pinch her throat just above her collarbone. It seemed to stop it. She had seen her mother do it, and for the same reason.

"Wake up," she whispered to the others. Cynthia—the permanently miserable Cynthia—pulled away from Emily's hand on her shoulder. "Mary," Emily prompted. But Mary was awake, she realized, moving like an automaton, twisting up her hair, pinning it under her cap.

"I shall freeze to death on this side," the girl complained. "Cyn, you take it tonight. You're like a hog as 'tis. Your hog's backside'll keep you warm." She turned round to Emily, her face an indistinct blur in the shadows. "Why is it so bloody cold?" she demanded.

"I think it snowed," Emily told her. She felt her way to the end of the room and the thin curtains. "It looks different, the light." Then, from the window, she saw the snow lying on the lead of the roof and stuck in the twists of the chimneys, fancy spirals in the half darkness.

"No wonder," Mary muttered, pulling on wool stockings from under her pillow so that her feet need not touch the bare floorboards. "No bloody wonder."

"Miss Dodd will hear you," Emily warned, her hand on the door.

"I don't care if she does," Mary whispered back. "She's got a piece of felt on her floor. She's warmer than us. Any more of this, I shall go home."

But they both knew that would never happen. Mary needed her fourteen pounds a year to send back to her father; she couldn't afford to be fired by the head housemaid for her language, and a single insolent word could do it. Mary would go to bed at night and Emily could hear her swearing into her pillow, but downstairs she was as they all were: eyes averted, head bowed, utterly silent, scrubbing carpets and grates on their knees.

There was a narrow stair down to the first landing; beyond that, a stretch of corridor led to the servants' stair at the far end of the house. Directly below was the master's bedroom; the girls were taught to walk lightly on the boarded floor. Not an echo, not a word. It was a maid's job more than anything else to be invisible, a kind of wraith every morning carrying coal to every bedroom. Breathless, boneless wraith. Until the hand touched the hair on the back of her neck, until it stroked the flesh of her arm below the turned-up sleeve of the dress.

Emily screwed her eyes shut on the servants' stair, and stopped.

The housekeeper had caught her crying here a week ago—come running up the stairs before Emily could right herself. "What's the matter with you?" Mrs. Jocelyn had demanded. "Get out of the way." Emily had done as she was told. Nevertheless, it was strange. She thought that she had forgotten how to cry. The shame and terror had wrung it out of her. Mostly she would stand in those lost moments with a dry mouth and dry eyes, staring into the future, beyond grief. He'd taken her heart, she'd thought then to herself. Taken it, broken it, left it staggering through each hour like a faulty clock trying to keep time.

She went as quickly as she could down to the basement, and met Alfred Whitley by the kitchens. "Give me the coal," she hissed at him, snatching the bucket he had brought. She was sorry for her rudeness afterwards; Alfred was willing, if stupid. His mouth always looked too big for his open, gormless face, and his nose permanently ran and he would wipe it on his sleeve. "Like a wet weekend," John Gray, the estate steward, had said. "That's what you get out of the village. They don't breed brains down there. Just muck."

Still, poor Alfred. Poor Alfie. You had to feel for the lad. Only thirteen, and with the worst of the jobs, the hallboy. Though he seemed not to care, standing in the yard cutting a hundredweight of logs, hair plastered to his head in the rain. They never let Mr. Bradfield, the butler, see Alfie in one of the boy's states: exhausted, muddy, wet, sitting on the back step with a mug of cocoa. Mr. Bradfield would have kicked his sorry hide. Mr. Bradfield liked his steps nice and clean.

Emily was dodging the butler's room now. She could see the oil lamp lit in there; there was a glass panel in his door. She hurried past with the coal scuttle, climbed a second stair, and pushed open the green baize door to the house.

This stair brought her out on the south side, next to Lord

William's study, and the archive, and the library. Emily disliked it here: not so much the study, which was a pleasant little place with a fine desk and a small fireplace where she now lit the first fire, but the archive containing all the Roman relics that had belonged to Lord William's father. All the shelves had to be dusted, with their stained alabaster birds and cats, and little sculptures and pots, and bones dug up from Beddersley Hill, where they said that ancient kings were buried. They were all funny things, strange things. They made the hair prickle on the back of her neck. She hated the elongated eyes of the cat statues—two of them, one on each side of the door.

Seeing the fire catch, she put up the fireguard and went back to the hallway, crossing the marble floor under the high, vaulted arches. This was the oldest part of the house, what had been the main house before Lord William had extended the whole place fifteen years ago with Lady Cavendish's fortune. They said that the money from the wool mills was the only reason that Cavendish had bothered with a bride, but Emily did not know anything about that. To her, the great hall seemed stranded in the center of the modern additions: heavy wood beams far above. Alfred had lit the oil lamps by the entrance and the main stair. They were pools of color in the dark.

Emily went into the drawing room. There was an urgent need to be fast at this time of day. There were five fires to light on this floor, and then the bedrooms by six o'clock, or soon after. Cynthia and Mary helped the maid of all work stoke up the kitchen fires, sweep out the corridors, and take tea and toast to the upper staff: Amelie, the ladies' maid; Mr. Cooper, the master's valet; and Mrs. Jocelyn. The last month they had also been helping the scullery maid—it was rightfully her job to make sure the kitchen was clear—but Enid Bliss had bronchitis and could not breathe when she got up, a fact that the three chambermaids had been trying to hide from the housekeeper.

Emily was still counting to herself as she worked. There were three sets of guests here already, so that was eight rooms upstairs. Her fingers flew over the paper, kindling, and coal. Finishing, she wiped her hands on the apron, stood up, and immediately felt the familiar swing of sickness. Waiting for it to subside, she looked around. Hundreds of shapes inhabited the shadows: chairs, tables, lamps, occasional tables with flowers, others with hothouse plants; shelves with pernickety little flower-girl porcelain that Mr. Bradfield claimed was so expensive; fire screens, footrests. "I shall hoist the complete collection into the river one day," the mistress was supposed to have said, annoyed to find the parlor maids still polishing the furniture after breakfast. Or so Mrs. Jocelyn claimed. "A progressive woman," was the housekeeper's verdict. "I doubt she means it. The class of furnishings are so important."

Emily had found it funny. Not the remark, but the voice. Mrs. Jocelyn couldn't keep her Leeds accent out of her mouth, though she tried. Twenty-seven years in the Cavendish service, and there was still the broad, flat sound of Hunslet in Mrs. Jocelyn's tone.

Emily gazed into the middle distance. Had Mrs. Jocelyn ever been married, really? Every housekeeper was called "Mrs.," married or not. But she couldn't imagine anyone ever clasping Mrs. Jocelyn in his arms, holding her close, kissing that plain face. She had a ring on her finger, but that meant as little as the title; she might have put it there herself. It always flashed brightly as Mrs. Jocelyn fervently clasped her hands at morning prayers in the hall. Emily wiped a hair out of her eyes. Still, for all that, she might have had someone to love her; there might be a Mr. Jocelyn somewhere out in the wide world. Mrs. Jocelyn might have grasped what it took to make a man adore her. Which was far more than she herself had done. She gripped the sides of her skirt, her heart thudding. There was nothing to see: no, really, despite all that there was in this room, all that there was all over this enormous house, there was nothing to see. Nothing but night. She'd never be in the light again. Never, never.

She went to the drawing room door, sick in her heart, sick in her soul, sick of the rooms and the stairs and the fires and the secret hand that had touched hers, sick of him, sick of the abyss crawling towards her as if it were alive. It would writhe out there in the dark, sticky with guilt, like tar in the road that stuck to her shoes in the summer, and one day it would catch her by the ankle and drag her down. "God help me," she murmured, and turned out into the hall.

Lady Cavendish was six feet away, standing near the bottom of the main stairs.

"Oh, ma'am," she whispered. She didn't know what to do with herself. Lady Cavendish never came downstairs at this time of day. None of the family did: None of them ever stirred from their rooms until breakfast. Emily tried to step back against the wall. That was what she was supposed to do if any of the family appeared: flatten herself against the wall and look at the floor.

"Is it . . . Malham?" Lady Cavendish asked.

"Maitland, ma'am." Emily dared a glance upwards. Her mistress was looking at her amusedly. She was wrapped in some astonishing coat all lined with dark fur, under it she wore a pair of matching slippers.

"I'm rather out of place, Maitland," Lady Cavendish said, still smiling. She leaned forward. "But I've come to look at something."

Emily said not a word. Her mistress brushed past her, walked along the hall, the wrap trailing on the marble floor. Then she looked over her shoulder. "Is the door unlocked?" she asked.

The front door of the house was massive: Mr. Bradfield would open it in an hour. "No, ma'am," she replied.

Her mistress stopped. "Oh, it's tiresome," she said, as if to herself.

"One is a prisoner in one's own home." She said it lightly, walking back to the stair. "I suppose in time Amelie will bring me tea," she remarked. "Will you tell her I am waiting?"

Emily stared at the other woman, aghast. The servant hierarchy dictated that no mere housemaid could speak to a lady's maid. Even the head maid would approach Amelie only in the direst emergency. "No, of course you can't tell her," Lady Cavendish mused irritatedly, seeing Emily's expression.

"If you please, ma'am, I can go to tell Mrs. Jocelyn."

Her mistress looked down at her from the fifth or sixth step up. She was such a pretty woman, Emily thought. Beautiful, in fact. "Like a bird in a gilded cage," Mr. Bradfield had once said. She looked gilded now: pretty hair and pretty clothes and very pale. Perhaps she was ill, Emily wondered. You had to be ill or mad to go wandering about downstairs at this time of day, hadn't you? But her mistress was leaning slightly towards her, putting a finger to her lips, the smile broader than ever. "So naughty of me to come down and disturb you," she said. "But I shan't breathe a word. And neither shall you."

Emily looked again the floor. Not a word. Not breathe a word. She was used to that, all right.

She could hear the swish of the gown on the steps, and then she heard her mistress's voice. "There is a great tree down in the drive," she called carelessly. "That was what I was coming to look at. I can see it from my room—it is near the house. You might, all the same, tell Mrs. Jocelyn that."

By seven o'clock, the "outsiders" were all out in the drive of the house: the head gardener, Robert March, and the three undergardeners; the carter and farrier, Josiah Armitage, his son, Jack, and the two stable boys. Alfie was sent to help them, kitted out in a stable blanket with an old leather strap serving as a belt around his waist.

The great beech tree lay on its side. It had been in full leaf the previous year, and the remnants still clung to the branches. Robert March scratched his head and declared it a mystery. The old tree—the drive had been planted in 1815—must have been weakened at the root, he decided, though there was no apparent cause. All of them looked down the length of the drive at the five-hundred-yard stretch of beeches whose branches met overhead. "We don't want no more of the buggers down," March was heard to mutter as he and the boys took to the axes and saws.

It was cold, hard work. Once the smaller branches were removed, March set the farm boys to cut them down further and pile them in the wide loop of the drive before the house, feeling his way through the snow for the low metal wire where the grass and the gravel met. It would all do for kindling, some for hurdles; nothing would be wasted.

Josiah Armitage looked over at March: the seventy-year-old Yorkshireman was hunched over his work, great clouds of breath standing out like a halo around him. March was heavy and broad, and his face permanently florid, but Josiah knew better than to suggest he should slow himself down. March was bitter and fierce; he should have been a drill sergeant. Josiah had seen undergardeners quake under his scrutiny, and last summer March had fired a man for nothing more than going down to the village to attend his wife, who was in her fourth day of labor with their first child. The man had come back grinning, triumphant. But not for long. March had caught him by the collar and taken him down to the end of the drive and kicked him out. It was the very next day that Josiah had seen March tenderly pollinating in the greenhouse, twisting a fine three-haired paintbrush in the tomato flowers as if nothing had happened, and there was not a family newly desperate for want of a "character"—the passport to another job.

The garden boys and stable boys slaved under him now, hacking at the tree without looking up. At last, March straightened. "Go get the horse," he told Josiah. "Horse and hay cart both."

Josiah leaned on the ax he had been wielding and looked March in the eye. Sweat was streaming down the carter's face.

"If you'd be so kind, Mr. Armitage," March conceded.

Josiah and his son went off through the snow, wheeling out over the lawn so that they did not walk directly in front of the house. March watched them go; behind his back, his undergardeners smirked. If March was stone, Armitage was Yorkshire flint—brittle and cutting, tough as the long winters. He took orders only from Lord Cavendish; the boy Harry had almost been brought up hanging on Armitage's every word while his own father was away in London for the eight years he had been an MP. Harry was often silent around his father, and his father was short at best around his son, but Harry had talked long enough and loud enough with Armitage all his childhood, and Harry even now would have lived in the warmth of the stables alongside the horses, given half a chance. March knew that as well as anyone, and it looked hardly about to change, even if Harry was nineteen this coming year.

It began to snow a little again around ten o'clock; briefly, March saw Lady Cavendish at the window of the morning room, her hands wrung in front of her in an anxious pose. When she stepped away, the front door opened. William Cavendish, dressed in a greatcoat, came out and down the long flight of sandstone steps.

Seeing the earl walking rapidly towards him, March plucked at the rim of his hat. "M'lord."

Cavendish shielded his eyes against the snow with one gloved hand. "How much longer?"

"The Shire's being harnessed," March replied.

"And what of the remaining trees?"

"Seem a'reet, m'lord."

"Get the men down the drive and clear the snow back as soon as the horse comes. I want to take the car to the station at twelve."

March nodded. He waited for William Cavendish to say something else: perhaps that the staff could take a hot drink at the back doors, or at March's own cottage in the walled kitchen gardens. But Cavendish said nothing. He simply walked away.

The Shire horse came in a quarter of an hour. Josiah Armitage was on one side leading by the rein, Jack on the top of the cart. The three coming through the gentle snow—a fine white curtain and the horse itself grey with great white-haired hooves—looked like ghosts, scribbles on a grey page, until they were almost upon the drive. Then the Shire—nineteen hands high and weighing a ton and a half—came into focus, breath steaming. Ice granules were forming on the condensation on the harness and the padded collar around the horse's neck. The boys stopped cutting. Alfie put one hand on the collar, reaching up to do so, and the horse turned its massive, ponderous head to look at the boy. Alfie laid his face against the warm flank. "Wenceslas," he said. "Old mate, old mate."

NOTES

NOTES

NOTES